THE SPECTER OF SEDUCTION

Pluto's Snitch #3

CAROLYN HAINES

KaliOka Press

For Lucille Armstrong, related by choice if not blood

CHAPTER 1

R eginald Proctor slowed the rented car at the vine-
covered portal. We'd arrived at Waverley Mansion in
the Black Prairie section of Mississippi and, if the
entrance said anything, it was isolation and neglect. We'd traveled a good distance through intolerable August heat and bad
roads, the car thumping and creaking as it hit one pothole
after another. Relief swept over me. We were here at last.

For one brief moment, the afternoon silence was filled with
the calls of wild songbirds, as sweet as the scent of the honey-
suckle that surrounded us. The aggressive vines had climbed
the brick portal marking the entrance to the mansion and
leaped into the dense trees, creating a curtain of pale gold
flowers. The August sun filtered through the poplars, cedars,
and oaks of all variety with an intense green light that was
almost preternatural. The raw beauty made me lean out the
window and inhale, but seconds later, a swarm of yellow flies
dove at us from the thick woods. Another moment of motion-
lessness and we'd be drained.

"Hang on, Raissa." Reginald swatted a fly. Blood bloomed on his neck where he'd squashed the biting insect.

"Go! The Sheridans are expecting us." Had been expecting us for a while. The journey from Montgomery had taken an hour longer than we'd anticipated. Once we'd left the main road, we'd had to avoid washouts, move fallen tree limbs and other hazards, and had slowed to a crawl. Each mile into the heart of the woods told us more than we wanted to know about the isolation of Waverley, a once majestic jewel in the crown of the Confederate states. "You would think in 1920, someone could maintain the road a little better," I grumbled, hanging on as the car sped through a large puddle.

"They said the estate had been left to ruin." Reginald depressed the clutch as he eyed the crumbling brick portal almost obscured by vines and underbrush. The driveway before us was narrow and rutted. Volunteer beech, maple, and oak crowded in tightly. Full with summer greenery, the path was beautiful but dense.

Reginald and I had come to Waverley House at the behest of the new owners who were experiencing difficulties with their eight-year-old daughter, Amanda. Since moving to Waverley Mansion, the child had begun to display behavior that frightened them. She'd taken up with an imaginary playmate she called Nan. Plenty of children living in secluded areas had imaginary friends, but there was more to the matter. Waverley was reputed to be haunted and this unseen friend, Nan, was coaching Amanda in behavior that was naughty at best and dangerous at worst.

Amanda had begun to sneak out of the house and roam the woods in what her parents described as a feral state. She seemed attuned to a different reality—one her parents didn't see and couldn't share. Each week she grew more distant and peculiar.

As investigators in the Pluto's Snitch detective agency, Reginald and I were here to attempt to solve our second case. If a spirit haunted the old mansion and was somehow controlling the girl, it was up to us to find it and root it out.

"Can you go faster?" I asked Reginald. Our last case in Montgomery, Alabama, had concluded only two days before. We'd barely had time to compare notes before we'd received a letter begging us to come to Waverley House. Because the plea was so desperate, we'd rented a car in Montgomery and journeyed through Alabama's wild and hilly terrain, crossing at last into Mississippi. At Columbus, we drove over the Tombigbee River and found ourselves in a part of the state where the rich black earth produced fine pastureland and lush green fields filled with cattle.

Reginald swerved as he obliterated another yellow fly. "These damn flies are trying to suck us dry." He pressed the gas pedal and shot along the narrow drive that wound and curved through beautiful woods. The flies followed us in a swarm, buzzing loud.

Ready or not, it was time to meet Royal and Anne Sheridan and their daughter, Amanda.

As we dashed down the driveway, I tried to push back the misgivings I felt. Reginald and I had agreed to come to this isolated estate without investigating the circumstances or even the people we'd agreed to work for. I'd spoken with Uncle Brett, my only relative, on the phone. He'd been reluctant for me to travel to Waverley until he'd had a chance to investigate the Sheridan family, but I hadn't waited.

My thoughts drifted back to my uncle's home, Caoin House, and how much I missed him and the location. A flash

of yellow moved across a clearing to the right of the drive and
I sat up straight. It was a young woman rushing through the
trees. She ran hard and fast, looking back over her shoulder as
if someone pursued her. Someone she feared. Her left cheek
bore a long scratch and blood dripped down her jaw and onto
the collar of her dress.

"Hey!" I waved out the car window.

"What is it?" Reginald slowed the car.

"There's a young woman running." I pointed to the now
empty woods. There was no trace of anyone or anything.

"A real woman or something else?" Excitement laced Reginald's voice.

"I thought she was real." She'd been so solid, so contempo-
rary. "She wore a yellow dress, a summer dress. Not something
Zelda would wear. Modern but more conservative." More like
something I would choose. I didn't say it out loud, but I could
still see the gauzy material floating out behind her as she ran.
"And she had a bob. She was modern." That spoke against her
being a ghost. But the way she'd disappeared—into thin air.
That was not a trait of a flesh and blood woman.

When the car stopped, I got out and stepped into the
woods. Silence had fallen. The birds no longer sang, and an
eerie stillness had settled in. Not even the flies were moving.
Reginald joined me. We walked into the clearing and stopped.
There was no sign of the girl. The hair along my neck stood on
end, a warning.

"You didn't see her?" I asked Reginald.

"No." He offered me his arm when I stumbled in a bit of
deadfall. "I didn't see anything. Yet you saw her clearly." More
than anything, Reginald wanted to see a ghost. He didn't
bother to hide his disappointment.

I nudged him a little. "If ghosts are running about the

woods, this could be a good opportunity for you to practice your second sight. But to be honest, that young woman was a bit old to be Nan, the playmate."

"I'd know that if I'd seen her." He took out his cigarette case but didn't light up. "Looks like we might be useful here after all. I was beginning to regret coming to this backwoods location."

There was no point in lingering in the clearing. The stillness had passed and now the sound of yellow flies and mosquitoes warned of their bloodthirsty return. "Yes, maybe we can be of service. It would be good to help this family and then return to Mobile. I find I'm missing my uncle."

"Yes, Caoin House has grown on me too," Reginald said. "Though I should find an apartment in Mobile. I can't remain living on your uncle's generosity."

"He's thinks you're the bee's knees." I squeezed his arm. "He loves having you there. And it isn't like the house is crowded." Caoin House had over sixty rooms and three wings. I was glad for Reginald's company. And the truth was we hadn't been at Caoin House much because we'd been working.

"We can discuss future arrangements when we return to Mobile. We need a little office somewhere." He handed me into the passenger seat, then slammed his door and started the motor. We coasted down the driveway and into a gentle curve.

The first view of the house through the crowded trees reminded me of a fairy tale setting. The architecture of Waverley House was unique. The original owner had built a four-story house with a central rotunda. This octagonal-shaped room that topped the house peeked through the tops of the trees. I knew from research that spiral staircases curved up to each floor and continued on to the next. I'd read about the history of the house in a book I'd found in the Sayre library, the home where we'd stayed during our case in Montgomery.

The design of Waverley allowed for the opening of windows in the fourth floor rotunda that created a draft. Hot air was pulled up and out. It was said that Waverley, when the house was maintained and in its prime, had been one of the wonders of the South. In a land where summer could prove suffocating, the house was always cool and beautifully crafted.

At last the whole house came into view. Sadness, a sense of acute loss, fell over me with such poignancy that I almost asked Reginald to stop the car. Almost. We continued to a stop at the front of the house. The Sheridan family had only moved in during the spring, and though they'd brought in crews to renovate the old mansion, the work was slow. New boards replaced those that had rotted on the front porch, and painters on scaffolding worked to scrape away the old curling paint applying a new coat of pristine white, repairing window sills and other issues as they primed and painted. In time, the magnificence of the house would be restored.

"Royal! They're here!" Anne Sheridan was a lovely woman with blond curls pulled into a messy bun. She wore a man's shirt and loose britches, and she held a paintbrush in her hand as she hurried down the porch toward us. "Welcome." Her smile was warm but also tense. "I'm so glad you're here."

"The road proved challenging," Reginald said as he got out of the car and shook her free hand.

She came around the car and hugged me when I stepped out. "It's rained every day for the past two weeks. That makes travel, and renovation, so much harder. The workmen have been staying at a private home to prevent unnecessary travel. We're hoping September brings drier weather."

"It is August in the South." I liked Anne instantly. She was a pretty woman, fragile though determined not to be. Her eyes were the same blue as the pattern of my mother's favorite china.

"What are you painting?" I asked. The white enamel paint was slowly leaking from the brush onto her hand. It would take a scrubbing with turpentine to get it off.

"The kitchen cabinets," she said. "I simply had to paint them. The workmen are concentrating on the outside of the house but I had to do something. Cleaning and painting, that has been my life these last few months. I just can't put my dishes or staples away in cabinets that look so..." She faded, and I wondered how and why this delicate woman had chosen to come to the wilds of Mississippi to salvage a mansion. She would be more at home serving tea in one of Mobile's society salons.

"Royal will be here soon," she said. "He must have gone around back. Come inside and I'll make some lemonade. You look hot and tired. I am so thankful you agreed to come here and help with our...problem. Mr. Proctor, Madam Petalungro spoke so highly of your work with her in New Orleans. She said you were well versed in the methods of the spirit world. And Mrs. James, I am aware that you have a real gift. Thank you for coming here. If you can help my daughter, I don't care what it costs."

There was no sign of Amanda, the child, but I didn't want to ask. Not yet. If the child knew why we were there, it would be best for her to approach us on her own. "Do you have a young woman, probably late teens or early twenties, working here?" I asked.

"No, it's just us, the carpenters and yard workers, the governess Constance Nyman, and the horse trainer who lives on the property, but not in the house. And there's Fancy, who's

technically the cook but who helps with everything. She has a
cabin in back, as does Amos, the gardener. Why do you ask?"

"I sure could use that lemonade." I didn't want to stand in
the yard discussing a potential ghost. It would be better to
probe this topic when we were inside and more comfortable.

Reginald got our bags out of the car and carried them
inside as Anne led the way. We stopped in the foyer, taking in
the grandeur of the house. The central portion of the house
was open all the way to the fourth floor rotunda. The staircases began on either side of the central room and curved up
to the second floor. Each room on the second floor opened on
an interior landing that gave a view of the rotunda. The stairs
continued in a circle and then lifted again to climb to the third
floor and on to the fourth. The house was a true architectural
wonder.

"Your rooms are on the second floor," Anne said. "Please
leave your bags here and I'll have them taken to your room.
Fancy helps me with the cleaning and cooking. Once we have
more rooms renovated we'll hire more staff. Come into the
kitchen, if you don't mind. We can talk while I squeeze the
lemons. We've all become a jack-of-all-trades here while the
renovations are happening." She smiled, but there was tension
beneath the warm expression. "It's almost impossible to hire
anyone to work here. It's so isolated. And...well, the house has
a reputation, as I mentioned."

We did as she bade us and followed into a bright and sunny
room connected to the main house with a dog trot or covered
walkway. Many houses were constructed with a detached
kitchen in case of a fire. Waverley Mansion still relied on a
wood-burning stove. The newfangled gas or electric stoves had
not made it this far into the deep rural areas. It would be some
time before phones and electric power came to the Sheridans.

Reginald and I took a seat at a stout wooden table, and I could see the work Anne had been engaged in with her paint brush. One wall of cabinets glistened in the afternoon sunlight, the paint still wet. She put her brush in a bucket of turpentine by the back door and stood on the steps to wash the paint from her hands. The pungent scent of the turpentine reminded me of one of my mother's friends, an artist. She'd always smelled of paint thinner and I found it comforting.

When Anne returned, she took the lemons from a bowl on her counter and began cutting and squeezing them. Before she finished, a black woman came into the kitchen. Without a word she eased Anne away from the chore and began to make the lemonade.

"This is Fancy," Anne said, making introductions.

"Take your guests to the front parlor," Fancy suggested. "I was just in there dustin' and it's cooler in that room. Don't open them draperies, though. Mosquitoes are buzzin' to get inside."

"Thank you, Fancy."

We followed Anne back to the main house and the front parlor, a beautiful room centered with a grand piano and an arched alcove. Bjorn Norquist, the man who'd designed and built the house, had designed the alcove as the setting for family weddings, funerals, and christenings—the official celebration of family events.

Reginald went to the piano and struck a simple melody. "Do you play?" Reginald asked our hostess.

"Not well. Amanda has a talent for it. We'll hire a music instructor once we're truly settled in. Constance knows the basics and is teaching Amanda to read music." Anne frowned. "My daughter seems more interested in riding her horse than playing the piano, though. This horse obsession is a new phase, one she's acquired since moving here." She walked to the window and looked out. "I begged Royal not to buy her that horse, but he wanted her to ride. There are fox hunts here. They're part of the social world that Royal enjoys. Bird hunting, fishing, those things. I never understood killing things for fun."

I knew the world of plantation homes and fox hunts, though I'd never had a desire to participate. I'd taken riding lessons and could control a reliable horse, but my skills stopped there. Reginald had never ridden. His world had been the city, where he could either walk or find a carriage, or now rent a car.

"Where is Amanda?" I was eager to meet the young girl.

Anne's expression shifted to a carefully controlled neutral. "She's up in her room, I believe. Shall I get her?"

I wanted to ask about the young woman I'd seen before the child joined us. "Let's talk a moment first. What does your Constance Nyman look like?" I asked.

"Tall, thin, blond hair. She's pretty in an austere way, though she's in her forties now. Never married. She's devoted herself to instructing children in their lessons and deportment."

Marriage was the natural path for a woman. Then childbirth and assuming the role of wife and mother. It was dictated by society, with rare exception. Old maid schoolmarms were something of a joke. I'd been saved by that description only because I was a widow. My husband had died in the war.

"Did Constance move here with you?" I asked.

"No, she joined us several weeks back, and we're so fortunate to have her. I was afraid once she saw how far from West Point we were, she wouldn't stay. She's still young enough to want a social life, and she certainly won't have one here."

"And Amanda, does she have any friends?"

Anne shook her head. "There are so few children here. We make it a point to take her into town for church and social engagements, but she'll be schooled here, at least for the next two years. Perhaps by then the roads will be improved."

It would be a lonely two years for an eight-year-old girl. Many children grew up on farms, but they had the interaction of school days and at least the chance of friendships.

Anne's brow furrowed. "Amanda doesn't make friends easily, and she's gotten off on the wrong foot with some of the young girls in town."

"How so?" Reginald asked.

"She frightens them with her stories," Anne said. "I don't know where she comes up with the things she does. They are macabre and grotesque." She swallowed. "She says Nan tells her about them."

"Her imaginary friend?" I asked.

"Yes. And a wicked friend she is."

"I saw a young woman in the woods," I said carefully. "Youngish late teens or early twenties. Could this be Nan?"

Anne chuckled mirthlessly. "No, I suspect that's one of the college girls. They're a plague."

"College girls?" I was totally lost.

"The Mississippi State College for Women in Columbus. The women going to school there are mostly privileged and moneyed. They think the law doesn't apply to them."

"Why are they coming here?" I asked.

"They come with the young men from the Industrial and Mechanical state college in Starkville. Waverley has been a trysting ground for these students for decades." Anne poured more lemonade for us.

"Why would students drive from Columbus and Starkville

all the way here?" The grounds were lovely, but there were beautiful stretches of woods much closer to the schools.

"The legend goes that young women become lusty and sexually hungry when they come on the grounds here. Ridiculous, but so far we've been unable to keep them off the property completely." Anne looked down at her hands in her lap. "We've stopped in town to talk to the sheriff, but there's little he can do. Royal shoots at the students. Not at them, but over their heads, trying to frighten them away. It's dangerous for them to be here. They've scared us a few times when they've been running around late at night."

Reginald's gaze met mine. Perhaps our mysterious young woman in the woods was less imaginary and far more muscle and bone. And it might explain some of Amanda's older notions. A lonely child would be drawn to a college girl.

"I saw someone in the woods along the driveway coming in," I said. "A young woman who could easily have been a college student. Yellow dress. Bobbed hair."

Anne rose to her feet. "That sounds like one of the provocateurs. They're smart young women. I daresay her car was parked in some lane just out of sight."

"Could we meet Amanda?" I asked.

"Yes, let me bring her down." She left us in the cool parlor.

"Haunting or not?" Reginald asked. He was counting on my sixth sense to answer the question.

"I can't tell. The child will provide the answer."

CHAPTER 2

Amanda Sheridan was a beautiful child. She had chestnut ringlets that framed a lovely face and large, gray eyes with dark lashes. She dragged a dolly behind her—one that had seen a lot of wear. When she looked at us, she was serene and considering, which was a bit startling for an eight-year-old.

"Hello, Amanda," I said, dropping to one knee so that I was on her level. I wanted to put her at ease.

She ignored me and looked at Reginald. "You think I'm sick, don't you?"

I tried to hide my reaction, but the child had startled me. Apparently her mother, too. Anne put a hand on her shoulder. "Are you not well, Amanda?"

"No, Mother, I'm fine. But you think I'm sick."

Anne cast a furtive glance at me. "No, darling, I don't. I think you're precocious."

"You're worried that something is wrong with me. Because of Nan." She looked at Reginald as she spoke. "You're a doctor, aren't you?"

Reginald laughed. "No, Amanda. It would be hard to find a term to describe me, but I think gambler and reprobate might come close." He won her with his easy charm. She smiled at him. "And her?" She pointed at me.

"She's a writer," he said. "She writes ghost stories. Her first one is going to be published this fall in a big magazine."

"You're here to see Nan." She turned to me, her gray eyes far older than they should have been. "She'll be happy to see you."

My body felt as if an icy wind sliced through me. I needed no other explanation about why Amanda Sheridan found it difficult to make friends. She was a changeling, an unexpected child. I could almost believe the fairies had played a role in swapping an older, wiser fairy child for the Sheridan daughter.

"Amanda, Mrs. James and Mr. Proctor will be staying a few days. I hope you'll help me show them a good time while they visit."

"Shall I play the piano for them?" she asked.

"Of course." Anne was startled by the request.

Amanda walked to the piano and sat down on the bench. Her feet didn't touch the pedals, but she sat up tall and held her hand over the ivories. She leaned slightly forward and began to play Beethoven's "Fur Elise."

Her audience was transfixed. When she finished, we applauded. Reginald went to her and congratulated her.

"I didn't realize you'd progressed so," Anne said. "That was...wonderful."

"Constance has been teaching me." Amanda slid off the piano bench. "Isn't this a lovely old thing." Her hand ran over the dark wood of the piano. It was a huge piece. "It was made in South America. Mahogany. It was a birthday gift to Olivia Norquist, the daughter of the man who built this house."

"How lovely that you know so much history about your home," I said. "This is a beautiful and unique house. I'm sure you're excited to live here."

"It's better now," Amanda said. She walked to the window and pushed back the draperies to look out. The sun was so bright it seemed to pull the color from the grass and trees. "Yes, it's better here now."

"Better than what?" I asked. There was definitely something unusual about the little girl, but I couldn't tell if it was supernatural or not.

"Better than when I first got here. There's no one about for miles, you know. If the house caught on fire it would burn to the ground before anyone even knew it."

"What's your dolly's name?" Reginald asked. Amanda had dropped the doll beside the piano bench and he picked it up and handed it to her.

"She's Penny," Amanda said, reaching for her. "She's old."

"Little girls love their dollies," Reginald said, handing her over.

"Yes, little girls do." Amanda looked at him and smiled sly like a fox. "Mother, I'm going to ride Moonglow. You know there's going to be a show at the Nelson's plantation. They'll have jumping. Wouldn't that be something to see?"

"We'll discuss it with your father, but you know you can't ride astride like you do here. It would be a terrible scandal."

"Oh, my, a scandal." Amanda laughed and it was clear she was mocking her mother. "I would think someone who claims to see ghosts would be even more of a scandal." She walked out of the room, and I had the distinct sense that an older presence had just departed.

"See," Anne said, tears filling her eyes. "That's not my daughter. Amanda is a sweet child, a young girl."

I had to agree. The person who'd just left the room was neither sweet nor a child.

CHAPTER 3

With the loan of a veiled hat for me and a kerchief to tie over Reginald's lower face and neck, we took a walk down the driveway before the setting sun truly brought out the bloodsuckers. As bad as the flies and mosquitoes were during the hot hours, they multiplied by the thousands at dawn and dusk.

My long-sleeved blouse and ankle-length skirt gave me plenty of protection, with the veil. Reginald, too, seemed comfortable as we strolled toward the clearing where I'd seen the female. Apparition or corporeal being, I intended to find out. There would be evidence of a physical body moving through the clearing, and Reginald and I needed to know if we were dealing with the influence of an older college girl on Amanda or something from the dark side of the River Jordan. I'd still like to meet Royal Sheridan, but I knew Anne was not equipped to handle the challenge her family faced. Ghost or naughty young woman, the person influencing Amanda had to be caught and stopped.

"What do you make of the child?" Reginald asked.

It was amusing that he thought I might have more insight into her behavior than he did—because I was female. My experiences with children had involved the older teens I'd taught in high school, those who had already begun to form their own personalities. Amanda was truly a child. At eight, she should be innocent and trusting of her parents, agreeable, and happy. She was loved and had many entitlements.

"That was no child," I answered. "She was very mature. Did you see Anne's face when she began to play? She's far surpassed her mother's expectations, and apparently in a short time."

"Which leads me to believe the child is being haunted," Reginald responded.

"Yes." He was the logical member of our agency, and he was adept at reading the living in a way I could only envy. Reginald's years in an orphanage and growing up on the streets in a hard life would serve him well in our new occupation as spirit detectives. "Her mother said she had a natural talent for the piano."

"You're correct. We can't take that one thing as proof one way or the other." He pointed down the drive. "The clearing is right up here."

"Thank goodness. The veil and long sleeves are doing their job, but I'm sweltering." Sweat was running down my spine, pooling at the cinched waist of my skirt. The sensation was unpleasant.

We stepped into the clearing, and I did my best to recreate the fleeting image of the young woman in yellow. At the trunk of a big sycamore, I had a clear image of her hand pushing off the pale, smooth trunk as she ran. "Here." I searched the ground for some evidence of a footprint. The leaves were so thick, it was impossible to determine anything.

I traced the path I believed she'd taken, hoping for some

THE SPECTER OF SEDUCTION 19

evidence that would resolve our question. No matter how hard we looked, the woods remained pristine, undisturbed.

"Ghost?" Reginald said, his grin a little wry.

"I wish we could set a trap." I was tired from the journey and a little cranky at the isolation. I wanted to call my uncle in Mobile. He'd put out feelers about the Sheridan family. Not because I suspected them of anything at all, but because he was my uncle Brett and since I'd moved into Caoin House last June, he'd taken on the role of parent and protector. And I was glad for it. My heart needed a haven to heal from the losses I'd endured.

"What might a ghost trap entail?" Reginald asked. "If I could only see the spirits like you do, I could help you more."

"If I could only deduce the hearts of the living like you do, I could help myself."

He chuckled. "You are my friend, Raissa James. And the best partner. I don't believe in the god of gifts, but someone was looking out for me when our paths crossed."

It was a peculiar statement, and one that deserved exploration. "If you don't believe in God, how can you believe in spirits?"

"I didn't say I didn't believe in a divine entity. I said I didn't believe in a god who bestowed gifts on his favored children like some ancient Santa Claus. In most instances, we make our own luck and good fortune. Good deeds are their own reward."

Had I not been close to fainting from the heat, I would have enjoyed a spirited argument. Not that I necessarily disagreed, but my parents had taught me the joy of a solid debate with a matched opponent. And Reginald Proctor was that, and more. I also couldn't help but wonder if his lack of belief was the thing that kept him from seeing the spirits that deviled me. This deserved full exploration—once we were out of the steaming woods.

"I don't see anything," I said. Disappointment was evident in my tone.

"Me either, but it was the place we had to start. Let's head back to the house. It is amazingly cool there. The house is remarkable. And I saw a bar fully stocked with whiskey. I'm afraid I've gotten spoiled with ice in my drink. Such luxuries aren't available here, but a measure of neat whiskey would be greatly appreciated."

"Yes." I wasn't a big consumer of spirits, but this day deserved a cocktail. In a land where liquor was illegal, everyone seemed to have plenty of it. I would just be glad for the cool parlor and something with a bit of calming influence to drink.

We set off along the drive at a slow pace. It was too hot to hurry, and every step produced another slither of sweat down my body. I was caught up in the sensation when a gunshot blasted through the quiet woods. Reginald instinctively grabbed my arm and drew me into the trees on the verge. "That wasn't far away."

"I know." It didn't appear that anyone was shooting at us, but I wondered who might be hunting so close to Waverley Mansion. Amanda had gone to ride her horse. It wasn't safe for her to be in the woods if someone was shooting.

The sound of someone crashing through the woods came from the north, and Reginald and I began to run down the drive. As we rounded a bend, I saw a horse and rider. The animal was almost silver, a horse made of molten light. The young girl astride the animal wore an expression of fierce joy. I didn't think the horse was running away with her.

Horse and rider jumped a fallen tree and disappeared down

a trail that cut through the woods. Amanda ducked branches and rode with abandon.

"She is an excellent horsewoman," Reginald said.

"She's a danger to herself." I was all for riding, but she could break her neck.

"Do you think Anne knows how wild Amanda is on horseback?"

"I don't think she has any control over that child."

We walked back to Waverley Mansion in silence. I carried dread in my chest. I didn't know what was wrong with Amanda, but I knew she was in real danger.

We arrived at Waverley just as a man carrying a shotgun came out of the woods. He approached us and shook Reginald's hand, introducing himself as Royal Sheridan. He was a good-looking man with a suntanned face and gray eyes with laugh lines around them. Today, though, there was a deep furrow between his brows.

"Damn college kids," he said. "I was warned about them, but I thought a few weeks after we'd occupied the house, they'd take the hint and steer clear. It's not like there aren't plenty of isolated places for them to park and pet." He shouldered the gun with ease. He was comfortable with firearms.

"The road in here is pretty tough. You'd think they could find a location with easier access," Reginald pointed out.

"It's the legend. It draws them like flies to honey." Royal signaled us up the steps and into the house. "Let's find a cool spot and have a drink."

We settled in the parlor, the piano a reminder of Amanda's new talent. I had a lot of questions, but observation would be my first recourse.

"Let me get you a bourbon," Royal said to Reginald. "And you, Mrs. James, what would you prefer?"

"Bourbon is fine for me." I liked that my answer was unexpected.

Royal went to a sideboard where glasses and a decanter of amber liquid were arranged. He poured three glasses and uncorked a bottle of wine and poured a fourth glass, I supposed for his wife.

"The bourbon comes from a family recipe," he said. "It's a hobby of mine. There's an art to good 'likker', as my granddad called it."

I sipped the drink, surprised at how smooth the taste was. "It's very good."

"Generations of Sheridans have perfected the distillation process."

"Prohibition has made bootlegging a booming business," Reginald said. "A lot of rum comes into New Orleans from the port, but corn grows well in Louisiana, and bourbon is a favored drink,"

"That's true." Royal visibly relaxed.

"It amazes me that people think laws will prevent people from participating in their vices." Reginald was enjoying the bourbon.

"Prohibition won't last for long, though. Folks already see that the new law isn't making things better. I was at the capitol in Jackson last week and heard the lawmakers arguing like coon dogs at a tree. The cost of enforcing the anti-drinking laws is hitting the state budget hard. And it's only driven the liquor underground. State's not getting any taxes for illegal hooch." He shrugged. "The noble experiment is a failure. Smart folks see that."

"A lot of churchgoers would disagree." Reginald sipped and sighed with contentment. "This is good. You do have a talent."

"What folks say in church and what they do on a Saturday

night are two different things. Some of the people marching to stop the sale of liquor were my granddaddy's best customers. And they don't feel a bit of shame at their hypocrisy. They view it as expediency. They have to project a certain image, even when everyone knows it's fake. Pander to the womenfolk who see liquor as Satan's handmaiden. The truth is, people want their small pleasures. You can take that to the bank."

The conversation stopped when Anne joined us. She found her glass of wine on the hunt board and sat beside her husband on the sofa. She looked less tense, and I realized she had no clue about the way her daughter was riding through the woods.

"Constance will join us," Anne said. "Amanda is finishing a riding lesson. Once she's cleaned up, we'll have dinner."

Reginald's glance told me to hold back on what we'd seen with the girl and horse. We had to win Amanda's confidence if we were to work with her. Tattling to her mother wouldn't benefit us.

When the governess entered the room, Royal stopped in mid-sentence with some story he was telling Reginald. He got up and poured another glass of wine and handed it to Constance Nyman as he made introductions.

"Mr. Proctor and Mrs. James will be staying on the second floor with you," Royal said. "I'm sure you'll be glad of the company." He turned to us. "Constance isn't the flighty type, but she's been hearing noises in the night."

I leaned forward. "What kind of noises?"

"Doors opening. Footsteps." She shrugged. She was a lovely woman with blond hair pulled into a rather severe bun at the back of her head. She was slender and would have been willowy in her youth. Her dress was a plain summer frock that hit mid-calf. With a bit of make-up and a smile, she could have been a fetching woman, and she was still in her prime. I wondered why she'd agreed to come to a home so far away from any social activities. Maybe the Sheridans threw parties or fetes. That would at least give her an outlet. It seemed unreasonable that she'd given up on marriage and a family of her own.

"We're very interested in anything out of the ordinary," Reginald said. "Raissa is an author. She writes ghost stories."

"She's to be published in the fall," Anne said. "Her first publication."

Constance surprised us with a warm smile. "So you're here for stories about Nora Bailey, the notorious Union spy who infiltrated the Norquist family and provided information about a Confederate attack that ended in tragedy for the boys in gray."

"Nora Bailey?" I invited more information.

Anne went to the hunt board and retrieved the liquor and refilled our glasses. "It's an exciting story with romance, betrayal, and a brutal death. Waverley comes complete, not only with wild sexual impulses but also stories of the fallen South."

"I can't wait," Reginald said. "Tell us."

"The story is really Anne's to tell," Constance said. "She shared it with me."

"But you're the better storyteller," Anne said. "Please."

Constance nodded, then leaned back in her chair. "Nora Bailey came to Waverley House in the third year of the Civil War. She was a guest here, a young woman one of the Norquist sons met while visiting New Orleans. Nora had no family, and she moved from place to place, visiting those who had plenty of space."

"That wasn't uncommon for young women back in that time," I said. "Often the young women went to households where it was hoped someone would find a love match for them."

"And that's what happened," Constance said. "Waverley Mansion was built by the Norquist family. Bjorn and Marketta were the parents. They'd come here from Sweden, where Bjorn had manufactured weapons and munitions. He'd been very successful with his work but wanted to start his own company."

"A lucrative profession in a country headed into war," Reginald said.

"True. The factory is gone now but it was on the Tombigbee River, which made it easy to ship weapons. It's easy to see now why Nora wrangled an introduction to Francis Norquist and got herself invited here. But let me tell you about the family. There were three boys and three girls." She waved a hand toward the rotunda. "The girls occupied the second floor, where we'll be staying. Helene, Marguerite, and Olivia were the girls. The boys had the third floor, probably in the hopes that they wouldn't be able to leave the house without their parents knowing. From all accounts, they were handsome hell-raisers." Constance shot a look at Anne that I didn't understand. "The boys were Burton, Jedidiah, and Francis. All were in the Confederate cavalry and rose to high ranks. It was Francis who fell in love with the fiery Nora. It was said she was a beauty with a love of adventure and a strong will. A perfect match for Francis, who was known to be the best dancer in the South."

Constance was an accomplished storyteller. She'd swept us up into the tale with little effort.

"Imagine the parties that were held here, even with the war raging. The Norquist boys would ride home together whenever they could, often bringing other young officers to court their sisters. When Francis met Nora, everyone on the property knew he'd fallen for her. And she for him, or at least so it seemed."

I had a very bad feeling this story did not have a happy ending. "Was he killed?"

"That might have been kinder," Constance said.

That sounded even more ominous.

"What happened?" I didn't want to know but I had to. Constance had compelled my interest.

"Nora was a Union spy. She'd come to Waverley Mansion with the express mission of seducing one of the Norquist sons so she could obtain information about military plans. I don't know if she picked Francis because he was the highest ranked of the boys with more access to valuable information, or if it just happened that he was the one who fell for her."

"She betrayed him." This hit me hard, because my husband had died on the battlefield in France. The idea of betraying a soldier—it simply was wrong.

"Yes, she betrayed him. She used him to learn of a Confederate maneuver that likely would have turned the course of the war. She reported the plan to her Union handler, who in turn got the information to General Grant. The Confederates were flanked on both sides. There were few survivors."

"Francis was killed?" The battle played out in my mind. The noise and fear and blood—it was the stuff of my nightmares. No human deserved to die in such confusion and horror.

"Yes, he was eventually. All of the Norquist boys died in battle. Before that, though, Nora's role was revealed. She was hanged from the big magnolia in the front yard."

"Hanged?" I was stunned. "They hanged a woman?"

Constance sat up taller. "They hanged a spy. Not a woman,

a spy."

"I suppose it's Nora's ghost that lingers here," Reginald said.

"If she's here, it isn't by choice." Constance went to the hunt board and refilled her glass. "I don't believe Nora's spirit would want to remain here. It was said she never struggled when they caught her and pronounced her guilty. She didn't attempt to save herself."

"She really loved Francis," Reginald said. "That's even more tragic."

"There was a painting of her here at one time," Constance said. "It was said that visitors would often see the woman in the painting in the house or around the gardens. Several visiting men have reported that she comes to them in the night, alluring and amorous. The story is that as long as the painting exists, Nora is trapped. She can never find peace until the painting is destroyed."

"Was it painted here at Waverley?" Reginald asked.

"Yes, by the famous portraitist Julian DeWitt. It was said that he fell in love with Nora too. He was visiting at Waverley, painting the daughters' portraits, when Nora arrived. He fell for her instantly. The legend has it that Nora was completely irresistible when she turned her attentions upon a man. She had quite the reputation. At any rate, DeWitt left shortly before she betrayed Francis. It would have been so much better if she'd left with the painter and never completed her mission."

The story had left me depressed and unhappy. I missed Alex. More than I wanted to admit on most days. His death had been in another war on a different continent, but his loss was felt as keenly. The hopes of so many young men had been broken on a field of blood, and all for what? Money was the coin of those who fought wars. Death was the payment to the soldiers who answered to the bugle of patriotism.

The sound of light footsteps came to us and we ceased the conversation. It could only be Amanda. Spies and hangings were not fit topics for a young girl. She came into the room with a solemn look. Gone was the wild pleasure I'd seen when she rode her horse.

She took a seat between her parents, her posture perfect, her demeanor proper.

"Did you have a nice ride today?" her mother asked.

The corners of her mouth lifted into a smile. "I did. I saw our guests walking along the driveway. Did you have a nice walk?" she asked. Even her simple question seemed so mature.

"Yes." She was toying with us, waiting to see if we'd tell on her for riding so dangerously. I played along. "I'm sorry we didn't meet your riding teacher. Perhaps he should accompany you when you ride about the property. What if you fell? How would your parents find you?"

"No need to worry. I'm very accomplished. Even Newly says so. Mother, what about the horse show at the Nelson's on Sunday? Can we go? Please. I do want to enter Moonglow in the jumping classes."

Anne looked at her husband with some exasperation. "She can't ride astride. Why don't you insist that she use a sidesaddle like a proper lady?"

"Proper ladies don't have much fun," Amanda said.

Constance stood up. "I think we should review some lessons before dinner." She held out her hand. Amanda gave the governess her fingers and rose. "More lessons. I shall be the smartest horsewoman in the South."

She followed Constance out of the room, but she looked back at me and winked.

CHAPTER 4

Waverley House was the perfect setting for one of my stories, and when I went to my room on the second floor, I got out my pen and paper and began to write. I missed the typewriter I had at Caoin House. I'd become addicted to the speed with which I could type, my fingers keeping up with my thoughts. Working in longhand had become tedious, but I had no option. The muse had paid me a visit and soon I was lost in the world of my imagination.

"Framed Alive" was the title of my newest story. It would be loosely patterned on Nora Bailey, a woman whose past sins prevented her from finding peace. In my story, the spirit of a young woman had been imprisoned in a painting. Not dead and not alive, she haunted a lovely mansion in New York City.

The Sheridans had conveniently provided mosquito netting that allowed me to leave the windows open, and I also left the interior door to the rotunda ajar. This allowed a cross draft that made the room comfortable in the night air. It was a lovely room, complete with a small sitting room and space for at least two beds, though only one occupied the room. An old armoire stood in shadows in a corner, and there were feminine chairs and a small table by the window. In the winter, that would be a wonderful desk. Now, though, I wrote in bed by candlelight to stay within the insect netting.

Even as I created my ghost tale, I couldn't completely forget about Amanda. The child unnerved me. Perhaps she was merely precocious, having spent the majority of her time with adults. Time would tell.

I wrote until my eyes began to close, and I blew out my candle and settled into the soft pillows. The delicious meal of fresh garden vegetables and a fish caught that morning in the Tombigbee River had relaxed me. Only thoughts of Amanda troubled my mind.

I awoke after midnight, aware of noise in the hallway outside my door. Constance had reported strange noises, and I wondered if this might be the imaginary playmate, Nan. The thought sent a spear of cold fear into my heart. Ghosts were often not sinister, but they could be, as I'd learned in my brief career as an investigator of the terrain ruled by the mythological Pluto. He was the ruler of Hades, the land of the dead, and some dead had unfinished business with the living.

The noise came again, a soft shush, pause, shush, pause, shush. As if someone dragged a foot or was pulling something along the floor. What mischief might Nan be up to? It was my job to find out.

Reginald's room was across the rotunda from mine, and I saw his door was also ajar for the cooling draft. Constance's quarters were next to mine. She'd shown me her beautifully appointed room that included a private bathing area, newly installed by Royal Sheridan, a morning room with a fireplace, and a comfortable sitting and sewing area. Constance was talented with needle and thread. She was making a riding habit for Amanda, though I wondered if the child would willingly give up her breeches for even the most lovely female attire. I did believe she was safer astride, particularly if she insisted on riding like a hellcat and jumping fallen trees. That women should risk their necks in a side-saddle for propriety didn't sit well with me, and I had some sympathy for her desire to ride like the boys.

I stood at my door and studied the landing that circled the rotunda. Nothing appeared amiss. I was about to return to my room when I heard something downstairs. The shush, pause, and now a thump. Thump, shush, pause, thump. Like a head bumping down stairs. The thought came to me unbidden and with it a quiver of fear. My imagination was certainly in overdrive.

I retrieved my robe and slipped into it, belting the sash as I started down the curving staircase. If someone was in the house, I would find them. If it was a spirit, I wanted to see what it looked like. If it was Nan, I wanted a look at her.

At the ground floor, I stopped in front of the Sheridans' chamber. Several rooms comprised their quarters, and beside them was the only locked door in the house. Amanda's room. Since she'd taken to midnight ventures into the woods, her parents had moved her downstairs and locked her door at night from the outside.

I touched the doorknob. To my surprise it turned easily. Amanda's door wasn't locked at all. I stepped into the room to find her bed empty. The child was gone. She'd either escaped or been taken, and I wondered if the noise I'd heard was someone physically removing her. I needed to sound the alarm. I returned to the rotunda and froze. Amanda stood at the open front door in her pink nightgown. She looked so young and vulnerable. Then she laughed softly and ran into the night.

Without thinking I went after her.

The grass was thick with dew, and I followed Amanda into the woods. She'd found a deer trail that was wide enough for her to run. Taller, I had more difficulty, but I followed, my breathing harsh in my own ears. The silence of the woods struck me. Now was a time when insects, birds, and the small mammals should be active. This was prime hunting time for raccoons and opossums and squirrels, and in some instances, for the larger nocturnal creatures. However, nothing moved in the dense woods except for the child and me.

Amanda seemed to know where she was going, and I followed, realizing that if I lost her, I might not be able to find my way back to the house until daylight. Still I pursued the flash of her pink nightgown through the moon-glazed trees. I came upon a stables in a clearing. Moonglow, the magical silver horse that belong to Amanda, whinnied from a lush pasture. The horse watched the woods, prancing up and down the fence line.

I turned back to the child, and Amanda had disappeared. The dark woods crowded close upon me. Ahead, a warm light burned in the cabin beside the stables. I'd have to go there for help getting back to Waverley. I was a fool, out in the night in a gown and robe. As I approached the front door of the cabin, it opened and a tall, dark-haired man stepped out. The horse trainer, Newly Castor. It had to be. He was broad-shouldered and lean, a man of action. The look he shot me made my breath catch. Though my gown was modest, I felt suddenly revealed.

"Come here," he said, and I had no will to evade him. Rather, my imagination teemed with memories of his kisses and passion. I knew this man in the most intimate way. And I liked what I knew. I went to him and kissed him wildly, without restraint. His arms and lips were familiar, and I ached for him. Hungered for the wild rush of pleasure he gave me with his touch, his nearness. I'd never wanted anything more than to be with him.

"I can't live without you," he said.

That it was true gave me immense satisfaction. Only I could provide what he needed. "I'm here."

"You can't go back to him."

"Tonight I'm here with you." I stopped his words with a long deep kiss and stepped back to drop my robe and gown to the ground. The cool rush of air against my bare skin was exhilarating.

"Raissa!"

The one word was like a lash cutting into my flesh. I spun around to see Reginald coming toward me. His face reflected horror.

"What are you doing?" he demanded, picking up my gown and pulling it over my head. In a moment he had my robe wrapped and belted around me. "What on earth are you doing out here taking your clothes off?"

I couldn't answer because I didn't understand. I was in the middle of the Sheridan's front yard, not in the woods or at the stables. And I was alone. My entire reality had shifted, and I didn't know how. There was no handsome man waiting to take me in his arms. Reginald, my friend and partner, was the only other person about.

"What time is it?" I asked.

"After three in the morning. I heard something in the house and when I went to check on you, I realized your bed was empty. Then I saw you standing out here taking your clothes off."

"I don't know what I was doing. I thought I was...with

someone. A dark-haired man who smelled of leather and hay. He was at the stables. I thought he was the horse trainer..." My voice faded as did my thoughts. "How long have I been out here?"

"I don't know, but let me get you inside."

I followed obediently. "It was so real, Reginald. I was in his arms, kissing him. I was starved for his touch." I choked up. I hadn't felt so alive since Alex left for France—and never returned. "I have no idea who this man could be."

"Did you see anything else?"

"Amanda! I was following her into the woods. She's not in her room."

"No, I'm not." The voice came from the upstairs window in my room. Amanda sat on the window sill watching us. "I won't tell anyone," she said, then ducked back into the house.

"There is something very wrong with that child," I said. "And with me."

"Then I'd be willing to venture there's something very wrong with Waverley Mansion," Reginald said. He put his arm around me. "And we'll get to the bottom of it. I promise you. Now let's go inside. Tomorrow we can continue the investigation."

Fancy came from the kitchen with her arms loaded with platters of scrambled eggs, bacon, and the tiny tea biscuits that I normally adored, but my stomach churned and I couldn't eat. A young black girl followed her with a silver service of coffee. It was three times the food we could eat.

"We feed the workmen," Anne said. "If they're staying in the area, there's no place for them to get food."

I thought of the man I'd met last night. Or thought I met. Or dreamt. Could it have been a workman? I'd stayed awake the remainder of the night fretting over my behavior. I'd

THE SPECTER OF SEDUCTION 35

stripped myself naked in the front yard of a home where I was a guest. An eight-year-old child had likely seen me behave in such a reckless and wanton fashion. And I had no explanation for it.

"Chin up," Reginald whispered to me as he pretended to pick up his napkin from the floor. He sat to my right, and a good thing. I needed the support.

"Did you sleep well?" Anne asked.

Constance and Amanda joined us at the table, saving me from a lie. The child dug into her food and ignored me.

"Yes, the night was cool with the draft coming through the windows. The mosquito netting was genius," Reginald said. He was well-groomed, but fatigue touched his eyes. He was worried about me too.

"Yes," I said, unable to force out additional words.

"I slept like the dead," Amanda said, finally glancing up at me. She smiled.

The child...was simply not right. "I thought I heard you outside last night, Amanda." I would not let her bully me with her knowledge of my indiscretion.

"They lock me in my room," she said. "I can't get out."

"It's for your own protection," Anne said. She looked at me. "We aren't cruel, but we're terrified she'll fall in the old cistern or wander into the woods. There are still bears out there. And some wild cats. And plenty of snakes. I've been told there are alligators in some of the ponds and at the river."

"I agree. The woods aren't safe at night." How well I knew that. Something was amiss. "Reginald and I might drive into West Point. I need to call my uncle and let him know we arrived safely. Could we pick up some supplies, perhaps?"

"That would be extremely helpful," Royal said with a flush of happiness. "I have so much to do, but I was going to drive

into town for some things the workmen need. Are you sure
you wouldn't mind?"

"We're happy to do it," Reginald said. "Make a list. And if
you need any food supplies, Anne, we can get those too."

"You are a blessing," she said.

Not so much a blessing as a pair of gumshoes on a case. My
goal was to speak with some of the members of the local Episcopal church, the sheriff, and a married couple my uncle knew.
I needed to find out what reputation the Sheridan family had
in town. Something had happened to me last night, and I
couldn't say whether I'd been given a drug or not. There had to
be an explanation for my behavior, and I intended to find out
what it was.

But first, I would find the stables and speak with the riding
instructor. I would learn a lot from him.

CHAPTER 5

There was no escaping Reginald as I made my way toward the stables, using the directions Constance gave me. She was curious about my desire to see the stables and Moonglow, but she didn't ask the questions I saw in her eyes.

Reginald was not so shy. "What do you think you'll find?" he asked.

"I don't know, but I have to look. I kissed a man. It couldn't have been a dream. It was too real. I'd rather know now if it was Newly Castor than have him come up to the house." I walked fast. I'd worn long sleeves, but I'd forgotten the veil, and once we were in the woods, the yellow flies swarmed around our heads. I stopped and grabbed Reginald's arm. "Last night I wasn't bitten by any insects."

His eyebrows moved up. "Which means you didn't leave the front lawn. If you'd gone into the woods..."

He was correct. "So my visit with the horse trainer, or whoever he was, *was* an illusion."

"Which would mean you were drugged." Reginald sounded

grim. "Why invite us here only to harm us? It doesn't make sense. I'm glad we're going into town. I'll take the bank draft from Royal and leave it at the local bank to be sure it clears. There is some madness here, but we won't be double-crossed out of the jack he owes us."

I was more worried about my conduct than money, but Reginald didn't have a wealthy uncle. "Nothing that's happening at Waverley makes any sense. The child is... provocative. I wouldn't say she's haunted. But she's definitely under the influence of someone older and more sexually experienced. She knows things a child shouldn't know."

"How did she get out of her room?" Reginald asked.

"I don't know."

"Ghosts normally can't turn locks and keys."

He had an excellent point. Most spirits were unable to manipulate physical matter. They could appear as visions, spirits, an echo of the past. But I was learning that there were those more powerful entities that could move objects. The hideous monkey jigger from Caoin House came to mind. Reginald's unconscious fingers tapping out Morse code. Yes, there were some entities that had gathered tremendous energy—and used it. Nan could have let Amanda out of her room. It *was* possible.

My thoughts carried me through the woods and to the clearing where Moonglow stood at the wooden pasture fence, calling out toward the woods, just as she'd done in my nocturnal ramble. The stables centered the clearing, and the cabin was to the left, just as I'd seen it last night. As if my dream were re-enacting itself in broad daylight, a handsome, broad-shouldered man stepped out of the cabin. His dark hair, longish and combed back from his face, was tied in a Scottish queue that was long out of fashion.

He saw us and came our way.

"Is that him?" Reginald asked.

I studied him. He had the body build, the dark-hair, the purposeful stride, and the unrelenting gaze of my dream lover, but it was not him. "No," I whispered.

"Hello," the man said, coming forward. "You m-m-ust be looking for Amanda. She isn't scheduled for a lesson until after n-n-nine."

"She rides dangerously," Reginald said, a bit of heat in his voice.

"I would control her if I could," the man said, his tone deliberately casual. "She's a spoiled ch-ch-child who does as she pleases. The best I can do is teach her to be as safe as p-p-possible."

An interesting response from the man who'd come from Kentucky with the horse to train Amanda. I'd heard the entire story from Constance, who heartily disapproved of Amanda's riding activities. Not because it was dangerous, but because it was unladylike.

And Constance hadn't mentioned Newly's slight stutter. But why should she? It didn't matter to his profession.

"Aren't you in charge of her lessons?" I sounded like a schoolmarm, even to myself.

"I'm in charge of lessons. Amanda is apparently in ch-ch-charge of everything else." Newly Castor looked toward the house. The fourth floor rotunda rose above the treetops. "The Sheridans are nice p-p-people, but the daughter is...a handful."

"Have you noticed anyone else in the woods?" If my romantic partner of the previous evening wasn't Newly Castor, then who was it?

"Kids from the schools over at C-C-Columbus and Starkville. Strange that local kids stay away from here. It's the college students. They have cars and money to do what they want, I guess. They c-c-come here to make love in the woods. It's like a challenge or game to them."

"A challenge?"

"B-b-because of the legend. The girls come to prove they can't be seduced and the guys come to give it their best shot. From what I've heard, true or not I can't say, but something about this place does get under a girl's skin." The more he talked, the less he stuttered, which indicated he was getting more comfortable with us.

"Did you see a young woman in a yellow dress yesterday?"

"I did," Newly said. "She was with a young m-man over in the back garden beside the hydrangeas. They were pretty involved."

A nice way of saying they were making love. The memory of my behavior the past night made a flush rise to my face. There was something about Waverley Mansion that impacted a woman's sexuality—and control. I wondered if Constance had felt the pull of sexual longings. She was cultured, refined, and kept her own counsel. Whatever impulses she might have felt, I would likely never know.

"Amanda was riding like a hellion," I said. "This obviously isn't news to you, but she could so easily get hurt. I don't think the Sheridans would recover."

He nodded. "I try. I c-c-can't set restrictions her folks won't enforce."

"I understand." I had one more question. "Do the college students usually show up in the daytime or at night?"

"Both. You'd think the bitin' bugs would keep them away."

"Yes, you would." Another good point I hadn't considered. "We're going into town. Is there anything we can pick up for you?"

His eyes lit up. "Would you d-d-drop a bridle at the boot-maker's shop for repair?"

"Happy to do it."

"Be right back." Newly hurried into the stables and returned with a beautiful leather bridle. "Right here." He pointed to a frayed bit of leather. "C-can't have it break on the girl."

"Ab-so-lute-ly not." I smiled. Since leaving Zelda and Tallulah back in Montgomery, I'd fallen out of the use of modern expressions. It felt good to use one, especially since at Waverley Mansion, I felt I'd gone far, far back in time.

WEST POINT, Mississippi was a thriving little city that sprang to full life after the laying of rails for the Mobile and Ohio Railroad in 1858. The railroad tied West Point to vital river trade on the Tombigbee River close to Waverley Mansion.

Beyond the tracks, the picturesque town, the seat of Clay County, was centered by the courthouse. Progress in the form of paved or brick streets and automobiles had come to West Point, and the downtown stores and cafes were active. As we drove along Main Street, I took note of the more conservative attire on the store window mannequins. The role of women was deeply struck in the Deep South—females were wives and mothers, providers and nurturers who made a home for their families. Modern antics were frowned upon.

One shop, Step In Style, featured flapper dresses with cloche hats in one window and a male mannequin in slacks and a maroon and white sweater with the logo of the men's college in the second window. He held a megaphone, as if he might be yelling at a football game. Football was a popular pastime in areas that boasted a college team. The world was changing rapidly, and the influence of the young would only grow stronger if the towns and communities were to survive. The days of obedient women and young men with destinies cast by their family names were fading into the past. I saw both the good and the bad in the change. The impact of the war and the resulting emotional scars rippled out like rings around a stone dropped in water.

"It's a nice little town," Reginald said.

"Yes." I glanced at him. Reginald was not a small-town man. The anonymity of a big city worked better for his lifestyle. There were too many nosey gossips in small towns to allow comfort.

"Think how the railroads are opening up so many towns. And of course better roads and cars."

"This is a good life." Flowers bloomed on private lawns and around businesses. Pride in the city was apparent.

"There's a nice feel to this place," Reginald said. He offered me his cigarette case, but I shook my head. I was not completely successful at being a modern woman. I wasn't much of a drinker, and cigarettes made me cough. We went past a public library, a place I might need to visit at a later date. Now we were on a tight schedule.

Reginald and I drove to the home of Edward and Callie Ledbetter. Edward's father had been a riverboat captain for my uncle. After graduating high school, Edward had worked for a year on the Queen Cleo, one of my uncle's steamboats. Uncle Brett was exceedingly fond of the young man and had grubstaked his mercantile venture—a wise move on Uncle Brett's part. Edward was doing very, very well and had repaid the debt with interest.

Callie, a handsome woman with dark hair and a shirt-waist dress in pale lavender, came to the door at Reginald's solid knock. Uncle Brett had sent a telegram telling her of our arrival in the area. "Come in, Raissa. We've heard such wonderful stories about you. And it's so good to meet you, Mr. Proctor." She led us into a parlor where a small table had been laid with refreshments. "The tea has just steeped, but if you prefer coffee..."

"Tea is lovely," I said and Reginald nodded.

We'd just gotten through the niceties when Edward joined up. After a few moments of casual chit chat I turned the conversation to the Sheridans.

"Your uncle said you were working on a case there," Callie said, unable to hide her curiosity. "What kind of case?"

"We solve mysteries." Reginald kept it light. "Things that go missing, relatives who can't be found, fine art that's been stolen, that kind of thing. It would seem we have a knack for such things, and in the process, Mrs. James and I are able to travel and gain experiences for her stories."

I admired the way he skirted our true mission—that of hauntings and other supernatural events. There was still great resistance from most people to accept that beyond this reality, there was another realm, and that sometimes spirits lingered, crossing into our world with potentially devastating effect. An angry spirit, as I'd learned recently, could generate dense energy, and a ghost determined to manifest would sometimes take control of another person.

"How exciting," Callie said. "To be honest, I'd hoped you'd come to help that little girl. Amanda. She's not a healthy child."

"In what way?" I asked.

"She's not mentally healthy. Many of the young girls her age aren't allowed to play with her, not even after church. Of course Amanda isn't in town often enough to really develop friendships, and that's hard on a solitary child."

Callie was as lovely and friendly as Uncle Brett had said. And she seemed willing to volunteer a lot of information. To my relief, Edward and Reginald left the parlor to go outside and smoke. The door for more intimate conversation was opening wide. "I do find Amanda strangely mature." I stepped into the subject with care.

Callie snorted. "That child knows things she shouldn't. Now Anne and Royal seem like nice people, but someone took that little girl's innocence. She knows grown-up things. Nice people don't talk about this, and Edward told me to stay quiet, but since you're in that house, please see if you can make sure that child isn't being...harmed."

I understood her meaning clearly. She was worried Amanda was being abused. "I don't see Mr. Sheridan harming his own daughter. He seems devoted to her welfare."

Callie twisted her napkin in her hands. "I hate to imply such a dastardly thing, but something is wrong with Amanda. That horse trainer..." She didn't finish and didn't look at me.

"I've spoken with Mr. Castor. He didn't strike me as a deviant." There was no more polite word.

"He's a hard drinker, a brawler, and a gambler. The sheriff has locked him up several times." She sighed heavily. "Of course a lot of men behave that way. It's not Christian to imply such things."

"I'll do my best to determine if the child has been used in such a fashion." The prospect made me want to run for Caoin House and Uncle Brett. It was one thing to search for ghosts but another to probe a case of incest or child abuse. "I'll also speak with the sheriff before I leave town. If there is even a chance something like this is happening, you have my word that I will end it."

She shook her head. "Sheriff Gaines has been called out to Waverley House more than once, but it wasn't for the child."

"For the college students trespassing?"

"Oh, that too, but I was referring to the moonshining."

Callie was full of information that struck me like a bat. "Royal is a bootlegger?"

"One of the biggest in the region, so I've heard. The sheriff's gone out there to try and catch him at it, but so far no luck. Folks around here wonder where he gets his money, though. Waverley isn't planted in any crop and he doesn't raise beef, hogs, or chickens. He's spending a fortune on renovating that house, and the horse he bought for Amanda cost nearly a thousand dollars. That's a fancy price for a child's toy."

I liked Callie, but the pettiness of her judgment was becoming more and more clear. I wondered what she would say about Reginald if she somehow deduced his romantic preference when our backs were turned. "Amanda is a serious equestrian. It's her passion."

She looked up at me. "You're right, Raissa. I've heard she's very accomplished, and to be honest, some of the plantation girls are pea-green with envy over her riding and her horse. They've been the best riders for too many years, and they hate having an outsider come in and steal their thunder. Especially one so young and so...daring."

"They've seen her ride?"

"There are shows at different plantations. I've seen her jump fences taller than her horse. She never hesitates. By the way, the Nelsons are hosting an event with jumping and dressage, all very European. They say it's as refined as ballet."

"I'd like to see that."

"The event is Sunday. Everyone is welcome. We take picnic refreshments and find a shady spot to watch the young riders. This type of riding has become popular among some of the families who have dreams of participating in the Olympics. The Germans and Swedes dominate now, but, with training, that could change. Americans can do everything better than anyone else."

"And women? Do they allow women riders?" I'd not kept up with athletics. My world had been focused on war.

"There have been a rare few female competitors. Tennis, of course. And equestrian events. It really isn't ladylike for a woman to straddle a horse."

I tried not to smile and failed. Callie rejected all modern ideas where a woman was concerned. I'd known many people like her. Change made her uncomfortable, and not to change was a challenge that also made her uncomfortable. "I know. Isn't it wonderful? Amanda and her peers are refusing the limitations imposed on our gender. If Tennessee ratifies the Nineteenth Amendment, we'll be able to vote for president."

"Voting is a far cry from straddling a horse." Callie's back was up.

"For some, but not for all." I spoke as gently as I could. "Amanda has talent. She shouldn't be penalized because she was born a girl." I thought perhaps I'd stumbled upon Amanda's secret dream. She had her heart set on competing in the Olympics, and she had no one to share her desire with. This could be a huge advantage for me, and while I worried about the dangers of her riding, I had to admire a child who knew so thoroughly what she wanted to do. Such focus was a type of genius to my way of thinking.

"Do you find all this obsession with changing the role of women to be healthy?" Callie had seen my smile.

"I do," I said. I might fib about my job here to keep the gossip down, but I had to stand up for Amanda's dream and for other women. I thought of Zelda and her foolhardy bravery at deliberately baiting the Montgomery matrons. Her life would have been easier had she taken her modern ways to New York and stayed there, but she had too much courage and heart to do that.

"Young women are behaving dangerously. They're ruining their chances at security. You know, why buy the cow if you can get the milk for free?"

"There's a vast difference between riding a horse and becoming sexually loose."

"There are some who would argue that the two go hand in glove."

I nodded. "There are always those who find a belief system that helps them suppress others. My mother often spoke of the time when Negroes didn't have the right to vote and were considered three-fifths of a human. Obviously a false belief." We had gotten dangerously off track. "But we're so lucky to live in times where people can choose what to believe, aren't we? Uncle Brett believes that Edward is a business genius and the luckiest man alive to have married you."

"I adore your uncle. I have an aunt who might take a shine to him. What do you think?"

"We must attempt to match-make." Uncle Brett had a lovely female friend, but there was no need to tell Callie that. I'd turned the conversation, thank goodness. "I understand the Sheridans attend the Episcopal church in town."

"When they come. The road is not good, as you know, and it's a long drive."

"Your minister's name is?"

"Lewis Brock. He's a lovely man." She frowned. "Maybe he could speak with the Sheridans."

"If that proves necessary, I'll certainly speak with him about it." I didn't want Callie sending a minister out to meddle in what might be a family nightmare.

Reginald and Edward returned, and for another half hour we talked about Uncle Brett's steamships and a new invention he was working on. When we took our leave, I gave Callie a hug. "I'll let you know if I find anything untoward."

CHAPTER 6

T he Clay County Sheriff's Office was similar in smell, set-up, and attitude to the ones I'd visited in Mobile and Montgomery Counties. I could only describe it as dominatingly male. Sheriff Walter Gaines, a middle-aged man with a trim build and impressive mustache, looked up at me, as did four deputies who edged toward fat. None of them spoke to me. Only to Reginald.

With practiced ease, Reginald maneuvered us into the sheriff's private office, though it was clear that none of the lawmen felt I belonged there. The good wife let her husband handle matters of the law. Women without husbands or fathers or brothers—they relied on the kindness of strangers.

It took about five minutes of Sheriff Gaines hemming and hawing before I excused myself and left. It was hot as Hades outside, but Reginald would be able to learn far more from Gaines if I wasn't around. We'd learned to play to our strengths.

It was the perfect opportunity to stroll downtown, and I did so, going straight to the Step In Style shop. I was curious about the proprietor who flaunted the community norms. To my surprise, the shopkeeper was a young woman who looked like she should be in a college classroom rather than running a business. She wore a smart dress banded at the hips, no stockings, shoes with a lot of straps and several strands of beads. Her bobbed hair was marcelled and her dark eye makeup was offset by bright red lipstick. I'd walked into the den of a flapper.

"May I help you?" She came over, taking in my dress rumpled from the car ride and the heat of the day.

"I'm visiting in the area and liked your window display. I'm Raissa James."

"Edith Keller." She laughed out loud. "My display window is a topic of hot debate. Everybody in this dump thinks it's their beeswax to tell me how to sell glad rags. Bunch of Mrs. Grundys, if you ask me."

I liked her grit, and her modern lingo made me miss Zelda even more. "I like the dress in the window." I didn't need a new dress, but I had earned some money selling my first story. I wondered who supported this store.

"Something fetching for a special man?" She grinned.

"No, just in case. A girl can hope, right?" I was, perhaps, five years older than she was, but I felt ancient in comparison. She was all bright hope and unafraid defiance.

"You're a looker. Guys should be buzzing around like you're honey." She cut a sideways glance. "You don't want that. You've been hurt."

"And you're perceptive." With my eyes misting over, it was pointless to deny it. "My husband was killed in the war."

"I'm so sorry."

"Me too. I'm visiting with the Sheridans at Waverley Mansion."

"The folks with the little bad girl."

"Bad?"

She shrugged. "That's what I've heard. Folks are scared of her."

"She's eight years old."

"Folks around here get an idea and they can't let it go. Someone said she was in cahoots with the Devil and now folks are afraid of her. The other little girls were mean to her, if you want to know the truth. Amanda is a sort of tomboy—she likes being outside and wearing pants and riding horses, and they made fun of her. I got the idea she didn't take that lying down, and she got back at some of them."

"How? She's eight!"

"Kids are mean. Six or eight or twenty-eight. They pack up against you, find a weakness, you're a goner."

I was suddenly struck by the memory of a cool fall day on the playground when a couple of girls decided to target me. I had been shy and quiet. It was a misery for the rest of the year.

"Amanda has a governess, and she's a remarkable horse rider."

"Yes! She has that horse trainer. He's a real Valentino!" She gave a little shimmy. "I'd like to throw a bridle on that man. Have you met him?"

"I have. He's a looker."

She sighed. "He comes to town and stays in the speakeasies, and I can't go in there. My reputation is bad enough. Hey, maybe you could tell him about me."

"Maybe." I lifted a shoulder. "I don't know how long he'll stay. I don't think his position is permanent."

"There are plenty of horses need training around these parts. He could stay busy as much as he wanted. Now that folks don't have to ride horses, it's become a real ritzy thing to do. Upper crust and all of that."

"Have you met the governess, Constance Nyman?"

"Only at church. She's the perfect fire extinguisher. I think if she smiled her face would crack."

I tried not to laugh but I couldn't stop myself. "She's pretty nice, just very serious."

"You think?" She straightened a display of belts. "When I was a fish, I used to go out to Waverley Mansion with a group of girls and boys. You know, danger and booze, good combos for a necking party."

I'd missed those days, but I could imagine. "Did you ever see anything?"

"No but I will say that something does go on there. My roommate went out to Waverley with her fly-boy and three months later he was wearing a set of handcuffs and she was sewing a layette. They're still married and got two kids, so it worked out."

"Did she say she was influenced by someone or something at Waverley?"

"She insisted. Said she knew what she was doing, but it was like someone else was inside her and she was outside, unable to stop it. Joey, that's her guy, said she was too hot to handle. Got them both in the frying pan. Her daddy actually had a shotgun at the wedding, just in case Joey tried to dodge."

I felt for the young woman in question. I'd married for love, and it had been momentous. I knew girls who'd married out of necessity—pregnancy, economics, status, parental expectations, a desperate need for a family. The fairy tale romance and wedding was rarer than most people realized. For the term of my romance, I'd been the luckiest girl in the world.

And then I was one of millions who endured loss and grief. Life could be both sweet and terribly bitter.

I pulled my thoughts back to the moment. "Your friend said she felt she lost control of her body?" My libidinous romp on the lawn of Waverley stung me with shame again.

"That's what she said, but what else could she say?" Edith was a practical girl.

"Perhaps. I have another question. Is your shop here successful? I mean you're offering city fashions, not the more traditional styles."

"The young people swarm in here, looking to see what's new. High school girls and boys. Sales should pick up very soon as the high school graduates prepare to leave for school in September. They may not buy modern styles to wear in West Point, but they want to be modern on the campus, away from the nosy neighbors who wag their tongues all over town."

"Excellent point." I had to give it to Edith. She understood her audience and their needs. "Have you met Anne and Royal Sheridan?"

She rolled her eyes. "Not them, but that girl of theirs. She's something else. She sneaks over here and tries on dresses that are inappropriate and too large. It's like she thinks she's taller and bigger and older than she really is. But she's quick. She comes up with some comments that make me slap my knee."

It was the same description of Amanda—too mature for her age. "Has she ever said anything about her home circumstances?"

Edith thought a moment. "She said one time that she was going to be a famous equestrian. I had to ask her what that meant. A famous horse rider. Of all things for a young girl to dream about, riding horses. I grew up on a farm. I was never so glad when we could finally afford an old jalopy. Why would anyone want to ride a horse when they can ride in a car?"

I picked up a beautiful scarf. As soon as the weather turned, it would be a beautiful addition to my wardrobe. "Do you know if anything untoward ever happened out at Waverley. I hear the place is haunted."

"The old folks tell how the ghost of a Union spy hangs out there."

"No dead children?" I was thinking more of Nan.

"Not that I heard. They hanged that woman, Nora something. Hanged her from the big magnolia tree in the front yard. They caught her lover and roped him up beside her."

"One of the Norquist boys was murdered?" This Constance had skipped.

"No, it wasn't her fiancé, it was her lover. A doctor on the plantation next door. He was a Union sympathizer and the man who took the information she gathered and got it across the Confederate lines."

"Do you remember his name?"

"No, sorry. It's been a long time since I sat around on the front porch listening to Gramps and Mawmaw tell stories. I'm here at the shop most of the time."

"That must have been terrible for Francis Norquist. It was said he loved Nora deeply."

"Her body disappeared from the tree. Folks say he cut her down and buried her against his family's wishes. She's supposed to be buried on the property, but no one can say for sure when it happened. It's all just talk and legend now."

The bell over the door jangled and my new friend stood up tall and straight. An unhappy woman and her daughter came into the shop. The girl went immediately to several short dresses that would look adorable on her. The mother frowned, hesitating in the middle of the store.

"If I can help you, please let me know," Edith said. "I'll have more dresses coming in next week."

"I'm going to school at Columbus," the girl said, though she didn't look old enough to be a high school graduate. I could tell I was getting older now because everyone looked younger to me.

"I can show you some sketches of college fashion if you'd like." Edith was closing in on a sale.

"Thank you," I whispered to her and left so she could run her business. When I turned the corner and the courthouse came into view, I saw Reginald leaning against the car smoking a cigarette.

"How'd it go?" I asked, refusing his offer of a smoke.

"Sheriff isn't much of a lawman, but he's a great politician. Said there weren't any bootleggers in Clay County and that young folks will be young folks and no point getting too upset over any of it. The only real information I got was that he didn't much care for Royal Sheridan. Seems like the county is considering doing some work on the road to Waverley Mansion instead of funding the sheriff's budget. I'd say a conflict of interest."

Reginald had the most acute ability to sniff out people's real motives

"Let's stop by the church and then run the errands for Royal and Anne," I suggested.

"That's a plan."

CHAPTER 7

Reverend Lewis Brock was a white-haired gentleman who puttered as we talked. Reginald and I introduced ourselves, explaining that we were visiting at Waverley and that I was a writer of ghost stories. It was a profession that held no appeal for him.

"Thank you for taking the time to talk with us," I said.

Lewis Brock was a man who did not do well with stillness. As we talked, Reginald and I followed him around the lovely sanctuary of the Episcopal Church of West Point as he returned hymnals to their holders in the backs of pews and examined kick marks where some child had swung his feet in boredom striking the pew in front.

"Some parents have no respect for God's house," he said as he wiped at the marks.

"It was probably a child," Reginald observed.

"Yes." He looked up and I had the uncanny realization that he knew it was a child and which one. A child he didn't like. "This younger generation has no respect or discipline. Why if

I'd dared to kick a pew during church service, my mother would have grabbed my ear, dragged me outside, and switched me until I knew better."

I ignored that bit of child-rearing advice and complimented Brock on the beauty of his church. It was a lovely building with vaulted ceilings and colorful stained glass windows that cast kaleidoscopic patterns on the polished hardwood floors. Had the minister been able to control his nervous cleaning, it would have been a place of serenity.

"How long have you pastored here?" I asked.

"Five years or so. West Point is a growing community. I'm lucky to have active church members, those who value the work of a man of God."

"Of course." I couldn't tell if he was difficult to talk to or if he simply didn't want to talk to us.

"Have you had any reports of...unusual things happening out at Waverley Mansion?" Reginald got right to the point. He didn't care for Reverend Brock.

"Other than ghosts, hangings, spies, a horse trainer who drinks and brawls, and a child far too advanced for her years?" He waited to see our response.

"Anything you might describe as occurring from the spirit world?" Reginald didn't back down.

"No, I don't believe in ghosts or hauntings. I do believe that undisciplined children can create a world of mischief. That's what's going on at Waverley and nothing more."

I wondered about Callie's belief that Amanda might be an unwilling participant in an incestuous relationship. The minister appeared to believe that Amanda was willful and her parents too soft on her. It was a sentiment I'd heard before.

"I've been collecting anecdotes regarding the history of Waverley Mansion. I'm sure you know everyone in town.

Maybe you could point us to a local historian or someone who knows local stories. I do write fiction, so I'm not all that concerned with facts. I'd just like to know the lore about the Waverley."

"I don't deal in lore, so I'm afraid I can't help you."

Wouldn't or couldn't. I wanted to ask but didn't. It wouldn't do a bit of good. "Thank you, Reverend." I signaled to Reginald that I was ready to go. He took my elbow to escort me out into the bright sunshine. When we were almost to the car, he leaned in to whisper, "I'll be right back."

Before I could protest, he was gone. I waited ten minutes in the car and when he returned, he lifted one eyebrow. "Like the sheriff, the preacher man doesn't really like to talk to women."

I understood. I had stepped out of my approved role, and the best way to deal with an uppity woman was to simply ignore her. "Thanks for going back."

"I didn't find out much except that a lot of people think there's something going on at Waverley Mansion. They don't necessarily believe in ghosts, but they do believe the place 'isn't right' and that it has impacted the Sheridan family. Seems there was another family who moved in and didn't stay longer than eight weeks. That was years ago. Brock didn't know how to get in touch with them."

"Let's get those supplies and get home. I wonder if Anne has any old photographs of the house and the Norquist family."

"Never hurts to ask."

FANCY BROUGHT four boxes of things down from the fourth floor and left them in my room. After the heat had driven us

into a long nap, Reginald and I sat at the little table by the
window and began our search. The house was cooler than any
place I'd been all day, but it was still uncomfortably warm.
Nonetheless we needed to work if we were to find anything
helpful to Amanda.

A soft tap on the door made us both look up from a ledger
of estate accounts that we were pursuing. Anne stepped into
the room.

"Have you discovered anything that might help?"

"Not yet." Reginald was kind but firm. "This could take
some time, Anne. We're not certain what we're looking for.
Maybe we can visit a bit with Amanda tomorrow. See if we can
get this Nan to appear."

"Perhaps tonight after supper. That's when...Amanda is
sometimes the most strange."

"Sure. We'll see what we can do."

"Anne, do you know who these people are?" An old tintype
had been stuck in the pages of the journal. It showed four
women and four men, all very young and handsome. They were
seated in the front parlor of the house, the women on a sofa
and the men standing behind them. When I looked closely at
the men, I almost dropped the picture. The man I'd kissed was
there. A man who died years before and yet I'd shared a
passionate kiss with him.

Anne didn't notice my falter, but Reginald shot me a
curious look. Anne took the picture and studied it. "Six are the
Norquist children, but I can't identify the other two. If I had
to guess, I'd say that dark-haired one is Nora. She's pretty. The
other is likely the local doctor. Calvert something."

Reginald stood to look over Anne's shoulder. "That one?"

"Yes. The girls are Helene, Marguerite, and that one is
Olivia. The boys are Burton, there, behind Olivia. He's the

youngest. That's Francis, and the older one, Jedidiah. They were all killed in the war. I think Francis grew reckless after what happened with the spy."

"And the daughters? What happened to them?"

"Their prospective beaus were all killed, from what I remember. I think they moved away and died as spinsters. That's when the house was abandoned. It's sad to me. A once-proud family that descends into ruin. When there aren't children, there's not much to pin the future on."

I studied the photograph and pointed to the beauty that might be Nora Bailey. "Did you ever see the portrait of her that Francis commissioned?"

Anne sighed. "No. I haven't. But I haven't looked. There are trunks and paintings and things up on the fourth floor. To be honest, we've been so preoccupied with the physical renovation that we haven't gone through any of the memorabilia. I need to do that."

"I can help. It might give us some leads about this Nan."

"Sure. Just be careful. The stairs up to the fourth floor are narrow."

"My daddy used to tell me I was as sure-footed as a goat."

"Okay. Dinner will be at seven. Maybe the day will cool, but Fancy is making a cold soup and some vegetables from the garden. The only thing that appeals to me is a glass of cold tea. What I wouldn't give for some ice. If the county improves our road, we'll be able to get deliveries of ice and milk. It's either that or Newly's going to have to learn to milk and churn butter."

The image of Newly Castor doing either chore was amusing. "Thank you, Anne." She looked so fragile and worried that I put a hand on her arm. "We'll get to the bottom of this. Has Amanda mentioned Nan lately?"

"No, strangely she hasn't."

"I do need to talk with her."

"She'll finish her lessons at five. Either before or after supper would be good."

"I'll meet her in the parlor. Maybe she'll play for me again."

Anne bit her lip. "Can she? I don't know that she will ever play like that again. And it scares me to death." She turned and left the room, leaving a lingering sadness behind.

I kept the photograph of the Norquist children and the woman I presumed to be Nora Bailey and the journal of accounts for Waverley Mansion. The other boxes Reginald and I returned to the storage rooms on the fourth floor. The spiraling staircase was a challenge as the steps did narrow greatly up to the fourth floor. It took us two trips, and then we found some excellent afternoon light and settled on the floor with more boxes in front of us.

I'd always been interested in history, and whoever had packed the boxes of Waverley Mansion had done so with great love. Invitations for weddings and parties that pre-dated the Civil War were in abundance, giving a clear picture of life at Waverley before it all went to hell. The Norquist daughters were the social elite, invited to hundreds of luncheons, rides, dances, and sleep-overs at different plantations. Oak Alley, a nearby mansion, hosted as many parties as Waverley Mansion, and I discovered it abutted the Waverley land. The house was columned and gracious, and a tintype of a gathering of young people on the front lawn took my imagination back to a time when graciousness was an art.

A lifestyle and a culture that embodied so much beauty and blood had been destroyed by greed and war, and it had all been unnecessary, to my way of thinking. There could be no moral argument for slavery. A peaceful resolution should have been found. But that was more than fifty years past, yet the scars still lingered on the earth, but even more on the psyche of the people.

"Let's go through some of those old paintings." Reginald pointed to a sheet-shrouded mound against the wall. When we pulled the sheet back, he was correct. Framed portraits and landscapes were stacked one against the other.

"Do you suppose we'll find the DeWitt painting of Nora Bailey?"

"It would be helpful. Do you think you saw Nora's ghost in the woods?"

"No. Her dress was modern."

"And a ghost can't assume modern garb?" Reginald teased me gently.

I thought a moment. "You know, I can't honestly say. Why not? Why would they have to dress in the time period when they died?"

Reginald held the first painting as I gently flipped the stack one by one. "Some of these could be valuable. That's a Bennett." Clayton Bennett was a famous Southern portrait painter.

"Is this one a DeWitt?" Reginald asked.

My hopes jumped. If we could find a painting by Julian DeWitt, we might be on the trail of the Nora Bailey portrait that had gone missing. The painting Reginald held was of Olivia Norquist, not the spy. Olivia was a beautiful girl with tawny hair and grey eyes. I had no doubt she'd been a popular belle.

We'd gone through all of the paintings, including some incredible landscapes and more portraits of the Norquist family—all were handsome people with square jaws and the look of Swedes or Norwegians. In looking through some letters and documents, I'd learned how Bjorn Norquist had come to the property along the Tombigbee River and built this house on a design he'd hoped to patent and sell to others in the South who wanted a cooler home. He'd brought a now-abandoned spur of the railroad to Waverley for transport of goods from the river landing into West Point. He'd been an entrepreneur with an eye on the future.

The death of his sons in the Civil War had broken him. He'd lived until 1868, and then died, a man in his late fifties who'd lost his will to live.

"I guess the girls left Waverley after he died." I couldn't see Marguerite and Helene, both war spinsters, staying here alone without a man. Olivia had married and moved to San Francisco. I'd found several letters to her sisters begging them to move out to California with her. Eventually Helene and Marguerite had followed her to the west coast. And there they'd disappeared. Their link to Mississippi had been dissolved permanently when Waverley became the property of the state for failure to pay taxes.

"The family has surely been plagued with tragedy." Reginald folded up the last letter and put it back in the file.

"I think of the families with two or three children who died. That was common. I simply am not strong enough to endure the death of a child." After losing Alex, I doubted I'd ever risk having a child. My losses of both parents and then Alex had come too fast and too hard.

"Don't dig a hole and climb in until you have to," Reginald said. "I'm going out on the balcony for a smoke. I'm afraid to light up in here. I might start a fire."

"That's using your noggin. I'll come out for some air in a minute." The storage room was musty and even the semiliquid outside humidity would be a nice change. Before I left, though, I wanted to go through another box of letters.

I picked up a packet tied with a red ribbon and realized after opening the first one that these were love letters to Francis from Nora. Her penmanship spoke of a bold person, one who took action and didn't hesitate.

"My darling Francis, it's been two months since we were together and I find I can't sleep at night. My dreams are hot, fevered, and filled with memories of your touch, your kisses, your body pressed against and into mine. You are the giver of intense pleasure, and I want to do the things that bring you gratification.

"I have begun to touch myself, pretending it is you. I blush at the way my body writhes and longs for you."

I put the letter aside and found my heart pounding. Nora was an uninhibited correspondent, and compared to her, I felt like a callow fool. I'd never been so free in writing my husband and it was one of my deepest regrets. I could have given Alex something intimate and real, though he was an ocean away. I simply hadn't known how to be so sexual with pen and paper.

"Raissa?" Reginald stood in the doorway. "Do you want to clean up before dinner? It's five. And you have a meeting with Amanda?"

"Yes, I do." I answered both questions at once, stood up, and brushed the dust from my skirt. My face was flushed, but I knew Reginald would attribute it to the attic and the heat. "What are you going to do?"

"Take a stroll to the stables and talk with Newly Castor. He's around here all the time. Surely he's seen something and maybe he can shed some light on Amanda's imaginary friend."

"Good idea. Do you think we should plan a séance

tonight?" If Nan was around, I wanted to meet her and get an idea of what she wanted, or needed.

"See how the meeting with Amanda goes. We don't want to put her in a corner if she isn't ready to work with us."

"You're right." As usual, Reginald's level-headedness was a boon to our work.

CHAPTER 8

Fancy was busy in the kitchen, and the Sheridans had retired to their room. Reginald had gone to the stables, and Constance had decided on a walk around the gardens. She was an avid horticulturist who knew a lot about the native plants growing at the mansion. Waverley had a full-time gardener, but we'd yet to meet him.

I asked Amanda to join me in the front parlor. She agreed without hesitation, and we took our seats on facing chairs, a small table between us.

"Shall we call up the spirit of my imaginary friend?" she asked, watching me carefully.

I was slightly taken aback, but I tried not to show it. "Would you like to do that? Have a séance?"

"Isn't that why you're here. To send Nan packing?"

"Only if you want her to go."

"Mother hates her. So does Father, though he tries to pretend he doesn't believe she's here."

"Tell me about Nan. Is she a young girl like you?"

"Am I young?" Amanda cut a look at me that gave me

pause. In her cool gray eyes, I saw the confidence of a young woman, not a child.

"How old are you, Amanda?"

"Eight."

"Really? You seem much older."

She shrugged. "I thought you were interested in Nan."

"I am. But I'm also interested in you. See, Nan wouldn't be here unless you wanted her. That's how it works. She might be in the house or around the yard, but she wouldn't be in you, and that's where she is, am I right?"

"You're not dumb."

"Tell me how you met?" I'd had no experience dealing with a person, especially a child, who'd lost the defining line between herself and another entity. And there was always the chance that Amanda, or Nan, was playing with me.

"I was in the back garden, digging around in a bare patch of dirt. Amos came over and told me to find another place to play. He said that patch of dirt was cursed."

"Amos is the gardener?"

"Yes, Amos Plackett. He's nice. He tells me stories when he's resting. I hate it here because there's no one around for miles."

"I know you're lonely here. Maybe when they work on the road you'll be able to go to the public school."

"The other children don't like me."

"And why is that?"

"I tell them the stories about Waverley Mansion. They say I scare them." Her smile was mischievous and sinister. "And I do. I like to. They're such scaredy cats. I can make Margaret and Hattie cry." She shook her head slowly. "They are so stupid."

I could see why the other children didn't want to play with

her. "Before you came here to Waverley, did you have play-mates your own age?"

"Yes. I lived in town and went to school. I was the teacher's pet."

"And then you came here."

"And Nan became my only friend."

"What does Nan look like?"

"Close your eyes and I'll tell you."

I didn't want to admit it, but Amanda made me uncomfort-able. Despite that, I had to win her trust. Whatever was going on with her, everything would go smoother if she believed I was there to help her. I couldn't allow her to see that I was ill-at-ease. "Okay." I closed my eyes.

"I'm going to play the piano, and you'll see her." Amanda's footsteps went to the piano. She began to play Chopin's Prelude in E minor. "Keep your eyes closed," she directed.

I leaned back in the chair trying to clear my mind. I had no idea what Amanda expected me to see, but I was willing to experiment.

The music, tinged with sadness, flowed through me and once again I was amazed at the emotion with which Amanda played. She was equally accomplished on the piano and atop a horse. Whatever else was going on with the child, she was immensely gifted.

An image began to appear in my mind. I was in the rotunda of Waverley Mansion, standing at the door to the parlor. Above me on the second floor was the laughter of several young women. Outside the front door, other houseguests chat-ted. It was a party, one of the many winter gatherings that kept the local residents from total isolation.

The weather was mild and the day sunny. I started toward the front door, but the murmur of voices in the parlor stopped me. The hint of secretiveness drew me like a bee to honey. The door was open and I peeped in to find Francis, Jedidiah, and Burton, along with several other Confederate officers, leaning over a map that had been placed atop a beautiful piano.

"We can bring the weapons and ammunition up the Tombigbee to the landing here. The Henry rifles and Colt revolvers will turn the tide, I know it." Jedidiah tapped the map with force. "The rail spur here at Waverley will allow us to get the munitions to the main rail line and then we'll be able to transport them to our troops."

"The soldiers are in desperate need of food supplies too," Francis said.

"We'll load some flour and meal for them," another young man said. "We have to move quickly. They can't hold back the bluecoats much longer."

"The guns will be here in four days," Francis said. "We have to be ready to move them immediately."

"Then we know what we need to do."

The laughter of the young women upstairs moved onto the balcony above the rotunda and I stepped back into the doorway of a bedroom, out of sight from the second-floor landing. My heart was pounding. I had to get out of the house.

"Nora, you look like you've seen a ghost." The voice came from behind me. Olivia had come from the library and was looking at me with open curiosity.

"I went out on the back porch and there was a huge rat. It stood up on its hind legs and challenged me." I managed a shaky laugh.

"I'll get the boys to look for it. I'm sure it wants inside to be warmer." Olivia brushed past me and went to the parlor. "Gentlemen, we need assistance. Nora was challenged by a wood rat."

Francis and his brothers came into the rotunda. "I'll save you from the vermin," he said, brushing a hand across my cheek. I pressed into his hand, closing my eyes so I couldn't see his handsome face, the grey eyes that looked at me with such adoration.

"Thank you."

"No rat is going to upset my fiancée."

And the men strode out to the back porch to search for the errant rat.

A hand grasped my shoulder and shook it. When I opened my eyes, Amanda was staring at me. She shook my shoulder lightly again. "You fell asleep," she said. "Mama is ready to serve dinner."

I sat up in the chair, disoriented.

"Did you meet someone?" she asked.

"Yes, but it wasn't Nan."

"I know. Well, maybe next time." She left me and I had the uneasy idea that she knew exactly what I'd dreamt.

THROUGHOUT SUPPER, I was still reeling from the dream. It had been so real, so visceral. I'd felt what Nora Bailey felt, and it was disconcerting. She had feelings for Francis, a deep attachment and sexual longing. Yet, I knew from the legend that she betrayed him and his brothers and the family who had so graciously welcomed her into their home.

As I forced myself to eat the crisp cucumbers marinated in vinegar and salt with tomatoes and sliced onions, I tried to settle my emotions. The cold supper was light and perfect for the hot day.

"Where's Daddy?" Amanda asked.

Until then I hadn't really noticed that Royal was absent.

Since we'd brought the supplies he requested, he'd been working on the estate.

"One of the workmen saw some of those college kids in the woods. He went to run them out." Anne looked worried.

"They just come back," Amanda said, buttering a slice of bread. "He can't stop them."

Anne spoke softly. "He believes if he makes it uncomfortable for them, they'll stop."

Amanda only stared at her mother. She had a way of making it seem she knew things she couldn't possibly know.

"Have you spoken with the schools?" Reginald asked. "Surely they can put some pressure on the students to stop."

Anne nodded. "That's an excellent idea. When we go to Columbus, we can stop at the school there. If the girls refuse to come here, the boys won't have much incentive."

Reginald took over the table conversation, telling a few stories of his years in New Orleans and the many celebrities he'd met. He was aware that I was unsettled, and I greatly appreciated his efforts to keep the conversational ball rolling smoothly. At last the meal was over and he suggested we take a walk before night fell. I needed to speak with him, so it was the perfect opportunity.

We left the house behind and headed toward the back gardens. Amanda had mentioned a bare spot on the grounds, and I found it with ease. I also found Amos Plackett, the gardener. He was a bent, older man who'd once been a slave. Now he had a small cabin that had originally been quarters for the Negroes.

"Weather's coolin' off a little," he said amiably. "Nice evenin' for a walk."

"Yes, sir," Reginald said. "It looks like you have your work cut out for you, bringing these gardens back." An acre or two had been cleared and re-landscaped but the tangled mess of the former gardens stretched all the way to dense woods.

"Yes, it's comin' along, but it takes time. I kept the vegetable patch going after the sisters left, but the rest was too much. 'Course I was a young-un back then. I had to hire out to the other folks along the river to make ends meet. End of the day, I didn't see a need for fancy gardens in a place no one ever came."

"What about the young people who come to pet and neck?"

He chuckled softly. "They ain't lookin' at flowers, I can tell you that for sure. Those young'uns don't care about flowers or shrubs."

"They really upset Mr. Sheridan." I put that out for consideration.

"Lots of things upset the owners of a place when folks trespass."

"Why is this place bare?" I looked at the circle of earth that was beside a beautiful patch of lilies, some with double-petaled blooms that I'd never seen before.

"That's where Mr. Francis took the body of his fiancée, that spy, after he cut her out of the magnolia tree up front. They wanted to burn her, hangin' in the tree, but he stopped it. He tricked 'em into riding off and then he brung her back here and hid her so they couldn't find her."

For a moment, my heart squeezed with anguish. "Is that true, Amos, or just part of the legend?"

"It's true. I was a little boy, and I saw it. He cut her down while the others had gone to get that other one and some kerosene and a torch, and he brung her here and hid her under leaves until the crowd got tired of searchin' and went on and burned the other one."

"The doctor."

"Yes, he was a doctor. He helped my mama bring me into this world. Folks said both of us would have died without Dr. Marcus from over at Nine Oaks. Sat with my mama for two days."

"How did Nora Bailey and the doctor get caught?" Amos seemed to have more pertinent information than anyone else on the plantation.

"That Sherman sent the bluecoat soldiers down to waylay the train with all the guns. The Confederates knew someone had sold them out, and it wasn't long before they came to the fact that it had to be Miss Nora."

The past settled over me like a wet wool blanket, suffocating. I'd been part of this, at least in my dream. "That must have been terrible for everyone."

"Bad times back then. I was just a small boy. That night I thought they'd kill us all. The white men were so angry. They'd lost loved ones and a big important battle."

"What did Francis do with Nora's body?"

"When everyone was gone and the place was quiet, he took her out to the family cemetery and buried her. Took down what was left of that doctor and buried him too. That broke Mr. Francis. Wasn't three weeks later he was killed in a cavalry charge. Some said he rushed into the bullets like he wanted to die."

"Why would Nora betray a man she loved?" I asked the question of myself as much as Reginald and Amos.

"She believed slavery was a bad thing," Amos said. "She loved Francis. She did. She loved that painter man too. And the doctor. Miss Nora was a sweet young woman when she came here. Then she changed. She couldn't settle on one man. She had a hunger in her that had to be fed. And that's what ultimately got her kilt. They was on to her, and she met that doctor back yonder in the woods. One of the Norquist girls, Olivia, come up on them and seen they was makin' love. Then it wasn't hard to put two and two together."

"Only disaster could come from that." Reginald looked beyond us into the woods. "To be betrayed in that fashion must have cut Francis Norquist to the bone."

I followed his gaze. Beyond the cleared garden was thick woods, and I thought I saw movement there, the flash of pale green. When I didn't see it again, I realized it was merely leaves in the breeze. Amos continued talking, almost as if he'd been waiting a long time to tell this story.

"Mr. Francis, he didn't want to believe it was Nora, but once they caught her, she confessed and told how she'd done it and why. She bragged about the men. Old Mr. Norquist sent riders into town for the sheriff. The word spread and neighbors came here. They were all out at the front of the house and they had Miss Nora inside. My mama told me to get in the woods and hide. She said a mob could do anything, even to a child. So I came back here and hid. I heard what they did, up in the front. The crowd broke into the house and brought her up to the front balcony. They hung her in that old magnolia. I stayed out here in the woods all night, and that's how I knew Mr. Francis brought her body back here and hid it."

"What a terrible tragedy." Reginald put a hand on my back to steady me. Worry brought his eyebrows together in a knot. "You okay?"

"Yes. It's just hard to imagine how many people died and were hurt by all of this. It's no wonder folks haven't let go of the war. Brother against brother. Lover against lover. Every family faced terrible choices."

"Yes, ma'am," Amos said. "All those boys killed. You can't

know the joy Burton and Francis brought to this place. Jedidiah was more serious, but those two young men..." He chuckled, "lord they could devil those girls. Had them squawking like wet hens. After they was gone, this place was like a grave. Women folks got no one to marry or love and no hope of meetin' anyone. Losin' all the young men took away the future for every person living in these parts. Homes gone. Livestock gone. Fields and silos burned. White folks suffered hard, but so did the darkies who stayed on the land. Nothin' left but hard times. Lotta folks in these parts came close to starvin' to death. Women folks with no men to garden or tend the livestock. What livestock there was left after the soldiers and riffraff came through."

"But you stayed?" I was curious why.

"My mama stayed. She loved Miss Marketta. Stayed with her to the bitter end. That woman just lost her will to live. She was childlike, and Mama stayed to tend her. Mr. Norquist stayed in the woods, huntin' and fishin' for several weeks. Brought in meat, but he was no company for his wife or daughters. And one day he just didn't come home. It was months later they found his body."

"Did he take his own life?" Reginald asked.

"Folks couldn't tell, but that wouldn't surprise anyone."

"And after they were all gone, you stayed." Reginald made it a statement, but he was asking why.

"Mr. Norquist gave me my cabin and two acres of land right here. It's mine until I die. I have a well for water, the river for fishing, the woods for squirrels and deer. I had my garden. I could make do just fine and help out some of my neighbors to get enough money for the things I couldn't raise myself. No reason to leave. And I knew the white folks would be back one day. This place calls for a lovin' hand. Someone would come. Maybe someone to set the past to rights."

"And what past needs justice?" Reginald asked.

"You're here for that child. I know what you do. You've come to rid her of the ghosts."

"So you believe she is haunted?" I asked.

He considered for a moment. "Not sayin' it's a ghost like most people think, but there's somethin' powerful here. Somethin' that has a big need. You gotta figure it out to fix it. Now I need to weed those day lilies or Miss Anne will be disappointed. They got a loggin' crew comin' in to take down all those trees that pushed up beside the driveway and clear out the scrub oaks in the front yard. Waverley Mansion is going to look like she did a hundred years ago."

"Thank you, Amos." Reginald shook his hand and we took our leave, following a path into the woods.

CHAPTER 9

Dusk was falling over Waverley, and I found myself relaxing as I told Reginald of my experience with Amanda at the piano.

"So the child manipulated you into a dream so she wouldn't have to talk to you." He lit a cigarette, and I stood close to him, hoping the smoke would keep the biting insects at bay.

"She did. She's much too clever to be eight. I'm wondering if somehow an older woman is her playmate, someone telling her things that aren't appropriate for her age."

"It sounds like the only explanation, unless you want to think the child has consorted with demons."

"Hardly." It was peculiar that I believed in ghosts and life after death, but I had a hard time swallowing the idea of a demon. My first case at Caoin House had involved spirits trapped because of cruelty and brutalities. Our second case had been more peculiar, with a past life taking control of a young woman to extract revenge. Now this—an older spirit influencing a child.

"What's our course of action?"

"I think we should try a séance." I knew the risks, especially after our encounter at Roswell House.

"Okay. I'll speak with Royal and make arrangements. Who should attend?"

"The family, Constance, and the horse trainer."

Reginald exhaled a cloud of smoke. "Really?"

"Yes, Amanda trusts him. And his presence here isn't accidental. We need to find out why. By the way, he has a chick-a-dee at the dress shop who'd like to know him better."

"No match-making, Raissa." Reginald was serious. "That's the quickest way I know to get into the middle of something that can go bad very quickly."

He was right, but it was hard to resist. I liked Edith Keller, and Newly was certainly a handsome man. He could have a good career working at different plantations. Tin Lizzies and jalopies were becoming increasingly popular, but many still rode horses or carriages. The elite would always use horses for sport, and if Newly had the knack of making those riders look good on their mounts, his bed would be made here for the rest of his time.

"We should turn back," Reginald said. "It's getting dark, and we still have some blood left. In fact, it's strange that we haven't been swarmed."

I turned around, suddenly tired. It has been a long, long day. The flash of green caught my attention, and I stopped suddenly enough that Reginald bumped into me.

"What?"

"There." I pointed, and he started forward as he caught sight of the movement.

"It's someone in the woods," he said. "Let me see if I can catch them."

"Be careful."

He tore through the underbrush off the path, and I started after him. We were fifty yards off the path when a gunshot blasted. I ducked and dropped to the ground instinctively.

"Hello!" Reginald called out loudly, also ducking. When we both stood up, hoping the shooting was over, whoever we'd seen in the woods was gone. I was more than ready to return to the house and broach the subject of a séance with the Sheridans. At least no one would be blasting away in the house.

We waited several minutes and then walked back the way we'd come. We'd just arrived back at Waverley when Royal came out of the woods carrying a shotgun and a brown jug. It didn't take a detective to deduce that he was the person who'd discharged a weapon and that the jug contained whiskey based on his family's recipe. He was cooking hooch back in the woods, which might explain his determination to run the trespassers off. Callie Ledbetter had spoken the truth when she said Royal was moonshining.

"Hope I didn't startle you too much," he said. "Those damn college kids. I caught a couple in the woods again. I shoot over their heads, hoping it scares them enough so they don't come back."

"You did give us a start," Reginald said. Like me, he didn't care for firearms. Guns were meant to kill things, most often people.

"I always shoot way above the trees," Royal said. "The noise sends them running like scared rabbits. They know they're trespassing. They just don't care."

"What if Amanda is riding?" I asked. "Aren't you afraid you'll panic her horse?"

"Not Moonglow. That animal has one thing on her mind— jumping. I have to say Newly Castor wasn't lying when he told me about her."

"Do you expect Newly to stay on teaching Amanda?"

Royal sighed. "That's what Amanda wants, and he's worked miracles with her. But Anne wants Newly and the horse gone. She says Amanda is too masculine."

I considered his words. "I wouldn't say that. She's willful."

"Now that's an understatement." Royal motioned toward the house. "The bugs will be out in full force in another ten minutes. Let's head inside."

It was the perfect opportunity to raise the possibility of a séance.

Reginald reached for his cigarette case in his pocket but came up empty. "I must have dropped it," he said.

"Go on with Royal. I'll get it." Reginald would be far better at convincing Amanda's father of the need for a séance than I would. "I remember where we were smoking."

"Are you sure?" Reginald looked concerned.

I wanted nothing more than to be out of the reach of the bugs, but it was best I retrieve the lost item. "It won't take ten minutes. I'll beat the mosquitoes." Before he could resist, I took off at a jog down the trail that wound through the woods.

Intent on accomplishing my goal, I wasn't paying close attention, until I heard the voices in the woods. A man and a woman were arguing. I hoped it wasn't another college couple come to test the legend of Waverley Mansion. I slowed so I could hear better and finally stopped behind a screen of thick privets. I recognized the slow stutter of Newly Castor.

"We have to s-stop."

"No." The one word held anguish, and I was shocked to realize it was Constance Nyman who spoke. I'd never seen the woman display any strong emotion. "I can't live without you, Newly."

"Then we s-s-should leave together."

"And live on what?" The cold edge of practicality was in Constance's voice.

"I'll get a j-j-job training other horses."

"The Sheridans are paying me handsomely to be here as Amanda's governess. They pay so much because this is an isolated hell."

"Then we t-t-tell them."

"No. They won't accept us together. They'll fire us both."

"Then we'll move on. We can f-f-find other work."

"I need to be here. At Waverley."

I eased closer and saw Constance pacing. Newly stood stock still, misery on his handsome face. "Constance, that child is going to catch us, and then we're g-g-going to do her more harm. Somehow she knows more than a child should."

Constance stopped. "I have the sense she's in danger. I can't leave her, Newly. I can't. Her parents mean well, but they aren't prepared for what's here at Waverley."

Newly's face darkened. "I knew there was something off about this p-p-place. That child has changed in the short time I've been teaching her. What *is* here? What does it want?" Newly sounded as disconcerted as I was.

"I don't know, but I can't abandon Amanda. I can't." Constance turned abruptly and stared into the woods. "Someone is there. They're watching us. I've sensed it for a while now."

"Who?" Newly asked.

I stepped out of the fringe of shrubbery, driven partially by a swarm of mosquitoes. "It's me. I came to look for Reginald's cigarette case." I walked toward the area where Reginald had been smoking. The silver case glinted in the dying sunlight. It must have fallen out of his pocket. "Here it is." I picked it up, eager to get back to the house. Reginald would be very inter-

ested in what I'd learned about the governess and the horse
trainer.

"Raissa, walk with me," Constance said.

She suspected that I'd overheard her and Newly's declara-
tion. I had to decide if I was going to pretend otherwise or
confront the truth. I fell into step beside her.

"I have c-c-chores at the stables. Excuse me." Newly went
in the opposite direction.

"Newly and I were discussing Amanda. I want her to ride
less and study her French more."

"She loves that horse." I'd made my decision. Whatever
was going on between Constance and Newly was their
business.

"She wants to be a professional horsewoman." Constance
sighed. "That's not a life for a young woman. Not a young
woman from a good family. It would almost be better if she
wanted to be on the stage."

Although everyone was fascinated by actresses such as my
friend Tallulah Bankhead—I'd met her on a previous case—the
acting profession was still considered scandalous by many religious people. In some rural churches, theater was equated with
Satanic activity. Women riding astride and jumping horses over
fences would also be viewed as aberrant behavior. I'd expected
Constance to be more progressive, though. She was educated.
She'd traveled. The world was a bigger place than the mores
and traditions of the Deep South, where women had always
been viewed as ornamental bearers of children.

"She's very talented. I've seen her ride. She is fearless."

"Is that a good thing for a young lady who will almost
surely spend her life under the thumb of a husband?" She
glanced at me when I stopped. "Do you think I'm a single
governess because I have no suitors?"

"I haven't given it any thought at all," I said. "I just accepted that you'd chosen to rear the children of others. For whatever reasons."

"You're a modern woman. You aren't willing to accept the choices others make for you. You want to be a writer, which I'm sure raises eyebrows in polite Mobile society."

"I do."

"You choose your friends and make your own decisions about what's right and wrong."

"I do." I wondered if she was referring to Reginald and what must surely be a puzzling relationship to those on the outside. "Each person should be free to find his own happiness, and that goes for Amanda, too. She loves riding."

"And what happens when she is forty and no longer in the show ring and no man has made an offer because she is a scandal?"

"Men are changing too, Constance. Maybe she'll find a man who values her because she is fearless and bold." I was neither fearless nor bold, but I had chosen a profession—writing and solving mysteries—that put me at odds with the majority of women who sought to be homemakers and mothers. And sometimes I wore britches. My romantic prospects were bleak based on those standards. And I wasn't even really a modern woman.

"Be realistic, Raissa. You have a wealthy uncle who can indulge your whims." She smiled to take the sting away. "I checked you out when I heard the Sheridans talking about your detective agency. And you're a widow. You married and entered proper society. Death robbed you of your husband, and while it may sound cynical, that's an acceptable end to your marriage. It has left you free to be more independent. Amanda doesn't have either luxury. Her father is a bootlegger, and she'll never have a husband who can take care of her unless she adheres to conventions."

"I'm not denying your point." I stopped and found myself surrounded by the wonderful scent of sweet autumn clematis. The vine had covered some scrub bushes. "But she is eight years old. Let her have her dreams. Chances are she'll discover boys and yield this horse ambition on her own."

"And if she doesn't?"

"Then you'll have prepared her for a life where she must make her own way. She will be an educated woman with more choices than you or I had."

"You were a school teacher."

She had done her research. "Yes, and I enjoyed the job. I intended to return to Savannah and teaching, but Uncle Brett made it too difficult for me to say no to him."

"If only we all had an Uncle Brett."

"Yes, he has greatly changed my life." I wouldn't deny it. A rich uncle made things much, much easier, not because I expected money from him but because I knew if I needed it— or anything else—he would be there.

CHAPTER 10

While Anne was reluctant to hold the séance, it was Constance who demonstrated the most resistance. I wondered if it was because Newly Castor was attending. Their secret would be difficult to hide if they were in the same room for any length of time. Electricity practically crackled between them. To my surprise, Royal insisted on the séance and on all attending.

"It's for Amanda," he said to Constance. "If Raissa and Reginald can't help her, I don't know what other options are open to us. She grows more and more distant and isolated from us each day."

"Okay." Constance capitulated. "I'll attend. But I can't guarantee I'll participate. I don't believe in conjuring ghosts or speaking with spirits."

"I don't know that we can do either," I told her. "We can try. I want to see this Nan that Amanda says is her friend. It will give me a better understanding of what's happening with the child."

"Now that would be impressive," Constance said. "What do I need to do to prepare?"

"Meet in the front parlor at midnight," I said. Twelve o'clock was a time often cited as receptive to contacting spirits. Some called it the "between time," when one day was ending and another beginning.

While Anne set up a card table for our séance, I pulled Reginald aside. "You know we can't call Madam if something goes wrong. There's no phone service and it would take too long to get into town and find a telephone." Madam Petalungro was a highly-regarded medium in New Orleans. She worked with Arthur Conan Doyle and others in the spiritualist movement, and she'd been Reginald's mentor when I met him. Working a case in Montgomery, I found that I desperately needed her expertise. Luckily, I'd been able to get a long distance call through to her. There was no phone service at Waverley Mansion.

"We have to proceed with caution." Reginald remembered the dangers we'd faced once we stirred up the entity at Roswell House. "We can't afford to unleash something we can't control."

"I know." I felt the burden of my responsibilities. "But we have to try."

"Madam always said to be careful of issuing invitations. Be alert, but don't invite. Let's see what comes up, and if you have any hesitation, break the connection."

I nodded.

"Try to rest for an hour or so," Reginald said. He brushed my limp hair from my forehead. The heat of the day and the excitement had taken its toll on me. I was sweaty and tired.

"Maybe a cool bath." That would reinvigorate me; maybe

take the slump out of my shoulders. I needed to do something to get my second wind.

"I'll share a drink with Royal and make sure he's aware of what might happen."

"And Amanda? Should I talk to her?"

"I don't think so. I don't think you'd actually be talking to the child." Reginald held my gaze. "I look at her, and I don't see a child at all. She's something else now. Let this evening play out."

As I soaked in a tub of cool water, I considered the dangers in front of me. I could be injured by an aggressive entity if I allowed it to connect with me. But it was clear Amanda had already formed a bond, and it was her that I feared for most of all. When I was dry, I stretched out on my bed for an hour, waiting for the appointed time. I found I couldn't relax, so I wrote on my story. Slipping into my fictional world was a release. I'd completed two more stories which I thought might be publishable, and F. Scott Fitzgerald had offered to read over them for me. I only had to return to Mobile, type them up, and mail them off. My work as a spiritual detective had given me much fodder for my fiction.

I wrote by candlelight. A breeze filtered through the wide-open windows, and outside the night birds called. An owl was on the hunt. I heard his cry and even the flutter of his wings. I put down my pen and paper and went to the small balcony and looked out over the front lawn that was silvered in moonlight. An early dew had dropped and caught the pale glow of the moon. It brought to mind Amanda's remarkable horse, Moon-glow. The beautiful animal had an almost pearlescent glow to her coat.

Amanda had a right to compete in equestrian competitions if that was her heart's desire. I believed that. But Constance also had a point. The child would be shut out of polite society if she pursued professional riding. It simply wasn't done.

I didn't have to decide Amanda's future path. All I had to do was discover if something unnatural was influencing her. Then her parents would take charge.

I gathered candles, writing paper, pencils, and a clump of sage to burn if I felt dark spirits were too close. These were the tools I'd use for the séance. At last the hour approached and I went downstairs to find Reginald sipping a neat bourbon. Royal and Anne had chosen not to drink. Newly held a glass of wine, and Constance looked to be sipping water. It was time to gather around the game table, which was the perfect size.

When we were all seated, I asked that we join hands. In my limited experience, I'd performed one real séance—with near disastrous results—and attempted to manipulate another, which also held many surprises for me. My experience was minimal, but I'd studied the procedure. Resting in my room, I'd clarified what needed to happen. I had to meet Nan and see if I could determine what she wanted. By my understanding, she was a child, a lost little girl. I didn't view her as a malignant spirit, and I wanted to help her move on to the afterlife. If she was stuck here at Waverley Mansion, she might remain for a long, long time if I couldn't help her. I would help Nan which would, in turn, help Amanda.

"We're here to speak with Nan," I said clearly. "Our energies combine to assist her in manifesting so that we can speak with her. We are friends who wish only to help her."

A heavy silence fell over the room. In the candlelight, the faces across from me looked haunted and gaunt. I was as worried for the living as I was for the dead. Anne was edging closer and closer to a breakdown. I could feel it. Royal had no idea what to do to help her or his daughter. Newly and

Constance worked so hard to put up a cool exterior to each other that I could almost sense the blood thrumming in their veins. I wondered if anyone else felt it. Only Reginald was fully aware of what could—and should—happen.

"I call upon the spirit of Nan here at Waverley Mansion," I said. "I want no other; I'm here for Nan. I want to help you, Nan. Your friend, Amanda, wants to help you. Please show yourself. If you can tell us what you need, we'll help."

Anne coughed lightly and cleared her throat. For a moment I thought she was going to faint, but she straightened her back and lifted her chin.

"Nan, if you can hear us, please come forward. We're here to help."

A clock in the parlor ticked off the seconds, and the curtains fluttered in an unexpected breeze. A chill touched my ankles gently, but there.

"She's here," Amanda said, and for that instant she sounded like a child. She wasn't afraid--she was warm and innocent, almost happy to be with her friend.

"Where is she?" Constance asked. She looked around the room. When she started to stand, I stopped her with a warning.

"Don't break the circle, please. Hold onto Amanda's hand and Reginald's. Everyone remain seated. Look into the flame of the candle and concentrate on offering energy to Nan so that she can manifest. You may or may not be able to see her. It doesn't matter. We only need to determine how to help her."

"I want her to leave my daughter alone," Anne said.

"Please," I said softly. "Breathe deeply, stay calm, focus on the candle." The solitary flame in the center of the table burned brighter for a moment. Newly, who'd been silent, gasped.

"She's here," Amanda said again.

I looked toward the lovely alcove Bjorn Norquist had built into the parlor. I'd been told the area was used for weddings and funerals. Bjorn had planned to see his daughters married in that alcove, and his grandchildren christened. None of that had ever come to pass.

"Where is she, Amanda?" I could tell that the young girl saw something I couldn't. It was disconcerting that Amanda's abilities were more acute than my own. She was attuned to Nan. They had a bond.

A cold sensation brushed the back of my neck, and a child's hand touched my bare arm. "I'm here," a little girl said.

"Listen," Reginald whispered. "She's here."

Anne began to weep silently as Royal tried to comfort her without letting go of the hands he held.

"Are you Nan?" I asked.

"Yes, that's what I'm called." Her voice grew stronger, though I couldn't yet see her. "It's my pet name, not my given name. No one ever uses my real name. It's a secret."

"Why are you here, Nan?"

"Where else would I be? This is my home."

I could see her clearly in her blue dress with a large collar. She was a slender child, tall, perhaps seven or eight, with chestnut hair streaked with blond. Dark shadows smudged beneath her eyes. She looked troubled and afraid.

"Are you Nan?" I asked again. I'd been tricked before.

She nodded slowly, glancing at Amanda as if the little girl could lead her to the right answers. "I am."

"And Waverley Mansion is your home. You live here?"

"I do now, but I don't want to anymore."

I looked across the table at Amanda. She was staring exactly at the spot where I could see Nan. I wondered if anyone else saw her, but I thought not. No one else had spoken out.

"If you don't like being here at Waverley Mansion, why don't you leave?" I kept my voice low and easy, the same way I'd question any child.

"No one knows what happened to me, and they should know." Her voice grew stronger, darker, and deeper. "They should pay."

The chill around the child intensified, and even those who couldn't see her shivered in the cold wind that suddenly filled the room. Despite that, I clearly felt her hot fury. She stayed because her anger held her here. But anger at what? Or whom?

The candles on the hunt board across the room guttered, and I could see my breath even though the night outside was near eighty degrees. "She's here," I told them. "She's a beautiful young girl." I described her and the dress she wore.

"What does she want with my daughter?" Anne demanded, her voice breaking. "Make her tell you so we can stop this. I want my little girl back."

Reginald scanned the room with his gaze. He lingered on the place where Nan stood, but I didn't think he could see her. Only Amanda seemed capable. "Is this your imaginary friend?" I asked Amanda.

"This is Nan." Amanda was completely unfazed. "She's nice. She's shown me the gardens and the cemetery and so many places on the property where we can watch the college students. They kiss and kiss and kiss."

"I should shoot them," Royal said savagely. His wife shushed him.

"What else has Nan taught you?" I asked.

"She taught me to play jacks." Amanda laughed like the

sweet young girl she should be. "Nan is so lonely here. Everyone else has left, but she can't go."

"Why not?" I had to get Nan to admit to her powerful emotions or else she'd be bound here. Sometimes the needs of others anchored a spirit to this realm, but sometimes it was the negative energy of the spirit itself. Release only came when a spirit was ready to let go.

Everyone at the table was riveted, watching Amanda because they couldn't see the little girl in the blue dress who walked around the table and stood at Amanda's side.

"Tell her the truth." Nan spoke to Amanda. "Tell her."

Amanda shook her head. "It's not my story to tell."

Nan's face darkened, and for a moment I thought I saw the outline of her skull beneath the tender skin of a young girl. "Tell the truth and shame the devil," Nan said.

Amanda cried out in pain.

"What does she want Amanda to tell?" Anne asked, her fear growing by the moment. "Stop this, Raissa. Make this creature leave my child alone."

"I'm trying." I looked at Reginald. We didn't have a single trick or idea. This child, Nan, was very strong. And while she wasn't what I'd call a malevolent spirit, she was unhappy and angry, and she was firmly attached to Amanda.

"Nan, tell me the truth. I'll tell others. I promise."

Nan backed away from Amanda and in less than two seconds she was standing right beside me. The air around her was frigid. "Find my body."

"What?" I couldn't believe what she was saying.

"Find it. Find the truth."

"I will," I said with as much resolve as I could muster. "I promise you. I will find it and tell the truth."

"Find what?" Reginald asked.

I didn't want to say in front of the others. "Nan, you have to let go. You can move on if you wish. You have my word I will do everything in my power to fulfill your request."

"Tell the truth and shame the devil." Nan's voice was singsong, but her words held meaning.

"What is your real name, Nan? I'll find what happened, but I need a starting place.

"Watch this." Her neck snapped at a grotesque angle. "That's how it was done." Other loud snaps made her back bend in unnatural ways.

"Nan. Stop!" I spoke sharply, and Reginald started to rise from his seat, but I shook my head. "No. It's okay."

Bent and broken, Nan stared at me. "She's going to hurt her. She is. Amanda is special, and she will take her if you don't stop it." She straightened up, the broken bones reassembling. "She's coming now. I have to go."

The chill dissipated. The room was once again warm with a humid breeze flowing through the windows.

"Nan!" I called to her, but she was gone.

"She's left us," Reginald said. There was a sheen of sweat on his forehead, and I wondered what he'd experienced. Reginald was always cool.

"What has she done to my child?" Anne demanded. She could sit no longer and pushed back from the table with such force her chair fell over. The candles in the room flickered and went out. It was Nan's final comment.

Anne went to her daughter and pulled Amanda to her breast, rocking her. "I won't let her harm you. I won't."

Amanda spoke softly. "She's not the one you should be worried about."

Her words made me inhale sharply. "Who should we be worried about?" All along I'd felt that Nan wasn't the problem

I'd been sent to resolve. There was something much darker at Waverley Mansion.

"You'll know soon enough," Amanda said. She stood up, easily pushing her mother away. "Now I'm tired." She left the parlor and I could hear her footsteps in the rotunda as she went to her room.

"Can you rid her of Nan?" Royal asked me.

"I think so, but I'm not sure that's going to solve your problems."

Newly had been completely quiet. He cleared his throat softly. "She n-n-needs that horse."

I had to agree with him. Nan wasn't the problem with Amanda, and the one thing that kept her tied to her family and Waverley was Moonglow.

"Try to keep her safe," Royal said to Newly. "I know you can't make her ride with common sense, but try."

"I will."

I had a question for the trainer. "Do you know who Amanda was talking about, the person we should be worried about?"

He glanced at Constance. "Check the cemetery. I see her there a lot. She's visiting someone, and I have to say it gives me the willies whenever I see her there, talking away to empty air."

I would do that.

CHAPTER 11

Exhausted from the long day and the emotional turmoil of the séance, I retired to my room. Reginald wanted to talk, but I needed to reflect on Nan and what I'd learned about her. Anger bound her spirit to Waverley Mansion, and I wondered what had happened to a child so young that could make her that filled with fury. I also accepted that it would be up to me and Reginald to find out Nan's story. No one else had the tools to look except Amanda, and I knew better than to count on her for help. Amanda was a sensitive. She saw spirits in great detail and perhaps with more talent than I had.

But she would not be inclined to send Nan away. Nan was her only playmate, and in a way I didn't blame Amanda. The isolation had to be unpleasant. Back when Waverley was built, the plantation was something of a small town all on its own. There were slaves, family members, craftsmen who made clothes and shoes and put up food. A child would have plenty of other children about. I'd often wondered how a little girl or boy who played with the Negro children as friends could grow up to see them as property. To sell them—or worse. How did one sell a friend? It was a puzzle of the human's ability to put greed above all else.

I'd left my writing supplies on the small table by the window. A breeze fluttered one of the pages to the floor and I bent to retrieve it when I froze.

Scrawled across the bottom of the page in handwriting that looked tortured were the words, "Get out." The ink had blotched and spotted and the paper was deeply grooved by the force of the hand holding the pen.

Instincts kicked in and I crouched, looking about the room. Someone had been in here. But who? Everyone in the house had been with me in the parlor. Fancy didn't sleep in the house but was quartered in her own cabin deeper in woods near Amos Plackett. The help had all gone home after supper.

Which led me to believe that whoever had been in my room and left the message was not anyone living at Waverley. Or anyone living at all. This was a message from the dead. In order to hold the pen and write, the spirit had to be powerful. And likely dangerous.

I wanted to go to Reginald's room to show him, but it was almost two in the morning. The new day would be starting soon, and we had plenty of work to do. My room was empty now, and if I roused Reginald's protective emotions, no one in the household would sleep. I believed I could release Nan quickly, move her into the realm where she belonged. After that, we'd have to reassess.

I restacked my pages, putting the one with the ghost writing on the bottom. I used a small vase as a paperweight. Pulling on a light nightgown, I climbed into bed. After I blew out the candle, my eyes adjusted to the darkness, and I took in the unfamiliar furnishings, the deeper shadows in the corners of the room. Waverley House was haunted, but I wasn't afraid of Nan. She was a lost child. Tomorrow I'd do my best to discover her identity and what had happened to her. My best guess was that she was a guest here at Waverley Mansion, one who had died of an accident. Children often didn't understand the dangers around them. A high fever could have taken her life—any infection for that matter. Life for a child in the 1800s had been fragile.

I let my thoughts wander back to my childhood, secure and loved with parents who indulged my curiosities. They'd educated me, knowing it would set me outside the normal realm of female experience. They'd brought me up to see myself as a person first, a woman second. I was not a flapper or stage actress like Zelda or Tallulah. I didn't crave that limelight or the role of party girl. I wasn't a trend setter. But I wanted to be a writer, a field usually reserved for the masculine. I could only hope my gender wouldn't be held against me.

A night bird nested near my window and began to sing a sweet five-note melody. Dawn would arrive quickly. I closed my eyes. Almost immediately I fell into a deep sleep. Once again I traveled the woods surrounding Waverley Mansion. This time I was with a blond young man who made me laugh. He held my hand tightly and looked back at me, breathless with our daring, as he pulled me through the woods.

"Come on," he said. "We're almost there."

I followed, pretending I felt lost, but I wasn't. I knew the woods far better than he'd ever know them. We came upon a small clearing beside a little stream that flowed fast over rocks and sand. A plaid blanket had been spread over a bed of soft ferns. Beside it were a basket of food and a bottle of wine. The young man had brought a picnic for us.

We tumbled on the blanket, all arms and legs and bodies

thrashing as we laughed, exhilarated at the feel of each other. "A drink?" he asked.

I didn't care for alcohol, but he was nervous. "Sure."

We shared the bottle of wine, passing it back and forth as we sat on the wool blanket beneath a chestnut tree in a small clearing. The weather was fine, crisp and cool, and I noticed the clunky-heeled shoes I wore. I wanted to touch my face, to see what I might look like, but I didn't. I wasn't myself—I was someone else entirely.

My forest green skirt came just below my knees. As he looked, I pulled the skirt higher, offering a glimpse of my thighs. I wanted him to put his hand there, to move it higher up my leg. He kissed me with great ardor, and I kissed him back. When he pulled slightly away, I took his hand and put it on my inner thigh. "You can touch me," I said. "I like it. And I'll touch you."

He inched his hand up, at last understanding what I wanted. I wasn't going to stop him. Kisses were nice, but I wanted more. He was merely inexperienced. I would have to show him.

The sound of glass breaking caused me to sit up in bed, completely confused as to my whereabouts. I threw back the sheet, my body reeling from the intensity of the dream. My heart pounded—something had startled me awake but since I wasn't exactly certain where I was, I couldn't think clearly. A noise outside the house made me walk to the window.

A sharp piece of glass pierced the bottom of my foot. The pages of my short story caught a gust of wind and blew up into the air in a mini-cyclone. I remembered putting the small vase on top of them. Obviously it had blown off the table and broken.

I lit a candle and sat down to examine my foot. The cut

was small but the piece of glass was still there. I pulled it out and tore the bottom of my nightgown free to make a bandage. It wasn't a serious wound, but I didn't want to track blood across the hardwood and rug. The wound was oddly not painful. Truthfully, I was still disoriented. I'd been in the woods with a young man, ready to make love. My need for him was far more intense than the cut on my foot. And none of it made sense.

When I'd fully come to my senses, I gathered up the pieces of the broken vase and the pages of my story. I could see the glimmer of dawn out the window, which meant it was close to five o'clock in the morning. It was pointless to try to sleep. I didn't want to risk another dream—I feared I would lose myself in the tangle of my erotic needs. I'd loved my husband deeply and experienced a deep intimacy with him. But the dream I'd just experienced was so different. I had no deep feeling for the young man in it. I wanted only the release of a sexual climax. I didn't even know the man or care to know him. The experience—even though it was merely a dream—was highly unsettling.

I felt I'd lost myself.

I sat at the window waiting for light until I heard the sound of Fancy in the kitchen preparing breakfast. I examined my foot. The cut was small and had sealed cleanly. A day or so of being careful and it would be scabbed over and then healed. I hoped the vase wasn't a family treasure.

I dressed and went downstairs, eager for coffee. The fog of the night clung to me, and I needed to be alert. When I went into the dining room, Amanda was already seated at the table. Her hair was braided and she wore breeches and a white shirt with riding boots.

"Do you have a lesson on Moonglow today?" I asked.

"Yes. Tomorrow is the big show at the Nelson house. I'm going."

"You're a fine rider." I poured coffee and sat across from her. "I know it must be hard to want to be something that society frowns on. I'm aware of the difficulties you face. You shouldn't be limited because you're a girl."

"I don't care. I will ride. And I will win. That's what they can't argue with—my winning."

She had a point. "Tell me about Nan," I said. "What do you know about her? I'd like to help her but I'm not sure how to go about it."

"She wants to leave here." Amanda frowned. "She can't. Something happened to her here, and until she knows what, she's stuck."

I'd heard that before, from Nan herself. "Thanks." My appetite had vanished. Though I knew I should wait for Reginald, I decided to see if I could find the Norquist family cemetery. I didn't know what I expected to find, but I needed to look. And I needed some time alone. The dream had truly rattled me to my foundation.

Royal was already outside supervising the workers, who were repairing a water cistern. In a few hours they would all disappear, and I wondered if the renovation was a ruse for workers who helped with the moonshine operation. Anne had not arisen. If Constance was awake, she hadn't come downstairs either. I stopped by the kitchen and told Fancy I would skip breakfast, but I did refill my coffee cup and started down the driveway through the thick dew. Luckily I had good shoes and socks to keep my injured foot dry.

I should have asked directions to the cemetery, but for some reason I hadn't. Maybe I didn't really want to go there.

Maybe I only needed a solitary walk. Or maybe I wanted to see if I would be led there.

My nocturnal episode had left me disturbed and unsettled. At times like this, a solitary walk often brought the calm I needed. When I'd lived in Savannah, I'd often walked along the water. When Alex was alive, that was one of our favorite haunts. Now I was an inland girl, and while the bloodsuckers made a walk an exercise in annoyance, I had to get out of the house and on my own.

Instead of heading down the drive, I angled to the side lawn, stopping to stare at the enormous magnolia tree in the front yard. Nora Bailey, Union spy, had died there, hanged as a traitor. Her lover and co-conspirator, Calvert Marcus, a medical doctor from a nearby plantation, had also been hanged. It was too easy to imagine the grotesque scene. The doctor's body had also been doused with kerosene and burned. Francis had saved Nora's remains from the flames.

I went to the patch of barren ground where Amos had told Reginald and me that Nora's body had been hidden. The ground was completely bare. Not a blade of grass or even a weed, though the lawn around the patch was lush. I picked up some of the dirt— it was black and loamy. I could see no reason why it didn't support plants, unless the ground was afflicted with a curse. Soaked in dark blood. The thought made me uncomfortable. What was I dealing with? Amanda had implied that Nan wasn't the real danger here. Nan had said the same. So if not Nan, then who? Or what?

My two "dreams" had given me more than enough clues to believe that Nan had a companion spirit here. Nora Bailey. She'd been described to me as a woman with fiery passions, and I'd certainly felt those fires kindled in me. Was Nora able to take possession of Amanda's body? Was that why the little girl was so mature in her speech and behavior? Or was Nora more of a confidante, an unhappy, vengeful spirit who was using a child to wage war on a family that had done her no harm.

I left the barren ground and found a trail that wound deeper into the woods. I recognized the bark of oaks and dogwood trees. In the spring this would be a paradise of white blossoms. Crepe myrtle edged the yard now, the bright fuchsia, lavenders, and whites scattered on the ground in a magical blanket. In the unrelenting heat, it was hard to believe that cooler weather would ever arrive, but the passage of time couldn't be stopped. August still reigned, but October would return.

The path meandered through the woods where early morning light, as pale as lemon gauze, filtered through the green leaves. The deeper into the woods I walked, the louder the birds became. I recognized the trill of a mockingbird and the scolding of a blue jay. A fat gray squirrel perched on a branch watching me. The small creatures were safe from my intentions. I only wanted a walk.

I came upon a line of cedar trees, the dark green fronds full and heavy. They'd been planted closely together, creating a wall of evergreen. The line was straight, as if it had been shot for a surveyor's instrument and they stretched for at least a quarter mile. Determination was either a character strength or a weakness, depending on who you spoke with. I walked down the line looking for an opening to see what was on the other side.

At last I found a place where several branches had snapped off, either from wind or the weight of water in the dense boughs. I struggled through and found myself in a cemetery. I shouldn't have been surprised, but I was. My intent had been to find the Norquist Cemetery, and I had been led there by intuition.

The burial ground had been sadly neglected. Scrub trees and brambles covered many of the graves. In a few, the marble slab had broken and caved in revealing the tomb beneath. Black lichen covered many of the headstones, and time had worn away the names, dates, and epitaphs.

I found two graves with wonderful old marble headstones of two angels, one playing a lute and the other a horn. A wrought iron fence enclosed the two, separating them from the rest of the graves. I entered the enclosure and used a bit of sand to rub the moss away from the inscriptions. Bjorn and Marketta Norquist. They rested here on the land they'd loved.

With that as an anchor, it was easier to find the graves of the three boys, Francis, Jedidiah, and Burton. They were included in the plot to the left of their parents protected by the lovely wrought iron fencing,. I knelt at Francis's grave and read the inscription. "A heart too true for worldly love." He died in a charge at Holly Springs, as had Burton, the younger brother who followed him wherever he went. Jedidiah fought and died at Vicksburg, one of the most brutal sieges in military history.

I was surprised to find a plot for Olivia Norquist. I knew she'd left Mississippi, but apparently her body had been brought back to Waverley. She'd only lived a short time after the war ended. The other two sisters, Helene and Marguerite, had left the South and had not returned, even in death. If my memory served me correctly, they'd moved out to California and lived together, two war spinsters. At least they'd had each other, which was more than a lot of Southerners had after the war and reconstruction.

There were other graves, none with the beautiful sculptures of the Norquist family. As I moved around the cemetery, locating a grave here and there, I found Amos Plackett's mother buried under a big sycamore tree. She'd been loyal to the Norquist family and though she had a simple stone, she was here with those she'd served so loyally. One day Amos would be here too, I felt certain. And there was a grave marker with only one name. Bertha. The granite marker was unusual, especially if Bertha was a slave. And there was a strange symbol etched into the stone beside her name. It looked like a chicken track. She rested beside Amos's mother.

Would the Sheridans continue the tradition of burial on the grounds of Waverley? It was more popular for the wealthy now to buy a plot in town where a funeral company hired gardeners to tend the graves and keep them neatly ordered. Others sought burial in church cemeteries.

My husband was buried in France, in a grave I'd never visited and wasn't likely to ever see. I didn't mourn his anonymous burial though, because I knew his spirit was not in the ground, only bones and skin and hair. The important part of him was gone from this plane, though on occasion he'd paid me a visit to bring comfort or support.

I was leaving the family plot when I tripped on a root or something and went sprawling. I wasn't harmed, but the wind had been knocked from my lungs. When I drew a few ragged breaths, I looked to see what had caught my foot. A carved lamb was nestled into the grass and weeds. The small headstone had been obscured by brush and briars, but I recognized that it was a child's grave. None of the Norquist children had lived to reproduce. Was this the final resting place of Nan? Maybe Amos could give me some help. Or perhaps some of the older neighbors. War survivors still lived in the area. Maybe someone would remember a child at Waverley.

I'd found the principle players of the Norquist family, but if Nora Bailey was buried nearby, I hadn't discovered her grave. It made perfect sense that it wouldn't be marked by a headstone. After their sons were killed in the war, I didn't think Bjorn and Marketta would spend time or energy marking the grave of the woman responsible for their deaths.

I cleared the grass and weeds away from the child's grave. "Nan?" I said. "Is this you?"

The morning was growing brighter and sunnier, but I felt a cool darkness shift over the landscape. And then I saw the child in the blue dress. Her collar was so large it covered her shoulders and hung down her back in a square. The frills of her blue dress spoke of a child who enjoyed being dressed. Her hair was in shiny ringlets, held back with a bow. She was a pretty child, dainty and haunted.

"Nan?"

She stepped forward. "Yes."

"It's time to leave."

"Who will play with Amanda?" She had the ability to communicate clearly and with seemingly little effort. This was very rare. Most spirits talked in symbols and hints that had to be deciphered. Nan was strong.

"She will go to school and ride. She needs to make friends, living friends. She can't do that as long as you're here."

"I can't go."

She seemed to gain in density and detail. I noticed the black-strapped shoes she wore. She was dressed for church or a social outing. She was dressed like a child who came from money.

"What happened to you?" I wanted to help her. But I couldn't unless she gave me some clues.

"The stairs. Tumble, tumble, tumble." She made a circular

motion with one hand. "Down to the bottom." Her head snapped and fell to the side. I heard the bones crack, and I wanted to cry. "It hurt, but not for long."

She'd broken her neck in a fall down the stairs. The Norquist family had nothing but bad luck. "I'm so sorry."

"For the best. For the best. Everyone said so."

I could hardly look at her with her head angled to the side. I couldn't imagine losing a child in such a way. Or any way for that matter. "I'll tell the Sheridans about your grave. I'm sure they'll get a headstone for you."

"No!" She was on top of me before I could move. "No! It's a secret. No one must know."

"Why is your grave a secret?" I didn't understand at all.

"Many things were secret. I couldn't go to town. I couldn't go to school. It was all a big secret."

"Were you ill?" Sometimes if a child had an abnormality, they were hidden away, but Nan looked perfectly fine—except for the broken neck.

"Woodshed."

I didn't understand what she meant. She was growing tired, and her communication was less clear.

"What woodshed?"

"Woodshed baby."

At last the truth struck me. She was an illegitimate child. A woods colt was the expression the child was trying to use. "Who was your mother?"

She showed the first sign of emotion. Fear. "No. No!" She faded in and out. "No tell!"

She'd be gone in a moment, unable to sustain the energy necessary to show herself—if this was her true form. I'd been tricked into sympathy before by malevolent spirits. I also remembered Madam's sternest admonishment. "Remember, spirits lie." Not always out of spite or personal gain, but the spirit world was not the same as ours. Things were more fluid, and for some spirits, the past was a minefield of half-memories and emotions that didn't always reflect the truth.

"Nan, I'll help you if you let me." But I spoke to empty air. She was gone.

I heard someone coming through the woods and I looked up to see Amanda astride Moonglow. She was at the edge of the cemetery watching me.

"Are you going to help Nan leave?" she asked. The horse pawed the ground, impatient to go.

"I will if I can. Here she's between realms. She's neither dead nor alive. You can see how that isn't good for her."

"I can." She circled the horse. "I want her to go."

"What has she told you, Amanda? Do you know what happened to her?"

"She fell down the stairs in the house."

"Fell?" I had a suspicion that perhaps Nan's death wasn't an accident.

Amanda shrugged, but when she looked away, my suspicions were confirmed. "Who pushed her?"

Moonglow snorted and pawed more fiercely. She was one of the most beautiful horses I'd ever seen, and she had the same spirit as her rider.

"It's Nan's secret to tell."

"Do you know?"

She nodded. "The others don't want anyone to know."

I nodded because emotion closed my throat. A possibility occurred to me. What if Nan was Nora Bailey's daughter? That would thicken the stew.

"How long have you been able to see spirits, Amanda?"

She shrugged, and Moonglow quieted for a moment. "It's

easier here. The other children hate me because I tell them. They're babies. They're always afraid."

I could see that. I'd thought Amanda was demonstrating sexual maturity in front of the other children, but it wasn't romantic maturity. She'd been scaring them with stories of what she saw, of ghosts and spirits and dark emotion. I could help Amanda, because I understood.

"I saw spirits when I was a child, but I taught myself not to. After my husband was killed in the war, I began to see them again. Not all the time, but enough."

"I want them to go away."

"Maybe I can help you, if you'll let me."

She bit her bottom lip. "Maybe." She squeezed her calves into Moonglow who took off like a shot. "Be careful here in the cemetery," she called back to me. "You're never alone."

CHAPTER 12

I watched her ride away, a delicate young girl on the back of a powerful horse. She had what it took to be a true competitor. Would she have the chance, or would gender dictate the limits of her life? It made me angry to think about it.

My clothes were sticking to me in the sweltering heat and humidity, and I wanted to go back to the house and consult with Reginald. Now that I suspected the underlying cause of Nan's tenure in Waverley, it was up to me and Reginald to free her spirit. Our first chore would be to figure out whose daughter she was and then who had killed her. Surely if Nora had brought her daughter with her to Waverley, there would be some records.

Reginald had far more experience in digging into real facts than I did. Once we learned the truth, I felt Nan would willingly depart. And once that was done? Something else lingered at Waverley, but we'd been hired to help Amanda. Beyond that, we had no obligations.

A bright flash of color through the trees caught my eye and

I paused to watch a scarlet tanager settle on a branch. I'd never seen one of the songbirds so near. It trilled at me, and I moved closer. The little bird seemed to have no fear of me. When I was almost upon it, the bird darted to a far corner of the cemetery.

As I walked toward it, a sudden sadness fell over me, a sensation as thick as the humidity. It slipped over me like a second skin, and I wondered if I had the will to walk back to the house. I had lost all hope. My arms and legs grew leaden, and breathing became a burden. The idea of simply curling up on the ground was overpowering. The morass fell over me so suddenly that I had no defenses.

I knelt in the grass and weeds, wanting just to lie down for a little while, to allow the dark emotion to pass. I was so alone, so absolutely alone. There was no point in going forward. I'd done things that were unforgivable. I was unloved, unwanted. It would be so much easier just to go to sleep and never wake up.

An overpowering urge to cry took hold of me. I dug my fingers into the thick grass and wailed, not caring who heard. I tore at the grass and sobbed. I'd never been caught in such a maelstrom of wretched emotion. I keened and pulled up clumps of grass, throwing it up and away, digging deeper. My fingers scraped against something hard beneath the carpet of grass. The emotional storm was beginning to pass and I caught my breath. Whatever was beneath the sod was solid and cold. I worked the grass free.

"Raissa! Are you hurt?"

Reginald came striding into the cemetery. "What are you doing here? I heard you crying." He knelt beside me. "Can you stand up?"

I nodded, wiping the tears from my face. "I was just so sad

I had to lie down, but I'm okay." Reginald's presence slowly expelled the bone-weary sadness. I leaned against him while I took deep breaths. "Here. I've found something."

He turned my face to examine me. "You don't even look like yourself. Do you want to return to Mobile?"

"No." I pulled up more grass, revealing the cool marbled stone. "Look."

He bent to examine the small area I'd cleared. It was a pale white grave slab. Reginald started pulling up the grass and together we cleared an area large enough to read the inscription, "Death Yields Before True Love."

We looked at each other. "Nora Bailey," we said together. We'd found the grave of the notorious spy. Amos had told us Francis had brought her to the family cemetery and buried her in secret. Someone, likely Francis, had put the slab over her grave as a final remembrance. Or someone who loved Francis had done it to honor him.

"He loved her even if she betrayed him and his family," Reginald said. "His brothers died because she gave family secrets to the enemy. That's bitter and tragic."

I wondered if the onslaught of grief I'd experienced came from Nora. Maybe she'd felt remorse at her actions. I only knew I didn't want to visit that well of despair again. It had caught and shook me like a rat in a terrier's teeth. "Now that we know where she's buried if we discover she is still haunting the grounds, maybe we can help her find peace too."

"Two ghosts for the price of one?" Reginald asked.

I only smiled. "Whatever it takes, right?"

"As long as you're not hurt. I won't risk your health," he said. "When I saw you rending the ground and crying...it scared me. I'm not picking up on the energy here that you are.

What I'm seeing is a little girl who is very disturbed and my partner who has lost control of her emotions."

"I'm okay, and I think we can help Amanda. Just know that Nora Bailey isn't done with Waverley Mansion. Not yet," I said. "Not by a long shot." And I knew she wasn't done with me, either, but there was no point upsetting Reginald more than he already was.

We made it back to the front lawn of Waverley when a patrol car bumped down the drive. I recognized the lawman who got out looking like an old west caricature of a wild and woolly sheriff. His longish hair and handlebar mustache were neatly groomed. He was trim and fit, his gun holstered on his hip and his badge pinned to his shirt pocket. He came toward us with purpose.

"Mr. Proctor," he said, "I need to speak with Royal Sheridan. Where is he?"

"Royal was on his way to work on the renovation when I saw him about an hour earlier. Anne will probably know where to locate him. You should speak with her."

"Thanks. Mrs. James." He tipped his hat and stepped past us and went up the steps to the front door. He knocked and entered before he had an invitation.

"I think he has a bee in his bonnet," I said. "Butt me." I wasn't a big smoker, but my cemetery episode had left my nerves frazzled. Reginald offered me a cigarette and lit it for me, trying to hide his smile of amusement. My previous attempts to smoke with the poise of a modern woman had ended in coughing fits. This time was no exception.

He took the cigarette from my hand. "Tell me what happened. Talking will be better than a smoke."

We settled on the porch steps, and I told him about the emotions that had swept over me. Not my emotions—those belonging to someone else. I could only assume it was Nora since I felt certain I was at her grave.

I was almost finished when I heard voices raised in the house. Anne was yelling at someone, and she wasn't the type to yell. Whatever was going on, we needed to break it up. Reginald and I hurried inside to find the sheriff with his hands on his hips, angrily demanding that Anne tell him where Royal was.

"My husband is working on the property. I don't know where."

"I came to tell him face to face if he shoots at another kid, he's going to jail." Gaines's face was red with anger. "I've warned him twice. He can't go shooting at people. Next time it's jail."

"My husband has a right to protect our property from trespassers. It would seem to me your job would be to arrest those trespassers, not harass a taxpayer."

Anne had more backbone than I'd given her credit.

"You tell him what I said." Gaines had removed his hat but he put it back on. When he saw me and Reginald, he grimaced.

"Sheriff, can I help you?" Reginald asked pointedly.

"You should mind your own business." He looked Reginald up and down. "Stay out of things that don't include you."

Constance and Amanda had come halfway down the steps. It was Constance who took control of the situation. "Sheriff Gaines, I don't think you should come into a constituent's home and intimidate the woman of the house. I believe if the churches knew how you spoke to Mrs. Sheridan, the membership would be shocked."

Gaines threw back his shoulders. "Who are you to tell the law how to conduct business?"

"I'm an educated woman who has studied the laws

outlining the duties of a sheriff. Browbeating a woman in her own home isn't part of your job."

I glanced at Reginald who was equally impressed with the exchange. Constance had surprised both of us.

"If you have business with Mr. Sheridan, I suggest you leave him a message setting an appointment time." Constance came down the stairs to stand directly in front of the sheriff. She was a tall woman, and she met him eye to eye.

"I don't want an appointment. I want Sheridan to stop shooting at people. That's why I'm here. Tell him." Gaines stomped around me and Reginald and went out the front door.

Anne staggered, but Reginald was at her side, a supporting hand on her arm. "I'm okay," she said. "Royal has complained to the sheriff more than once about those trespassers. The law won't do a thing. That's why Royal shoots over their heads. What else can we do to keep our property secure? We're so isolated out here. Any of those people could be up to mischief."

We settled Anne in the parlor with a glass of cold tea. Constance and Amanda returned upstairs to finish their study session. Constance was as reserved and proper as if the sheriff's visit had never occurred. Amanda gave me a wink as she ran up the stairs behind her governess. I was surprised to see the girl in a dress and attending to her studies. Only a short time ago she'd been in breeches astride her horse. I hoped I'd made a bond with the child.

We sat with Anne for half an hour before she was calm enough to retire to her room to rest. As the day moved toward lunch, Reginald and I were left to our own devices. We decided to return to the fourth floor and go through more of the trunks and artifacts that had been tucked away for years, which brought up an interesting question.

"Reginald, why hasn't someone broken into the house and taken these things?" I waved my hand around at some furniture under dust cloths, the trunks with memorabilia, the beautiful dresses from another time carefully wrapped in sheets with cedar chips to keep moths away. "There have been college kids on the property for decades, and you know they came into this house to explore. Yet not a single piece of furniture has been broken and no one has done damage to the house. None of the vandalism one would expect. They didn't even take souvenirs from this room. That's unusual."

"It is." He sat back on his heels before a trunk of old letters and journals. "Juveniles often tear property up, but not here. Not Waverley. Maybe they were afraid of whatever lurks here."

An interesting thought. "I'll have to ask in town next time we go. I need to post a letter to Uncle Brett, and I want to talk to that minister again."

"The minister? Why? He was particularly unhelpful."

"Yes. I want his explanation of what's going on here on this property. It should prove enlightening as to the community's attitude toward Waverley Mansion. I mean the local kids knew it was here and didn't bother anything. Why? It's as if a protective spell has been cast." Even saying the words made my skin crawl. Not so long ago I hadn't believed in spells or ghosts. Now, I was a lot less judgmental and a lot more willing to believe in things outside the normal range of experience.

"We'll drive back into West Point Monday," Reginald offered. "The horse show at the Nelson plantation is coming up. Do you want to stay or go back to Mobile? We can leave here, Raissa. We came to help and we've tried, but after seeing you in that cemetery today, I think we should go home."

"I want to stay."

Reginald considered for a long moment. "Then I'd like to

see the Sheridans interact with the neighbors. The horse show will be a good opportunity."

"Good idea." I stood up. "I want to get some paper and a pen from my room." Something nagged at the back of my mind. "I'll be right back."

The house was quiet. I didn't know if Constance and Amanda were still studying, but I didn't hear them. Constance was well versed in the foliage that grew around the estate, and she was helping Amanda make a book of various leaves and plants and their uses. It would be a handy document to have in the house. I would make one for Uncle Brett at Caoin House when I returned. He would value it more than anything else I could do for him.

I opened my bedroom door and stopped. Something was off in the room. I couldn't put my finger on it exactly, but I hesitated to enter. The skin along my arms prickled and pulled. "Hello," I said, feeling silly, talking to an empty room. Spirits didn't normally answer. At least not many of them.

I stepped into the room and the door shut behind me of its own volition. The sense of being imprisoned came on me strong, but I fought the desire to turn and run. The room was full of midday shadows cast by the sun coming through the windows. I went to get my papers and felt the crunch of glass beneath my shoe. I remembered then the breaking of the vase and the strange writing—had it been a dream? I'd forgotten all about it in my morning adventure in the cemetery. Now I couldn't decide if it had ever happened.

Except for the glass beneath my shoe—glass that I'd picked up once before.

The pages of my story were scattered across the floor, exactly as they had been in the episode from the night. Had I dreamed it or lived it and was it happening again? I couldn't say. Time had telescoped and left me stuck in this moment that was like an echo. The air pressed against my skin, and the light came through the window with a rare intensity. I could feel the blood race through my veins. I stepped closer to the window, though I hadn't intended to do so. The heel of my shoe crushed a page of writing.

I wanted to bend down and pick up my story, but I couldn't. The sense of being completely out of control of my physical being set up rising panic. I could feel my heartbeat increasing, my lungs working to pull in oxygen, but something else held me in an iron grip, unable to truly breathe or move.

Something had been written on the bottom of one page. I remembered it, but I couldn't remember what the words were. I wanted to pick up the pages and look, but I seemed frozen, standing at the window.

I glanced outside and gasped. A young woman stood at the edge of the yard, behind a brace of dogwood trees. She wore a navy-blue dress with a big sailor collar in some type of nautical print, sleeveless and short. Her pale hair was tucked beneath a straw cloche hat, and she had a spark of mischief about her. If she was even real. I had to question everything I saw and felt.

She slipped through the trees, glancing over her shoulder as if she were hiding from someone—a game. She didn't seem worried or upset, more playful. And then I saw why. The young man who darted out of the woods was laughing and calling out to her. I couldn't hear what he said, only the teasing note in his voice.

She ducked back into the woods and ran, her bare legs flashing in the sunlight that penetrated the trees. And then she was gone. The young man in his white shirt and carrying a boater hat ran after her. The sound of their laughter carried to me. He jumped a clump of underbrush and disappeared.

I was completely unprepared for the shotgun blast that seemed to come from the front yard. A covey of quail burst into flight, their wings fluttering like my constricted heart. Royal came out of the woods toting his shotgun. And I was released from my paralysis.

I grasped the window sill and leaned on it, inhaling deeply. It seemed ages since I could pull enough air into my lungs. I bent down and picked up my pages. The writing had been on the last page, which was missing. I knelt and reached under the bed, my fingers groping in the darkness created by the dust ruffle. At last I felt it and pulled it out.

I took it to the window to examine the bold strokes of the pen that said, "Get out."

Fear punched into me with a visceral force when I realized the two words had been written in my hand.

"Raissa, are you okay?" Reginald knocked on the door and opened it. "What's wrong?"

He was beside me, his arm around my waist. My legs were a bit shaky and I let him seat me on the bed. "What is it?" he asked.

I handed him the paper and watched his face as he read it. "Who wrote this?"

My mouth was dry, and my tongue made a strange clicking sound when I tried to talk. "I did, I think."

"Who do you want to get out?"

"Us." I was afraid. It was fear that threatened to silence me now. "There is something here, and it's able to connect with me and control me. I'm afraid, Reginald. I'm afraid that when I'm in its grip, I may not be able to come back."

"We'll leave in the morning. I know you want to see this through, but not when you're susceptible to the entity," he said. "I'll explain it to the Sheridans now. Maybe Madam can recommend someone else for this job."

I nodded, feeling like a weak sister. "I'm as useless as a flat tire."

Reginald chuckled. "You're one of the bravest people I know. There is an art to life, Raissa, and knowing when to avoid a confrontation is a big part of having a good life."

"I feel like I'm losing myself," I said. "I have strange dreams. Desires that are bigger than me." I didn't know how to tell him about my sexual appetite without being too bold and improper, but he was my partner. He needed to know what was going on with me. "I feel like someone else is taking me over, imposing her will and desires on me. I feel her...appetite. She wants sex. It's terrifying."

"We'll leave now. We can make it halfway home, maybe stop in Meridian. There's an opera house there, the Grand Opera House. Maybe they'll have a performance. We could do with a little culture." He nudged my shoulder. "We'll find someone to help the Sheridans and I'm sure we can find a case to work on closer to Mobile."

He was making the best of me tucking my tail and running. I loved him for that.

CHAPTER 13

After a modest drink of Royal's whiskey that went down like smooth heat, I'd calmed considerably. Enough to convince Reginald I wasn't ready to quit Waverley Mansion. Not when I felt so close to resolving the issues of Nan and possibly Nora Bailey.

Reginald and I were seated in the beautiful parlor. A breeze came through the front windows. The house was quiet. Anne was still in her rooms, and Constance and Amanda were either upstairs or outside. Royal hadn't returned. The last I'd seen of him, he'd been chasing the students who were trespassing on the property.

I settled into a velvet covered chair and put my feet up on a hassock. I was exhausted, but my fear and anxiety had subsided. Reginald was a friend who made me feel secure.

"Do you remember writing the words 'Get Out'?" Reginald asked. He had stopped pressuring me to leave Waverley because he'd accepted it was useless. I was as mule-headed as he was.

"No. I honestly thought someone else had written them. But it looks like my handwriting."

"Tell me about the dream."

I'd only given him bits and pieces. I was embarrassed at the intense level of desire that had overtaken me for a complete stranger, a man whose face I couldn't remember but my fingers longed for the contours of his flesh, the feel of his body pressed into mine. But how could Reginald interpret events if he didn't know the truth? I gave him the basic details.

"And you felt the desires of this entity?"

I nodded, unwilling to meet his gaze. "I was obsessed with making love with the gentleman." The words were shocking, even to me. Nice girls didn't have such thoughts. Well, they did but didn't admit them.

"Did you know what she was thinking or just what she was feeling?"

It was the ultimate question. "Only feeling. And I can't truly say it was a woman. It was so...aggressively sexual. What if it was Francis?" There had been a real masculinity about the sexual desire—no tender feelings at all. Just a drive for satisfaction, as I understood how men often felt.

I had a sudden flash of insight. If I could access the entity's thoughts, I would know who it was for certain. To willingly allow myself to be overtaken by such raw emotions came with risks. I could easily behave inappropriately, but Reginald could prevent that. With force, if necessary. "Do you think you might stay with me tonight? Maybe I can allow this entity more access and figure it out." Once before, in a Tuscaloosa hotel room, Reginald had slept on the floor beside my bed to keep me safe.

"Of course I can stay with you, but I don't think this is a wise move."

"You can wake me if I dream too deeply. Or if I do something...too bold." Reginald understood I might have no control over my own actions.

He hesitated. "What if I can't wake you? What if you *are* overtaken by this thing?"

"Just don't let me do anything scandalous. You'll be able to wake me. If not, restrain me until you can get me under control." I believed the spirit wanted to use me long enough to gain the satisfaction it sought. It didn't want permanent possession, not like the issue we'd had with Camilla Granger. That had been far more complex than a simple possession.

"Raissa, I have some reservations about this plan." Reginald was worried. He brushed at his neatly trimmed mustache. "This is nothing to play with, and I don't have access to Madam if something should go wrong. I'd have to drive into West Point to find a telephone. Anything could happen while I was gone."

He had a point, but one I wasn't willing to concede. "I'll be fine. I just know it."

"Let's see if we can find any survivors of that time period. Surely there's someone around. If we can get a lead on what happened to Nan from someone living..."

"Amos would be the most likely to know if anyone is still around these parts." Reginald's idea was better than mine. If it worked. But resolving Nan wouldn't necessarily resolve Nora.

"Let's at least ask him. If he knows anyone, now would be the perfect time to visit them. I think Royal and Anne need some privacy when he comes back inside. He's going to be put out about the sheriff being here."

"I'll leave a note in the kitchen if Fancy isn't there."

I ran upstairs and grabbed my little notebook and a pencil. The kitchen was empty so I scrawled a note and left it under the salt shaker, then met Reginald in the backyard where he was already talking with Amos.

Amos scrutinized first Reginald, then me. "I haven't been by to see Miss Coralee Hemptead in a spell, but she' be the one to see. She and Miss Marguerite were best friends. She was here all the time. She a nice lady. Kind to everyone."

"Does she live near?" Reginald asked.

"Across the creek, but the water is down now. It should be fine to go. Sometimes, when the water was up, Miss Cora would stay here at Waverley for weeks at a time. She loved it here." He sighed. "She loved Mr. Francis, from what my mama told me. Such a shame he didn't love her back. Things might'a turned out a whole lot different for the Norquist family."

"Where does Miss Coralee live?" I asked.

"When you leave the driveway, take a right. Go 'bout a mile, you'll cross the creek. Then another mile, there's a shell drive to the right. That's Miss Coralee's place. Run down somethin' awful, but she lives there. I don't know how she stands the loneliness. Everyone she knows is done gone."

"Thank you, Amos."

"Wait a minute." He went toward his cabin. Ten minutes later he was back with a paper sack filled with sweet potatoes, squash, and three bright red tomatoes. "Tell her I sent this. I worry she doesn't have enough to eat, but I don't have a way to get to her. I can't walk far like I used to. Miss Coralee's older than me, and far as I know, she doesn't have anybody."

Reginald took the sack of vegetables. "Is there anything else we should take her?"

"A pint of Mr. Royal's whiskey wouldn't go amiss. And some honey Miss Constance got from that old maple tree. She'd like that, I know."

"I'll get it." I left Reginald talking with the gardener while I went to the kitchen, hunting for a jar of honey and the boot-legged whisky. Luckily Fancy was back and she helped me find the goods. "Mr. Royal will be tickled to share with Miss Coralee," Fancy assured me. "He takes her provisions when he has time. He'll be happy you're doing it today."

I took her at her word and called to Reginald from the back porch. Together we walked around the house to the car. It was going to be a hot drive, but if we wanted to return before dark, we needed to get moving. We couldn't count on the road to be easy. Coralee lived farther off the beaten path than Waverley.

When the car was moving, the drive was pleasant, and I found myself drowsing as we passed beneath a canopy of leaves. To my left I caught a glimpse of three soldiers in gray, haggard and watchful. They stood almost invisible in the thick trees. They watched us, as if they hoped for a ride.

The war was a long way from over in these parts. I wondered if we stopped and searched the area if we'd find three graves, the final resting place of fallen soldiers, or if these were men who'd been on the march to battle or home but never came to the end of their earthly journey. Whatever their reason for lingering, they touched me with sadness. They had the look of the lost about them. I considered asking Reginald to stop and let me see if I could release them, but when I looked again, they were gone, evaporated like a thin mist.

"What did you see?" Reginald asked. He knew me too well.

"Confederate soldiers. The Norquists weren't the only family to lose their sons, brothers, and fathers."

"I've never understood the allure of war, of fighting for what? A cause? Slavery was a cause? One man's cause is another man's prison."

"I agree." I thought of my Alex. In my dreams I saw the

bullets tear into his body, the way he twisted and fell on a field littered with the dead and dying. The war to end all wars. To stop the Kaiser. I'd be willing to bet that a new villain would arise before too much time passed. There was never an end to the people who let greed and vanity push them to do dreadful deeds. "Do you think people will ever learn to live in peace?"

Reginald didn't answer for a long time. "I think that the human animal is badly flawed. Greed is the basis for most disputes, personal or global. As long as there is greed, there will be wars. Young men will be duped into fighting. Old men will grow rich."

"I'm almost sorry I asked." I sighed. "I wish I could disagree."

"If you see those soldiers on the way home, tell me and I'll stop. It can't hurt to try to help them."

Reginald was like that. Willing to help. "Ab-so-lute-ly." It was the one modern phrasing I could actually say with conviction. "There's the driveway."

Reginald slowed at a white shell drive that disappeared in thick trees more badly overgrown than Waverley. How in the world did Coralee Hempstead stand it out here so alone without even electricity or a telephone to connect her to the modern world? In such a short time I had grown spoiled by the new inventions of the modern age.

"Are you ready?" Reginald asked.

"I am. I hope she can help us. I hope she will."

We bumped down the driveway that wasn't as rutted as Waverley's because it had so little use. In a clearing rapidly being overtaken by trees and vines was the ruin of what had once been a lovely plantation house, two-storied with large white columns on the front. The white paint had curled and flaked away, and some of the wood work appeared to be rotting. Another ten years of neglect, and the house would collapse in upon itself.

A rocking chair had been placed on the porch, and a small woman, her lap draped with a quilt despite the heat, rocked back and forth. Her hair was pulled back in a feminine bun, and she wore a neatly starched and ironed dress from another era. The creases were as sharp as knife blades.

She saw us coming, but she didn't miss a beat of her rocking. How many other visitors had come down her driveway bringing news or questions? Her serene expression gave nothing away. We stopped and got out of the car and approached.

"Can I help you?" she asked. Her voice was strong, and I was surprised to see she wore powder, rouge, and lipstick. She'd had no way of knowing company would arrive, so I assumed she dressed carefully each day. The way a proper lady was taught to do.

"Miss Coralee," I said, "Amos Plackett sent you some vegetables, and Royal Sheridan sent some other treats."

Reginald was holding the sack and he walked to the edge of the porch and put it at her feet. "Would you have a few minutes to talk with us?" he asked.

"Time is the only thing I have plenty of," she said. "I'd offer a chair, but I don't have any more."

"We can sit right here." I jumped up to the edge of the porch and made myself comfortable leaning against one of the columns. It was hot, but the shady porch cut the heat by quite a bit. I made the introductions and told her we were guests at Waverley.

"Those new people there are nice. I've waited a long time to see that place come back to life." She nodded slowly. "Yes, it's time. The past has ruled there long enough."

"So you've met the Sheridans?" Reginald asked casually.

"Mr. Royal is kind enough to check on me. The girl. Yes, I've met her. She rides over to visit with me. She's an extraordinary child."

This was an unusual turn of events. I hadn't anticipated that Amanda would ride so far from home. It was slightly peculiar that a young girl would ride to spend time with an older woman. Children were generally caught in their own fantasies and whims, unwilling to take the time to hear the interests of a past generation.

"Amanda is an excellent rider," I said.

"She puts me in mind of Nora Bailey. That woman tore up the countryside riding hither and yon, up to her tricks. She was a sight on that horse. Francis bought her a fine black gelding, perhaps the finest horse in the county. And it suited her. Both loved a challenge."

She'd brought up the reason for our trip without any prompting. This might be easier than I'd thought. "We've heard a lot about Nora this week."

"You would. She destroyed that family. She might as well have struck those young men down with her own hand. They died because of her." Coralee's eyes grew flinty hard. "I hope that bitch is burning in hell."

It was a shocking statement coming from such a well-groomed, elderly woman. She looked like someone who would offer tea and *petit fours* for an afternoon social.

She smiled at my shock. "You think I should be kind and loving, like an old woman. Maybe I would have been that grandma if Francis had lived. If I'd ever had a chance with him. But I didn't. Not after that vile bitch caught his eye and bewitched him. She could churn butter with her tail, and she liked to do it. She had a talent for nasty, and poor Francis followed her like a lovesick puppy. That cunning bitch shook the sheets with any man who didn't run away from her. Francis wasn't enough. She had to have that artist. The doctor. Lord knows who else. But Francis couldn't see it. Not until it was too late."

Reginald cut a glance at me, and I knew he was thinking about the dream I'd shared with him, the sense of being overtaken by salacious impulses. "Tell us about Nora," he said. "We ask because there are things happening at Waverley that defy logical explanation."

Coralee was old, but she was completely alert. She assessed the undertones in Reginald's remark. "You want to know why she serviced every man who came her way?"

"That would be helpful," Reginald agreed, a tiny flush of color touching his face. Talking about a woman's sexual proclivities with an elderly lady wasn't exactly his forte.

"She wasn't a common whore. I'll give her that." Coralee motioned for Reginald to hand her the bag of vegetables. "Did Amos send me a nip of Royal's moonshine?"

"He did." Reginald fished it out of the bag and handed it to her.

"Royal Sheridan brews a fine batch of whiskey. If the country wasn't so stupid for prohibition, he could make a good living. As it is, paying off the lawmen and revenuers cuts into a man's profits." She tilted the bottle up and took a swallow before she put the cork in and put it back in the bag.

She was a sharp tack, and living alone in a crumbling old plantation hadn't dimmed her brain at all. "Miss Coralee, do you think Nora loved any of the men she was involved with?" I needed to know more about what motivated her. I'd felt her impulses—or I now believed it to be her—the strong desire to make love with men, the need to draw them to her. But I didn't understand.

"Can a nymph experience love?" she asked.

"A nymph?" I knew the stories of mythology and the wanton women who lived in the woods and seduced men. They were wild and free and lived for sexual pleasure. Nora Bailey was no nymph. She'd been a devious and calculated spy. Perhaps Coralee was half a bubble off plumb after all.

"Yes, if you understand the true identity of those creatures. My daddy sent me off to Massachusetts after the war to study. There were no boys left to marry. My friends were all gone or dead. I went to school to be a teacher, but Daddy didn't calculate that there wouldn't be any schools in Mississippi able to pay teachers. My northern education held no value back here in Mississippi. After the war, there was nothing down here but hunger and death. I knew I'd never fit in up North, so I came home. There were Negro children here and over at Waverley, Nine Oaks, different places. I taught most of them to read and write. Folks paid me with vegetables and eggs, and sometimes a chicken or roast. I got by."

She was rambling, and Reginald shifted on the porch. I felt his frustration. We'd been very close to finding out something we needed to know about Nora.

"Those must have been hard times. But when the Norquist children were all alive and Waverley was a show place, I'll bet you loved visiting there." I had to get her back on track.

"The house was an architectural delight." Coralee looked beyond me into the woods, and likely into the past. "There were dances. Oh, you wouldn't believe. All of the girls would be up on the second floor, getting ready, and when the band struck up, we would come down that staircase one after the other. The young men would stand in the rotunda and simply gawk at us. I felt like a princess."

I could easily picture the scene she described. Waverley was meant for laughter and parties. The fall from a love of such beauty and grace was hard to accept, but that time was gone from the South and everywhere else.

"How did Nora Bailey come to stay at Waverley?" I asked. I wanted to ease into the questions about her possible child and what happened to Nan.

"Francis met her in New Orleans. I'm sure she seduced him, turned his head clean around. She could drop a man to his knees with one long heated look or a flutter of her eyelashes. She had a power. At any rate, she told him she had nowhere to go, no family and no place to live. New Orleans was coming under attack. Francis brought her here, a place he thought she would be safe. He never understood that she was never in danger. He and his brothers were the ones who would suffer."

"Was Nora Bailey traveling alone?" Reginald asked.

Coralee frowned. "What do you mean? Alone?"

"Was there anyone with her? A child?" Reginald clarified.

She shook her head. "I don't think so. A child would have greatly hampered Nora's seduction schemes. She didn't have a motherly bone in her body. All she wanted was a man. Any man. She was a nymph, and the men crawled on their bellies to be with her."

It could be said that Coralee was bitter because she loved Francis, but I suspected her hatred for Nora stemmed from more than jealousy. Nora had been instrumental in killing hundreds of young Southern men and ending the South's chances to win the war. She would be anathema to anyone who loved their homeland and their people. I could never support a fight to retain slavery, but I understood how hard it was to lose the people one loved.

"There was a child at the house," Reginald pressed. "A little girl. I think her name was Nan. Do you know anything about her?"

Coralee's attention snapped back to us. "I think you should leave. Thank Amos and Mr. Royal for me. I appreciate the gifts."

Our dismissal was so brusque. I didn't understand what had gone wrong. "Was there a child?" I asked.

"Young woman, I'm not going to talk about that. What's done is done. There's no undoing it. Telling tales won't help the child or anyone else." She stood up from the rocker, her quilt falling to the floor. Reginald picked it up and handed it to her as he gained his feet on the ground. "I have to go inside."

"Thank you for your time," I said. The only thing I could say for certain is that there was a child at Waverley. She'd said as much. And Nora hadn't arrived with a child—or if she had it was well hidden. But something was very much off about Nan. That she was illegitimate was a fact she'd told me herself. I had one more try. "I know Nan was illegitimate. What I want to know is what happened to her. Please, it could help Amanda. There's something very wrong at Waverley, and it is Amanda who will pay the price if we can't help her."

Coralee stopped halfway to the front door. She turned to face us. "I felt sorry for Nan. She was a living reminder of the shame, and no one in that family could afford to truly love her."

"Who was her mother?" I asked.

"It doesn't matter."

"I'm afraid it does matter. Was it Bjorn or one of the Norquist boys?"

She started to go inside but stopped. "No one ever knew the father. Just leave it alone. You want to find a villain, look into that fancy doctor that threw Olivia over for Nora Bailey. Olivia's heart was broken. That bitch Nora Bailey did more damage to a good family and even though she hanged for it, that wasn't punishment enough. They were going to burn her, but someone stole her body."

After all these years, Amos had never revealed to Coralee that it was Francis who'd cut Nora down and ultimately saved her body from desecration. He'd given her a final resting place. I wasn't about to reveal that secret.

"Who would have wanted to hurt Nan?" Reginald asked gently. "It's important, Miss Coralee."

"Look into that fancy pants doctor from Nine Oaks. Calvert Marcus. He was oh so handsome and smooth. Women for miles around would pretend to be sick just to spend a few minutes with him touching their foreheads or checking their pulse." Her lip curled. "I'd be willing to bet he's the one who pushed that little girl down the stairs. Nan followed him around like he was Santa Claus. She was under his feet all the time. No telling what she saw, him snooping all over Waverley Mansion for his Union causes. I think he had to shut her up." Her eyes were flinty. "They hanged Calvert Marcus, and they burned him, and it still wasn't enough." She went inside, letting the door slam behind her. She might be an elderly woman of a certain societal level, but she had a yen for blood.

CHAPTER 14

We returned to Waverley, both of us quiet. It was reprehensible that Nan's father pushed her down the stairs and killed her because she wanted a small sign of affection from him. Calvert Marcus was a medical doctor and a spy. His first loyalty had been with the Union army, and I wondered if he'd worked Olivia to worm information from her, just as Nora had obviously manipulated Francis.

The Norquists family had played a big role in the Confederate army, one large enough to attract the interest of two spies.

I heard Anne in the parlor when we entered, and Reginald waited there while I ran up to my room. When I entered, I stopped. The bedsheets had been torn from the bed and scattered about the room. An oil lamp had been knocked over, and the flame sprang to life, moving toward the soaked sheets. Before I even thought, I ran forward and grabbed the quilt and beat the flames out.

"Help!" I cried. "Help, someone!"

Footsteps pounded up the stairs and Reginald burst into

the room. Between us, we managed to suffocate the flames. The floor was scorched, but I hoped it could be cleaned. The wood planking was thick and solid oak.

"What happened?" Anne asked. The look on her face told me what she suspected.

I told her how I'd entered the room, saw the disarray and just as I was about to call for help, the flame had made it to the oil and conflagrated.

"Who did this?"

I shook my head. "We've been away." I left it at that.

"No one has been in this room." Anne was clearly worried. I didn't want to add to her worry by telling her that it might not have been a corporeal being who caused the damage. "Amanda came in from her ride and went to her room. Constance is with her. Has been since she returned from her lesson. Fancy is in the kitchen. No one here at Waverley could have done this. *Would* have done it."

I nodded. Movement near the edge of the woods caught my eye and I moved closer to the window. Constance and Newly Castor were engaged in an intense conversation. She glanced toward the house, and then she ran into the woods. Newly followed her.

"I need to speak with Amanda," I said, aware that my comment came out of the clear blue sky. I didn't wait but slipped out of the room and down the hall to Amanda's door. I knocked and when there was no answer, I opened the door.

Amanda was nowhere to be found.

Had it been a ghost that tried to set a fire in my room, or had it been an eight-year-old child who might not want me to uncover the secrets of Waverley House?

· · ·

WHEN WE GATHERED FOR SUPPER, the atmosphere around the table was unusually tense. The fire, the visit from the sheriff, Amanda's absence —too many things were happening.

Amanda, unwilling to talk about where she'd been all afternoon, arrived late and ate with concentration, seemingly in her own world. Anne fanned herself and sipped a glass of wine. She had no appetite for food and kept shooting worried glances at her husband. Royal stabbed his roast and washed it down with neat whiskey, his countenance dark and angry. Constance kept her gaze on her plate and ignored the rest of us, but I intended to buttonhole her before she retired for the evening.

Reginald and I had agreed to let the idea of another séance rest for the evening. The mood was all wrong. Royal was on his way to drunkenness, and Anne was unwell. She was so pale she might have been mistaken for a ghost. I left Reginald smoking on the porch with Royal, and I followed Constance to her room.

"May I have a word?" I asked her.

"I'm very tired. It's been a tedious day. Amanda disappeared and had everyone in an uproar, as you know." She looked at me with frank curiosity. "Then again, you and Mr. Proctor disappeared also. I thought Amanda was with you."

"Reginald and I had some business." I brushed her unasked questions aside. "I want to speak to you about Amanda's friend. Nan. I have to figure out who her parents were."

Surprise flitted across her face, but she covered it well by adding, "It's a mystery. Nan was probably the get of one of the Norquist boys. From what I understand, the girl was sent here from New Orleans when she was a toddler. It wasn't uncommon for boys to sow their wild oats without real consequences. Their families took in the children, raising them as distant relatives."

I nodded, not really surprised that Constance had used deductive skills to get to that point. Constance was educated and observant. If the ghost of a child lurked at Waverley, it would have to have some connection to the past. "What about the daughters? Could one of them be Nan's mother?"

"Doubtful. Even with great care it would have been hard for a Norquist daughter to have a child out of wedlock."

"I believe Nan was murdered. Who would want to kill a bastard child?"

This time she couldn't cover her concern. "You can't go around saying things like that. You have no proof the child was killed."

"I have all the proof I need. And I'll soon have the tools to set Nan's spirit free. She wants everyone to know what happened to her. She lingers here because her murderer was never acknowledged, much less punished. I'll find out the truth, and then her spirit will move on as it should have decades ago."

"Do you really think it will be that simple?" Constance asked.

For a moment I wondered what she knew that I didn't. Clearly she thought she had information outside of my grasp. Was it something Amanda had revealed to Newly? "I saw you with the horse trainer." It was time to put my cards on the table. "I don't care what goes on between you, but let me recommend that you be honest with the Sheridans. Amanda is behaving like a much more mature child. It's clear to me you and Newly are romantically involved. I hope the two aren't connected because she's witnessed your romantic meetings."

"Of course not!" Constance was indignant. "How dare you."

"I'm not accusing. Take my advice, Constance. Just be honest. The truth will serve you better than deception."

Constance opened her mouth slightly and inhaled. "Are you going to tell them?"

"No, I'm not saying a word. It isn't my business. But they'll find out and then the Sheridans will feel betrayed. I've seen you and Newly together twice. Not exactly what I'd call discreet. It would be better to tell the Sheridans the facts. They value you and Newly. That you're in love shouldn't matter to them. It's the sneaking around that would disturb them. Or at least that's my opinion."

For the first time since I'd met her, Constance seemed to loosen up. The rigidity of her proper posture relaxed. "I never expected to fall in love with him. I'm a woman of a certain age. The fluttery stomach and—" she shook her head. "I'm sorry. I sound ridiculous. Like a school girl. But my feelings for him are a gift. One I thought had passed me by."

"You sound like someone in love." I remembered how Alex's voice could make me want to dance and sing. His arms around me were the safest haven I'd ever known. Those were things no woman should deny herself. Time or age didn't diminish the desire for partnership. Beneath her proper rigidity, Constance needed the same things that most women valued.

"Love hasn't been an option in my life," Constance said. "Responsibility has been my stock and trade. Newly is a surprise. To both of us." Her expression softened and she looked years younger. I hoped for her that this love would carry her through the rest of her life. But I wasn't at Waverley to play Cupid. I had a more serious job.

"Tell me what you've learned about Nora Bailey since you arrived here. I've heard she was very beautiful, but that she betrayed everyone who loved her. That she had uncontrollable sexual impulses."

Constance snorted. "Really? Uncontrollable? Do you believe that or is it just another excuse for a woman who couldn't live without going after every man she met?"

It was a loaded question for me. I hesitated with my answer and Constance continued to talk as she tidied the items on her dressing table. Her hands found a beautiful glass perfume container, bright red, and I realized it was shaped like the scarlet tanager I'd seen in the graveyard.

"These modern young women have no impulse control, and they believe it makes them original and brave. It only makes them fools. The men sleep with them, have a laugh, and move on to the next conquest. Marriage has only ever been the safety net for a woman. Either that or a career, as we both have chosen. From what I've learned of Nora Bailey, she was a skilled courtesan. She used her body to gather information and manipulate men for comfort and provisions. I've always viewed that as prostitution."

One thing I'd learned about Nora Bailey—she brought out people's passion. Even sixty years after the fact, those who hated her did so with a depth of emotion. Even people who were far outside the impact she had during the war. "Do you have any idea where the painting of her might be?"

Constance realized I wasn't going to leave, so she waved me onto a chaise near the window. She took a plump wing chair that had been placed in front of her cold fireplace. In the winter it would be the perfect reading chair. "Would you like some tea? Fancy said ice was delivered this morning, so I can chip some for our drinks."

"Not right now." I wanted to continue our talk without distraction. "What about the painting?"

"You know the legend?"

I'd put together some elements, but no one had ever told me the entire story. "Please, I'd love to hear it."

"Amanda told me. She heard it from some of the girls at the church in West Point. When she told them she'd seen Nora Bailey's ghost, that's when the trouble started with the girls. They were afraid of Amanda because she claims to see dead people. That girl makes her own problems by making up such a thing."

"I believe she does see ghosts." It was a relief to tell Constance. "If she has this gift, she needs to learn to use it, not allow it to negatively impact her life."

"Gift?" Constance almost rolled her eyes. "I'm aware you can see spirits, but would you really call it a gift?"

"We shall see, I suppose. If I can help Amanda and Nan, maybe it is a gift."

"You are a do-gooder, aren't you?" She stood up and went to the window.

I was a little taken aback. "I like to help people."

"I didn't mean to sound...judgmental. It's just that so few people truly care what happens to others. It's refreshing to see someone who honestly has compassion."

We'd strayed from the portrait yet again. "Tell me the legend about Nora's painting, please."

Constance looked out the window, and a slight smile lifted the corners of her mouth. Night was falling, and I wondered if I might be interfering with a rendezvous with Newly. Was he waiting for her as the gloaming fell over Waverley? The quicker she told me about the portrait, the sooner I'd be out of her room.

"I shouldn't bring up this foolishness."

"Horse feathers." I used another modern phrase that was somewhat lighthearted—and a contrast to my do-gooder label.

"I'd really like to hear it. I never know what things will help me with a...case." I'd almost said haunting.

Constance nodded. "Okay. Before I moved out here with the Sheridans, I did ask around about Waverley. I'd been working in Tupelo, and even there rumors about this old plantation were everywhere. Before the war, it had been some place. There's a warehouse on the river, and the old Waverley Ferry was in use all the time. The Norquists were an old, respected family. There was talk of subdividing some of the property to build a town to rival West Point and Columbus. But the war changed all of that, and then the railroad came through and the river wasn't as important."

My uncle had foreseen the death of the steamship, which was why he was busy with another invention. A secret he refused to talk about. "Those must have been grand days for the plantation owners and the elite. Not too thrilling for those who worked the fields."

She raised her eyebrows. "A suffragette, a spiritualist, *and* an abolitionist?"

I smiled at her teasing. "See, I can be a smidge more than just a run-of-the-mill do-gooder."

Constance shook her head as she laughed. She was quite pretty when she smiled. "I can see that. I didn't mean to press on a bruise."

"I want to hear about the legend. I had no idea Waverley's reputation was so widespread." It was a little concerning. I'd discovered that rumors of hauntings were often based on fact or at least sensitivity to the spirit world. Stories of the Waverley ghosts had spread far and wide. "So what's the story?"

"Waverley is supposed to be haunted by the ghost of Nora Bailey. Not hard to guess she would haunt the grounds since she died a violent death, but not before her actions would cause many horrible deaths. What she did crippled the Confederate forces this side of the Mississippi. Her betrayal of Francis and the Norquist family was catastrophic."

I had no desire to debate the merits of spying. "I wonder what she was really like. What she wanted? What she hoped to gain by spying for what was considered the enemy in her homeland?" I wondered what I would have done had I lived at a time when my beliefs were in conflict with the land I loved.

"She wanted fame and money. You don't think she did all of this for free, do you?" Constance unbuttoned the top button of her blouse. With the door closed, the room was warm. "She was kept by numerous men who all fell in love with her, and she betrayed them all. When she died, she was a wealthy woman. The story was that while she was living in New Orleans she was the mistress of a pirate, a man who ran the Union blockades and brought slaves from the Caribbean into New Orleans to auction, even though it was against the law. He was a ruthless man and she profited from his willingness to sell flesh. Yet she supported the Union's determination to stop slavery. She was a hypocrite."

I understood Constance's frustration. "Nora did pay with her life."

"And think how many lives she ruined."

"They said she was beautiful." Could any woman be so lovely that a man lost his good sense.

"I understand she was. Not just in appearance. She had a way about her that made every man think he was something special. It was her talent."

I'd known a few women who were popular with men. They were sought after as dates and dancing partners, sometimes as wives. Some were physically beautiful and some were not. It was more about what the men saw reflected back to them than what the women actually looked like. It sounded like Nora was the perfect mirror for a man to see himself as powerful, desirable, unique, and fabulous. That was indeed a valuable gift.

"You know a lot about Nora."

"Nora and other women like her. As a governess, I've worked in homes where the wife became a work horse while the husband fancied himself free to do as he pleased. It takes a certain kind of woman to involve herself with a man she knows she can never have. The temporary is good enough for those women, and they bleed the men dry while they can. The good wife endures in silence."

She was right about that. The double standard for men and women chafed me greatly. Men could do as they pleased. Women could only move within the proscribed social mores of their communities. Even I, a widow, could never be seen in inappropriate circumstances with any male, much less take a lover. But a man could do anything. Nora had defied that, and much more. "Did Nora truly fall in love with the doctor at the nearby plantation?"

"I don't know. The stories I heard were about her prowess between the sheets. She was accomplished and sexually ravenous. I don't know that she had the capability to really love anyone."

"And the painting?"

"It disappeared the night she was hung. Francis had commissioned it from Julian DeWitt. The artist was here painting the Norquist daughters. DeWitt stayed to paint Nora, who sat for the painting for months as he worked. It took him four times longer to paint her than the others. It was said that he called her the perfect model, that the light infused her skin and she knew how to hold a pose."

"The artist was yet another of her conquests."

"Yes, DeWitt loved her too. Luckily he escaped with his oils and his life. So many others didn't."

"What kind of portrait did he paint? I mean, what was she doing in the portrait?"

"She's standing on the staircase, her dress lifted slightly as if she's stepping down. The angle of her hands was exquisite. The story goes that it is so life-like, it looks as if she's walking out of the frame. And for a time it hung above the staircase. That was where Francis put it. The night she was hanged, it was taken down and never seen again.

"I'd really like to find the painting. I think it might help resolve matters here."

"Anne doesn't have a clue where it might be. When she moved in here, it was already gone. For decades teens and curiosity seekers came in and out of this house. The painting was probably stolen."

"Isn't it odd that no one damaged the house?" I was still smitten by that fact. "And of all the things not taken, the painting was the only one that was."

"Waverley has her own power," Constance said. "I don't believe in ghosts or hauntings, but there are places that do possess unusual qualities. This house is so...perfect here. It suits the land. If Bjorn Norquist hadn't built it, someone else would have. Can't you feel that? It had to be here, exactly as it is. Even the trees have grown in the exact place to perfectly frame it."

Constance's observations made my skin tingle. She might not believe in ghosts, but she was a sensitive. To places. She had a kinship with Waverley that went beyond the ordinary. This was a subject I'd have to delve into with Madam when I had a chance to speak with her again.

A light tap at the door sent Constance to open it. She invited Reginald into the room. "Did you put Royal in a better mood?" she asked.

"He's angry. He feels the law won't help him protect his land and intends to penalize him when he tries to do it himself. Why won't the sheriff help him protect his property?"

"Good question," Constance said. "There's bad feelings between them. Sheriff Gaines has a reputation for graft. I'm thinking Royal refuses to pay for the sheriff's favor. Today looked like Walter Gaines came to squeeze some money out of Royal. You know, pay up or feel the brunt of my displeasure. From what I understand, the other bootleggers pay a tidy sum to the sheriff to look the other way."

Reginald nodded and joined me on the chaise. "I think you've pegged it, Constance." He looked from me to her. "I don't want to interrupt your conversation. I'll retire to my room."

"No, you'll want to hear this," I said. "I'm learning about the legend of Nora Bailey and the painting."

"The missing painting," Reginald said. "Where could it be?"

"Somewhere on the grounds, if Nora is haunting this place," Constance said. "The legend is that Nora steps out of the painting and takes on human form again. She wanders the grounds of Waverley until she finds a...host. Then she possesses the young women who come here to pet with their boyfriends, causing the girls to go farther than they normally would. That's the draw for the trespassers. That's why those young people keep coming back again and again. The boys know Waverley does affect the young women."

Royal had his work cut out for him if the young people truly believed the grounds of Waverley were some kind of aphrodisiac. "So the last time the painting was seen, it was hanging in the first curve of the staircase?"

"Anne had the wall painted twice, but the outline of where the portrait hung is still there. A little creepy, isn't it?"

"Yes." There were lots of creepy things about this estate. I'd check it out the next time I went downstairs.

"You've figured out that it was Nora who killed Nan, haven't you?" Constance asked.

The question caught Reginald and I completely off guard. "Nora? Why?" Coralee had been certain it was Dr. Marcus who'd killed his own child.

"I think the little girl was always lurking in corners, hiding in the woods. From what I could gather, she was a mousy child, a loner who pried and snooped. I believe she saw something she shouldn't have. Whether it was Nora in an indiscretion or Nora searching desk drawers and reading private mail, I don't know, but it's easy to assume this. Think about it. Nora couldn't afford to be revealed as a spy until her work was complete. She killed Nan to silence her."

I didn't have a response. Thousands of soldiers had died because of Nora's spying. Thousands. Was it so hard to believe she could eliminate one child?

"If what you're saying is true, Nora was a terrible person. Amoral."

"What type of person would it take to be such an excellent spy. A spy has to win the confidence of the very people she intends to sacrifice. And according to the people who remembered the Norquist family, Francis did love her. More than his own family."

"War is dirty work." Greed and betrayal were facts of war, along with cowardice and courage. "You've given me a lot to think about, Constance." I stood up.

"I'm going to retire," Reginald said, also rising. "I need to think about all of this, Constance. I have to admit, it never occurred to me that it would be a woman responsible for the deliberate death—the murder—of a child."

"Me too." I wanted a word with Reginald before we parted ways for the evening. And I thought we might be holding Constance up from meeting Newly. She'd glanced out her window more than once, and I'd heard the call of a songbird repeated at least three times. It might truly be a songbird, or it might be Newly signaling that he was waiting for her. If I had a man I loved waiting for me, I'd want to spend as much time as possible with him.

"I think I'll go out for a bit of air." Constance followed us out of the room. She was almost down the stairs by the time Reginald stopped at my door.

"Do you think Nora Bailey killed a child in cold blood?" he asked.

"It's a lot to take in." I didn't know what I believed. Constance seemed sure of her facts and assumptions, but I reserved some doubt.

"Are you okay? You're pale." Reginald said

"I'm going to write for a while." I wanted to think about Nora Bailey. There was a way to connect with her if I could figure it out.

"If you decide to go outside, get me."

I nodded. The problem was that sometimes I ended up doing things I hadn't anticipated.

CHAPTER 15

My candles were nothing but burning wicks when I finally decided to call it a night. I'd finished one story. It would require a lot of re-working, but I could go to bed well satisfied with my efforts.

The night creatures were out. Once I blew out the candles, I stood at the window and listened to the birds and small animals. Benedict, Amanda's pet cat, came out of the woods, head high, tail straight in the air. Owls and cats could see better in the dark than any other critter, or so I'd been told. The black cat often hid in the bushes outside the mansion, slyly hunting. He'd been in a hydrangea earlier in the day. He was a fine specimen of a cat and made me long for a pet of my own, but if I traveled a lot with my business, it wouldn't be fair to the pet or to Uncle Brett to saddle him with the care.

The cat stopped on the lawn and looked up directly into my window, as if he sensed me watching him. He was tensed for action, yet also relaxed. Felines had mastered the ability to hold two conflicting actions at once, like certain classical dancers who embodied motion in stillness. Benedict stared up at me.

"What do you see, pretty kitty?" I whispered softly. He stretched out, tilted his head as if he could hear, though it was impossible. Very slowly he stood and came out from under the bushes. His back arched and his tail fluffed, and he hissed, then darted up to the front porch.

The air around me turned freezing, and in one instant I could see my own breath. I knew if I turned around, Nora would be in the room. I wasn't afraid of her, but I wasn't ready to confront her either. I wanted to know what Nora had been in life before I attempted to draw her out in death. In my gut, I accepted it would come down to a personal battle between us. Nora wanted something from me, and she was a woman who often got what she wanted.

I turned to face her and stopped. The silhouette, highlighted by moonlight, was that of a grown woman. She wore a ball gown that emphasized her slender waist, pulled in even smaller by a whalebone corset. The low-cut gown revealed full breasts and pale, smooth shoulders. Her hair was piled in ringlets on top of her head and secured with several bows that matched her dress. She was a vision of Southern femininity, circa 1860, before the deprivations of war hit.

"Nora," I said. "At last."

"Come to me." She spoke the words in a deep voice, seductive, hinting of many pleasures.

I was afraid of her. She was powerful, and she was sizing me up. "No, I won't. Not yet. But we will confront each other." My heart was pounding, but I refused to back down. "You must leave, though I suspect your fate is not one you will enjoy."

Somewhere on the first floor, a clock chimed. My room was filled with the lovely scent of wisteria. The summer was too far gone for the purple flowers to be blooming—they were some of spring's first belles. But the smell was unmistakable, and it came with such violent force that it was almost suffocating. I counted ten chimes of the clock.

"My place," Nora said. "My home. Forever."

I couldn't show my fear. Madam had told me to always hold my ground. Once a spirit was aware they could manipulate a living person, they were in charge of what happened next. "No, Nora, your time has passed. You belong with the dead. You deserve your judgment." I'd never felt such harshness toward a spirit before, but Nora Bailey had harmed so many.

Her image wavered, fading and then returning. My teeth chattered from the cold. "Get out! Or die!" Her words were an assault.

Before I could respond, a vase of cut flowers on the vanity flew across the room and struck me in the side of the head, shattering. I gasped and almost fell as water and zinnias splattered down me, but I righted myself. She'd hurled the vase with great strength, and the blow had left me a little addled. When I looked around again, the room was empty.

A light tap at my door let me know that Reginald had heard the ruckus. He came in and helped me into a seat. I was covered in water and blood. The vase had cut my scalp just above my ear, and it was bleeding profusely.

Reginald lit a candle and examined the wound, pressing a clean cloth against it to try to stop the blood. When the flow had slowed to a trickle, he examined it. "You should be stitched," he said. "It's a good gap."

"Can't we just bandage it?" A doctor would be a long drive on a dark and lonely road, if we could find one willing to treat me. There was no phone to call and alert a medical person that we needed his attention. We might arrive at his house only to discover he was out on another call. "Or wait until tomorrow?"

Anne Sheridan entered the room with a candle in her hand. With her hair down her back in soft curls and her nightgown flowing about her ankles, she was a delicate, ephemeral creature. "What happened? Are you okay?"

"One of the entities doesn't want me here." I suspected who'd started the fire in my room, too. Which meant that Nora perceived me as a danger to her. That was one positive to take from the incident. "I'm fine, Anne. Really."

Anne brought her candle close to examine the wound in my scalp. "You need to have that stitched. You don't want that gaping open, Raissa. And you sure don't want it infected."

"That's exactly what I said." Reginald patted my arm. "I'll drive you to the doctor."

"Newly can stitch it." Anne left and returned with Constance. "Get Newly. Tell him to bring his kit."

"He's a horse trainer not a doctor," Reginald objected.

"And he's stitched up animals worth thousands of dollars. He's very skilled," Anne said. "One of the workmen sliced his thigh open. Newly stitched him up and it healed with only a thin white scar. Better than what the local barber can do. He's good at this, I promise. I trust him more than Doc Little. He's a nice man, but a little shaky."

"Get Newly," I said.

"I'll be back as quickly as I can," Constance said.

"Should Royal go for him?" Reginald asked.

"He's asleep," Anne said. "And best to leave him that way. He was far from sober when he finally went to bed."

"Where's Amanda?" I asked. Everyone else in the house was awake and in my room. It was curious the child hadn't come to investigate the commotion.

"I'll check on her on the way out." Constance took a lighted candle. "I know there's a flashlight in the parlor. Would it be okay—"

"Certainly," Anne said. "Take it and be careful in those woods."

"I will." Constance disappeared and I heard her footsteps on the stairs.

"Let's go to the kitchen and put some water on to boil," Anne said. "We need to clean the cut before he closes it up. We can't have any dirt in the wound. If we do that part now, it will make the stitching go quicker."

With Reginald's help, I was almost across the room when I heard Constance call out. "Anne, it's Amanda. She's gone."

The air rushed out of Anne's lungs all at once and she faltered, stumbling. She recovered and inhaled. "That child is damn clever. She can pick a lock." She took hold of my elbow to give me support. "Now let's get you down to the kitchen. I think this has gone far enough, Raissa. You've been injured, your room set on fire. It's time to back away from this. I'm going to send Amanda to a boarding school. I've been thinking about it for a long time now. Royal is opposed, but he thought the horse would help. It's just made her more willful and wild. She's beyond my control, and she needs to be some place where she has to bend to authority. Before she's ruined completely. The notions she takes in her head…I've had enough! If a change of scenery doesn't return her to the normal girl I love, then I'll explore medical care. But this can't go on. She's going to harm herself running around in the night."

It was the longest speech I'd ever heard Anne give and told me how desperately worried she was. My head throbbed, and I didn't know if I agreed or disagreed with her decision. The final say was hers and Royal's. If Amanda were my child, I'd be worried sick by her behavior, and Anne was right to be concerned that she was out in the night alone. There were predators in the woods, and Waverley was isolated.

"Reginald, go look for her. I'm fine."

"Once I'm sure you're—"

"No, I promise you. I'm fine. Amanda is the one who may be in danger."

He nodded. "I'll check back in a bit. Constance is going to the stables. I'll go toward the river."

"Thank you!" Anne touched his arm. "Thank you. I appreciate all you've both done. It's just time to yield. I want to move away from Waverley."

"We can discuss this when Amanda is safe and Raissa is stitched. Just watch over her." He ran down the stairs and out the front door.

Now I had to wait for Newly to ply his needle and thread. It wasn't an event I looked forward to.

Anne stoked the stove and put water on to boil. I knew the preparations for stitching a wound. I'd read about the treatment of soldiers on the field of battle. Those descriptions didn't bring comfort. "Anne, I think you should wake Royal and let him hunt for Amanda." Having met the full force of Nora's power, I had grave concerns for the child.

"You're right." She wiped her hands on an apron that hung by the kitchen door. "I'll be right back. Newly should be here soon. Then he and Constance can help hunt."

"I'm fine." I waved her out of the room.

The kitchen was Fancy's domain, and while I'd offered to help with the chores of food preparation—and that help had been declined—I hadn't spent much time in the room. It was connected to the main house by a dog trot and was obviously part of a much older structure, likely the original dwelling at

Waverley. The stout walls were thick logs, but modern glass windows had been added, though they were open because of the heat. Royal was building a kitchen onto the main structure of Waverley in anticipation of electricity and the diminished likelihood of a fire caused by the cook stove.

A noise outside the window drew my attention. I stood, glad to find my wooziness had passed. My head was still wrapped in the cloth Reginald had used to staunch the blood flow, and I held it in place with one hand as I leaned over the sink to look out the window. The moon was occluded by a thin cloud. It broke free and silvered the side yard with pale light. Waverley was such a beautiful place. Even with the troubles it harbored, the magnificence of the land couldn't be denied.

A figure flitted through the trees, a darker shadow in among the gray and green. Someone was out there.

"Raissa?" Anne had returned and spoke from behind me.

"Yes." I followed the movement outside the window and leaned over the sink for a better view.

"Raissa?"

I heard Anne call my name again, but I was right there in front of her. And I couldn't look away from the yard or I'd lose sight of the movement I was tracking. "Yes. What is it? I think there's someone out in the yard." Something flitted from the trunk of one tree to the next, a little closer to the house. In the pale light it could have been a person or a deer. Or something else. It was the latter that made my skin prickle.

"Raissa?" Anne was growing more insistent.

"Just a minute. I see something and it could be Amanda." I strained to see into the gloom of the yard, but all I caught was movement. I couldn't identify what made it.

"Raissa!" The voice was dark and oily, and I whirled around to discover that Anne was not in the room with me. The entity that stood in the doorway had the features of a beautiful woman. She wore a ball gown of pale green in the style of a Southern belle. Her hair was pulled back with intricate braids and coils and held in place by ribbons. The skin of her bare shoulders was creamy, untouched by the hot Southern sun. Nora Bailey had returned, and this time her figure was denser, more detailed. "Need you." She floated closer.

Intuitively I understood the danger. Nora had changed her mind about my potential use. Nora meant to take me. To possess my body if she could. I'd played with the idea of letting this happen, because I felt if I understood what she wanted, then I'd be better able to combat her. But I'd counted on Reginald's help, and Nora had come at a time when I was alone and weakened by my injury. If she took over now, I might not be able to force her out. She was very dangerous. Her strength was greater than mine.

I dared not show my fear. "You should be glad I'm here. I can help you move on." Even as I said it, I realized Nora had no desire to leave Waverley place. She had everything she needed here—all of the young women from the school that she could possess and manipulate to gain the sexual gratification she desired. The conquest of the young men. Those things fed what passed for her soul. I understood what she had become. Not a nymph, but a succubus. She was that thing that fed off the carnal pleasure she achieved from bewitching men, and she used the bodies of anyone she could to do so. She left behind her a path of complete destruction. I didn't know if she'd been this creature during the Civil War, and that had led to her conquests of so many men. If she possessed me, would I become a cunning, insatiable woman who took whoever I wanted to my bed? Was Nora Bailey possessed by this creature

—or had she been the creature from its inception? So many questions, and I had no answers.

"Need you!" She came closer, calculating her best move. I'd read only a little lore about succubi, but I understood she had to touch me. In legend, Lilith, Adam's first wife was considered the original succubus after she laid with the Archangel Samuel. These were demons who prayed on human weaknesses and desires. She came toward me, hand outstretched. Her features were so beautiful, her curves lush and desirable. I stepped back. I had to fight.

I was overwhelmed by the smell of wisteria, followed immediately by the gagging odor of decomposition. She might look beautiful, but beneath the veneer of a belle was a dead person, a corpse, a demon brought back to life by wickedness.

"Where is that painting of you?" I asked.

She recoiled, and I knew I'd scored a well-placed arrow. The painting was important, and she knew it. Reginald and I had to find that painting.

"You can't run." She reached her hand toward me and I felt the pinch of bitter cold.

Where in the hell had Anne gone? And Reginald? I was alone. More alone than I'd ever been before. She exerted her will on me, and I was weakening.

"Allow me to help you, Nora. If you're still trapped inside, I will release you. I can free you." I didn't retreat but held my ground and chose to appeal to a spirit that might be held captive. "You are a dead thing, a woman who betrayed those who loved her. Perhaps your place in Hell awaits you. I can't judge you. Maybe you were forced to act against your will. I don't know. But surely an ending is better than this torment of constant madness."

She cocked her head as if studying an insect. "No. No." She spoke softly. "You will obey."

She rushed forward and grasped my bicep. Her touch was icy and hot, simultaneously. My arm went numb, and I lost the ability to speak. I tried to put up a wall in my mind, to block her entrance into my thoughts, but she was powerful. She wanted to feed, and she was very hungry. I felt her hot desire for a man, the terrible, churning need for sexual contact.

She was pulling my body, clutching at my breast bone as she fought to enter. My arms and legs were leaden, but I continued to struggle against her. I had only my will. I was not a quitter, but with each passing second, I felt more of her need and less of my own determination to fight.

"Raissa!" Reginald burst into the room. Behind him were Newly Castor and Constance.

Nora stood directly in front of me, her hand clutching my breast bone, lifting me. I was helpless to stop her. Reginald's face was frozen in horror, and Constance hid her face against Newly's shoulder. They wouldn't be able to see Nora. To them I would appear suspended in air.

"Dear God," Newly said, transfixed by what he was witnessing.

"Release her!" Reginald stepped forward into her space, and I saw his breath frost. He grasped my shoulders and pulled me toward him, surrounding me with his very flesh.

Her grip on me weakened, and I wrested free of her. I burrowed against Reginald, and she was gone. The scent of wisteria filled the kitchen, sweet and overwhelming.

"What is that smell?" Constance asked. "Flowers of some kind?"

"Raissa," Reginald said, easing me into a chair. The wound on my head had reopened and blood slithered down my ear and cheek and onto my blouse. Constance found another towel and set to work applying pressure.

Newly stepped up and examined the wound. "It shouldn't take more than seven stitches. Let's get this done."

"Where's Anne?" Constance asked.

"She went to wake Royal. She's been gone a while." The words had barely left my mouth when the sound of a gunshot echoed from the house.

For a moment we said nothing. It seemed as if the shot reverberated in the room, striking us all to silence as the implications rained down on us.

"Oh, no." Constance gasped. "I ran into some of those college students in the woods. That's what took me so long. I convinced them to leave, but not quickly enough, I guess. I left them and went to get Newly and came straight back here."

"Check for Anne and Royal," Reginald told Constance. "Quickly, please." He signaled Newly to work. "We need to get this closed up."

The episode with Nora had left me weakened and pliant, which was possibly a good thing as Newly cut away the hair around the wound. He used a chip of ice to deaden the scalp as much as possible, but I was very aware of the piercing needle and the pull of the thread through the tough skin. I could hear the thread sliding, the sound almost more unpleasant than the sensation.

"You're very stoic," Newly said as he worked. "A lot easier than a horse."

He made me smile, and I could see the relief on Reginald's face. "What happened in here?" Reginald asked.

There was no point hiding things from Newly. He'd seen me, four inches off the ground, suspended in the air. "It was Nora. I know what she is now. Whatever she was in life, she is something ugly and dangerous in death." I was reluctant to name her a demon in front of Newly.

Reginald clearly wanted to discuss the incident, but Constance had returned empty handed. She was still pale, and Newly was finishing his work. Now wasn't the time. And we had much research to do if we intended to combat Nora. Reginald and I would not be leaving Waverley Mansion, not until the Sheridans and all who set foot on the property were safe.

Newly finished his stitching and was putting his tools away when Anne lurched to a stop in the doorway. I hadn't believed things could get worse. I was wrong. Blood covered the front of her nightgown and her hands.

"Help," she said, staggering.

Reginald caught her before she hit the floor. "Are you hurt, Anne?"

"No, it's a man. In the woods. Shot. He's been shot. He's still alive, but not for long. He's bleeding so much."

"Where is Amanda?" Reginald asked.

"I don't know." Anne shook her head and wept. "They're all gone. All of them."

My scalp was on fire from Newly's ministrations, but the leaden feeling in my limbs had passed. I would have bruises from the grip Nora had used on me, but otherwise I was fine. Now, though, we had a gunshot person in the woods and Amanda and Royal were still missing.

"Where is the man who was shot?" Reginald asked Anne. "Tell us where to find him. Maybe we can help him."

I shared a glance with Reginald and knew we both feared it might be Royal Sheridan who was wounded. We had to go and look. If the person was still alive, we might be able to offer aid. And it it wasn't Royal who was wounded, there was a very good chance he was the person who had pulled the trigger.

CHAPTER 16

R eginald urged me to remain in the house, but I had
no intention of doing so. The men rushed out the
door, following the directions Anne had given to find
the wounded man. Constance and I helped Anne to bed. She
was breathing, but I questioned if she was truly alive. She'd
fallen into a place in her mind where no one could rouse her.
She'd retreated to the safety of her own thoughts or memories.
She wasn't a vigorous woman at the best of times. I feared she
was in shock and needed medical help, but before someone
could drive to town to look for a doctor, we had to find the
wounded person, Royal, and Amanda.

Once Anne was settled beneath a light sheet and breathing
regularly, Constance took my elbow. "We should look for
Amanda. The men will find the wounded person. We need to
locate that child."

I agreed, and I knew that staying inside Waverley offered
no protection for me from Nora. "If I begin to behave in a
peculiar way, you must restrain me. Do whatever you need to
do. Then make Reginald take me immediately to New Orleans.

He may be able to find help for me there." I grasped her wrist and held it. "Promise me!"

Constance frowned. She wanted to question my demand, but there was no time. "I promise." She pulled free of me and retrieved the flashlight. Without further comment, we headed into the woods.

While the men sought the wounded man, we were looking for a young girl who knew her way around Waverley's grounds in the dark. Amanda was a child that had gone feral in some regards. She was as much nocturnal creature as eight-year-old girl. And I was certain she had help from the Great Beyond. I only hoped it was Nan who was guiding her. Nan was a lost child. I knew for certain Nora had no good intentions for the child. If Constance was correct in her assumptions about Nora, she was not only a spy, traitor, and seductress, but a child murderer. A woman who used and eliminated anyone who got in her path.

We left the front lawn and entered the woods. When I'd agreed to come to Waverley Mansion, I hadn't envisioned spending the August days and nights in the woods. It was hot and humid. I could feel the hair at the nape of my neck curling in the damp heat. I was at my wit's end.

"Amanda!" Constance yelled. We had no hopes of sneaking up on her, and it was possible if she'd been sleepwalking, we might startle her awake, which could be good or bad.

"Amanda! Call out to us." I brushed away the bloodsucking insects that had found our scent. But there were also the magic of lightning bugs flitting in front of us, and the sounds of birds startled from their sleep. The night held a completely different kind of activity than the daytime—more secretive, more furtive.

Constance led the way through the thick tangle with the

flashlight. She pushed through the undergrowth, and I did my best to stop slender limbs from slapping me in the head near my stitches. After what I'd gone through to get them in, I didn't want them pulled out. "Amanda!" I called. "Amanda!"

Constance was following what seemed to be a deer path though the darkness. As she swung the light from side to side, shadows jumped. She was so on edge that she started and fell back against me several times.

"Amanda! Amanda!" we called into the night, which seemed to drink our voices, leaving only darkness and our panting as we pressed on.

"She used to like to play in the old warehouse on the river," Constance said. "It was instructive for the role the Tombigbee played in development of Waverley and this area, and also the Civil War. She really loved the old building." Her voice broke. "She said she was never alone there. Never alone. Why didn't I question her?"

"I hope it's Nan, and not...."

"I should have paid more attention. I thought it was just her fancy. And once Moonglow arrived, Amanda lost interest in her studies." She ducked under a tree that had partially fallen over. "Maybe she's there, hiding."

I didn't answer. It was pointless. If she was there, we would find her and between the two of us, we would bring her home.

We both called over and over as we hurried toward the river and what could be another terrible tragedy. I had no doubt Amanda had been warned away from the water, but she was a determined child. Warnings wouldn't slow her down. But other than ghosts, what possible attraction could an old landing and warehouse hold for a young girl. "How much further?" I asked.

"Not far. The old ferry is right up here, just above the

warehouse."

"Is the ferry still used?" I asked.

"Not since the bridge was put in, but some of those college kids will try anything. The old ferry is still there. They can pull themselves across the river if the water is low and the current not too strong. They leave their cars on the Columbus side and come over on the ferry. When they've had their fun, they go back. It's one reason Royal has had such a hard time catching them. Those young people are willing to take such risks. No one maintains those ropes and if that ferry broke free, no telling where it would end up. But you know young people; they believe they're invincible." She sighed. "But they aren't. No one is."

We burst into a clearing, and slowed to a stop. The night was shockingly quiet. Here along the river I could hear the waves lapping gently against the shore. The moonlight tipped the gentle swells of the river that looked slow and lazy, but I knew the Tombigbee had swift and treacherous currents in some places. Water could be so deceptive.

To the south of us, the warehouse, black and filled with shadows, loomed. I started to the riverbank, afraid of what I might see floating near the wharf but afraid not to look. Amanda courted death with her riding, with her wildness. I hoped she hadn't found it in the river.

I took a deep breath of relief when I didn't see anything in the water. I'd truly dreaded what I thought I'd find. "She isn't here," I said.

"No. I don't see her. I don't think anyone is here."

"Is that a car across the river?" I almost didn't believe that I was looking at a newer model Ford. It was a smart car, green with yellow trim. The ferry bobbed gently on our side of the Tombigbee.

"Oh, no," Constance whispered. "I'll bet it belongs to those college students I tried to run off.

"Do you think Royal would really shoot someone?" He was hot-tempered and aggravated about the trespassers, but to shoot a young person set on mischief was an extreme action.

"I don't know. He's changed since he came to Waverley. They all have. Anne is so much weaker, and Royal is angrier. The child...she's more mature and willful." She touched my back. "We should leave. Amanda isn't here. I don't know where that child could be."

"I'm telling you, I feel like skinning her alive." That was a dire threat one of my grade school teachers had reserved for the worst behaved children in the class. The vividness of the punishment had stuck with me, but now I understood exactly how my teacher must have felt. Had Amanda done what she was told, none of us would be out in the woods.

Constance clucked softly. "Royal and Anne have no control of her. She respects no one but Newly and that imaginary friend of hers, Nan."

"A poor murdered child."

Constance put a hand on my shoulder and stopped me as I was about to reenter the woods. My head hurt, I was hot and tired. I wanted to find Amanda and go back to my bedroom.

"Do you hear that?" she asked.

I hadn't heard anything, but I hadn't been listening. I stilled my body and focused. Something was coming through the woods. And it was coming fast. Constance and I were standing in the open. I didn't know whether to hide or hold my ground. If it was Royal and we ran, he might shoot us. If it was someone else, we might come under fire if we stood out in the open.

"Help!" The cry came from the woods. It was a woman, and she sounded terrified.

"Help!"

"She's that way," I said, pointing. "Let's cut her off."

Constance and I took off toward a point where I thought our path would intersect with the distressed woman. I'd rushed into the woods when I saw her darting through the trees. I realized I'd seen her once before, on the first day I arrived at Waverley. She'd been running in the woods then too. She was one of the young women from the college in Columbus. She'd been in the woods with a young man. I'd assumed she was a ghost, but I'd been wrong.

"Hey!" I was almost on her, but she gave me a terrified look and ran the other way, darting like a rabbit chased by a fox. "Hey! Stop." I outdistanced Constance and went after the woman. "Stop!"

When she didn't heed my call, I gave a last burst of speed and caught her. I grabbed her arm and pulled her around. Blood covered the front of her short dress. She sobbed and dropped to the ground, crying into her knees. "Don't hurt me! Please don't hurt me!"

"Who are you?" I asked.

"My name is Penelope. Penelope Lott. I'm a student at the college in Columbus." She raised her tear-stained face. "You have to help me. He's going to kill me."

"Who?" I asked.

"The man who owns this land. He shot Ashland. He killed Ashland!"

She was almost incoherent with her grief and fear and emotion. "Who is Ashland?" I put a hand on her shoulder to steady her and she flinched.

"He's my boyfriend. We came here for a picnic. Ashland

said it would be fun. He promised we would be safe. I told him after last time we shouldn't be here but he thought it was a lark."

"Where is the injured man?" Constance asked gently. She'd caught up with us, and while she struggled to regain her breath, she knelt beside the young woman.

"Back there!" Penelope pointed toward the direction she'd come from. "I left him. I had to run away to find help. But the man tried to kill me too! I got away."

"You saw your friend get shot?" Another kind of terror was taking hold of me. Royal was volatile about trespassers. And he had been drinking heavily at dinner. Had he deliberately shot someone?

"I saw it. That man, the one who owns this place, pointed the shotgun right at Ashland and pulled the trigger. It was terrible. He cried out and stumbled backwards, and his whole chest was covered in blood. I tried to stop the bleeding, but I couldn't. I couldn't." She sobbed uncontrollably. "Blood was bubbling at his lips. I couldn't help him."

Constance pulled her into her arms and rocked her. "You're okay now," she said. "You're okay. No one will harm you."

"I have to help Ashland, but there's nothing I can do." She cried harder. "I told him not to come here. I told him, but he said it was magical, that I would want to make love with him. And I did. But now he's dead."

I caught Constance's eye. "Can you get her back to Waverley without me? I can't wait. I have to get back to Waverley. Now."

She nodded. "I'll join you when she's calmed down."

"I'm going to look for Amanda." And Reginald. If this terrible thing had truly happened, we would have to call the sheriff. It was the only path open to us.

CHAPTER 17

I raced against the clock as I ran back toward Waverley Mansion. Surely the young man was not dead. He had to be alive. Maybe the young woman was hysterical and her boyfriend hadn't suffered such a severe gunshot.

The image that stayed with me as I dashed blindly through the woods was the bubbling of blood on his lips. Punctured lung. One of Alex's soldier friends had died in his arms from a gunshot into his lungs. Alex had held him, unable to stop the inevitable. He'd written in great detail how helpless he felt. That frothy blood was a sign of imminent death. Penelope had to be wrong about what she'd seen. Royal was an angry and erratic man. And he'd been drinking heavily. But he would not have shot an unarmed college student no matter how mad he was. It simply could not be true.

I ran hard, pushed by my thoughts, until I burst into the front lawn of Waverley. Amanda was sitting on the front steps, singing softly to herself. I recognized the song, "Buffalo Gals." As she sang, Amanda began to dance across the porch. Fury propelled me toward her.

"We've been looking everywhere for you."

"I know." She shrugged one shoulder and sat down. "Here I am."

I grabbed her arm and fought back the desire to shake some sense into her. "Your actions have consequences, Amanda. Serious ones. Get inside that house right now."

"You can't tell me what to do." Her face held all the defiance of a young woman.

"Oh, I can and I will." I pulled her up. "I don't know exactly what's going on with you, but I will find out. And I will stop this. Because if I don't, you're going to find yourself in extremely unpleasant circumstances. If Nan is influencing you, you'd best tell her to back off because you are one step from being sent away to boarding school." I meant to frighten her. And Nan. Or whoever was influencing her. "The step after that is an institution. I've seen what that's like and you don't want to end up there."

She bit her bottom lip, and tears formed in her eyes but didn't fall. I'd finally gotten her attention. "Go sit with your mother," I said. "She isn't well and she needs attention. Do not leave that room, do you hear me? There's someone in the woods with a gun, and a man has been wounded."

"Is it Newly?" She was at least concerned.

"No, someone else. If you father comes in, try to get him to stay with you and Anne."

"Where's Reginald? And Constance?" For the first time since I'd come to Waverley, I heard her sounding and behaving like a child.

"She's helping a young woman we found in the woods."

"Penelope?" she asked.

"How do you know her?" I couldn't believe Amanda knew all of this and had never spoken of it to her parents.

"I saw her on the lawn earlier in the evening. That's why I went outside. She and her boyfriend were sneaking around the property. I told them Daddy would be furious, but she was laughing. She said they came here a lot to neck in the woods. She said Waverley had a special magic for lovers."

"Did you see your father out in the woods?" I asked.

She shook her head. "No. Not tonight. Other times, though. He's out in the dark a lot. He's always looking for those people who are kissing."

I hoped she'd only seen kissing. That was bad enough. I felt a desperate need to run into the woods looking for Reginald, but while Amanda was willing to talk with me, I had to try to anchor her to her parents and Waverley. My biggest fear was that she would give up her connections to the real world, and then...I didn't know what would become of her. Would she die or simply drift into the dream world that now held her mother? Once a person truly let go of reality, I didn't know where they existed.

"Amanda, Nan must leave. Her family and others who love her are waiting."

"She's my only friend here."

"Aren't there any other little girls who ride horses?" I had to reach her, to give her something real to hold onto.

She thought about it. "Hester rides."

"Does Hester live close enough to go on picnics? To ride to the creek? Things like that."

"Yes. She's just past Miss Edith's place. Not so far."

It was a wonderful opening. "I met Miss Edith. She loves that you visit her."

Amanda was very still before she spoke. "She said I could be anything I wanted. She said I should never give up my dream. Women who yield are crushed. That's what she told me."

So Miss Edith Keller was one of the influences working on Amanda. I should have guessed. "In some ways she's right, but in others, not so much. You have to decide how to balance what you want against what you're willing to give up to have it."

"You want to be a writer. Women don't write stories. It's inappropriate." She said the last word stiffly, as if she'd rehearsed. I wondered if Constance or Anne had said that in front of her.

"Yes, I've heard that before." Even though I needed to be on the move, to find Reginald, to drive to town for help, I sat on the steps beside Amanda. "I write under a pen name. Initials and my last name. Few will know I'm a woman. It's very different from jumping horses in a show ring." I smiled at her. "And a lot less dangerous."

"Moonglow would never hurt me. She loves me. More than anyone else does."

I believed her. I'd seen her atop the horse. They had a special bond. "Amanda, what do you know about Nora Bailey. She's here too. You see her, I know."

She didn't deny it, but she looked down at her bare feet, covered with dew and blades of clipped grass. "I don't want to talk about her. Sometimes she scares me."

"She's powerful, Amanda. And I believe she is...evil." How to warn a child against an entity who'd likely presented herself as a playmate, a friend, though Amanda had the sense to be wary of her. Amanda's isolation and loneliness were almost palpable. How easy it would have been for Nora to deceive her, to lure her. But why? What could Amanda offer this demon?

"She says I'm good enough to ride in big competitions."

Flattery was such an effective tool. "And you are. But you don't need her to tell you so. It's your parents you need to win over, and you can do that by completing your studies, by being a loving daughter. Making your parents worry is only going to work against you."

"I don't mean to do that. Sometimes I do things and then later I don't know why I did them."

"You need to fight that, Amanda." Now my concern for the child outstripped worry for a wounded trespasser.

"How?"

That was the question. "Think of a wall of white light all around you. A bubble may be a better description. When you feel an...influence, create that bubble in your mind." This was one of the techniques Madam had instructed me to use when I felt my own will slipping and another trying to take over. Those of us who were sensitive to spirits and entities had to learn how to safeguard ourselves.

"Did Mama tell you I dreamed about Waverley Mansion before we moved here?"

I did not want to hear this. "No, she didn't. You dreamed you were moving to a wonderful house, or you dreamed of this place specifically?"

"This place. I saw it, all surrounded by the woods and falling apart. When I dreamed it, the house was in much worse shape. The walls were all messed up with the plaster falling down. The floors were uneven and had fallen through in places. It was terrible. I didn't want to come here at first, but then it wasn't so bad."

Precognitive dreams were an area where I had no knowledge. I'd never even asked Madam about them. Reginald, who'd worked with her for several years, might have some guidance. But why would a young girl in the central part of the state dream of a mansion in ruins that she'd never visited? The sinister implications left me short of breath.

"You must have heard your parents talking about Waverley?"

"No. In my dream, other people lived here. They laughed, and they ran up and down the stairs until the grownups fussed. The boys and girls snuck kisses and sang and danced. Not like it is now with Mama and Daddy. And Constance. No one laughs here now."

Amanda's loneliness had focused her as a serious equestrian, but it had also opened the door to relationships with the dead. It was not a healthy thing for her. When this was settled, the Sheridans needed to make arrangements for Amanda to have more social interaction. Perhaps if the spirits were put to rest, Amanda wouldn't frighten her chums.

"We'll talk about this tomorrow, after breakfast. Right now, you need to go inside and be with your mother."

"She's afraid of me." She looked out toward the woods. "If you send Nan away, I won't have anyone except the grown one."

"I intend to send them both away, Amanda. You need to find flesh and blood friends, other young people to play and laugh with. You should be at sleepovers and ice cream parties at that nice hotel in West Point. I'm sure Hester and the other girls who love horses would so enjoy riding through the woods here at Waverley. There's a world of fun out there with real children."

"I'd like that."

At last I felt a real glimmer of hope that this could be resolved. "I have to go look for Reginald. Promise me you won't go back into the woods."

"I won't."

"You could be accidentally shot." I had to impress on her the danger.

"Okay." She walked slowly to the front door. "You won't leave until I have new friends, will you?"

"I'll stay." I couldn't stay long, but I wouldn't leave the child alone at Waverley without Nan.

The door slammed and I took off toward the stables, running as fast as I dared in the darkness.

CHAPTER 18

The scene I found at the stables was worse than I'd feared. Reginald and Newly, soaked in blood, sat dejectedly at the kitchen table in Newly's cabin. On the floor beside them was the body of a young man. His shirt had been pushed into the flesh of his chest by the scattershot of a shotgun. It was impossible to tell where bloody cloth ended and flesh began. He was a young man, only a few years younger than me, which put him in his early twenties. It was likely he attended the state college in Starkville for young men. He'd traded a promising future for the thrill of trespassing and necking with his sweetie.

I walked to the body and studied the face that had once been handsome and square-jawed. His eyes were glazing over with the opaque film of death. Soon he would likely be another of the dead who haunted the grounds of Waverley.

"He was dead when we found him," Reginald said. "No sign of Royal, either. We brought him here because it was too far to carry him to Waverley, and we thought it was more than Anne could take."

"His name is Ashland Pratt," I said.

"Oh, no." Newly stood up abruptly. "This is bad."

"Why?" Reginald sat up straight, but he didn't stand.

"Ashland Pratt is the son of Buckland P-P-Pratt. He's a member of the Mississippi legislature and a lawyer. This is his only son. Pratt, Senior, is going to hit Royal with everything he has. The boy was a known juvenile d-d-delinquent, but Buckland got him out of all the trouble he got into. The boy felt there were no boundaries."

"This *is* bad." I wanted to do something for the dead young man, but he was now beyond my reach. "He was with a girl, Penelope Lott. We found her running toward the river. She said they'd come over to Waverley by way of the ferry. They left their car on the other side of the Tombigbee. She saw Royal shoot this young man."

"Shit." Newly paced the small room. "She saw it?" He turned to me, as if I could tell a different story. "If she s-s-saw it, Royal is cooked. They'll hang him."

Reginald shot me a look and I knew we both thought of the history of Waverley. Hangings were common on those grounds. "Perhaps he was provoked," Reginald said. "If this young man threatened him..."

"No." I couldn't hide the facts. "Not the way the girl is telling it. She was hysterical, but she was clear. She said Royal shot him point blank."

"It's possible he was possessed," Reginald said, but he offered it as a last hope. Even if it were true, it would not stand as a defense for killing a man. Not in rural Mississippi or likely anywhere else. The best it could gain Royal was an insanity defense. Hanging might be a better choice than being locked away forever in an asylum.

"What are we g-g-going to do?" Newly put the question squarely before us.

"We have to call the sheriff." As much as I disliked Walter Gaines, there was no way to avoid telling him what had happened. If we got him first, it would go better for Royal than if Penelope Lott told her story first. "I'll drive to West Point and find him. Tell him what happened."

"Bring a doctor," Reginald said flatly.

"I don't think it will help. He's dead."

"For Anne," Reginald said. "This could snap her mind. She isn't strong."

I nodded. "Do you want me to drive there? We could put the body in the car and I could take it to the sheriff." I didn't relish that idea, but it would give Reginald and Newly time to find Royal, to sober him up, to seek the truth and prepare for the consequences.

"No, there's no point. Let him rest here." Newly swallowed. "I don't know what else to do." He got a sheet from his bed and covered Ashland Platt. "Why couldn't those kids just s-s-stay away from here?" he asked. "They had no business on the land. They knew it upset the Sheridan family. I've caught them in the pasture with Moonglow, m-m-messing around. They could have harmed the horse or gotten themselves kicked or stomped. There's no telling what mischief they've gotten up to. In the winter they s-s-start fires in the woods."

The list of complaints about trespassers was valid, but it wouldn't matter. Even I knew that. "I'll be back as quickly as I can."

"Call your uncle while you're in town, if you can," Reginald said. "I think we're going to be here longer than we first anticipated."

I didn't care for the sound of that, but I recognized the

truth. Anne would need support. And I'd just made a break-
through with Amanda. Reginald and I might resolve the
haunting of the house, but it would take a lawyer to resolve the
legal issues Royal faced. And still he hadn't been found. He was
wandering in the woods with his gun.

"Constance and the girl, Penelope, are coming back from
the river. You might want to see if you can corral Royal and get
him in the house. Maybe sober him up if you can. If he's drunk
and belligerent, it won't help his cause. And he already hates
the sheriff."

Reginald nodded. "Drive safely."

"I will."

"Watch the l-l-livestock loose on this road," Newly said.

"I will."

I went back through the woods to Waverley to get the
rented car. It was a good thing Uncle Brett had encouraged me
to learn to drive. It had come in handy more than once since
the summer had begun.

ORDERED thinking was the only thing that I could do. I
hurried down the path I'd come to know almost as well as my
name. I could only hope Amanda was still in the house with
Anne, and that Constance and Penelope had returned. The
trail from the river was a good distance, but they should have
arrived back at Waverley. It might be wise to take Penelope to
West Point with me. I could tell her that Ashland Pratt was
dead when I had her alone. My gut told me I had to spare
Anne all scenes and emotional upsets that I could.

Movement to my right made me pause. Was it someone
from Waverley or another young trespasser? Or Royal, with
a gun?

I saw them then, the dead soldiers. They rose from the leaf-strewn forest floor like wraiths. Thin as rails, their raggedy uniforms hanging on skeletons, they came toward me. The gaunt faces and tormented eyes looked into me and past. They stepped by me as if I weren't there, on a patrol or mission or perhaps seeking a final resting place.

"God rest you," I said to them, knowing that my words held no power. These men were part of a time and place lost long ago in the past. They had nothing to do with me or Waverley Mansion.

I drew in a deep breath, calming my racing heart. And froze. From the south, I heard soft murmurings and laughter.

"He never comes out this late," a young man said. "Come here."

"Make love to me," a woman answered. "Touch me. I want to feel your hands all over my body."

I couldn't believe it. Another young couple had come to test the legend of Waverley Mansion and to risk their lives for a thrill. Ashland Pratt lay dead not half a mile from them, and they had no clue of the danger they faced.

The couple was hidden from me by a dip in the land. I could smell water, and I knew a creek ran through the property. Obviously the couple had gone there for their rendezvous, planning to stay cool in the creek. Alex and I had such a secret place, and the ripple of the cool water over heated flesh had been double enticing. I didn't blame the young people for their appetites. I worried for them because they danced with danger.

I stepped off the path with some regret. It was pitch dark in the woods, and there were deadfalls and downed trees that could easily twist an ankle or worse. But I had to send the lovers on their way.

I topped the rise and looked down the incline, steeper in places than I'd thought possible, to see the couple on the bank of the running creek. I could hear the water and more. The girl sat atop the young man, and he moaned with pleasure. She bent over him, kissing him, her hair hiding their faces.

"Excuse me. You have to leave." I felt like some horrible schoolmarm interrupting their moment of intimacy. I knew how precious those moments might be, and also how costly for the girl. Pregnancy was a high price to pay if the girl was unwed. I had no time to linger and wait for them to finish.

I made as much noise in the shrubs as I could. The couple was locked in their passion, oblivious to my presence, though I was now making no attempt to be quiet.

"Hey!" I stepped closer. "Hey! You have to leave. This is private property. Leave for your own sake."

They continued making love. He grabbed her waist and flipped her beneath him. His body was lean and young and beautiful as he drove into her.

"Stop!" I picked up a fallen limb and threw it. Though it landed close to them, they never acknowledged it.

"Don't stop," the girl said. "Never stop. Tell me you love me."

"I love you," the man said. "I'll love you forever."

They seemed caught in some place and time that excluded me. I didn't exist for them. I noticed their clothes scattered about on the leaves. Her white chemise gave me my first clue.

The man's body blocked my view of her face, but I suspected I would know her. "Nora!"

She turned to face me at the sound of her name. Her smile was victorious. "You came. I knew you would."

The man stopped moving, and Nora sat up and pushed him away. She had no more use for him than an old shoe. He slumped over, and she pulled herself out from under him. "I've been waiting."

I looked at the man's face, which had slowly begun to fade into gray. From the photo I'd seen in the attic, I realized it was Burton Norquist, Francis's younger brother. The young man who'd followed him into battle and died. He'd been having sex with his brother's fiancée. Because Nora Bailey wasn't just a beautiful woman, she was something much older and far more evil. I understood her power over the men she entranced. She made them betray their loved ones, forget their honor. She was primal and powerful. And she came toward me, proud in her nakedness and sensuality.

I ran. I was terrified of her. I had no means to fight her, and I didn't want to be her victim.

I heard her laughter close behind me as I rushed through the woods and at last onto the lawn of Waverley Mansion. Several candles glowed on the front porch, and I saw Amanda waiting for me. "Now she's really angry," Amanda said. "She's going to make all of us pay."

CHAPTER 19

"Hurry inside." I put a candle in Amanda's hand and picked up the second one. "Hurry."

"Going inside won't help. She can come in any time she wants." Amanda had stopped in the doorway. "We should leave."

"Where's your mother?"

"In her room." Amanda looked past me to the edge of the woods. Whatever she saw made her eyes widen. I feared turning around to look, but I did. A beautiful Southern belle walked toward the house. She wore a ball gown. Her dark hair was piled on top of her head and held in place by ribbons. I knew her. Nora Bailey. And she was coming for me, just as she'd promised.

"Inside." I blew out the candles and threw them down as I pushed Amanda inside, slammed the door, and locked it.

"The door won't stop her. Nothing will." Amanda was afraid and also resigned.

"What does she want from you, Amanda?"

"She never says." She touched her chest. "I feel her here.

She wants...in."

My heart almost stopped. The protection of this child was in my hands, and I had no tools to fight Nora Bailey. "I won't let her hurt you."

Amanda looked at me, hearing the emptiness of my words. Her doubt was reflected in her face. "It's okay. No one can protect me here."

"Reginald and I will get to the bottom of this. We won't leave until we do."

"It's okay." She sighed heavily, the sound of a much older person. For months she'd been aware of Nan and Nora. She knew them better than I did. She'd carried this burden too long for one so young, and it had aged her in inappropriate ways. Her innocence could never be recovered, but I would not leave her to face this alone.

The moment passed, and when I looked out the sidelight by the door, the front yard was empty, but Nora hadn't gone. I knew that much. For the moment, though, she had withdrawn.

"How is your mother?"

Amanda looked up at me, eyes big. "She's asleep. She won't wake up. She isn't dead, though. I would know if she was."

Her words increased my worry. "I'll check her. Did Constance return?"

"No. I've been here alone. Always alone."

She almost broke my heart. "I'm sorry, Amanda. Let's check on Anne." I took her hand and led her to the suite of rooms her parents used. Where in the hell were Constance, Royal, and the young woman? It didn't make sense that they weren't back at Waverley by now.

We found her mother sleeping, as she'd said. I gently touched Anne's shoulder, but wherever she'd gone, she wasn't coming back right away. Her breath was shallow, but she remained still. I wondered if she ever would ever return to the living. I was afraid she'd made a choice to cut the moorings to this life and set herself adrift until her body gave out. I felt her forehead, which was hot, so I got a cool cloth from the kitchen and bathed her face and hands.

"Is she dying?" Amanda asked.

"No. I don't think so. I think she went somewhere to feel safe. Somewhere in her own mind."

"She hates it here. She hates Waverley. She won't say it, but I know she does."

"Why does your family stay?" There were other old homes, old plantations. Waverley was unique, but not worth the destruction of a family.

"Daddy has his business here. He says it's the perfect location. He has a free-flowing creek and lots of woods. No one comes out here very often, except those young people. That's why he hates them so much." Her voice almost broke but she recovered. She had amazing composure for a young girl. I wondered if her ability to see spirits was part of this. I, too, had been withdrawn and composed, older than my years.

"I don't think he hates them, Amanda. He's afraid they'll find something they shouldn't and bring the law down on him." I didn't want her to think her father had murdered someone out of hatred. She wasn't aware of Pratt's death yet, but she soon would be.

"Those college students are going to get Daddy arrested and put in jail."

She was only repeating what she'd heard her parents say, but it painted a very clear picture. Royal was bootlegging in a big way, far bigger than I'd ever suspected. At Waverley he had the perfect shipping hub. The young people sneaking around the property could easily stumble on his still, and that would in turn bring down the law. Making whisky was a very lucrative business for those who knew how to distill the spirit with potency and good taste. Royal had that skill in spades.

"Don't jump to conclusions, Amanda. A lot has happened here tonight. A lot of bad things. But we can still set things to right."

She didn't believe me. She didn't dispute my words, but she walked to the sidelights and looked out at the front yard. The sky had lightened slightly. Dawn was coming. Eventually.

I couldn't leave Amanda alone with Anne, even in daylight. The child had her limits too. And I couldn't leave Anne alone. Yet I needed to hurry to town and get the sheriff and a doctor. The task before me was impossible. I couldn't split myself into two people, but I could go a little distance into the woods and search for the governess. If Constance would only return I would be free to leave.

"Would you like to help me find Constance?" I asked Amanda.

"No. I don't want to go back in the woods. Nan says not to. She says it's dangerous."

I glanced around us but there was no sign of Nan. At least I didn't see her. "Is Nan here?"

"She's going to leave soon. She said you would help her. She said soon the truth would be known."

"I'm sorry, Amanda, but she doesn't belong here. It isn't right."

Amanda's smile was sad. "I don't belong here either, Raissa. Will you help me leave?"

I put my arm around her. "I will. If that is truly what you want, I believe your parents will give up this place and move to town. And I think it will happen sooner than you anticipate."

If Royal was found guilty of killing Ashland Pratt, I had no doubt Anne would act quickly to return to town. Waverley was too isolated without a telephone and electricity, too hard for a frail woman and a child.

"There's Constance!" Amanda pointed out the bedroom window. The two women were coming up from the back of the mansion, a direction that didn't make sense to me. They should have come from the east. "Who is that with her? What happened to her? She's covered in blood."

"It's one of the young women from the woods. She's not hurt." A lie of omission.

Constance led and Penelope followed, the blood on her blouse visible in the coming dawn light. Around them the woods were gray and misty. Soon the sun would burn the mist away, revealing intense green of every shade. And so much more. Things none of us really wanted to see. "Amanda, would you put another cool cloth on your mother's head?"

"Yes, ma'am."

"I'll be back soon." I hurried out of the room, closing the door. The governess took Penelope to the kitchen, and I met them there. "Amanda is home. Don't say anything in front of her about—"

"We have to find Ashland," Penelope said. "He's hurt."

"I'm sorry. He's dead." I thought it best to get the fact out quickly. "He was dead when Reginald and Newly found him. His body is at the horse trainer's cabin. They took him there, and they're sitting with him. I'm driving into town to get the sheriff." Now that Constance was at Waverley, I could leave.

"He can't be dead." Penelope didn't cry, as I'd anticipated. She was stunned. "He's only twenty-two. He can't be dead."

"I'm sorry." I put a hand on her shoulder but she jerked away.

"This is wrong. We were just having a little fun. That man

didn't have to shoot him."

"You were trespassing," Constance said softly. "I'm sure Royal didn't intend to hurt him. He always shoots over the heads."

"That's a damn lie. He pointed the gun at Ashland's chest and pulled the trigger. He wasn't twenty feet away. He was furious and so mean." Penelope was adamant. "Ashland was just standing there, holding his pants up. He wasn't armed. He was murdered!" She stretched the last word out into a wail.

She broke off in the middle of her cry. Constance gasped and I turned to look behind me. Amanda stood in the doorway. In her nightgown, with her hair tumbled over her shoulders, she looked like the child she was. A little girl whose father was accused of doing something terrible.

"Daddy wouldn't do that." She had a stout heart.

I went to her and turned her out of the doorway. This I'd hoped to avoid. "We'll get it sorted in the morning. Now that Constance is here, you should rest. We need to find your father."

"What about the dead man? The one she said Daddy shot?"

"Newly and Reginald are with him." I saw no point in lying. "I'll make you a pallet in your mother's room. You can watch over her while you sleep."

"Like the angels?"

Her question stopped me cold. I hadn't thought of angels watching over me in my sleep for many years. It had been a wonderful fancy my mother had given me, the idea of winged guardians of my sleep. I'd seen what I believed to be a succubus and accepted that completely, but an angel was hard for me to believe in. If only I could see one of those.

"Do you see the angels, Amanda?"

She paused at the door to her mother's room. "I don't see

them, but I know they're there."

"And they will watch over you and protect you." It was the flimsiest of guardianships, but it was one I could give a child for a bit of comfort.

Amanda entered her mother's room, checking the cloth on her forehead and dipping it again in the pan of cool water beside the bed. She put it back on her mother's brow while I got quilts and a pillow from a chifferobe and made a bed on the floor.

Anne never stirred, and my worry increased. What if she never came back? What would happen to Amanda? I had to fight back the tears. "Sleep tight. The angels are watching." I closed the door just before I sobbed. I allowed myself only a few seconds of distress and then returned to the kitchen. There was too much to be done.

"Someone must go to town. I can. Penelope, I'll take you with me because the sheriff will need to speak with you."

"No." She had wiped her tears away. "I want to go back to school at Columbus. I can't be involved in this. I'll be expelled from school. My parents will kill me."

My shoulders throbbed from tension. "You're in this now, Penelope. When you stepped foot on this property, you put yourself in the middle of it. Now a young man is dead and you're a witness to what happened. You have to step forward and tell what you know." My tone was harsher than I'd intended. "I'm sorry, but we have to go."

"I can go," Constance said. "I'll take her and get the sheriff. When Royal comes back, you'll have more influence with him. I'm hired help, but you are a respected visitor."

"Okay." Too tired to argue, I gave her the key to the rental car. "Please be safe."

"We will." She put her arm around Penelope's shoulders

and maneuvered her out the door. It seemed a bond had formed between the two women, one borne out of the trauma of the evening. I followed them to the front door. Above me on the second floor—which should have been empty—floorboards creaked. I cursed the lack of a telephone.

My energy was at its lowest point, and I couldn't afford another encounter with Nora now. Rest was out of the question. I looked in on Anne and Amanda. Both slept soundly. I found the flashlight Constance had been using and several candles and went up the stairs, circling and circling until I was at the fourth floor room where so much of the history of Waverley was stored. My intention was to grab some boxes with papers and letters and return to the front parlor where I could watch for Reginald and Constance to return. Soon it would be full light. Things were always easier in the light.

I was afraid, though I knew it was irrational. Nora or anyone else could reach me on the first floor as easily as the fourth. But as I entered the storage room, I felt far, far away from any other living person and very vulnerable.

The odor of old things surrounded me. Old furniture with a faint lingering of polish, old cloth, and old papers. Heat and humidity had done their damage, but many items were remarkably preserved.

In the far corner of the room was what looked like an old seaman's trunk, one that Reginald and I hadn't had time to explore. I went there first. The flashlight's beam was more reliable than a candle, but I didn't want to use the batteries up in case we needed it later. By candlelight, I began to go through the trunk. It soon became clear this was Bjorn Norquist's trunk. It contained letters from his family in Norway in a language I couldn't read. There were daguerreotypes of tall, light-eyed men, women, and children, and drawings of Waverley, with his notes on the edges about the capability of the house to draw in cooler air. There was also a patent on the design that had never been filed.

I dug deeper into the trunk and found a leather-bound journal. I recognized Bjorn's handwriting from other documents I'd examined, and I opened to the front page. There was no introduction or explanation of the journal, its purpose, or the author, but it was easy enough to pick up the pertinent details as I read.

April, 1860

The shock of Nan's arrival has lessened somewhat. She's been with a family in Vicksburg, and now they can no longer care for her. I was never told of her existence, and while she is unexpected, I find I'm charmed by the child. I often discover she is following me about the house or the lawn, and sometimes into the woods. She's a clever child and able to move without drawing attention to herself. This concerns me because there are abundant dangers in the woods. I've asked Olivia and the girls to watch her more closely, but they seem incapable of the basics of adulthood. I have spoiled my daughters. They assume someone else will do whatever they choose not to do. Life is not that convenient. If the rumblings of war are true, they will learn these lessons in a bitter manner. I pray for peace, and for the fortitude to get my daughters married and into happy homes.

So Nan had arrived at Waverley sometime before April 1860. Long before Nora arrived on the scene. They mystery of her parentage was as cloudy as ever. Whose child was she? A relative of Bjorn's, no doubt, for he was shocked by her arrival but took her in. It was possible he was shocked because the child was his, a pregnancy from a passing encounter. Or it could be the child was deformed in some manner. Children who were not whole or perfect were often sent to the country to live with relatives where they would not be in the public view so much. The ghost I'd seen was whole and perfectly formed, but ghosts were not always truthful. I'd raise the topic with Reginald and Amanda.

I rose and went downstairs for coffee. There was no sign of Fancy in the kitchen, so I ground the roasted coffee beans and put a pot on to brew. Thank goodness the fire in the stove had been banked. Waiting on the coffee, I paced until I held a steaming cup of the aromatic brew. And then I knew what I had to do.

Out of habit, I checked on Anne and Amanda, relieved to see they still slept. Amanda had been exhausted, and I hoped she'd continued in her dream state until I had solid answers for her about what would happen with her father. And where in the world was Royal? He wandered the woods at night sometimes, but he was normally home long before first light.

As I softly closed the bedroom door, I heard laughter coming from the second floor. Young girls giggled in the way of slumber parties and the silliness of youth. The sound had a strange echoing quality, as if the air was denser, pulling and tugging at the words.

"He's so handsome," one girl said. "Will you kiss him?"

"Of course."

More giggles.

"I'd like to kiss someone. I just don't know who yet." The speaker was a third girl.

"The wedding is never far behind the kiss."

"And we'll marry in the parlor. That's why Father built it. For weddings and christenings, the events of family. That's what he said."

"If we marry soldiers, we might travel and see the country. I've heard there are wonders to be witnessed in the mountains of the Carolinas. Waterfalls and caverns and great beauty. It's cooler there, and sometimes snow. Wouldn't that be lovely, to play in real snow."

"In the cities there are plays and concerts. It would be better to live in the city. Think of New York. There would always be something exciting to do."

When I stepped into the rotunda, the voices stopped, and I knew I'd disturbed a pocket of the past. No doubt that had been the Norquist girls, planning for a future they could barely imagine. They'd lived at a time when a young girl's dream could only be marriage and her own plantation where she would raise her children. The life, even for the wealthy wives, was not an easy one. It was filled with responsibilities, the care for all of the people who lived on the property. The tenure of Southern girlhood was so brief—many highborn daughters were married by the age of sixteen. The romantic dream of the mistress of the plantation was a far cry from the reality of the day-to-day life. Yet I understood the banter of the Norquist girls. They'd been trained to believe their ultimate worth would be found in their marriage and the men who desired them. And to the girls, marriage was a ticket to get away from the rural isolation of Waverley Mansion. How soon all of it would be gone—a reality they would never have wished for.

I carried my coffee to the storage room and began to read Bjorn's journal once again. The book fell open to a page dated Oct. 24, 1860.

. . .

"*My sons are eager for war. They gather with other young men and talk of the feats of bravery they'll perform on the battlefield and how they will fight for the South. They are young and can't know the horrors that await if the North and South cannot settle the issue of slavery. My own slaves will be freed. The longer I live in this society, the clearer I see how morally wrong it is. The black skin doesn't cover a black soul. We are all the same beneath the skin.*

The Waverley ferry is operating with a fine profit, and the steamboats stop at Waverley landing to take on cargo or disperse it. Waverley Mansion is becoming a destination. We have our own post office and a local doctor, Calvert Marcus, who is only a mile or so away. He is an excellent doctor and surgeon. He saved Heck's arm when he sliced it with a scythe and everyone said it would have to be amputated. He has expressed an interest in courting Olivia, and she finds his company quite pleasant. Not all marriages are based on romantic feelings, but I watch the two of them and I believe they are falling in love. Marketta is happy. Like all good mothers, she wants a love match for her children. I would keep it to myself, but I am glad to see the way Olivia and Calvert look at each other. I see a happy future.

Shopkeepers are opening businesses on the river dock. There is a lumber store and mill that has many customers. Merchants sell goods at the docks and Buford Crane has established a pub with food and liquor. Some of the homemade spirits are better than what is bottled by the big companies.

Helene and Marguerite think the war will bring the handsome soldier boys to balls and dances. They see the glamour of men in uniform, but not the cost. I will allow them their fancies until that is no longer possible."

I rubbed my tired eyes. Bjorn Norquist was not a happy

slave owner nor was he a warmonger. His views would not be popular with many people around him.

Bjorn's portrait still hung in the parlor, and I thought about his square jaw, the piercing blue eyes. He wasn't a fool, and he'd clearly seen what a war would do to the land he loved. Loss, loss, and more loss. His predictions had come true. He'd lost everything—his children. And finally Waverley Mansion itself.

I'd been sad when I entered the storage room, and now I felt a cloud of sorrow moving over me. I couldn't afford that emotion. I turned to the last pages and stopped at Aug. 22, 1864.

ALL IS LOST NOW. Tragedy has wielded a sharp blade, cutting through my children and my family with a brutality I never anticipated. The mob has hanged the bitch and traitor, Nora Bailey, but the damage is done. Francis is broken, and I fear he will run headlong into battle simply to end the misery he finds himself in. The doctor I so admired is a traitor to his country and a man who abused my family's friendship by breaking Olivia's heart and laying with my son's fiancée. The cost is high. Too high. And still the war drives on. There is no end to the bloodshed and misery for a cause that most know to be wrong. This is the price of not speaking out. This is the truth that will haunt me to my last days.

My children will die because a ruling class upheld an unsustainable way of life.

The blame falls squarely on the shoulders of men like me, those who were silent.

God help us all.

A GUST of wind caused the candle to flicker, and I looked up,

realizing that daylight had begun to filter through the window.
I gathered up the journal and other papers and took them to
my room. My body was exhausted, but my brain was on fire. I
felt a desperate need to do something, but I didn't know what.
Waiting was the chore in front of me.

I checked on Anne and Amanda, who thankfully continued
to sleep. I checked once more in the kitchen, but there was
still no sign of Fancy or any of the workmen.

As soon as Reginald returned to the house, we had to
release Nan. Nora was a more difficult matter, but we could
send the child on her way to the Great Beyond, where she
could find a measure of peace. First I needed to know whose
child she was and how she died. We had to act immediately. I
had a sense that energies were building in the house, things
that I didn't understand and couldn't control.

I poured another cup of coffee and took it up to my room
to continue my reading. I didn't think I could bear more of
Bjorn's pain, but I knew there had to be something in the past
that would help me address Nora. Bjorn had no love of her,
that was clear. But it seemed he wasn't part of the lynch mob
that had killed her.

I settled at my window perch to read, feeling as if I needed
to press the journal to my chest and absorb the facts. Reading
was too slow. I needed to know so much in so little time.

As I really examined the journal, I saw that entries were
daily up until 1862 when the war was fully upon the South. I
skimmed some passages of 1860 and early 1861, where Bjorn
documented the successes of his businesses and his children.
He wrote of his sons with great pride. Francis was his light. It
was clear Bjorn favored this son in his private thoughts. He
discussed marriage matches for his daughters, planning house
parties where young men could be introduced and travels for

Marguerite and Helene to Memphis where two young men of good families would be introduced. There were also comments about the selling of slaves, the expectation of crop yields, the planting of different grasses for hay and fodder. I could feel the expectation of the spring planting and the birthing of cattle and horses in his letters, and the heat of the hay field as the men worked to put up corn and hay for the livestock.

The journal gave me a sense of the rhythm of life at Waverley, the community, as much as the plantation. Bjorn was an accomplished writer, an educated man who spoke Norwegian, French, and English. He was well read and made sure his children, even the girls, had lessons. His wife, Marketta, was frequently mentioned as someone who helped him with decisions. They had come to this country and were building an empire for their children to inherit. Except the war changed all of that.

A PASSAGE in early July of 1864 made me smile.

OLIVIA WILL NOT CONTINUE *under the roof of Waverley much longer. The war has taken much from us, but it cannot take the joy of a joyous union. Dr. Calvert Marcus has asked for her hand in marriage. I was happy to answer in the affirmative. They will be wed in November, a double-ring ceremony with her brother, Francis, and Nora Bailey, a young woman who has been staying here at Waverley. She has no family, and so she will live here until Francis fulfills the duties of an officer of the Confederacy.*

Francis is quite smitten by Miss Bailey. I find her countenance pleasing, and her manners are impeccable. She is a refined pianist and speaks fluent French. Though she is impoverished, she had a broad education for a female. I had hoped that Francis would find true love with a local girl. Lucy Calhoun adores him, and her family is well respected throughout the state. Coralee Hempstead has loved him since she was a child, but he doesn't see her. I believe it is partially Nora's plight, a young woman with no family and no safe harbor from the cruelties of life, that makes Francis love her. He is a battle-hardened soldier, but he has ever been the one to find wounded animals and bring them home.

It will be good when the marriage vows are exchanged and Olivia leaves for Nine Oaks. There is tension between the females of the house. A battle without and one within. This is not the castle where I am king. Once the clucking has stopped, life will be more peaceful.

KNOWING what I knew about Nora made my chest ache for the Norquist family. I wondered if Dr. Marcus truly cared for Olivia, or if she was just a means to an end, another Southerner to exploit for information. Nora Bailey and Calvert Marcus had ultimately betrayed and destroyed the Norquist family.

I located the days of early August 1864, only a few weeks after this journal entry. Nora was living at the house, and Bjorn was disturbed by the impact she was having on his children. The girls didn't like her and resented her presence. The boys vied for her favor. Bjorn saw the dissent, but he didn't take action.

AUGUST 18, 1864

THE PORTRAIT of Nora Bailey is complete. Tonight we will celebrate the hanging of it on the wall by the staircase. It looks as if Nora is step-

ping out of the frame and into the rotunda. The painting is indeed a masterpiece, but one that I hope Nora and Francis take with them when they set up housekeeping of their own. The wedding is in the works for Thanksgiving. I hope so. Francis is deeply in love and I want my son to know the joys of marriage before he is called back to the thick of the battles. Olivia will wed Calvert and move to Nine Oaks. This will settle my household to some extent.

Contention between Francis and Burton has arisen, and I lay the blame at Nora Bailey's feet. There is something not right with that woman. She is beautiful by any measure, but there is a heat in her that concerns me. Men are drawn to her as if they catch the scent of something wild. She is discreet in her flirtations, but I have seen them. She comes in breathless, and soon a young man follows. He casts a searing look at her and she smiles and retreats. It is flirtation, but one I dislike. She treats Francis's heart with carelessness. She doesn't have the making of a proper wife, but he will not hear me on this subject. He is due to return to the battlefield and I will not break with him over Nora Bailey.

AUGUST 19, 1864

THIS MORNING I discovered Nora making love with Calvert in the stables. Those two will break the hearts of my children. Francis must report to General Lee in Virginia next week. When he is gone, I will put Nora out of the house. She will be gone when he returns and if I can arrange it, he will never know where she is.

I will break Olivia's engagement to Calvert and expose him for the unfaithful scoundrel he is. A doctor who cannot uphold a betrothal vow has no place in this community.

Steps will be taken.

CHAPTER 20

T he sound of voices drew me out of my reading. Reginald and another man were arguing. I rushed down the stairs and to the front porch to find Royal with his fists up, ready to fight Reginald. My dapper partner merely sidestepped each punch. Newly held a shotgun and watched. There was no danger of either man getting hurt, unless Royal fell and injured himself. He was staggeringly drunk.

"You can't tell me what to do," Royal slurred. "Castor, you're fired."

"Royal!" I snapped the word just as my mother had done when she was beyond the pale with my father. "Stop it this minute." I walked toward him.

To my complete surprise, he lowered his fists and looked at the ground, ashamed of his behavior in front of a lady.

"Where have you been?" But I didn't need an answer. He stank of drink and sweat and rancid emotion. Leaves and brush clung to his clothes.

"Asleep. In the woods." He pointed away from the house. "Back there. It got dark and I was tired."

"We found him stumbling around," Reginald said. "He was angry that I took the gun."

That was too bad, because he would not have his hands on a firearm. "Royal, you need to clean up. The sheriff will be here soon."

"Sheriff?" He was instantly belligerent. "That worthless skunk."

"He was using far more colorful language before you arrived," Reginald pointed out dryly. "At least he's cognizant not to curse in front of you."

"Royal, there's a dead man in Newly's cabin. He's been shot. He's one of the college boys, and as I understand it the son of a prominent citizen. There's going to be serious trouble here."

My words sobered him, and he stood a little taller. "He's dead?"

"Shot in the chest," Reginald said. "With a shotgun." He looked at the weapon Newly held, which was a 12-gauge double-barreled shotgun.

Royal shook his head. "I didn't shoot anyone. I saw those two, that girl and boy, and I shot over their heads. That's all I did. They ran like rabbits."

I took Royal's arm to guide him into the house. He had to clean up. He reeked of moonshine. "Ashland Pratt is dead on your property. Anne is so distraught that she's slipped away from us. I can't rouse her. Amanda needs you. I need you to sober up and speak with the sheriff."

"Okay."

I eased him toward the steps. "Newly, I haven't seen Fancy

this morning. Could you help me with wood for the stove? I'll need hot water for the bath."

"S-s-sure. I can handle the b-b-bath." Newly headed for the back of the house where the woodpile would be. He was eager to get away. Reginald stood beside me as we watched Royal enter the house. He didn't stumble but his gait was careful.

"Did he shoot the Pratt boy?" I asked.

"I don't know," Reginald said. "He doesn't know. I'm surprised he found the path home. Why didn't you go to town for the sheriff?"

"Constance went to town and took the young woman we found in the woods. Penelope Lott. She swears Royal shot the young man point-blank in the chest." I lowered my voice. "The spirits are active. I stayed to research the house and watch over Amanda." I quickly told him what I'd found in Bjorn's journal, and also the strange sensations and pockets of the past the house contained.

"I don't think the sheriff is going to want to believe Royal's side. There's bad blood there." Reginald took my elbow to assist me inside. "I need some coffee."

"You need some sleep," I said. "And so do I. Maybe we can catch a nap until the sheriff gets here."

Reginald nodded. "I'm worried about the Sheridans."

"You don't know the half of it. I've found some fascinating history." And I told him what I'd found in the journal as we walked inside.

"I need to think this through, but my brain is foggy."

"You need to sleep. Even an hour will help." I pointed him toward the stairs and gave him a push. After he was gone, I checked on the still sleeping Anne and Amanda. The child's face was so soft and innocent in repose. I wished I could secure angels to truly guard her. The world as she'd known it was about to change drastically.

I'D JUST DOZED off sitting in the parlor when I heard the sound of the piano. In a household torn apart, who was playing a war ditty, "The Yellow Rose of Texas?" I'd heard the song plenty of times, though the war was long over before I'd been born.

I sat up and felt my chest squeeze. Nora Bailey was at the piano. She put her entire body into playing the song, and when she began to sing, I was too afraid to move. No one else would hear her. She played and sang in a time long past, a dead and stagnant time and place. I'd stepped into another time bubble, and I didn't know if I was reliving her memory, or if her spirit was here, in the present, to torment only me.

I couldn't stop myself from watching her play. She was accomplished, something I'd never achieved though I'd taken lessons and practiced. Piano had never been my passion. I preferred writing, and I'd been fortunate enough to have parents who allowed me to follow my heart. Music, sewing, joining groups to perform good works—the normal activities of a young woman—had been a part of my life, but not the focus.

Nora loved the keyboard. Her fingers caressed the cool ivory keys, and she played with style and flair.

She stopped and swiveled on the bench to look at me. "Come and play a duet."

No. I would not. I would not participate in any activity with her, not even a piano duet.

"You can't escape me, Raissa. By the time you understand what I am, it will be too late. Nora fought me too, you know.

She tried to hold out, to keep a bit of herself. She didn't understand the desires I gave her body. And she fought. It only got her hanged, as you well know."

I wouldn't talk to the creature. It clearly wasn't Nora Bailey's ghost, which meant that it was a demonic entity, a succubus. It had taken control of Nora and destroyed so much. Her life, her love. Her future. The things Nora's body had done were not of her own choosing. I was slowly learning the demon's secrets. I knew to be careful. I would not engage in conversation.

"Flesh is merely flesh, but it is so nice to feel the sun warm my skin or the cool rush of dipping naked into a creek," she said. "I want flesh again. I want a living body to enjoy the pleasure it can give. I want...you."

The years that Waverley Mansion had been empty, this creature had roamed the woods taking advantage of the young who stopped in to neck and pet. Temporary possession. Now, though, it wanted much more. It wanted a permanent host, as it had enjoyed in Nora Bailey.

I tried to move, but I couldn't. She held me in a spell. I'd viewed Nora as the perpetrator of terrible actions, but she'd been more victim than anyone else.

The sound of a car motor released me. The creature in Nora's form vanished, a wraith disintegrating in swirling mist. I hurried out of the house and met Constance and the sheriff. They'd come in separate cars but had arrived at the same time.

"Where's Royal?" Walter Gaines asked. His face was red and the corners of his mustache twitched.

"He's inside. He knows you're coming."

"Bring him outside unless his wife wants to see him arrested."

"Won't you even listen to his side of things?" I asked.

Gaines had a grudge against Royal and he plainly relished the opportunity to lock him up.

"He's going to jail until I can prove he killed the Pratt boy. Things are gonna get hot. The boy's daddy, Buckland, has gone to Jackson to talk to a judge. He wants Royal to get the death penalty."

"Sheriff—"

"I'm here to do my duty. If he won't come out, I'll get him." Gaines brushed me aside and entered the house.

I waited. There was nothing else to do. In a moment Gaines came out of the house with Royal, who had at least taken a bath and changed into fresh clothes. He walked straight, and he nodded at me. "Take care of Anne and Amanda until I can get this cleared up."

"I will."

"I didn't kill anyone."

"I know." There was no other response. "We'll be in town to get a lawyer as soon as we can."

The sheriff pushed Royal toward his car, and in a matter of seconds they tore down the driveway. Constance stood emotionless in the lawn.

"You left the girl, Penelope, in town?" She would play a big role in Royal's trial. It would be good to keep tabs on her.

She nodded. "I left her in the sheriff's office giving a statement."

"She told Gaines that Royal shot the boy?" I asked.

"She did. Very emphatically. There was no trying to talk her down. She gave details. Royal is in big trouble here."

"What will happen to Waverley House?" There was little chance Royal would be found innocent.

"I suppose it will be sold." Constance looked up at the

house. "Such a shame. The Sheridans were bringing it back to its old glory. They've done so much work."

"This is terrible." My exhaustion, the fear of the thing possessing Nora, the seemingly impossible job of ridding the grounds of whatever she was, made me feel hopeless.

"Anne will be happier in a town. So will Amanda."

I didn't doubt Constance's evaluation, but it was a bitter pill. "Will you go with them?"

"I don't know. Once they're in an area with a school, it might be better for Amanda to attend with the other children. They won't have a need for me."

She had a point. "And Amos Plackett. Can he stay here?"

"I believe he owns his cabin and a plot of land."

I saw a bleak future. It seemed the Sheridans would fade from Waverley just as the Norquists had. There, and then gone. The house would remain, time would pass, and someone new would find the place and decide to bring it back to life. The demon that presented as Nora Bailey would seek another permanent host. The cycle would repeat.

"I'm going to check on Anne and Amanda." I needed to move, to do something useful, but I didn't know what.

"Get some rest, Raissa. You look exhausted. I suppose you'll be leaving soon."

Her statement surprised me. "I haven't finished what we came to do. This evening, I want to release Nan. She needs to be free."

Constance smiled. "Of course. I'll let Fancy know that we'll need something to eat."

"Where is Fancy?" I asked. "I haven't seen her all day."

"Mrs. Hempstead wasn't feeling well. Fancy went to see if she could help her."

"Should we start cooking?" I could at least chop vegetables since my cooking skills were minimal.

"You rest. I'll take care of that."

There was little else I could do. When I made it to West Point, I'd call my uncle. He'd help Royal find legal representation. He knew business people all over the South. It would be good to hear his voice. I was desperately tired and discouraged. "I'll try to sleep, but wake me in an hour," I requested. "There's much to be done before night falls again."

CHAPTER 21

I awoke with a start, gasping for air and thrashing to get out of bed. The slanting light of late afternoon told me I'd slept far beyond the time I'd planned. Constance had failed to wake me. I went to the window and looked out. It was after six, and the rumble of my stomach told me the first order of business was finding food.

At Reginald's door, I tapped lightly and heard him waking up. "Meet me downstairs." I was miffed at Constance, but it wouldn't do any good to complain. The hours were lost and I had been truly exhausted. Had Sheriff Gaines sent someone to retrieve Ashland Pratt's body? What had I missed in the six hours I'd slept?

Walking down the stairs, I stopped and examined the wall where the portrait of Nora Bailey had once hung. I could distinctly see the outline of the portrait. The paint was slightly darker where the picture had covered it. So strange since it had hung for only a few short weeks, certainly not enough to leave that lasting impression. I touched the wall and felt a buzz in my fingertips. Residual energy? I longed for a ten-minute conversation with Madam Petalungro. When I finally made it to civilization, I would call her too.

Reginald met me in the parlor, and we checked the kitchen only to find it empty. The house held the stillness that I associated with spaces long unoccupied. There wasn't a sound coming from Anne's bedroom, and I hated to go there. If I woke her, I would have to tell her what had happened. I didn't know if she was strong enough to endure Royal's arrest and accusation of murder. On the other hand, if she didn't awaken soon, I worried that she might not come back to us.

I tapped lightly on the door. When there was no answer, I peeped inside. Anne hadn't moved. She remained on the bed, her eyes closed, her chest moving shallowly. More troubling was the absence of Amanda. The child was gone. The pallet I'd made for her was on the floor and empty. I touched Anne's shoulder and shook gently. The need to find Amanda was greater than my desire to let her sleep. It didn't matter. She had gone somewhere she couldn't feel my touch or sense my desperation.

"Anne!" I shook her harder. "Wake up."

Her forehead was cool, and she wasn't in distress. She didn't have a fever, but something was very wrong with her. I'd sensed she was fragile, that too much stress could push her into breaking with a reality that terrified her. The drive to West Point at night could be treacherous, but we needed to get her to a doctor. I couldn't believe Constance had allowed me to sleep the afternoon away. And where was the governess? With relief I realized that Amanda was probably with her.

I found Reginald in the kitchen. "We should take Anne to a hospital. She won't wake up."

"And the girl? How is she?"

"She and Constance are gone."

"Let's grab something to eat. Maybe they'll return while we're eating. Then we can all head to town. Where in the hell are Constance and Amanda?" Reginald was tense and anxious.

And he was right to be. We faced a terrible choice—to take Anne for help and leave the governess and a child behind in a situation I knew to be dangerous—or to wait for their return. Each passing moment brought the night closer and closer. Darkness was not our friend. And then I remembered Amos Plackett.

"Let's see what Amos says. Maybe he knows where Constance went."

We hurried down the path to his cottage in the dying light. At least the intense heat was letting up. August would soon conclude, but until it did, the heat would be unrelenting. I caught a whiff of the promise of cooler evenings as I trotted beside Reginald, counting the days until autumn. Harvest time would be upon us. Pumpkins and Halloween and brisk nights when an open window invited only a breeze and not insects.

A low baritone sang the words to "Old Black Joe," the melancholy parlor song written by Stephen Foster."

Amos saw us and stopped hoeing. "Miss Raissa, is something wrong?"

"We need to take Anne to the hospital in West Point, and I want to see if my uncle can help find a lawyer for Royal." Amos knew the details of Royal's arrest. There were no secrets on a plantation like Waverley. "Constance and Amanda have disappeared and we need to find them right now."

"I saw Little Miss not ten minutes ago." He pointed to the woods. "Running through there like the devil was chasin' her. I called out but she didn't even slow."

"And Constance?"

He shrugged. "Not a hide nor hair of that teacher lady. Two hours ago she was headed toward the river down at the ferry."

"I wonder why she'd go down there. And why would she let Amanda roam freely?" I asked.

Amos looked me steady in the eye. "Miss Constance left here alone. Don't mean she'll be alone for long."

"Thanks, Amos." If Constance wanted to take some solace in Newly's arms, who was I to object, but her job was to care for Amanda. "If we have to take Anne to town, would you be able to watch Amanda?"

He nodded. "Sure. I'll watch her. Miss Anne, she don't have the strength of mind for the terrible things happenin' all around her. She should go to town and stay. Get away from here for a while. Take the young miss with her."

"I agree. I'll speak to Royal about it. Perhaps there are friends Anne and Amanda can stay with in town."

That would clear the deck for Reginald and I to do what had to be done at Waverley. The innocents would be out of Nora's reach when she started to fight back, because I knew she would.

"If I can find Amanda, I want to take her with us. She's not safe here." She had to be on the grounds, and the Nora creature had made it clear that Amanda was a target.

"Check the stables."

"Thank you."

Reginald and I turned back to Waverley, the house looming in the distance. I touched Reginald's arm. Someone was standing in an upstairs window. "Who is that?"

It was an adult, not a child. The form appeared slender, feminine. I thought I knew who it might be. Nora, or what passed for her. She was never far from Waverley.

"Raissa, why don't I go to the stables and see if I can find

Amanda? Would you get Anne ready to take to town? She'll need some personal things."

"Good plan." Like it or not, we'd be driving to West Point in darkness.

I made sandwiches and wrapped them for the drive. My stomach grumbled with hunger but my goal was to get Anne ready to leave. I found a bag for her things and packed what I thought she'd need. When I put her belongings and a sack of sandwiches on the porch, I saw Reginald jogging to the house.

"What's wrong?" I asked.

"Moonglow is gone. Newly has been looking for the horse and Amanda. She may have taken herself over to the Newman plantation for that horse show."

Amanda had really wanted to compete. She was a child and couldn't always be expected to use the best judgment.

Reginald continued talking. "We can stop by there on the way with Anne. The coroner has removed the boy's body, but he says it looks bad for Royal."

"How bad?"

"The coroner told Newly the county prosecutor is ready to file charges for murder. The sheriff and Pratt senior are asking for the death penalty."

"What are we going to do?" This was far more serious than I knew how to manage. Anne was no help. As far as I knew, Royal had no one to turn to but us,

Reginald was clearly torn. "I don't want to leave the child, but Anne needs help. And we have to find a lawyer for Royal. You should take Anne to West Point. I'll stay here and help Newly look for Amanda."

It was a poor choice. I didn't relish being alone on that road at night with a sick woman. If I hit a pothole wrong, I could knock a tire off. But we couldn't simply leave Amanda loose in the dark on her horse. One of us had to stay, and Reginald was not as easily influenced by the entity as I was.

"Okay." The decision was made. "I'll bring the car up to the steps and we can load Anne."

"Do you know where the doctor's office is located?"

"I'll find it. And I'll go to the sheriff's office to use the phone to call Uncle Brett. I can check on Royal while I'm there."

"Good. Get the car. I'll bring Anne out."

Reginald had parked the car to the side of the house and I ran to bring it around. I felt I was being watched, and I looked up to the third floor. Nora stood in the window. I couldn't read her expression. The light had all but faded and she was more of a silhouette. When I turned the key, there was no response from the engine. I tried several times. The car wouldn't start.

I knew where the key to the Sheridan's car was kept and I ran inside to the kitchen and retrieved it. Their vehicle was under a portico near the woodshed. When I turned the key and got no response, I knew this was by design. We were stranded at Waverley Mansion because someone, or something, didn't want us to leave. Newly didn't have a car—he'd come to Waverley riding Moonglow. We had no option but to hunker down in Waverley Mansion until the next morning.

Reginald arrived at the front porch with Anne in his arms. She was awake and looked to be much more alert.

"I don't need a doctor," Anne said calmly, "but I want to talk to Royal. I must speak with him."

"Of course," Reginald said. "Where is the car?"

"I'm afraid we aren't going to town. Someone's tampered with both cars. Neither will start."

"I'm not much at mechanics, but I'll take a look." Reginald lifted an eyebrow.

"Take Anne in the parlor. She has to try to eat." If we couldn't get medical attention for her, the least I could do was bolster her strength.

While he settled her into a chair, I heated some broth. She was able to sit up and eat, and she seemed to gain color. "Are you feeling better?" I asked.

"I've always been frail," she said. "I'm glad Amanda didn't inherit my constitution. She's strong and healthy. Royal wanted a boy, but he loves Amanda more than the moon and stars. He doesn't show his feelings, but he's been so worried about her."

"How big is Royal's moonshine operation?" There was no reason to beat around the bush.

"So you've figured it out." Anne wasn't surprised. "Respectable. His client list is growing day by day. The law against drinking has only served to give bootleggers a boom. Royal distills quality whiskey. He works hard at it."

"Does he have someone to help him?" I asked.

"Some local men work for him." Anne sat up. "Folks need to make a living and Royal offers them a job. It's honest work."

The sheriff wouldn't look at it that way. "So the workmen here at the house..."

"Mainly work on the still."

It made perfect sense because for days there would be no activity on the renovation projects, but I would catch glimpses of the men on the premises. It was also a possible lead to the person who had shot Ashland Pratt. If it wasn't Royal, then it could have been one of the workers. At least I had a hypothesis to offer the sheriff.

I left Anne in the parlor and stepped out on the porch where Reginald was waiting for me. "Someone messed up the wiring in both cars." He was angry and upset.

"I suspected as much."

"Raissa, it could be the person who killed Ashland Pratt is still lurking around this house."

"I've thought of that." But there was another possibility. "The entity that controls Nora Bailey is very strong, Reginald. She has the ability to take over young women. I know she's influenced Amanda. Possibly Constance. And I'm worried about Fancy. She hasn't shown up all day, and that's not like her. I don't believe she's sitting with Mrs. Hempstead all this time."

"I'd give a lot for one telephone call," Reginald said. "Anne can walk, but I don't know how far. We can't leave her here alone, not even with Newly and Amos."

"We should bring Newly to the house." He was a big, strong man used to wrangling livestock, but he would be no match for the entity who appeared as Nora Bailey.

"Reginald, we're not dealing with Nora Bailey's ghost."

"It's not the type of ghost I've ever experienced," he conceded. "What do you think it is?"

"A succubus."

He swallowed. "We need to talk to Madam. "

"We do. And this entity is powerful. She infects my mind, even though I fight her. She plays on human weakness and desire."

"I'd wondered about the Waverley legend of the young women who suddenly couldn't control their passions. So it's been this...demon all along."

"That should have been my first clue, but I thought the stories of succubi were just stories, part of the pantheon of gods and demi-gods. I don't believe in Zeus or Jupiter or Aphrodite."

"Maybe we should," Reginald said, and he wasn't completely kidding. His stomach grumbled with hunger, a moment of lightness we both needed. "Let's eat those sand-wiches you made."

"Good idea. Would you make us a drink?" I needed to calm the jitters that made me constantly look for evidence that Nora was near. I didn't want to spend another night at Waverley, but now there was no other option I could see.

Reginald returned with two glasses of whiskey. "If you think Fancy is at Mrs. Hempstead's, I could walk there," Reginald offered.

"That's a long trip in the dark. Too bad there's not another horse on the premises. I can ride. If Amanda would come home, I'd borrow Moonglow."

I unwrapped a ham sandwich and handed it over to Reginald. We were both starving, and for a few minutes we merely ate and sipped the whiskey Reginald had poured. The slow burn of the liquor was smooth and relaxing, and I sighed, a brief moment of contentment in a long day that was far from over.

"Listen." Reginald finished his sandwich and leaned forward.

I heard it too, the sound of hoof beats. Amanda came into sight, Moonglow an ephemeral blur of silver in the night. She rode up to the porch, her face alive with pleasure. She clutched a fistful of blue ribbons. "I won! I won all of my classes!"

No matter how annoyed I was with her, I couldn't step on her simple joy. "You're a wonderful equestrian."

"I'm sorry I'm so late getting home, but I talked with a trainer from England. He's interested in teaching me."

A door to a completely new world had opened for Amanda. For one evening, she had something wonderful and all her own to treasure. "I'm happy for you, Amanda."

"It was Moonglow. She knows exactly what I want. All I

have to do is think it, and she does it." Worry replaced her joy. "I'm sorry I left Mother. Is she still sick?"

"Your mother is better. Do you know where Constance might be?"

"She isn't here?" She looked up at the house and the joy left her face.

"What is it?" I asked.

"Constance is there, in the window, watching us. Waiting." The ribbons she clutched fell to the ground. "Can't you please take us away from here?"

"The cars aren't working," I said. "Amanda, would you mind letting me ride Moonglow over to Mrs. Hempstead's. I heard she's ill and Fancy is there."

"Ill? She was fine today. I saw her walking in her driveway when I rode by on the way to the horse show. She said she was going to make scuppernong jelly."

"Was Fancy with her?"

Amanda shook her head. "Fancy said she was going to make ice cream for us today since we had that block of ice delivered. She said Mr. Braughn had brought us some peaches and she promised she'd make ice cream."

I'd seen the peaches in a basket by the back door of the kitchen. When I'd gone for the car key, they'd been gone. "Reginald, would you walk with Amanda to the stables to take care of Moonglow? Please ask Newly to come to the house to spend the rest of the night." We needed to gather close. There was at least a sense of safety in numbers.

"Yes." Reginald caught my arm and whispered in my ear. "Are you looking for Fancy?"

"Yes."

"Be careful."

He'd followed the dark path my thoughts had taken. "I will.

I'll go to her cabin. The path is clear. Maybe she's not well today."

"If Amos is home, ask him to go with you."Reginald squeezed my arm. "Be careful, Raissa. I don't like leaving you alone here, but we can't send Amanda through the woods by herself."

"I know." I wanted Reginald at my side. He gave me confidence, and I needed that when I thought of Nora and what she might achieve.

"We'll come straight back. See you in an hour or less. Take a gun. There's a pistol in Anne's room. I saw it earlier."

I knew how to shoot, but I wasn't comfortable with a firearm. "I don't know."

"Promise me, Raissa. If one of the workers on the property is behind this, he may try to harm you. I realize a gun is useless against Nora, but it could save you from a mean person."

"Okay." I could carry it even if I didn't use it. "I'll get it."

"Be careful."

"And you too."

"I'm the wrong gender for Nora's interest, and believe it or not, growing up on the streets, I'm a pretty good scrapper. I don't like the idea of damaging my handsome face, but I can fight."

It was the perfect touch of humor to send us both on our way.

CHAPTER 22

Thank goodness Amos was on his front porch, sipping what looked to be a short glass of Royal's finest. Amos was so much more than a mere gardener. His claim to Waverley was greater than anyone else's, if serving the land were the measuring stick used to lay claim to a place. He'd held the property together for over half a century.

"Did you find Little Miss?" He asked when he saw me. "That girl does what she wants whenever she takes a notion."

"Yes, she'd been at that horse show. Thank goodness Anne wasn't aware she was missing all day." I swallowed a sigh and my frustration with Constance's lack of supervision. To be fair, though, we'd all been run ragged. "Amanda won a lot of blue ribbons."

"She shoulda been born a boy. Life would be easier for her." He nodded. "You should take her away from here."

"I'd like to take her and her mother, but the cars won't work. Anne is too weak to endure hard travel, so no one is leaving."

An expression that I read as fear passed over his face. "Your car and Mr. Royal's car both broken?"

"Yes, both."

"That's peculiar. How are they both broken at the same time?"

Amos was nobody's fool. He knew what I knew. "Because someone deliberately messed them up. Maybe Newly can do something tomorrow. In the dark, it's hopeless to try to work on them."

"You need me up at the Big House?"

"Would you walk with me to Fancy's? I'm concerned about her. Amanda rode by Mrs. Hempstead's today and Fancy wasn't there. She hadn't been there."

He stood up, his rocking chair creaking as he lifted his weight. "Fancy don't slack off work." He came down the steps, sprier than he had any right to be. Hard work had kept his joints limber and his frame slight.

"Amos, do you ever see unusual things in the woods at night?"

He turned away from me, looking into the trees that crowded so close to us. "I see things. Like them young people who come here. They're bewitched. This place puts a spell over those girls. They go chanky. Nothin' Mr. Royal does is gonna keep them away as long as those young men can come here and see their ladies crazy for lovin'."

"Have you seen anything else I should know about?"

"That school teacher likes the woods too. She's got business in the nighttime."

"I know Constance and Newly are sweet on each other."

"Sometimes she's not with Mr. Newly, but I mind my own business."

"What are you saying, Amos? Who is she with?"

"Growin' up a slave, I learned a long time ago not to put my nose in white folks' business. You ask Miss Constance."

I would do exactly that. "You remember Nan, the little girl who lived here before the war? She would have been close to your age. She came to live with the Norquists when she was small."

"I remember her." He looked past me. "Pretty little girl, but sad. She didn't have a place. Not a slave, not a Norquist. She was a ghost even before she died."

His words were as sharp as a blade. It must have been awful not to have a place in her own family. "I think she was murdered. I thought Nora Bailey had killed her, because she was in the way. But that's maybe not true."

He didn't say anything. The years of minding his own business had become an ingrained habit.

"Please, Amos. I'm worried about Amanda and Anne. I have to understand what happened to Nan, so she can rest in peace."

"I remember the day she died."

A chill traced over me, and in the distance, I saw her. She stood in the path, timid and quiet. She was a pretty child, but so sad. I'd thought it was because she was dead, but perhaps her life had been the real sadness. Caught between life and death, she was once again in a place where she could never belong.

"Tell me what happened."

"I wasn't in the house when she tumbled down the stairs. I only went inside to take firewood to the kitchen or sometimes to clean the fire grates and lay a new fire. Back then there was a big barn beyond my cabin. That's where the horses and mules lived, the work animals. My job was cleanin' the stalls and spreadin' the manure on the flowers. That wheelbarrow worked me." He chucked softly. "I loved being with the animals, hearing their sounds as they ate and slept. The day Nan died, I went up to the big house to tell Mama about a corn snake I'd caught. That's when I heard the hollerin'."

I let him tell the story in his own time as we walked through the woods. Nan stayed ahead of us, moving as we moved, always in the distance, disappearing into the trees. Amos couldn't see her, or he simply refused to look. I wondered if she was there to hear the story of her own death. I believed she might not know the truth of what had happened.

"Miss Helene come out the backdoor hollerin' and crying for my daddy. My daddy was Amite, and he doctored the farm animals. Folks said he had the touch for healin'. Mr. Calvert Marcus was a real doctor, but he was over at Nine Oaks. They got my daddy to help 'til the real doctor could get there."

"Was Nora Bailey living at Waverley then?"

"She was. Been here for a few months. That painter fellow, DeWitt, was here too. I'd seen Nora and him in the woods makin' love. My mama likta pinched my head off when I tried to tell her. Slaves didn't see things. A woman could strip naked in front of a slave, but he never saw it. Never acknowledged it was goin' on."

I'd been born over thirty years after the end of the Civil War. I'd known former slaves, but few talked about their life when they were the property of someone. My imagination supplied a lot of the details of those days, but it was very different to hear a former slave talk about them.

"Do you know what happened to Nan?"

"Broke her neck. On the stairs." He looked straight ahead. "Not too much more to go before we make Fancy's house. We should be seein' a light in her window soon."

I'd never been to Fancy's cabin, but I hoped he was right

about the distance. The woods seemed to close in on us, and Nan had begun to ease closer. There were huge dark pockets around her eyes, and the outline of a skull could be seen beneath the paler covering of skin. Nan was changing. How would she react if she heard the true facts about her own death? I didn't know, but we had to conclude her business here on the mortal plane.

"Amos, who pushed Nan on the stairs?"

He stopped, and I paused with him. "No harm in tellin' now, I suppose. Them Norquists are long dead and gone. It was Miss Olivia."

"What?" I stepped back, the branches of a bush grasping at my hair in a most unpleasant way. "Olivia? The daughter who was to marry Dr. Marcus?"

"Yes, ma'am."

"Why? Why would she harm a child?"

Amos looked around the woods, clearly ill at ease. "Let's move on. I want to check on Fancy and get back to my cabin. I don't take to runnin' in these woods at night. Lots of things out here I don't wanna see."

I understood completely. I kept pace with Amos, aware that Nan was no longer on the path ahead of us. She was near though. I felt a chill around me that belied the August night. When I looked beyond Amos, I saw her keeping pace with us just in the fringe of the woods.

"Tell." She looked at me and I felt the fierceness of her desire. "Tell why she pushed!" It was a demand.

"Amos, why would Olivia do that?"

"Nan was her child. Hers and a farrier who'd traveled through the area shoeing horses. Olivia got pregnant and she was sent to New Orleans to have the baby. A couple there took Nan, moved her up to Vicksburg, but when she was older, they sent her back to Waverley. I never knew why, but there was talk that Nan wasn't right. You know, right in her thinkin'."

"Why didn't you tell me this?" I asked.

"Not my place, Miss Raissa. This is white folks' business. Not mine. When all this happened, I was a little boy. I never knew if I heard it wrong or maybe was never told the truth. Time passed and I wondered if maybe I made it all up."

"Why would Olivia murder her own child?"

"She loved that Dr. Marcus and they were to be married. Nan was so quiet. She never said much. My mama called her Mouse. Said she hid in corners and only came out in the dark. Seems like Nan meant to tell Dr. Marcus that Olivia was her mama. It had been hushed up. Folks were told Nan was the daughter of a distant relative who'd died. I guess after all she'd been through, Nan wanted to be...seen. To be part of a real family, not an extra, unwanted person."

Sorrow is an inadequate word to describe what I felt. What kind of person would deny a child?

"Olivia killed her own child to keep her secret." The pressures of being a lady were intense, and a child out of wedlock would be the ruination of a woman's reputation. Chances are that Dr. Marcus would not have married Oliva if he'd known. But to push a child down a flight of stairs? It was horrific.

"Where is she buried?" I asked.

"Talk to Mrs. Hempstead. She knows more than anyone about those days. If she'll tell you. She keeps her tongue still."

"I will." We had come upon the small cabin where Fancy lived with her daughter, Betty, when Betty wasn't working in town. The cabin was dark and empty looking.

"I wonder if she went with Betty to a job," Amos said, but the undertone of worry was clear in his voice.

"Fancy!" I called her name, halting for a moment. My gut told me not to advance any further. "Fancy!"

There was no sign of life at the cabin. It was as if an evil enchantress had cast a spell. I expected cobwebs to suddenly appear and windows and doors to warp and creak open. But that didn't happen. The cabin was simply empty.

We went up the two steps to the porch. A pan of half-shelled peas sat on the floor beside a rocking chair. Dread overtook me.

"Amos, something is really wrong."

"Yes, ma'am, it is. We need to look inside. See what's what."

I didn't want to. I really wanted to run back to Waverley. To find Reginald and make the car work and leave this part of the country as far behind me as I could.

"You wait here," Amos said. "I'll go inside."

I didn't want to be a coward, but Nan stood at the edge of the porch. She shook her head at me, telling me to stay back, not to enter.

Amos creaked the door open and stepped inside. There was the flare of a match, and a kerosene lantern began to burn.

"Oh, dear lord," Amos said, his voice breaking. "Oh, dear Jesus, who would do this?"

I didn't cry out, but I knew before I looked that Fancy was dead. I walked into the house and surveyed the carnage. She was dead on the floor near the bedroom. She'd been stabbed repeatedly. She'd been dead a while because the flies were buzzing—I could hear them clearly once I stepped into the cabin. The blood had congealed.

"Betty?" I asked.

Amos checked the rest of the small cabin. "She's not here. Thank God she's not here."

"We have to make one of those cars run." I didn't believe that Nan, or the entity possessing Nora Bailey, had the ability to stab Fancy repeatedly. We were dealing with a flesh and bone killer, and one who had no aversion to blood. "We have to get Anne and Amanda to town."

"Yes, ma'am," Amos said. "We've got to do that."

"What can we do for Fancy?" I asked. It seemed wrong to leave her, so broken and betrayed.

"Nothin' to do for her now. We'll figure that out later. Look to the livin'. That's what my mama always said. The dead carry their own. We got to look to the livin."

We left the cabin, and Nan was standing at the edge of the yard. She looked right at me, a secretive smile on her face.

CHAPTER 23

Constance had returned when I made it back to Waverley. She was sitting on the front steps drinking a glass of water, breathless and her face and arms were scratched from the brambles and branches in the woods.

"Where have you been?" I asked.

"I saw someone and I went after them," she said. "I couldn't catch them. I got turned around in the dark, and it took me a while to find the path home."

She was lucky she hadn't been killed. "What did the person look like?" I asked.

"It was a man, tall and broad shouldered. He was fast, and he knew the woods far better than I did."

"Could it have been one of Royal's workmen?"

"I don't know." She used her arm to wipe sweat from her forehead and finally really looked at me. "Holy hell, what happened to you? You look like a corpse you're so pale."

"Fancy is dead."

The glass slipped from her fingers and struck the porch. It didn't break but rolled toward the edge where I caught it.

"Fancy is what?" The color had drained from her face.

"Someone stabbed her to death. Probably the same someone who killed that young man and blamed it on Royal."

Constance stood up. "Where is Amanda?" Her question carried a note of hysteria.

"She's with Reginald and Newly."

"We have to find her. Now."

She started down the steps but I grabbed her arm and stopped her. "She's safe. They're on the way here. I swear it. You don't need to be alone in the woods."

"What are we going to do?"

"Get one of those cars running and get to town for the sheriff and some help."

"Yes. Yes, that's what must be done."

Constance sat down on the steps again as if her legs had gone soft. "How has this happened? Who would hurt Fancy and why?"

"Because she must have seen something she shouldn't have seen." That was the only possible motive.

"What would that be?" Constance asked.

Before I could answer, Amanda, Reginald, and Newly merged out of the woods and onto the lawn like ghosts taking physical form. Amanda trudged forward, exhausted.

"Where have you been? You are going to be punished for this." Constance was aggravated, more at the events around us than the child, but Amanda was a handy target. She'd worried all of us.

"She was at a horse show." I put a restraining hand on Constance. "Let it go. It's too late to change anything now." I turned to Newly. "Could you look at the cars? We should go to town if we can." I didn't want to say anything about Fancy in front of Amanda.

"I can't guarantee anything, but I'll see what I can do."

"I'll help him." Reginald still held the flashlight. "If we can get one running, we will."

"I'll take Amanda inside and find something to eat." Constance said. Her anger had run its course. After they stepped inside, I motioned the men to come close.

"Someone murdered Fancy. She's dead in her cabin."

"We have to get into town with Anne and the child. Go inside. Lock the doors. Do what you can to barricade yourself in the house. If we get the car running, we'll head to town. If we don't, tomorrow one of us can ride the horse for help."

"Or we could take the ferry over to the other side of the river. Surely someone there has a telephone."

"We'll work it out tomorrow if we have to stay here," Reginald said. "Let's see what we can do about the cars."

I went inside to check on Anne and help Constance prepare something for Amanda and Newly to eat. It was going to be a long hard night whether we stayed or left for town.

AFTER HALF AN HOUR, the men gave up on getting one of the cars to run. We hunkered down in Waverley's parlor, waiting for the night to pass. Anne and Amanda, who knew nothing of Fancy's fate, were on the sofa, while Constance had taken a wing chair by the cold fireplace. I stretched out on the hearth rug with a pillow from my room. It was too hot to need a blanket, and I fell asleep the moment my head hit the floor.

At first light, Newly saddled Moonglow and rode to the Newman's plantation. He returned with a car they'd loaned him. There was no way to hide Fancy's murder from Anne, and I told her while Constance gave Amanda her breakfast. Anne wept, but she was able to pull herself together for the trip.

Royal's life depended on her coping. Amanda counted on her. She rose to meet those obligations, and I felt a glimmer of hope that the Sheridan family would pull through this.

We left Constance at Waverley to pack clothes for the Sheridans and herself. We dropped Newly off at the Newman's so he could ride Moonglow home and keep Constance safe. Anne, Amanda, Reginald, and I headed for West Point.

The clock in the courthouse square was chiming nine when we parked beneath a magnolia tree. Anne insisted on visiting Royal in jail and Reginald went to tell the sheriff about Fancy's murder. I took Amanda and went to the home of my uncle's friends, Edward and Callie Ledbetter. The news of the shooting death of Ashland Pratt and Royal's arrest for the crime was all over town. Callie's reception was cool—she was literally afraid of Amanda. But she couldn't harden her heart to a child. And she allowed me to use their telephone.

I wasted no time calling Uncle Brett, who immediately agreed to contact a lawyer for Royal. I knew he'd speak with the Ledbetters after I was gone, so I assured him that I was safe and in no danger, but I also told him the truth of what had transpired at Waverley. The murders of Ashland Pratt and Fancy upset him greatly.

"What's going on at that old mansion?" Uncle Brett asked.

"It's more than just a haunting, Uncle Brett. You could help me." I wasn't certain what resources West Point might have in regard to demonic possession. "I need any information you can find on a succubus."

"You're being serious?" His normal, easy-going tone had changed to terse worry.

"I am. It's complicated here. But I need to know how to fight one. I'm calling Madam Petalungro, but if you could also look. There were books in the Mobile library on various demons."

"Of course." He sighed. "I'd never have believed in hauntings and such if I hadn't seen it myself here at Caoin House. I'll do what I can. How can I get in touch with you?"

"I'll call you again as soon as possible. We'll do what we can for Royal, but Constance, Newly, and Amos are at Waverley. We can't leave them there for long."

"Perhaps you should all find a safe place in town."

"We might. I'm just not willing to give up on freeing Waverley of the past. Please send the lawyer for Royal over to the county jail."

"I'll take care of it. Be safe, Raissa. And hurry home."

"I will."

I hung up and called Madam Petalungro. She accepted the reverse charges, knowing I would make good on the cost. She also knew I'd never call unless I needed her advice. When she came to the telephone, I could tell she wasn't well. "I hate to burden you with this."

"Since I can't be there to help you, I can offer advice. Reginald is okay, isn't he?"

"He is." She knew something and was reluctant to share. I could hear it in her voice. She was worried. "What is it, Madam?"

"I had a dream about Reginald. He was in a cemetery, kneeling at a grave. Someone, or something, came out of the woods and attacked him. I woke up to his screams. It was terrible. Raissa, I'm not prone to prophetic dreams. I don't believe that's in his future. It's probably that he's been on my mind, a nagging worry. Just keep an eye out for him. He charges into situations when he should use caution. He's brave, and he needs to be smart."

She'd summed Reginald up very well. "We'll both be careful. I promise."

"Tell me what's happening at the house you're
investigating."

"I think it's a succubus, but one that's taken over the spirit
of a dead woman." It sounded preposterous.

There was a hum on the line, and I thought for a moment
the connection had been broken. "This dead woman caused a
lot of heart break?"

"She did. She was a Union spy in a household of Confederate soldiers. She betrayed the man she was engaged to marry.
He and his brothers were killed."

"I see."

I could hear Callie and Amanda in the other room talking.
Amanda sounded like a normal young girl, not the sly child I'd
first met. Callie was showing her a tea set she'd used as a child,
and Amanda was telling Callie a story. The dark influences
working on her had lessened.

"What can I do, Madam? There've been two murders, my
host is in jail and charged with a capital offense. I have to rid
the house of the spirits so we can try to help prove Mr.
Sheridan innocent of murder. And we have to find out who
killed Fancy, the cook."

"A succubus is a dangerous entity, Raissa. If this is truly
what you're confronting, you have to very careful. It can attach
to you."

"It wants to. It's taken me over—"

"You must not go back to that house!"

I wanted to promise I wouldn't go back, but I couldn't. "I
have to help these people. If I don't, what will become
of them?"

"If you yield to this entity, she will have what she wants

more than anything, which is a corporeal body to inhabit, a pretty young body that she can use for her carnal pleasure. You will lose who you are, Raissa, and I don't know that you will ever find your way back."

"What can I do to protect myself?" She had frightened me. I wanted to drive back to Mobile with Reginald and barricade myself at Caoin House with Uncle Brett and Winona and Travis, the people who worked for and loved my uncle. If I never set foot at Waverley again, it would be fine with me. Except I couldn't do that. Others were at risk.

"Carry iron on you at all times. Keep the fire poker by your bed at night. Some spirits can be temporarily damaged by striking them with iron. Keep your mind strong in your beliefs."

"Yes. I can do those things." I had my notebook and pen out and was making notes.

"These are merely precautions. If you speak with a demon, you are opening a door that's hard to close. It's good to have some protection with you at all times. You must find out who first called this creature, and why. It was brought with an incantation, an invitation. Then you must send it away."

"But whoever called it would be dead."

"Yes, that's true. Find a blood relative, someone who knows the truth. Once you've learned its secret, you can send the entity away. It was summoned to Waverley, and if what you say is true, this Nora Bailey was a victim of it. She may not have called it to her. And what of the child ghost, the playmate?"

"Nan. I believe she's ready to go. She was killed by her mother. She has to accept that and let go of the house."

"Be careful, Raissa. And Reginald must be on guard too. One haunting would be enough. A child murdered by her own mother—that might warp the child's spirit. Just because she seems innocent, keep in mind she may not be. The dead often lie."

A chill raced through me. "Madam, is it possible one of these entities killed the young man?"

"I've never known of a spirit firing a gun, but the more I work with the Great Beyond, the more I come to understand that anything is possible. Mr. Doyle was in New Orleans last week and recounted a story of a possession in London that made me believe the gates of Hell had opened. Do this. Remove all weapons from that house immediately. I'm serious. If there's even a chance these entities are powerful enough to manipulate a firearm, you can't risk it."

I would do that—I should have thought of it myself. Royal was gone, and I doubted Anne would be going back to Waverley with me. "I'll do what you say. If I need your help, I'll call again."

"Watch over Reginald. The succubus might want to inhabit your body, but it is the male energy that it thirsts for. If a man is drained for too long, death follows."

"I'll watch over him."

I hung up. I'd done what I could to prepare myself for the on-coming battle with Nora Bailey, or the creature inhabiting her ghost. Now it was time to go to the courthouse and see what could be done for Royal. I thanked Callie, who remained cool to me, and Amanda and I headed across town. The day was hot, and the sidewalk seemed to have absorbed the harsh sun. The bottoms of my feet were burning. We walked quickly from shade to shade, finally trotting up the courthouse steps. Anne needed to take Amanda to McGowin's Inn. The child looked exhausted, and when I saw Anne sitting outside the sheriff's office, I felt instant concern. What little strength she'd gained had been sapped.

"How is Royal?" I asked.

"He is innocent, but they won't listen to reason. The sheriff hates him."

She wasn't exaggerating, but I hoped the evidence that Fancy was murdered while Royal was in custody might help convince Sheriff Gaines that Royal was innocent. "Uncle Brett is sending a lawyer here to talk with him."

"How can I ever thank you, Raissa?"

"By taking Amanda to the inn and getting a room. You two need to stay in town to help Royal."

"And you?"

"I have an idea how to relieve Waverley of the haunting." There was no point going into any detail. Either she wouldn't believe it or the details would unduly upset her.

"I'd feel better if you stayed here in town. We need to bring Constance and Newly. No one should be at Waverley. There are killers there."

She was right, and that was one more reason we had to go back. "Shall I walk with you to the hotel? Reginald will bring your bags when he's done here."

"No, we can manage." She stood up and took Amanda's hand. "We'll be fine." Anne might not be strong, but she was determined.

When they were gone, I went into the sheriff's office and found Reginald arguing with Walter Gaines.

"He's a bootlegger and a criminal," Gaines said.

"Be reasonable, man." Reginald propped against the tall counter. "There's more going on at Waverley than you know. You just sent your deputy and the coroner to retrieve the body of a murdered woman. You can't pin that one on Royal. He's been in jail." Reginald saw me enter the room and waved me over, drawing Gaines's ire. The sheriff viewed both Reginald and me as interlopers.

"Could we have a word with Royal, please?" Reginald asked.

"I'm not running a boarding house or a social for Royal Sheridan." The sheriff unlocked a heavy door and took us back to five cells, only two occupied. Royal sat on a blue-tick mattress on a low cot. He rose when he saw us. The occupant of the other cell continued snoring.

"Dear god, what happened to Fancy? Anne didn't know anything except she was killed. Why? Who would do such a thing?" He rose and gripped the bars of his cell. "She never harmed a fly. I don't understand."

"Neither do we." Reginald reassuringly touched Royal's hand through the bars. "But we'll find out. And we'll find out what happened to Ashland Pratt."

"I didn't shoot anyone," he said. Leaning closer, he whispered, "I've tried to tell the sheriff, but he's convinced I'm guilty. I'm sure he's sending men and revenuers to search the woods for my still."

Reginald gave the sheriff a pointed look. "Could we have some privacy please?"

"You've got ten minutes." Gaines closed the door behind him.

"What happened?" Reginald asked. He'd developed a friendship with Royal that worked to our advantage.

"I saw a couple of those idiotic kids and I shot over their heads, like I always do. They took off running through the woods, screaming and laughing, like it was a game. I shot again, but high up. Not where it could hit them. I had a shipment to draw up and haul so I went back to work."

"Did you see them up close?" I asked.

"No, they were running away. But I did hear a third

gunshot. I don't know who fired, but it wasn't me." He gripped the bars. "I didn't know it was Pratt's son, Ashland. It doesn't matter who it was because I didn't shoot anyone. That much I know."

It mattered greatly that the dead man was a prominent citizen's son. The rich could afford more justice than the common man. "Tell me exactly what happened, please." I needed to visualize the scene. Pratt had been shot in the chest at point blank range. If Royal was telling the truth, and I believed him, had he fired the killing shot, it would have struck Pratt in the back, not the front.

"Where did this happen?" I asked him.

"I was on the west trail that runs by the little creek. I heard those kids laughing. I yelled at them, told them to get off my property now or I'd shoot them. They jumped up and started running away from me through the woods. Like I said, they were laughing and running, like it was a big game. I fired over their heads. When they laughed more, I fired again. The last I saw of both of them they were jumping scrub brush and headed for the river. Neither one of them was hurt at all. About ten minutes later, I heard another shot."

"Did they see your still?" Reginald asked. It was a smart question. It would go to motive if Royal truly faced trial.

"I don't know," Royal said, defeated. "I don't care if the students pet in the woods. It's the still. I can't have people wandering about the property all the time."

Reginald nodded and patted his hand again. "We'll figure this out. And we'll find the killer."

"What happened after that?" I asked. "You didn't come home until early the next morning."

Royal shook his head. "I was aggravated by those tres-passers. I went back to the still and sampled the whiskey, then re-stoked the fire. Keeping an even temperature is vital and I can't trust that to anyone else. The boys and I had another sample or two." A rueful grin landed and then disappeared. "We drank a little too much, and the guys took the shipment and left. Then I saw the woman in the woods."

"What woman? The one who was with Ashland Pratt?"

"I don't think so. It was dark, and I didn't get a good look, just a glimpse. She was watching me." His eyebrows lifted. "She was wearing an old dress, like from the past."

Nora Bailey. It couldn't be anyone else. She'd played a role in this fiasco. I should have known.

The door opened and Gaines returned with a dapper man in a three-piece suit. His pocket watch chain glinted in a shaft of light through the cell bars. "This is the lawyer sent around to represent Mr. Sheridan. He needs to speak with his client, so you've got to go."

"Royal, are there any of the workers on Waverley who might have a reason to want to harm you?" Reginald got the last question in before we were motioned out.

"Most of those men have worked for me since I moved in. Try Matthew Cooley. He just came on the crew. He's...a loner."

"Out." Gaines pointed at Reginald and me. "Now."

We had no choice but to leave the cells. At least Royal now had a lawyer.

When we were back in the sheriff's office, I turned to Gaines. He rubbed me the wrong way, and I felt Reginald's restraining hand on my arm. He knew me too well.

"Why don't you tell me about the dead Negro woman you found?" Gaines leaned on his desk, as casual as if we talked about a breakfast order. "Someone sliced her up pretty good."

"Her name is...was Fancy. She worked for the Sheridans since they moved into Waverley." I realized he should be talking with Anne or Royal. "We've only been at Waverley a few days so I don't have a lot of information."

"But you found her, right?" Gaines was sharper than I'd expected. He was driving at something, and I had a bad feeling he was trying to pull a net over me.

"When she didn't show up for work, I went to check on her, yes."

"And you found her cut up like a Halloween pumpkin."

"She'd been stabbed repeatedly." Reginald took over the story though he hadn't personally seen the body. "She was dead when Raissa found her. Had been for some time."

"And what made you decide to walk through the woods to her cabin?" Gaines asked.

"It wasn't like Fancy to miss work." I stared him down. It seemed I always found myself on the wrong side of the law. Not because of my actions, but because of my attitude. "Do you have any idea who did that to her?"

"We're investigating." Gaines had no intention of telling us anything useful. But at least he couldn't pin Fancy's murder on Royal, who'd been in the jail in West Point.

"Have you been able to find Matthew Cooley?" I asked.

"Haven't really been looking."

No matter. Reginald and I would find him. "I'd like to talk with Penelope Lott," I said. She was the witness that put the murder weapon in Royal's hand.

"You can't," Gaines said.

"Sheriff, we're assisting Royal's lawyer." It was a bit prema-ture, but it would happen.

"I don't care if you've been hired by the Pope. You can't talk to her because she's not in town anymore."

"What do you mean?" Reginald asked. "She's your eye

witness to the Pratt boy's murder. The defense has a right to interrogate her."

"She's gone. She went back to school over in Columbus. No point making her stay around here. She's just across the river, and I'll fetch her if we need her."

"She's at the girls' school there?"

"Yes. She's boarding there. She couldn't miss her classes or she'd be expelled. There was no need to make her stay here in West Point."

And no need to keep Royal locked up either, but I didn't say that. "Would you call the school and find out how to locate her?"

"Why should I?" Gaines asked.

"Because you're required by law not to block Mr. Sheridan's defense," Reginald said. He stepped between the sheriff and me. "If you try to impede his defense, it will come up in court."

"I can't impede the investigation, but I don't have to help you." Gaines didn't bother to hide his amusement.

"Do you have her home address?" Reginald asked.

The sheriff didn't say anything, but hot words sprang to my tongue. "You don't know how to get in touch with her? You have no witness, yet you're keeping Royal locked up, away from his family? This looks very bad."

Gaines rubbed his mustache. "She's living at the school. The girl won't be hard to find. She came forward voluntarily the first time. She'll do her duty in the courtroom."

"Let's go," Reginald said. "We need to get those cars fixed. I have to find a couple of parts. Newly thinks he can put them to right. And just so you should know, Sheriff, those cars were deliberately sabotaged. There's a lot going on at Waverley that you don't seem to be interested in."

"You should release Royal," I said, glaring at the sheriff. "If you don't have a witness, you have no proof Royal did anything wrong. I suggest you find Miss Lott and produce her. Or else let Royal go home."

"The only person going somewhere is you. Out of this office." Gaines pointed at the door. Reginald grasped my wrist and led me away before I did something I would likely regret.

CHAPTER 24

R eginald found the necessary auto parts at a garage, and after we stopped to tell Anne that the primary witness against Royal was missing, we headed down the highway to Waverley. I was sorely tempted to ask Reginald to change our course and head to Mobile, but I didn't. We had something to finish at the old mansion.

By the time Newly managed to replace the damaged parts on the Sheridan car and our rented car and we'd returned the Newman's vehicle, the day was gone. Dusk was settling over Waverley once again.

Constance and Newly sat with Reginald and me on the front porch. We sipped some of Royal's moonshine, too worn out to worry about supper. "Is there something we need to do at the still?" Reginald asked. "Royal said something about keeping an even fire going."

Newly shook his head. "I don't know much about making shine. I stayed clear of that part of the business."

"Are you familiar with Matthew Cooley?" Reginald asked.

"He's been working here about three weeks. From over at

Columbus. I gather he's had some experience cooking whiskey because Royal put him to work right away."

"I haven't seen any of the workers lately," I said. And until Fancy's murder, I hadn't given it a lot of consideration. They were in and out, sometimes painting the exterior, sometimes removing scrub brush, sometimes not in evidence. "Any one of them could have killed Ashland Pratt and Fancy. They're in the woods all the time. They come and go as they please."

"There are paths leading to the still from the west side of the property," Newly said. "Amanda rides her horse along them. It's a shortcut to the highway. I stay off them because I don't want to meet a load of shine going out. Royal likes his business dealings to be private and some of the men hauling for him don't like being seen."

"We'll check with the men at the still in the morning," Reginald said. "We should stay out of the woods at night. If someone is out there with a gun, running around in the dark it's an invitation to get shot."

The passing of time pressed hard against me. "Shall we attempt to free Nan?" I asked. The navy blue of true dark had begun to steal over the eastern sky. The lighter lavenders and pinks of sunset lit the west. A spangling of stars had begun to appear. If we were going to release Nan's spirit, now was the time. I'd wanted Amanda to have a chance to say her good-byes, but that wasn't going to happen. We needed to let Nan move on, and then we could deal with the Nora entity.

"Don't we have to wait until midnight?" Constance asked.

"I don't think so. Nan is strong and active and she wants release." I was worried. I wanted this over and done. "Shall we commence?"

Reginald pulled me aside. "Maybe we should wait. You're tired and you've been put through the wringer. This could be dangerous for you more than anyone else. What if Nora tries to take over?"

"I need the poker from the fireplace, and anything else iron we can find. Madam said that iron would help protect me."

"I have iron horseshoes in the s-s-stables." Newly was eager for action too. "Some are left over from the early days of Waverley. I can gather those."

"Thank you."

"There are cast iron pots and pans in the kitchen," Constance said. "I'll get those." She turned in the doorway. "What will the iron do?"

"Ward off the evil, from what Madam told me," I said. "Let's get busy."

An hour later, we were gathered at the dining table. I'd made a circle around my chair of horseshoes and cast iron skillets. Candles flamed on every available flat surface, including the china cabinet and several small tables. A large mirror above the hunt board gave us back our pale reflections.

"Please don't talk and don't get up for any reason. Don't break the circle. I'm going to call Nan forth. You may or may not see her, but if I talk to her, she's in the room. I want to tell her the truth I found about her death and then release her to the other side." It was best for everyone to know the intention of the séance.

We held hands, Reginald wrapping me in his strong protective fingers on one side and Constance on the other.

Even though the windows were open, the dining room was stifling hot. The air outside was still, the night clear. A hoot owl called from the woods with a who-who-who. I focused on Nan and my intention, ignoring the sweat that slipped down the small of my back.

"I call upon Nan, the spirit of a lost girl here at Waverley.

She died too young and in a violent fashion. We've come to help her cross over, to find the peace she deserves."

The stillness in the room grew heavier. "We're here to help you, Nan. Come and take the release. You'll be free, able to go to the other side. You're caught between two worlds now, and you can't rest."

The one candle in the center of the table flickered, but there was no other sign.

Reginald's fingers squeezed mine. "Perhaps she isn't ready, Raissa."

I didn't want to give up. "I know what happened to you, Nan. The unfairness of always being left out, of never having the thing you truly wanted. You longed to be part of a family. And I know you were deliberately murdered by the one person who should have protected you."

Constance inhaled, and across the table, Newly shifted in his chair, but no one broke the circle. Nan had come to me several times, without prompting. I didn't understand what held her back now. She wanted this. I'd found the truth of her death, the thing that had bound her to Waverley Mansion.

"Nan, will you come to me?"

An icy wind blasted into the room killing all of the candles. In the darkness, I felt Constance tense. Reginald said calmly, "Be still. Everyone just sit still. Raissa is in control."

I fought down the fear that threatened to overwhelm me. I couldn't help Nan if I was weak and cowardly. "Nan, please show yourself. I want to help you."

I saw her then, standing behind Newly. She wore a dress with a large lace collar. Her long hair was pulled back with a big bow. Her head snapped to her left shoulder, and I heard the cracking of bones. "Why?" she asked.

"I don't know." She wanted an answer to the question of why her own mother would murder her.

"Never one kind word or hug."

"I'm sorry, Nan. I wish I could change things, but I can't."

"Why didn't she love me?"

I felt the ache in her heart. "I don't know."

The child's grief and pain twisted my heart. "Remaining here at Waverley won't bring you the things you seek. Let go. You don't belong here."

She was suddenly at my side, her anger palpable. "That's what *she* said. I never belonged."

Her anger was hard. I had to remember she was a child, a lonely child who'd never known what it meant to be loved by her mother. "I want peace for you, Nan. To be where you do belong. You can only achieve that by letting go of this place."

"Amanda needs me."

"She'll make new friends among the living, as it should be. I did what you asked. I know what happened to you. I'll see that your grave is marked and that the truth is known. You won't be forgotten here."

"Truth?" The word wafted and echoed on a bitter breeze. My breath frosted as I exhaled.

"Truth is all I can offer. I can't undo what happened to you."

"What truth do you think you know?"

"That you were murdered by your mother, Olivia Norquist." Constance's grip on my finger was punishing, but I kept going. "That shouldn't happen to any child. I know that. But I also know that Bjorn Norquist and Marketta loved you. They welcomed you into their lives. You were not unloved."

Nan was suddenly reaching for me. Her fingers were bitter cold, but I didn't move. This child had been left alone in the darkness too long. I wouldn't back away from her. "I'll make sure the truth is known. You can rest easy now. You don't belong here with the living. You'll always be a mere shadow to those who are alive. You deserve more than that."

"Will I be loved?" she asked.

The heaviness in my heart was almost unbearable. "I believe you will. I believe you will find that."

"And Amanda?"

I nodded. "She will be fine. She must find her own path too. You aren't good for each other."

"Watch over her."

"I promise I will. Amanda will be safe." I meant that vow.

"Tell her goodbye."

I felt tears building. Amanda and Nan were both children who felt isolated and alone. For a while, they'd had each other.

"There's danger here." Nan whispered the words. "For her and for you."

I tried not to react to her warning. "For Amanda?"

"Nora wants her. If she can't have you, she'll take Amanda. I've tried to protect her."

I understood now that Nan's purpose at Waverley had always been two-fold. It wasn't just about the truth, but it was also about a vulnerable little girl who would grow soon enough into a woman, a vessel. Amanda was a sensitive too, and she could provide a new body for the needs of the entity that harbored here. I gripped Reginald's hand.

"Your job is done, Nan. I'm here now. I'll watch out for Amanda."

"She's coming for you. She is. If you interfere, she'll hurt you."

"Who brought the entity to Waverley?" I wondered if Nan even knew. Or if she could tell.

"She knows."

"Who?"

"Watch the front lawn, late at night. She's there. She's wicked. Don't let her hurt Amanda."

"I won't. I promise."

"She's coming now."

I sensed a change in the room, a thicker darkness and a cold that penetrated to the bone. "Go," I said to the girl's spirit. "Go now, before you can't."

She flickered twice and then vanished. The heaviness of the room lifted and I released Reginald's hand so he could relight the candles. I wanted to dissolve the séance before Nora put in an appearance.

"Nan is gone," I said.

"Was she really Bjorn Norquist's granddaughter?" Constance asked.

"Yes, I don't doubt it. What I understood from the journals I found upstairs and from Amos was that Olivia had a child out of wedlock. She had an affair with a farrier who traveled through and shoed some horses here. Olivia was sent to New Orleans, where she had the child and adopted her out to some distant relatives. When they could no longer keep Nan, she was brought here to Waverley, where she died when Olivia pushed her down the stairs."

"Why would a mother do that?" Constance asked the same question that deviled me.

"Because Olivia was in love with a local doctor. I believe Olivia was afraid that if Calvert found out she'd had a bastard child, he wouldn't marry her."

"Is she gone? This Nan?" Constance asked.

I nodded. "She's gone, but there is another entity here. Darker and more dangerous."

"I didn't hear or see anything," Constance said.

"I felt the c-c-cold," Newly said. "There was something here, Constance. You can't deny that."

"I don't know." She put her face in her hands and I thought she might be weeping, but she sat up. "I don't know what to believe. First it's Nan, a child ghost, and now she's gone. But suddenly there's another ghost here."

"Maybe not a ghost," Reginald said.

"Ghost, demon, who knows? Either that or you've found a honey pot with the Sheridans and want to stay on." Constance glared at both of us and stood up. "I'm exhausted. I need to lie down. Please excuse me."

We watched her exit the room, and I also felt the need to recline. "It has been a long, hard day. She's tired and upset."

"Tomorrow we'll look for Penelope Lott," Reginald said. "And Cooley. If he played a role in the deaths of Ashland Pratt or Fancy, we need to make him confess to it."

"And I'll see what I can find out about Matthew C-C-Cooley," Newly offered. "There are some places where men like him drink. If there are stories about him, I'll hear them."

"We should also look into Ashland Pratt," I said. "Somehow he doesn't strike me as an innocent party to any of this." Penelope Lott was also suspicious. The girl had leveled a death penalty charge against Royal and then disappeared. Perhaps the stress of what she'd seen had sent her home to her family, but we'd know more once Reginald had a chance to ask some questions.

It was difficult for me to go in the kitchen without thinking of Fancy and the kindness she'd always demonstrated toward the Sheridan family and me. What had she seen that put her in line to be murdered? I didn't know anything about her personal life, except that she lived quietly on the grounds of Waverley. Her daughter, Betty, had sent word that she would not return to Waverley. She would live in town with relatives. I couldn't blame her. Fancy was dead because of the events happening at Waverley place.

I toasted some bread and buttered it—a poor supper but it would suffice. The coals in the stove were burning low. I needed more wood if I meant to keep the fire alive until morning.

The woodshed was only twenty yards from the house, and the night was still. I took a candle for light. The biggest danger in any woodpile might be a snake or spider. I had to keep that in mind. The wood wouldn't bring itself in, and Newly and Reginald were having a smoke on the front porch. I wasn't about to let fear of the unknown take over my life.

I stepped outside, listening for any untoward noises. The night was beautiful, sparkling stars and a three-quarter moon that was bright enough to cast shadows. I'd never been afraid of the dark, but now I felt true danger. Nora lurked somewhere on the premises. Just because she hadn't appeared at the séance didn't mean she'd given up.

I made my way to the stacks of chopped and split wood. The stove wood had been cut into smaller sticks, and I put the candle down to stack the wood in my arm. One trip should be sufficient until morning. I worked quickly, finally blowing the candle out. I didn't have a free hand to carry it and the moonlight was enough.

The sweet scent of a heavy southern flower came to me. Wisteria. I walked around the shed and saw her. She stood between me and the kitchen steps.

CHAPTER 25

"I've been waiting for you." She solidified, taking on the form of a young woman very close to my age. She was beautiful. I could see why the flesh of Nora Bailey would attract this demonic spirit. What I had to learn was if a living, breathing Nora had summoned this demon.

"I know your secrets now." I had to brazen it out. My fingers found the pieces of iron I'd slipped into my pocket before the séance. Newly had also fashioned a necklace of sorts from pieces of horse shoes and hay string. It hung heavily around my neck.

I'd expected Nora to come at me when I was busy with Nan. I was glad the child's spirit had gone on without interference.

"And what good will these secrets do you?" she asked. "I rule at Waverley. Not you."

"I'm learning about you, Nora. I know your weakness, the thing you desire. And you won't have it."

"That's what Nora said. She was willful. When I was sitting for that portrait, she saw the trap. She knew what I intended, but she couldn't stop me. I picked her like a ripe plum, and I'll do the same for you." She came closer to me, gliding rather than walking.

The impulse to run for the back door was strong, but I'd never make it. If she realized how terrified I was, she'd finish me there, before I had a chance to save myself and what might be left of Nora Bailey.

"What's your name? Your real name. Not Nora."

"You're clever, aren't you?"

"Tell me your name."

"I go by many names. None you'd know."

"Why do you remain here?" But I knew the answer. When Nora Bailey was abruptly hanged, the demon was trapped. I recalled a story Madam had told me about a possession where the human had died suddenly and unexpectedly and the spirit was unable to leave or shift into a new host. This entity was waiting for a host.

"I've been waiting for *you*," she said. "You're the door. I thought I'd have to wait for the child, but you're here now. Ready for me."

She came closer. "You can't run from me. When I inhabit you, you'll feel everything. You'll be right beside me, sharing it all. You'll help me tease and torment those men, and finally drain them. And you won't be able to do a thing to stop it. You'll grow old, still lusting for the touch of a man's firm flesh until they shrink back from you in horror. This time, I'll know what to do. I won't be trapped in a dead body."

She was a terrible thing. A truly awful creature. I'd felt her temporary possession, those moments when I shared what was left of Nora Bailey, remnants of who she'd once been before she was corrupted. I would become that small writhing spirit, anguished and unable to completely die or escape, trapped in the flesh I no longer controlled. Trapped for eternity.

"You're perfect," she said, coming closer. The sense of tentacles sliding over my skin made me want to scream. "Firm and perfect. You'll do nicely." When she came to my shoulder, she pulled back abruptly. "Ah, you've found protection of a sort. It won't last long."

"I will stop—" I lost the power of speech. She exerted her will, blocking the words I wanted to say. She was giving me a small taste of what it would be like to be trapped with her. She wanted to make me afraid. She needed a wedge, and fear would give her that. "No!" I clamped down on my fear. My fingers found the necklace at my throat and gripped it tightly.

"I like a fighter." She inhaled and then exhaled and the scent of wisteria flooded around me. It was so dense it almost made me dizzy. "Men desire me. You'll share that, too. You'll be worshipped as a goddess of feminine wiles. That part, you'll like."

I understood something Madam had said. She'd warned me to hold onto who I was. I thought of Alex and my parents, of Uncle Brett—the people I loved. I clung to the identity of my memories and emotions. The pressure eased up and I stepped past her. "I'm going inside. If you could take me over, you would have." Whatever was missing, I had to find it before she did. The iron talisman had worked momentarily, because she hadn't anticipated it. But it wouldn't hold her back for long.

"I've waited a long time for another who can see the alter world. I can control those foolish college girls for a short time, but they would become little more than walking dead. You, though, you are capable." She licked her lips.

I'd never heard the term alter world, but I didn't ask. I kept walking, up the stairs and into the kitchen. When I closed the door behind me, I leaned against it and wept quietly before I gathered my frayed nerves.

NEWLY AND CONSTANCE had retired when I banked the fire in the stove and went out to the front porch with Reginald. When he offered a cigarette, I took one. My hand shook, and though he noticed, he didn't ask. Reginald had learned the art of patience. We smoked the cigarettes, then ate the toast I'd made, and Reginald poured us both another drink. I was glad for the bite of the whiskey and the warmth that seeped into my arms and legs. At last I felt as if my limbs were truly mine again.

"I'm afraid." I said it softly, when we were both near to finishing our drinks.

"I know. Me too. I fear for you."

"At least Nan is gone. I don't sense her any longer. I hope she's found peace and love."

"We could leave. Right now." Reginald offered me another cigarette. I took it, but I shook my head at the offered light. "I don't think the Sheridans are coming back here, Raissa. If we can't help Royal prove his innocence, they'll execute him."

"Yes, they'll hang him." The execution laws in Mississippi were the same as Alabama. Hanged by the neck, generally in the courthouse square. And when a powerful family like the Pratts was involved, a speedy trial often meant a rush to judgment and immediate execution. The sheriff had issues with Royal already which most likely had to do with a failure to pay "protection" to the sheriff for his whiskey operation. Royal had no friends who might help him or even slow things down for a true chance of justice. He had only us.

"Do you want me to sleep on the floor in your room?" Regi-

THE SPECTER OF SEDUCTION

nald asked. "I know you're experiencing things here that I can't imagine."

His compassion was almost my undoing. "It's Nora Bailey. Or the thing that she's become. She wants to take over my body. I don't fully understand, but I have the iron. It's a little necklace of bits and pieces." I pulled it from my blouse to show him. The old hay string wasn't attractive, but it did the job.

"We have to finish this business and get out of the house. We can rent rooms in West Point if we need to. This place is too dangerous."

"Tomorrow we can make arrangements." I had to agree. My last experience with Nora had taken a lot out of me. "I want to go to Columbus with you tomorrow." Reginald intended to find Penelope Lott. "To the girls' school. I'm hoping they'll have some reference books on the Greek and Roman pantheon of gods and demons. If I don't have a better plan when we finish, we can stop back by here, pick up Constance and Newly, and go on to West Point."

"Okay." He stood up and assisted me to my feet. "Let's get some rest."

I doubted I'd have much success sleeping, but we walked upstairs together and parted on the landing outside my room. "Are you sure?"

I nodded. "I'll be fine tonight." If Nora had the power to possess me this night, she would have done so at the kitchen door.

By the time I washed my face and hands, I was stumbling toward the bed. I fell into a deep sleep, unaware of anything around me. Whatever Nora's intentions for me, she left me alone until morning. I awoke at first light, my stomach rumbling and my eyelids feeling as if someone had thrown sand in them. I went down to the kitchen and put on the coffeepot, glad that I'd brought in wood and banked the fire.

When I had a steaming cup and another piece of toast, I went to the front porch. The front door creaked open and Constance came out, also in her nightgown. "I'm sorry if I was abrupt last night." She looked around the yard. "I don't think the Sheridans will be back. I'll be leaving today, too."

Her departure was unexpected. "You should at least talk to Anne and Royal," I said. "Give them a chance to decide what they want to do."

She shook her head. "It's time for me to go."

"And Newly?" I thought of Moonglow. What would happen to the horse if Newly left abruptly? I supposed I could take her to the Newman farm and ask them to care for her until her future was resolved.

"He doesn't know what I'm planning. I don't intend to tell him either."

"Constance!" She meant to truly vanish, severing ties with everyone here. "That's hardly fair."

"Life isn't fair. Not to Newly and not to me." Barefooted, she walked out into the dew-wet grass, turned, and examined the house. "When I first came here, I thought I'd stay for a long time. At least until Amanda married because that child isn't meant for public schools. She's far too sensitive. I saw this house and I felt as if I always belonged here."

"Give things a chance. Royal is innocent. I don't believe he killed that young man. If we can prove it, the Sheridans will be back."

"Innocent or not, I don't think it matters." She looked at me. "Of all the young men in the county, Ashland Pratt was the wrong one for Royal to shoot. Someone is going to pay, and Royal is handy. His guilt is irrelevant."

"Do you believe he shot a young man, a kid really, point-blank in the chest?" Constance had been with the Sheridans longer than I and she was acting as if she believed Royal was guilty.

"The girl said so."

"And the girl has conveniently disappeared."

"What? Penelope Lott is missing?"

"Yes, but I'm going to find her."

"How?"

I didn't know exactly, but I wasn't ready to give up. "Everyone leaves a trail. Everyone. I just have to pick up on it and follow it. Did she say anything to you when you took her to town?"

"She was so upset, we didn't speak of the shooting. She did say that Ashland was rash and impulsive and that he felt he could do as he pleased. She'd tried to talk him out of coming to Waverley."

"Did she mention her parents or home life?"

Constance frowned. "She didn't say anything useful. I'm sorry. Please don't tell Newly that I'm leaving." She put a hand on my shoulder. "Please. I do care for him, but he can build a life here. I can't. It's better to leave no hope."

"It's not my business." What she was doing wasn't right, but it also wasn't my place to try to make it right. "Will you tell the Sheridans?"

"I'll write them. They have enough on their plate. I hope you understand. You and Reginald will be leaving. Newly has job offers at other plantations. I would be here alone. I can't stop thinking about Fancy, about the way she was cut up. I don't have a dark imagination like you and Amanda, but I can't shake that business from my head."

The murder scene was vividly imprinted in my brain too. "I

understand that part, but I think you should at least tell Newly. It's clear he has feelings for you."

"And I for him, which is why I can't tell him I'm going. You don't know a lot about me or my past, but I've had my share of goodbyes. Too many—too many hard goodbyes."

I shook my head. "It's not my place to judge, Constance. Reginald and I are going to Columbus. Will you be here when we get back?"

"I don't know. I need to make arrangements, but I don't even know where to start. It's hard to do at Waverley. No telegraph, no phone, no car." She shrugged and laughed softly. "Without Amanda here, it is a bleak place indeed."

"Shall I send a car for you?" I could do that from Columbus.

"No. Thank you, though."

I rose from the steps and picked up my coffee cup. I was ready to start the day, to get busy and move things forward. "I'll bring some groceries when I come back. And a block of ice."

"That would be good. Now I'll get busy. Maybe the day will give me more courage and I'll stay at least until Royal is tried." She started to reach out to me but caught herself. "I do care."

I didn't blame Constance for her desire to flee. As I walked upstairs to dress, I found my own feet dragging. Waverley was like a huge energy drain. I knocked on Reginald's door to find him up and shaving.

"Meet me at the front door in ten minutes," he said.

I was in the car when he came down, and we drove away. Reginald hesitated at the crossroads. "I'm tempted to drive to the river and check the ferry," he said.

"Why?"

"The night you saw Penelope Lott, you said there was a car on the other side of the river."

"Yes."

"What kind?"

I thought about it. "It was a Chevrolet roadster. I couldn't see the color, but dark green or black. Light trim. Yellow, I think."

"Good."

"Why are you asking about the car?"

"Because that was how Penelope Lott got to Waverley. She came over on the ferry with the Pratt boy. His car has to be on the other side, and it might help us find her."

Columbus was a small city. It wouldn't be that hard to spot a particular car. Reginald was right. "Good thinking."

He turned away from the ferry and toward the main road. "First to the school."

Even though the day was humid and hot, the breeze in the car kept us comfortable. When we approached the outskirts of town, Reginald pulled into a diner. "I'm starving."

"I could eat too."

We went in and ordered breakfast, but it was clear Reginald was working another angle. He talked casually with the waitress about the town, the girls' school, local gossip. He was a handsome, polished man who put others at ease. Stella was the waitress's name—it was embroidered on her uniform. She was in her mid-thirties, the passage of time marked clearly on her face. Still it was easy to see the pretty young woman she'd once been.

"Those school girls sometimes stop by here, after they've been out to the river for a swim or such." She rolled her eyes, and I grinned. She had a big personality. "They go to classes to get an education, but they're a lot more interested in the boys over at Starkville than they are their books."

"Can you blame them?" Reginald asked. "Life is short, and young girls are finally getting a chance to have a little of the freedom men have enjoyed for such a long time. They should kick up their heels."

"Oh, they kick up their heels, lift their skirts, and do-si-do," Stella said. "But I don't begrudge them. I got married when I was sixteen. Got three kids at home. My husband was killed on the river."

"I'm sorry." I knew that pain.

"I miss him, but at least I got my kids."

"Do the young folks ever talk about that old haunted mansion across the river?" Reginald asked.

"Oh, that's all they talk about. The girls say there is something there. They get possessed or overtaken by something that makes them go wild." She laughed. "They swear it's true."

"Has anyone mentioned the shooting over at Waverley?"

"It's all over town," Stella said.

"Would you happen to know the female student, Penelope Lott?" Reginald asked.

Stella put her hands on her hips and leaned closer. "Some of the girls were in here late last night. They knew her name because of the Pratt boy. They said she wasn't a student. No one had ever heard of her at the school. But that boy that was killed, they knew him. He had the reputation of being a real horn dog, you know. He took more than one girl over to that old haunted mansion. I heard those girls saying some of the young ladies were aiming for revenge."

CHAPTER 26

Ashland Pratt's reputation came as no surprise to me or Reginald. Stella was a gold mine of gossip, but none of it helped us find Penelope Lott. A quick stop at the registrar of the school told us plenty. Penelope was not, nor had she ever been, a student there. Gaines had been had by a school girl.

We spoke with several young ladies, and none remembered Penelope at any campus functions, classes, or events. The classes were small and the students knew each other. "Girls pretend to be students here so they can date the boys from Starkville," one girl told us, "but that Ashland Pratt, he didn't care whether a girl went to school or not. He wanted one thing, and the girls I know were on to him. He couldn't get a date on a bet."

Except that he'd taken a girl to Waverley, and she'd accused Royal Sheridan of murder and then disappeared. We tried checking with personnel, thinking perhaps Penelope was an employee pretending to be a student. No such person had ever been hired. The trail of Penelope Lott had grown cold before we'd even caught a good scent.

"This stinks," Reginald told me as we walked up the steps into the cool interior of the brick campus library. "I'm beginning to think Royal was set up."

"To what purpose?" I asked. "Why would someone do that?"

"Jealousy, greed, revenge...the usual list." Reginald's frown was intense. "You don't have to say it, because I don't see how those motives apply either, but Royal isn't a killer. Not even drunk and angry. I have to believe that the property itself is the motive. Waverley Mansion, a place that was abandoned for many years. If Waverley is what's behind framing Royal, why didn't this person just buy the property before Royal did?"

"We should talk to the Sheridans about any other bids on Waverley."

"Yes, but right now the girl, Penelope Lott, is our best lead. She was the only witness, and it's her word against Royal's. He said he shot over their heads. If he was drunk and shot accidentally, that's a lot different than murder. She's painted Royal as a deliberate murderer. Why? We have to find that out."

The glimmer of hope he held out was dim, but I clutched it hard.

To maximize our time, Reginald took the list I'd prepared to the local market to pick up supplies while I worked in the library. The mythology section wasn't large, but it was respectable, and I found several references on female demons and entities that used sexual gratification as a tool to entrap souls. Was Nora Bailey a succubus? I honestly couldn't say. The books were vague and non-specific. The general information on different feminine entities that preyed on men through sexual wiles fit what was happening at Waverley. But there

were also differences. A true succubus had no need of a physical form. It worked its dark magic on the male during sleep
and dreams, slowly draining the male energy until only a husk
remained. Nora Bailey had been something else. She'd been an
insatiable temptress, one who drank attention and adoration as
much as the male's sexual energy. She was a huntress, too. She
identified her prey and then relentlessly pursued.

And now I was in her sights. It was my life—my soul—at
risk if I guessed wrong.

As I read the material, I tried to put into place what had
occurred at Waverley Mansion half a century earlier. I let my
mind relax, imagining Nora Bailey as she arrived at the beautiful old home. She'd been living in New Orleans, where she'd
fallen in love with Francis Norquist. Francis had extended the
hospitality of his Mississippi home because New Orleans was
under Union rule and considered dangerous to a delicate
flower of the South.

As a woman without family or home, Nora would have
been at the mercy of almost everyone. The information I'd
gleaned from Coralee and Constance indicated Nora had come
from a good Virginia family. Bad luck and bad decisions sent
her father to an early grave. Her brothers had joined the
Confederacy, and both had died of short rations and dysentery,
which might have been the impetus for her spy work.

She'd originally come further South in the hopes of marry-
ing, but without relatives to make introductions and arrangements, she'd ended up in New Orleans, where the old social
order was a bit more relaxed. New Orleans was a city of
intrigue, frequented by pirates and filled with officers from
good families. Beautiful and vivacious, Nora had been invited
to dinners and balls for her social skill, not her name or
inheritance.

Nora and Francis had met in the bayou home of a Southern sympathizer who was helping Francis gather needed supplies. Francis had sent Nora to Waverley, never imagining the fighting would move so near his family home. Or that something far worse than Yankees or starvation might be waiting for her.

And that was the key I sought. What had brought a female entity—this succubus creature—to Waverley? I'd discovered a few important facts. Nora was a sensitive, and the entity required someone with sensitivity to inhabit. Had Nora brought the demon with her from New Orleans—perhaps she'd been cursed by a jealous rival? Or had it been at the mansion, waiting for someone it could possess? The entity had implied that it finally wore down Nora's resistance at Waverley, but who had summoned it? That was what I had to discover. There was much to learn.

In the library stacks I looked up the Norquist family—the sons were lauded as brave Confederate soldiers. Bjorn and Marketta died shortly after the war ended of broken hearts, or so the history book implied. The girls abandoned Waverley and fled to the West Coast.

Dr. Calvert Marcus had a mention as a Union spy who was hanged and then burned by a mob. That these events took place at Waverley was never mentioned.

To my surprise, there was a photograph of the portrait of Nora Bailey created by Julian DeWitt. It was indeed extraordinary. Nora was luminous, glowing. And she looked real enough to step out of the frame and onto the staircase at Waverley, just as I'd been told.

While I had the opportunity, I looked up additional DeWitt art work. He'd been a sought after portraitist, and each painting was extraordinary. In a book of Civil War portraits I found each of the Norquist sisters, who were true beauties in their own right. Marguerite was slender and soft. Helene had brown hair and pale eyes and an elegant composure. Olivia radiated an intensity that made it hard to look away. DeWitt had also painted several other West Point and Columbus belles. They were gorgeous paintings that captured the subjects, but none were as alive as that of Nora Bailey. I could see what had attracted the negative spirit to her. Dark is always attracted to light.

When I'd gleaned as much as I could at the library, I walked to the courthouse to talk with the sheriff—and to borrow the telephone. Law officers weren't especially keen on allowing the public to use their telephone, but they couldn't really refuse since I could reverse the charges. And I had to speak with Uncle Brett and Madam.

The sheriff allowed me to use his office for the call, and a local switchboard operator made the connections to put me through to Caoin House. Uncle Brett answered immediately. He'd taken my request for research on succubi seriously, and he had some facts to share.

"Madam is worried about you and Reginald," Uncle Brett said. "We had a lengthy conversation last night. She consulted with some other mediums, and it's vitally important that you find out who summoned the succubus. Raissa, the creature is technically a demon, not a spirit. That concerned Madam greatly."

"And me too. She is...powerful and hard to pin down." I told Uncle Brett the difficulty I was having narrowing the source of the entity. "I don't think Nora deliberately summoned this thing. I don't."

"Then who?" he asked.

"Exactly the question I have to answer." I didn't want to

scare Uncle Brett, but he deserved to know the truth. "This spirit needs a sensitive to attach to. Nora was a sensitive. My understanding of the succubus is that a person can summon it for many different purposes, but it would be with that person. This entity at Waverley is...more than that."

"And it wants to attach to you?"

"Yes."

"I'd like to tell you to come straight home, but I won't do that. Please be careful, Raissa. Reginald is aware of this, right?"

"He will be, as soon as he returns from the store." I filled Uncle Brett in on what was happening with the Sheridan family. He promised to call the Ledbetters and prevail on them to befriend Anne and Amanda. "And I'm going to call Lewis Brock. I know he didn't impress you, but he is a man of the cloth. Just in case you need him. His brother is a lawyer in Mobile. I have some sway with him."

Uncle Brett lightened my load because he cared. He was always my support. "Thank you."

"Just promise me that you'll get out of that house. Stay in town. Do what you must to help the Sheridan family, but do not spend another night in that house."

"Uncle Brett, I promise you I'll take all precautions. Do you know anything about a painter, Julian DeWitt?"

There was a pause. "Why do you ask?"

"He painted Nora Bailey. I've been hunting the painting everywhere. It disappeared from Waverley the night Nora was hanged as a spy. It's an exquisite work."

"I've seen a photograph of the painting. Isabelle went to town yesterday and brought some books home from the Mobile library for me. She found material on the Norquist family and their role in the Civil War. The boys were considered to be great strategists. All three were killed. I'd mentioned Nora Bailey's name, and Isabelle found an article on the big scandal when a female spy was hanged. There was also a mention of the painting of Nora, and there was a bit of a story with it."

"What kind of story?"

"One that applies to your situation. The story goes that Nora's spirit can't rest until the painting is found and destroyed. That she's trapped in the painting."

"Was there any indication where the painting might be?"

"None. But after DeWitt fled Waverley Mansion, he went upriver to Tennessee. Nashville."

"Do you think he took the painting with him?" It wasn't a question I expected Uncle Brett to answer.

"I don't know, Raissa, but this sounds like an exciting hunt. Isabelle has been itching for an outing. Shall we drive up?"

"Yes." I adored Isabelle Brown, Uncle Brett's lady friend. Girlfriend sounded too undignified for people their age, but she was the woman in his life. I wished he would marry her, but Uncle Brett was not a man who could be pushed into anything.

"We'll leave today and overnight in Jackson, Mississippi. I have some friends there I haven't seen in years."

"Thank you, Uncle Brett."

"We'll bring these books. And Madam said to call her anytime. She was feeling better yesterday than she has in a while."

"I will." I could hear the sheriff and his officers outside the door. He was growing impatient. "I have to go. See you tomorrow." I hung up and gathered my purse. It was time to find Reginald and head back to Waverley if we were going to West Point for the night.

Where would one put a valuable painting? I wondered if it

had been destroyed by the Norquist sisters. I wouldn't blame them for burning the reminder of the woman who wreaked havoc in their family. And if they had burned the portrait, I had no idea what I'd do to attempt to rid Waverley of the dark wraith that had become Nora.

Reginald saw me walking toward the library and pulled over to pick me up. He'd found every item on my list, and some additional bits of iron for my pockets that he'd picked up in the local hardware store. It was long past lunchtime, so before we headed back to Waverley we stopped at a diner for lunch. The blue-plate special was meatloaf, and as we ate, I told him what I'd learned. He'd also discovered some interesting details.

"As it happens, I ran into a woman who has a Julian DeWitt painting of her great-grandmother," he said. "She said the painting was worth quite a bit of money, and she knew some of the stories about Waverley House. Even better, she knew gossip about the Pratt family." Reginald paused while the waitress topped his coffee.

"Something tells me the Pratts aren't on the up and up." I could see that coming a mile down the road. Privileged boy, prominent family, gets away with everything—never paying any consequences. The father would stretch the law to keep his son out of trouble, time and time again. Until Ashland stepped into something Daddy couldn't save him from.

Reginald leaned forward to keep his voice low. "Ashland Pratt was named in a paternity suit by another college student, but the interesting information is about the Lott girl. Mrs. Marshall, the woman I was talking with in the grocery, knows Penelope Lott. She said the girl showed up and took a room with her, stayed three weeks and left in a big hurry a few days ago. She was never a student at the school, and even when

Mrs. Marshall warned her about Ashland Pratt's reputation for despoiling and abandoning young women, Penelope was determined to go out with him."

"Where is Penelope now?"

"That's the interesting thing. Mrs. Marshall saw her this morning in front of the bank. She'd taken a job as a nanny for the bank owner, Mr. Cox."

"She's still in town?"

"Supposedly, but she's no longer staying at Mrs. Marshall's home."

"Then let's find her."

"I thought you'd feel that way." Reginald paid the lunch bill and we left the diner. He took a hard right, made the block, and headed for the bank. We weren't ready to give up hunting yet.

At the bank we were shown into the private office of the president, Franklin Cox, who was a stout man clearly aggravated by the mention of Penelope Lott. When we were seated at his massive desk, Reginald led the conversation with Cox, who sputtered with anger. "She took the job as nanny making us believe she'd be with us for the whole school year. My wife is livid."

"And she had letters of recommendation?"

"She did. I have them here." He brought three letters from the desk drawer. "You're welcome to them. I did check her out, and her former employers were highly complimentary."

Reginald handed the letters to me and I looked through the return addresses, delighted to see one came from Mobile, Alabama. Uncle Brett would check that for me.

"Have you seen Penelope today?" I asked, immediately aware that Mr. Cox was a follower of the "women should be seen and not heard" school. He addressed his answer to Reginald. His expression, as he noted my haircut, spoke volumes about his dislike for the type of woman I appeared to be.

"She was here for her final pay check. Maybe an hour ago. She said she was leaving town."

"Did she say where she was going?" Reginald asked.

Cox shook his head. "She didn't say and I didn't ask. She's an unreliable girl and she won't get a reference from me. She appeared to be something she wasn't. She kept her hair long and her dresses modest, unlike some women today. I knew the minute she got her hair cut last week it was going to be trouble."

"How did you come to hire Miss Lott?" Reginald asked.

"My wife spoke with some friends in Mobile who were happy with Penelope. She worked for them for a year and then said she was moving here to be closer to family."

"Did she mention who her family was?"

He hesitated. "No, she didn't. Penelope wasn't forthcoming about her past. I got the impression she'd had a lot of unhappiness. She was a bright young woman. She knew history, geography, math, and English, and she was better in the sciences than most men I know. In that regard, she was excellent. Broadly educated and also spoke French. She showed up on time and the children took to her immediately. It was a huge relief to Mrs. Cox to have her in the household. And then she suddenly quits. Such behavior is unheard of." He'd worked himself up into a loud huff by the end.

"That is very disappointing," Reginald agreed. "We appreciate your help. May we keep the reference letters?"

"Keep them. She'll never get another job in this city. It's best if all traces of her are removed. Mrs. Cox goes into near hysteria at the mention of her name."

We left the bank and once outside, Reginald burst into

laughter. "You should have seen your face! You were about to pop."

"Pompous old coot." It was the first disparaging comment that came to mind, and it made Reginald laugh more. "We have to work on your language. You need to modernize. You could call him an old money-bags or high hat with jingling pockets. Coot is a bit outdated."

I had to laugh too. Reginald was correct. My time at Waverley House had sapped all of the modern tendencies I'd learned from Zelda and Tallulah. I'd regressed back to the proper schoolmarm I'd been only a few months earlier

"If we stand out on the street in front of the bank and you smoke a cigarette, that will send a message." Reginald offered the smokes.

I shook my head. "It's too hot to stand here, for any reason. There's a telegraph office on Main Street. Let's go there and send Uncle Brett this address on Penelope's references. He'll check it."

"She was careful not to give any personal information away to the Coxes," Reginald said. "Let's hope she was careless in Mobile. I have a sense that she was here in Columbus for the express purpose of meeting Ashland Pratt."

His comment stopped me cold. "Why? What would be the reason for doing that? The young man is dead, and why would she want to involve herself in the death of a man she'd just met."

"You're assuming they'd never met. And what if this isn't about Pratt, but all about Royal Sheridan. It's possible he has a past, Raissa. Mr. Cox hired a young woman he didn't know and got snake bit. We took on clients we didn't know either. Keep that in mind."

. . .

AFTER WE SENT THE TELEGRAM, we drove around town looking for Penelope but had no luck. I wondered if she'd revealed anything about her ultimate destination to Constance. It was worth a few questions when we returned to Waverley—if Constance was still there.

We arrived back at the old mansion with plenty of daylight to pack up and relocate in West Point, away from the entity that lurked there. When we turned at the entrance to the driveway, Reginald slowed. It was almost as if we were driving into an area where the sunlight was muted. I put a hand on Reginald's arm. "I don't want to go to the mansion." I had a terrible feeling in my chest, as if a hand clutched my heart and squeezed.

Reginald idled the car. "I can take you to West Point and come back here for our things." He shifted into reverse.

"What about Constance and Newly. If she's still here, we can't just leave them." I was torn. The idea of the old house terrified me, but leaving Constance and Newly was unaccept-able. "Drive on." I gripped the door of the car.

"Are you sure?" Reginald wasn't sure, and that unsettled me.

"We'll get our things and those two and get out. Nora can have the place as far as I'm concerned. Uncle Brett and Isabelle will be here tomorrow. We came to release Nan, and we accomplished that. I do think we should all leave, until I have a chance to learn more about whatever is here. And until I have someone like Madam to counsel me." Reinforcements would be very welcome.

"We'll be out of here in fifteen minutes." Reginald drove slowly down the drive, and I remembered the first day we'd arrived. I'd seen the young woman running through the woods, a prelude to what was going to happen.

"Look!" Reginald slowed and pointed ahead. "It's Newly."

We sped up so that we were behind him, but he didn't turn around. Reginald tooted the car horn, and still Newly continued to walk in the middle of the road, ignoring us.

"What's wrong with him?" Reginald asked.

"Stop and let me out."

Reginald stopped the car and I dashed after Newly, who continued to walk, completely unaware of his surroundings. "Newly!" I caught his arm and turned him to face me. My heart pounded with fear. Newly looked at me with total blankness.

"Newly!" I shook him lightly just as Reginald joined us.

"Come get in the car," Reginald said, guiding Newly back to the vehicle. He offered no resistance or recognition. His pale gray eyes were glazed. "What happened to you?" Reginald asked.

But Newly was far away from us, trapped in a place where he neither saw nor heard us, but I was willing to bet it wasn't a pleasant place. His eyes mirrored empty horror.

"What's wrong with him?" Reginald asked.

"I wish I knew." I looked at his rumpled clothes, patches of dirt and leaves on his back and in his hair. "Maybe he fell and hit his head." There was no trace of blood or any other open wound.

We put him in the car and headed to Waverley. I dreaded what we might find there. We'd only been gone a short time, and something terrible had happened. I couldn't wait to grab my belongings and Constance and get off the premises. When I returned, I would bring Reverend Brock. I didn't care whether I liked him or not, he carried the authority of God with him, and I felt I needed more power than I possessed.

We parked in front of the mansion, and I knew instantly it was empty. The front door stood open, and Benedict, Amanda's cat, stretched and yawned on the doormat. "Constance!" I yelled for her as I got out of the car.

"She's gone. And the Sheridan's car is gone too." Reginald settled Newly in the car and gently told him to stay. "Grab your things," he said to me. "I'll get my stuff. We're leaving."

The purchases we'd made we left in the car, except for the block of ice. There would be no one at Waverley to use it, but it could cool the icebox for a little while. I hurried upstairs and packed my clothes, my writing, and emptied a pillow case. When I had put my things in the car, I lured the cat to me and put him in the pillowcase to take to West Point. I couldn't leave him to fend for himself at the old mansion. I didn't know when anyone would return to care for him. "Newly, hold the cat, please."

His hands automatically took the unhappy cat that thrashed about in the pillowcase. "I'll be right back." I had to tell Amos that we were leaving and give him the chance to go with us. Even if he went only as far as Mrs. Hempstead's, he would be clear of the property and the evil that lurked there.

There was a dangerous brooding quality over the mansion. The sun had disappeared behind a growing bank of clouds, and a cool wind whipped through the tops of the trees. On the fourth floor of Waverley, at the rotunda, a shutter banged.

She was there, standing at the window looking down at me. Nora Bailey. She was in no hurry, because she already felt victorious.

"Arg! Arg! Arg!" Newly uttered the weird, terrified sound and pointed up at the window. He could see her too. And he started to turn and climb out of the back of the car he was so afraid.

"Reginald!"

My partner came at the run.

"Hold him in the car, I have to get Amos."

"Hurry." Reginald physically restrained Newly in the car while I dashed around the plantation house to the small cabin in the back. Amos was already coming toward me, some clothes in a paper sack.

"You'd best get off the place," he said. "Things are stirred up good."

I took his elbow to hurry him along, and we jogged to the car. As soon as he was seated, I started the motor and wheeled around. I glanced once behind me at the house and saw her on the front porch. She was laughing. The fight was a long way from over.

CHAPTER 27

Coralee Hempstead was seated on her front porch, almost as if she hadn't moved since my last visit. She was shucking fat, plump ears of yellow corn.

"Amos," she said when she saw the gardener in the vehicle. "What brings y'all here looking like the Devil chased you down the road?" She eyed Newly, but said nothing.

"Bad things stirred up at Waverley," Amos said. "I thought I'd stay here for a spell."

"Of course. What about the rest of them?"

"Would you have room for Newly? And a cat?" I asked. There wasn't a doctor who could help Newly. If he had a safe place to rest, he might recover from the shock of what had happened to him.

"Of course." Mrs. Hempstead stood up. "I'll make some tea. Mr. Long down the road brought me a block of ice and I chipped some up. A cold drink will help that young man."

While she was in the house, I settled Newly in a rocker on her porch. Just getting away from Waverley seemed to help him. His color was better and he followed movement with his eyes now. "What happened to you?" I asked, not expecting an answer.

"Constance."

Reginald and I looked at each other. "What about Constance?" Reginald asked.

"She tried to kill me."

"How?" I couldn't grasp what he was saying.

"She, uh, she demanded that I make love to her. But she got on top of me and began to...take my life or maybe my soul." He looked away. "She was hideous. She wasn't a woman any more. She was a monster."

Reginald and I exchanged startled glances. Newly no longer stuttered. He didn't appear aware of the change. "Where is Constance now?" We couldn't leave her. We simply couldn't abandon her. And if what Newly said was true, it had been the entity, not Constance, that had attacked him.

"I don't know. She was in the Sheridan's car. She was laughing, like something truly wicked." He put his hands up to his ears. "And she was so strong. She didn't even look like herself. She was...hungry."

Newly was coming around at a rapid rate, and Amos had disappeared behind the house to bring in wood. Reginald and I sat on the edge of the porch near Coralee's chair. She came out with the drinks.

"Things finally came to a head at Waverley, didn't they?" Mrs. Hempstead served us tall glasses of iced sweet tea. I'd never tasted anything so good. "Amanda told me about you two. How you'd come to send her playmate on to heaven. That poor little girl."

"I believe Nan is at peace," I said. That was the one real

thing Reginald and I had accomplished. "But Waverley isn't at rest."

"No, it isn't." She settled back in her chair and picked up another ear of corn. She expertly stripped the shuck back. "I warned Amanda about the things that went on there. I tried to talk to Royal and Anne, but they wouldn't hear it. I knew the Norquist family, and I figured out what happened. I saw the altar Olivia built. I was there when she cast the summons. I know what she called down on that property. And I was there the day she killed her own daughter. I don't believe she had an ounce of remorse for pushing that little girl down those stairs."

"Olivia Norquist summoned the demon?" I'd never suspected one of the Norquist daughters. "Why?"

"She was in love with Calvert Marcus. The doctor didn't show interest in her, and she wanted to make him love her. She asked for the power of feminine wiles. She'd gotten hold of an incantation. We thought she was pretending, that she didn't know what would happen. We were wrong."

"How would she know how to do such a thing?" Young plantation women were protected from everything. It wasn't like they were schooled in curses and witchcraft.

"There was a slave from Haiti there. Bertha. She knew the hoodoo, and she told Olivia how to do it. That Fancy was her granddaughter."

I remembered the grave in the Norquist cemetery. Bertha's marker had contained her name and a strange symbol. Now I knew it was a hoodoo symbol. "What happened to Bertha?" I had a bad feeling.

"She fell in the well. She'd gone to get water and didn't come back. Somehow she fell right into the well. They said it broke her back and she drowned."

"She didn't fall into the well, did she, Mrs. Hempstead?"

"Call me Coralee. I don't have any proof, but I always believed Olivia pushed her. Olivia had a very direct way of dealing with people who attempted to thwart her desires."

Olivia had found a convenient way to eliminate those who stood between her and what she wanted. She pushed them into wells or down flights of stairs. A little shove, problem solved.

"And Nora Bailey?"

"Oh, Olivia hated Nora. Hated that she was beautiful and kind and that all of the men in the area flocked to her even though they knew she was Francis's girl."

"What was this thing that Olivia summoned?"

She shook her head. "I couldn't say. I never saw it, only what it did to Olivia. She was relentless in her pursuit of men. She'd already had a child out of wedlock, but she didn't care. And when she decided that Calvert Marcus was the man she wanted, she wouldn't let him rest. She was like a rutting cat, yowling and carrying on in the woods with him. The Norquists spoke of having her institutionalized, but the war was going on and no place was safe, not even mental hospitals.

"Was Calvert going to marry her?"

Coralee smiled. "I don't know. He had other ambitions, I'm sure you've heard. He was a devoted abolitionist. He spoke out against slavery, which made him unpopular to say the least. The community hated Calvert, and Olivia hated Nora, because Calvert would slip into a corner to talk to her. Spy business, but Olivia thought it was romantic. For revenge, Olivia made sure everyone knew Nora was a spy. The night Nora was hanged, Olivia was gleeful. Until the mob rode up with Calvert Marcus on a horse, hands tied behind his back, and hanged him from the same tree Nora was hanged from."

The scene she described was one of horror. "Francis cut Nora down."

"Yes, he loved her. And I believe she loved him until the very end when she changed and became...different. Then she was worse than Olivia. She sought out men to seduce right under Francis's nose. It was cruelty of the worst kind."

"Yet he cut her down and buried her." I paced the front porch, glad to see that Benedict had calmed in Reginald's arms.

"He did bury her. No one knew where, but I suspect it was in the family cemetery. He left some matters to attend with a lawyer in town and I think he had a marker put on her grave. That's just my suspicions, though." She looked into the distance, remembering. "Olivia took the portrait of Nora that Julian DeWitt had finished. Francis was livid, but Olivia refused to say where she'd hidden it. If her sisters helped, they never admitted it. It didn't really matter. Nora was dead and Francis followed her soon after. The painting was gone."

"You said Nora changed after she'd been at Waverley for a time. When did she begin to change?"

Her eyes narrowed. "She was there for several weeks before Francis came home. At first she was sweet and fun. Then she was...hard and calculating. She stopped talking to us girls. The men were the only thing that interested her."

"And Olivia took the painting?" Reginald asked. "Why?"

"She hated Nora. I remember that night Nora died. Bjorn Norquist was supposed to announce the engagement of Olivia and Calvert Marcus, but Olivia caught Nora and Calvert making love in the woods." Even after all the years that had passed, Coralee was still shaken by the memory of that scene.

I hated to interrupt, but I needed clarification. "Wait. Calvert had asked to marry Olivia? Was he forced into the marriage?"

Coralee rocked for a moment. "I don't know if I can answer that. He did ask. I don't know if Olivia said she was pregnant, or if Mr. Norquist convinced him he should do it to save Olivia's honor, or if Calvert was so intent on stopping the war that he was willing to marry Olivia for access to the plans the Norquist boys were making."

"Was Dr. Marcus in love with Nora Bailey?" Reginald asked.

"Perhaps. They were often seen together, but hindsight tells me it could have been the spying. It was all so outside the way I'd been raised, you see. I couldn't believe some of the stories about Nora. She was promiscuous, and right under Francis's nose. She became cruel, and she wasn't like that when she first arrived. She became another person entirely."

I was beginning to put together a sequence of events. If Olivia had summoned the succubus or whatever evil entity it was, then it had discovered an open door in Nora, who was open to the alter world, and it had transferred to her. I nudged Reginald.

"Was Nora romantically involved with the painter, Julian DeWitt?"

"There was talk. And that talk spiked a lot of jealousy. I tell you Olivia hated that painting. It was...incredible. Nora looked so alive. Her skin on the canvas was warm to the touch."

The clouds had darkened, and a wind fluttered the bright green leaves of the trees as the storm moved closer. Even though it was still afternoon, the day had darkened considerably. The weather perfectly reflected my mood and sent a flurry of a chill through me. A storm was coming.

"Where is the painting?" I asked softly. "Please tell us if you know."

Coralee shook her head. "I don't know. Olivia took it off

the wall while Francis was burying Nora. When he came into the house and saw it was gone, he went crazy. I thought he was going to strangle Olivia. He should have. She was a wicked person, and after that night, she grew more and more bitter."

"Did she ever marry?"

Coralee rocked for a moment, her hands stripping the ears of corn and silking them without conscious thought. "She left. Helene and Marguerite stayed on until the parents died, and then they left for the West Coast. I don't know what happened to Olivia. She was so unhappy and bitter, but she had an education, money in gold and not Confederate bonds, and a better chance than a lot of Southerners had."

"She never came back?"

"Not to my knowledge. As far as I know, the Norquist sisters left Mississippi and were never heard from again. Word came around that Helene married but never had children. The line died with the girls."

A family with six children, all dead within one generation, and a grandchild murdered. The war decimated numerous Southern families, killing off an entire generation and ending long lineages, but the Norquists had extinguished themselves. Where the daughters were concerned, though, it might not be a bad idea. I didn't know where spirits went when they crossed over, but I hoped that Nan wouldn't have to be near her mother. She deserved better.

"How did the Sheridans come to own the property?" Reginald asked.

"The place had gone up for taxes, but no one ever bought it. It had a reputation." Coralee shucked the last ear of corn and brushed the silks from her lap. "I'll can this corn and it'll make good soup this winter."

Reginald picked up an ear and sniffed it. "This will be good and sweet. There was one summer when I ran away from the orphanage. I was staying in the woods on the edge of a corn field. I'd eat three ears a day, because I didn't like the idea of stealing the farmer's corn. He knew I was hungry. He started leaving me sweet potatoes, and dried beans, and salt meat. He was a good man, but I loved that fresh corn."

Coralee assessed Reginald. "For a fancy man, you've got good values."

Trying to block my laughter, I snorted, which set everyone off. It was a brief moment, and we desperately needed the lightness. Even Newly laughed. "Coralee, do you believe Royal could shoot an unarmed man point blank in the chest?"

"Posh, that never happened. Royal blows hard but he's no killer. There's something else going on. There is true evil at Waverley. All those years it sat empty, no one managed to stake a claim to it. Folks came to look, and even though it was pennies to the dollar in price, no one wanted it. Until Royal and Anne. I told them Waverley wasn't any place for a young girl. I told them the truth. Whatever Olivia called up, it's been there ever since."

She was right about that.

"You were in love with Francis, weren't you?" Reginald asked gently.

Coralee sighed. "I was. Deeply. But once Nora Bailey came on the scene, he never saw me. I was the neighbor-girl. He'd grown up pulling my pigtails and teasing me. He never noticed when I became a woman."

My heart stung for her. Her love for Francis was the nugget she'd polished her whole life. The war had taken many of the young men of the South and North. Girls like Coralee had settled into a solitary life, knowing marriage and family were not going to be a choice. For a young woman from a good family, the only path was spinsterhood. Coralee had chosen to remain in her family home, isolated and away from the public eye. She wasn't even afforded the possibility of teaching or working in a church or as a nurse because she didn't live in town.

"What happened to the paintings DeWitt did of Helene and Marguerite?" I asked.

"I presume they took them when they moved West. They were beautiful. The last Confederate belles are what I called them. After the war, no one had money for portraits, or even fancy dresses to wear for a sitting. All of that was gone. Forever."

"Maybe Olivia destroyed the painting of Nora." I was musing aloud.

"Oh, no. She wouldn't." Coralee sat forward. "She wouldn't do that. She said more than once that she'd protect the painting forever."

"Why?" Reginald asked. "She hated Nora."

Coralee rocked a bit more. "She hated her, but that painting—she looked at it all the time while it was hanging near the staircase. I would find her standing there, staring, reaching out to touch the painting. Like I said, Nora was warm to the touch."

Reginald gained his feet and looked down at me. "We have to find that painting."

I nodded. The painting was the key.

"And Constance," Reginald said. "She's still missing."

"I believe she's gone." I put a hand on Newly's shoulder. "I don't know what happened to her, but she told me she was moving on. She didn't want to say goodbye to you." The horse trainer held a sweating glass of tea in his hand and stared out into the distance. He'd retreated back to some private place.

"Now I wonder if it was because she couldn't trust herself. Maybe she knew she'd fall under the influence of the...entity."

"You think she just left?" Reginald was skeptical.

"That's what she said." And I didn't want to spend time at Waverley looking for someone who was long gone.

"Coralee, Amos is here to help. Could you keep an eye on Newly for us?"

She nodded. "That boy needs to sleep. Nothing to help him but sleep. I've seen this before."

"Where?" I asked.

"Some of those boys coming out of Waverley. They were like the dead, like the Confederate soldiers I'd see as a child, walking home from the war. Skeletons and ghosts. They should have laid down on the battle field and just died. They'd been drained. That's the only way to describe it. Something got hold of them and drained them dry. They were like your friend, wild-eyed like a deer run into a trap. Mostly their girls, who didn't look much better, would put them in a car and drive them away." She shook her head. "They kept coming back, though. Why would someone return to a place where they were physically harmed?"

The power of the female entity, the sense of complete control. I understood how tempting it might be for a young woman. And for the male, that total sexual absorption. It would have been highly erotic. They weren't aware they risked their lives, possibly their souls. Had any of them been more acutely attuned to spirits, they might have died at Waverley.

"Did Olivia have any secret places at Waverley. Places where she might hide that portrait of Nora Bailey?"

The rocker creaked softly. "She fancied herself an artist. She was a fair painter if she was working with a still life, but she couldn't make people come alive. She set up her studio on the fourth floor. She said the light was best there because there are windows all around and her brothers left her paintings alone. Francis teased all of his sisters, and even me when I was visiting. He had a streak of mischief that could make anyone laugh, even Olivia, and she took herself very seriously."

The third floor, which had originally been the domain of the Norquist boys, contained bedrooms and a few small storage rooms. It was the fourth floor that reminded me of a light house, with open windows all around to allow the hot air to vent out of the house. One room was where I'd found the journals, and another was stacked with old furniture. I hadn't explored thoroughly. "Reginald, we have to go back there."

"I know. And there's no better time than now, before it gets dark."

Reginald helped Newly into the house. He was recovering, but it would take time. Coralee was right. He needed to rest. Amos came outside to speak with me. "You be safe, Miss Raissa."

I nodded. "Amos, did you know Matthew Cooley?"

"That man no good. He knew the moonshine business, but he was no friend of Mr. Sheridan's."

"Why do you say that?"

"He was stealing from Mr. Sheridan. He'd load the cars for delivering the moonshine, and he'd take extra for himself. Tell Mr. Sheridan jugs broke. That kind of thing."

"Royal wasn't a fool. He must have known."

Amos gave a lopsided grin. "He knew. I told him. He shoulda fired that man. Never let the fox in the hen house. Only trouble and grief can come from that."

Trouble and grief. Yes, Royal had a plateful of that.

"Thank you, Amos. Would you carry these supplies in for

Coralee? We won't need them at Waverley and y'all can use them here."

Reginald came out of the house and we got in the car. The storm lingered on the horizon but had moved no closer. Time to fish or cut bait.

CHAPTER 28

"First we look for Constance. If the car isn't around, we assume she's driven to town." I used my fingers to mark off the list of chores. "We have to find the painting. Do you want the house or the big barn in the back?"

"We should stick together." Reginald's frown drew his brows tight together.

"We can cover more ground if we separate."

"I won't leave you alone in there. That place works on you, and while you haven't been forthcoming about what you know, I can tell that you're afraid."

I was. Terrified. And I owed him at least what I believed I knew. "It's the painting, Reginald. Somehow, Nora Bailey's spirit is trapped in the painting. That was the spell or bargain Olivia made. Once the entity had shifted Nora out of her own body, it could take over her flesh. Olivia did this. She condemned Nora to an eternity of being possessed."

"That is distressing on so many levels." Reginald jerked the wheel sharply to miss a small furry creature in the road. "Sorry."

I pressed my hands against the dash and forced myself to breathe slowly. As we entered a section of road where the trees canopied overhead, I knew we were no longer alone. We weren't on Waverley property, but the woods were brimming with the dead. I saw their gray faces, a pale contrast against the trunks of the hardwood trees. Their uniforms were dirty and torn, a darker shade of gray. Had they ever been butternut, they were long ago worn and muddied into the non-color of the shadow men.

One stepped in front of the car. "Take me home," he said. "My wife is dying. My boy needs me."

Reginald sensed something and slowed. "What is it?"

"The dead. They're all around, watching." I'd never seen such a gathering of ghastly wounds. The men stepping out of the trees were missing arms and legs, eyes and hands. They were gaunt and hopeless.

Reginald, though he was going slow, drove through the man who'd spoken to me. I knew these spirits meant me no harm, but they impacted me with such dark emotional needs. The vortex of need pulled at me, and even Reginald felt it. He gripped the steering wheel and drove with a single-minded purpose.

"I wonder if these are all soldiers that died because of Nora Bailey's betrayal." I tried to avoid their hungry gazes.

"If we find that painting, we need to destroy it and make sure that Nora's grave is marked. Do you think she would have betrayed Francis and the Confederacy if she hadn't been possessed?"

"I don't know. It's impossible to know. I don't think she would have betrayed Francis though."

"So much death from Olivia Norquist. She put the blame for everything on Nora, but it was always her."

"And she will do a lot to keep that from being known." I had no doubt that while I would have to fight the succubus, it was truly Olivia that I had to banish from Waverley. She had started this horror, and at the root of it was her black spirit. The truth about Nan and her death had been told. The child had been released. The entity I called Nora was still there, though. The place seethed with her evil. And there was also a killer on the premises. It might be a remnant of the specter, but I believed it was a flesh and blood killer. He, or she, had taken the life of Ashland Pratt and Fancy. And they'd set Royal Sheridan up to take the blame for one of the murders.

We turned into the long drive that led to Waverley. In the late afternoon light, muted by the storm, the house rose white and proud among the green treetops. There was movement on the fourth floor, a shadow passing across the windows. "She's up there," I said.

"Constance?"

"No, Nora. Or what passes for her now." I gripped Reginald's arm. "If I begin to act...aggressive or sexual, promise me that you'll restrain me. Knock me out. Tie me up. Do whatever it takes to get me out of there."

"I will." He pulled the car to the front and stopped. "I will, Raissa. But you have to promise me that you won't put yourself in danger. If this gets to be too much, you'll let me know and we'll leave."

"I promise." Lying wasn't easy for me, but it was necessary. If I told Reginald that I might not be able to save myself, he would insist we leave. Now I had a stake in this outcome. Nora Bailey had been trapped for decades. I was here with the necessary tools to free her. If I walked away, the horrible events at Waverley would continue. An unsuspecting sensitive, like Nora, could get caught in the demon's need for new flesh

—and I had no doubt that was what the entity craved. It would consume whomever it could for the physical pleasure of a body.

And there was Constance. It was likely she was gone, but if she wasn't, she could be in serious danger.

"The risk isn't just from a spirit, Raissa. There is a murderer here. Someone who can use a gun and a knife."

"Fancy was butchered. Do you think Sheriff Gaines will even investigate?"

Reginald looked up at the house. "No. He'll put everything into convicting Royal of Ashland Pratt's murder. Fancy has no one to stand up for her. Not much chance Sheriff Gaines will put effort into figuring out who killed a Negro woman."

He was correct. If the victim of a crime was Negro, it was often uninvestigated. I had all I could fight against at Waverley. Taking on the justice system was pointless. "We'll figure it out. It has to be the same killer." The minute I said it, I knew it was true. Even though the Pratt young man had been blasted in the chest with a shotgun and Fancy had been murdered with a knife, it had to be the same person.

"What did Fancy see that she shouldn't have?" Reginald asked.

I felt he was delaying leaving me alone at the house, but I was glad for the brief respite from what I had to confront. "I don't know. And Pratt? I feel he was lured here by Penelope Lott."

"But why? She gains nothing. She's gone. I'm not disagreeing with you, but we have to figure out her motive."

"What happens to Waverley if Royal is convicted?"

Reginald motioned me up to the front porch and out of the scorching sun. "I'm sure Anne will sell out and leave. She can't run the moonshine business and she can't keep this place up, especially with Fancy gone."

"But anyone could have bought Waverley before the Sheridans did. It was on the market for years."

Reginald pulled out his cigarettes, lit one for me, and handed it over. "I know. If someone wanted the property, why not just buy it from the state?"

"What other reason could there be?"

"Payback to the Sheridans for some past incident," I suggested. "Someone who wanted the property but the Sheridans got it. Another bootlegger who feels Royal is cutting into his territory. I'm going to find out no matter what it takes."

Behind us the front door creaked slowly open. I heard the rustle of silk petticoats and the odor of wisteria came to me. I felt my knees give.

"Dammit, Raissa, you are too hard-headed." Reginald gently grasped my arm, holding me upright. "We aren't going in that house. I mean it. We'll come back with a priest. You stay here on the porch and let me grab our things."

For once, I wasn't going to argue. I felt physically ill at the idea of entering the house. The wave of sickness swept over me with fury, much like the storm that had gathered to the south. It had finally begun to move and a big thunderhead was approaching. Being trapped in Waverley with lightning popping outside was not something I wanted to happen.

"Hurry, please," I called to Reginald as he disappeared into the house.

I heard his footsteps going up the stairs, and I took a draw on the cigarette he'd left in my hand. It made me cough, but that was almost a pleasure since it was normal. There were so few normal things around me now.

I tossed the cigarette and paced the front porch. What was

keeping Reginald? Neither of us had much luggage. We only needed clothes for the next day. I went to the open door. "Reginald!" I called through the screen. "Do you need help?"

The clock in the front parlor struck twelve times, though it was afternoon. The sound of piano music drifted to me, a sad etude that ended as abruptly as it began.

"Reginald!" The stress was clear in my voice. "Reginald!"

Something had happened to him. He'd gone into the house and it had swallowed him whole. I had no choice. I pulled open the screened door to step inside, but before I could put a foot in, the heavy front door slammed with enough force to make me jump back with a cry.

"Stay out." The voice was neither male nor female.

Behind me, lightning flashed, followed by righteous thunder that shook the floorboards.

"Stay out!" The voice was like a gale wind, blasting me backward from the door.

"Reginald!" I called out for him, terrified for what might be happening to him.

"Raissa!" His voice sounded far, far away. Why had I ever let him go into the house alone? I'd assumed, wrongly, that as a male he was safe. But I thought of Newly, who had been almost catatonic. And Anne, and how the house pulled and drained her. No one was safe at Waverley. At the moment, though, Reginald was in grave danger.

Battling the force of the wind, I made it back to the door and pushed hard to open it. As suddenly as the wind began, it stopped and I stumbled into the house, almost losing my balance. The entity was toying with me. I heard the softest echo of a feminine laugh.

"Reginald!" But he didn't answer me.

I rushed up the stairs to his bedroom and found his suitcase packed by the door. My own suitcase was open on my bed, my belongings jumbled inside. This was where he'd been attacked. But what had happened to him?

I clutched the necklace of iron bits I wore and went back to the landing. Looking up to the fourth floor, I saw movement. Below me, in the rotunda, a harsh wind gusted. The front door slammed again, and as the storm drew closer, the house fell into a twilight dimness.

Where had Olivia conjured up this demon? I presumed it was the fourth floor, where perhaps I might find the painting of Nora Bailey, a woman likely maligned for fifty years. I wondered if she truly was a spy, or if her wanton behavior had simply given rise to ugly rumors.

I eased up the stairs holding firmly to the bannister. Olivia liked to push people to their deaths, and I wouldn't be a willing victim. I didn't know if she had the power to do that as a spirit, but I didn't want to risk a fall of over forty feet. I ignored the third floor and kept climbing.

My feet felt leaden, as if I couldn't lift them to the next step. She was sapping my will, as Madam had warmed me. Reginald wasn't the only one in danger. I forced myself forward. The sound of movement above me pushed me on. Someone was there. Reginald? Constance? Nora? Or something much worse? Dragging my legs, I fought against my own fear. I might be able to free Nora if I could find the painting, but how would I rid Waverley of the demonic spirit? I'd entered the house rashly, without a plan. If I failed, both Reginald and I would be lost, and how many others?

Olivia had summoned the demon through hoodoo. I had to figure out how to undo that summons and cast the demon out. First I had to find Reginald. At last I made it to the top of the stairs. The door to the storage room where I'd found Bjorn

Norquist's journals was open. I went there, fighting for each step. Dim light poured in through a window, but it was enough to see that a whirlwind had hit the room. Papers and memorabilia were scattered about the floor. The old leather trunk I'd admired was upended. Someone had been looking for something.

A dark stain on the floor was the first warning that someone had been hurt. I knelt and touched it, my fingers coming back sticky with blood. Beside the blood pool was a cameo that Constance wore each day. "Oh, no." The words slipped out. Three feet from the blood was a fireplace poker that had fallen from a set that had been shoved up against a hassock. The bellows were missing one arm, and the broom bristles had been burned away. I wondered if Constance had been struck with the poker. Why was she even in this room? Where had she gone?

I investigated the corners of the room, making sure Constance wasn't lying unconscious behind the furniture.

The room was empty. If I had plenty of time, I'd go through the papers, hoping to find something that I could use against the demon. That luxury wasn't open to me. My partner and Constance were missing. I looked about the room, checking behind old trunks and clothing covered in sheets, hoping to find the portrait of Nora Bailey. Luck wasn't with me. The painting wasn't in that room.

The sound of something dragging made me hold perfectly still. Sweat accumulated at my waist and slipped down my body, leaving a chill in its wake. The sweet scent of wisteria surrounded me, and I knew the demon was once again using the image of Nora Bailey. That was her scent.

I saw her in the doorway, as physical as if she were alive and breathing.

"Reginald!" she said, perfectly mocking my voice. "Oh, Reginald."

"Where is he?" I stood tall, even though I was shaking with fear.

"He's with me now, though he isn't really my taste, if you understand."

"Leave him alone." I stepped toward her. The slightest movement required all of my concentration.

"Or what?" she asked, then laughed. "You'll stomp your foot and demand that I obey you?"

I remembered what Madam said about the cast iron poker and I picked it up. "I'm going to send you back to the hell you came from." I was afraid, but I meant to fight.

"Really?" she almost purred. She stretched, a feline movement that she enjoyed. "I'm going to take you, Raissa, and use you in ways you can't imagine. Just breathe me in. I'll fill all those lonely, empty places inside you. You'll never be alone again."

Despite my knowing that she was a liar, I found her words seductive.

"All of those memories of Alex, the moments you shared, the intimacy that bonded you to him. All of those I can return to you. You can live in that lost time, Raissa. Never alone, always with Alex."

The scent of wisteria grew stronger, and she moved closer to me, a wraith of death in a beautiful antebellum gown, her cheeks pink with life force. Even though I knew this was an illusion, that the true spirit I confronted was dark and ugly, I was drawn to Nora's tender voice and kind face.

"I only want to help you, Raissa. Why would you want to stay so alone? Remember when you were wrapped in your parents' love? Feel it, the safety, the belonging. Let it flow over you. Remember the way you'd play in the rays of sunshine that came through the window while your mother made dinner in the kitchen. You had your fancy package of eight crayons, and you'd color. You'd hear your father's steps on the porch, and you'd jump up and run to him. He'd pick you up in his arms and hold you against his shirt that smelled of old books and ink. He'd kiss your head and brush your hair from your eyes with his hand. And you would see the love in his eyes. Wouldn't it be wonderful to feel that again? All the best moments of the past and none of the pain."

How did she know these specific memories that were mine and mine alone? I could smell the roast my mother cooked, a Thursday night tradition in our house. My blue crayon moved across the page, coloring within the lines I'd drawn for a butterfly, the anticipation of a hot supper fueling my hunger.

"Raissa, let me in." Nora held out her arms to me and spoke to me in the soft, cultured tones of a belle, a woman of good family and background and impeccable manners. I wanted nothing more than to melt into her embrace.

She came toward me, and the scent of wisteria grew stronger, so dense and rich that it was almost suffocating. My body urged me to run, to get away, but the compulsion to fall into her embrace was stronger. This was how she would possess me. This was what had happened to Nora Bailey. The entity would find a way to completely push me out of my body. She'd trapped Nora in a painting. She'd do the same to me.

"Don't be afraid." Her voice soothed me as she came even closer. She reached out a hand and touched my arm. I felt her hot need, the desire to have my very flesh. I drew back.

She laughed softly. "There's no escape, Raissa. I want to make it easy, but easy or hard, I will have you."

My only thought was to flee, but I couldn't move. She held

me, suspended in time and place. I lost feeling in my limbs, and I understood that I'd miscalculated by coming into the house for any reason.

Nora's image began to fall away, like flesh falling from a rotted corpse. Chunks dropped from her face, her arms, and torso. The dress she wore became the tatters of the grave, molded and decayed. All loveliness was gone, and what stood before me was the corpse, fresh from a grave. It too began to break down. The thing that was left was worse than I'd imagined. Elements of the feminine could be seen in its countenance, but the hollowed eyes burned with need. A few tufts of hair sprouted in ungainly fashion for its head. Its body was crooked and warped. It had come straight from hell, a demonic spirit with one goal, to feed off men. It required female flesh to complete the deed, and that would be my fate. I would be trapped there with her while she drew the life force from men until she left them dead or deranged.

A bolt of lightning struck a tree in the back yard, and the house rattled from the power of the blast. Ozone pushed out the wisteria smell, and for a second I was free of her.

"Reginald!" I screamed his name. He might not be able to help me, but he could knock me out. I didn't think she could possess me if I was unconscious. I looked at the closest object, which was the door frame. I ran at it full tilt and hit it hard. The blow stunned me and I fell to my knees. I literally saw stars, but I was still conscious. I slammed my head into the doorframe again, as hard as I could.

"No!" Nora screamed in rage.

I let go of consciousness and drifted into a black void.

CHAPTER 29

I came to consciousness when cold water splashed on my face. Sputtering, I sat up in the front yard of Waverley House with Reginald holding me loosely in his arms.

"That's quite a goose egg on your head. Two of them." He put a cold cloth on my forehead, which throbbed with true violence. I felt like my skull might explode at any minute.

"Raissa, who hurt you?" Reginald asked. "Are you okay?"

"I knocked myself out. She was going to take me over." The events prior to my spectacular head smacking came back to me. "Where were you? I thought she'd hurt you too."

"I was in Constance's room trying to see if she'd packed her things. The door to the sitting room slammed shut and I couldn't get it open. I heard you on the fourth floor. Or I should say I heard the commotion. When I finally got the door open, you were unconscious. I carried you out."

"She won't give up."

He eased me to a sitting position. "No, she won't. And that's why we're leaving. Forget your things. We'll buy some clothes in West Point in the morning."

I looked down at my dress, covered in dust and cobwebs and sweat. No respectable hotel would let us take a room. We'd have to impose on the Ledbetters to allow us to clean up at their home before we even attempted to go to a hotel. I laughed softly.

"You find humor?" Reginald asked.

"I was thinking how we had to clean up before we'd be able to take a room. After what we've been through, I'm worried about the proprieties of a hotel."

"It's the little guidelines that keep us from running off the rails, Raissa. I learned that in those years after I ran away from the orphanage. Total freedom is more of a prison than you'd think. Yes, we'll clean up first. We'll get some new clothes, and we'll have dinner at a nice café. If I had more grit, I'd rush in the door and grab a bottle of whiskey to take with us since I doubt West Point will flout the prohibition laws.

"I've never wanted a drink more, but not bad enough to go in that house. I found some blood and Constance's cameo, but no sign of her in the house."

"We'll come back with help. I won't let you go back in there, and I don't even want to be on the grounds. The Sheridan's car is gone. I'm pretty sure Constance left under her own steam."

"If the car is gone, she must have." The relief was immense.

"Let's go. It'll be dark soon and I want to be long gone from here."

We climbed into the car and Reginald turned the vehicle around, giving me a good view of the house. She was there, at the window on the second floor, the window of my room. She watched, completely in control. There was no air of concern coming from her. She was waiting. She knew I'd have to return.

I wondered if it was possible to protect myself.

THE SPECTER OF SEDUCTION

Reginald tore down the driveway like a bat out of hell. I grasped the car seat and closed my eyes. The quicker we left Waverley, the better. I was completely unprepared when Reginald slammed on the brakes. Only his arm, thrown out to stop me, kept me from smacking hard into the dash or windshield. But I had never been gladder to see a near collision in my life.

When the car completely stopped, I threw open the door and jumped out. "Uncle Brett! Isabelle! You came."

"Of course, Raissa. My dear, you're terribly washed out. And...dirty." Uncle Brett looked at Reginald. "You're in the same condition. Are you both okay?"

"Now I am." The back doors of the touring car opened and a short woman stepped out.

"Madam!" I ran to her and hugged her close to me. "Thank God you came."

Another man stepped out of the back of the car. A priest.

"I couldn't abandon you, dear. And this is Father McNeill. He accompanied me on the train from New Orleans."

"Yes, we joined up in Jackson and made that part of the journey together," Uncle Brett said.

"We've been worried sick." Isabelle put a gentle hand on my shoulder. "What are you doing here? We thought you'd be in town, but Royal Sheridan told us you wouldn't give up, that you'd be here."

"We were leaving." Reginald sounded a little sheepish.

"We'd come to look for Constance and get our things." I tried to explain, but I sounded like a fool even to myself. "We've had to leave without either."

"Where's the governess?" Uncle Brett looked around as if she might pop out of the woods. "She isn't in West Point. Or she isn't checked into the hotel."

His words reignited my worry, but I did my best to hide it.

"Are you sure Constance isn't in town? What about the Sheridan's car?"

Uncle Brett shook his head. "Let's get back to the hotel. We have much to do. Royal's trial is set for next Monday."

"Has the witness, Penelope Lott, shown up?"

Uncle Brett shook his head. "I don't know, but standing here in the woods isn't getting us anywhere." He looked around and I realized he was nervous. "Let's get out of here."

I caught the scent of wisteria, suffocatingly strong. The tree tops whipped in a sudden wind, and the rain came down in such a sheet that I couldn't see a foot in front of me.

"Get in the car!" Uncle Brett yelled. "Hurry."

In the heavy rain, I couldn't see the car. I stumbled backward and stepped in a mud puddle that sucked the shoe off my foot. Leaning down to find it in the pool of water that had accumulated so quickly, I didn't see who came up behind me. A moment later, I was pushed down and was being dragged into the woods.

"Raissa!"

I heard Reginald, Uncle Brett, and Isabelle calling my name. They sounded far, far away. The rain pelted me with such fierceness that it cut through my clothing, stinging my skin. The sky punished me. I rolled under the low-hanging limbs of a bush that gave some relief, and I managed to catch my breath.

"I've come for you, Raissa. It's too late for help now."

She was there, in her Nora disguise. "I won't do it. I'll drown myself in the mud puddle."

"It's not so easy to die."

She was righter about that than I wanted to admit. The rain had slacked up, strangling down to a steady downpour, and

I pushed myself to a sitting position. I'd crawl back to the car. It could only be a few yards away.

"Raissa!" I heard the fear in Uncle Brett's voice, and he sounded a distance away.

"Here!" But the word came out as a whisper. I looked around, puzzled. Even though it was still raining, I could see. I was in a clearing of trees. There was no sign of the driveway or the two vehicles. No sign of my uncle or Isabelle or Madam. They'd vanished.

I stood, my legs shaky. Leaning against a tree trunk, I tried to get my bearings, but I had no clue which direction was north or south. The woods around Waverley were thick and dense and difficult to travel, and I was in the middle of them. Only I wasn't alone.

Wisteria, thick and cloying. She'd isolated me and now she meant to make her move. I hurled myself forward, away from her.

"Don't run," she said.

My legs gave way and I fell back in the mud. I was going to die. Not in the literal sense of the word, but in a much worse way. The essence of who I was would be stuffed down into a tiny corner of my mind or heart or wherever the soul resided. I'd be stuck there, watching her use my body for her own evil purposes until she found a place to ditch my soul, a repository where I would be a prisoner. This was going to happen, and I couldn't stop it. But I would never quit fighting.

She came at me with the vengeance of a swarm of black wasps. I felt her at my nose and mouth, forcing and pushing her way in. It was over in a matter of moments. I rose from the mud, aware of the wet clothes clinging to my body. I could feel my own flesh—but from her perspective. My hands sculpted my curves, learning them, pleased with the firmness I felt.

"Raissa!" Reginald called.

The rain had almost stopped, and I heard him thrashing through the underbrush.

"Raissa!"

"Here!" I was surprised that my voice sounded normal, not like the honey-silk tones of Nora Bailey. "Reginald, here!" He came even though I didn't want him to. I knew she would hurt him. She would make me hurt him.

"Where's Uncle Brett?" She spoke and I wanted to tear my own throat out. She sounded exactly like me, and her intention was to learn where every single person was so she could plot her moves.

"He and Isabelle are in the house. We have to find that portrait, Raissa. Quickly. Come with me." He grasped my arm, but my body resisted.

The rain had cooled the temperatures, and the gathering night slipped around the woods leaving only a dim path to follow.

"Come on." He tightened his grip and tugged.

I wanted to tell him to run, to run fast and far away, to leave me to whatever fate was before me because there was nothing he or Uncle Brett could do. I tried to tell him this but all that came out was a guttural whisper.

"What's wrong with you?" He stared into my eyes.

I touched his face, running my fingers across his skin in a slow tease. "I can make you appreciate the things a woman can do." I struck a provocative pose. "Like what you see?"

No matter how I struggled against Nora, I had no control. I saw Reginald's shock, his unconscious pulling back. I moved into him, putting my arms around his neck and kissing him with searing passion. "I want you, Reginald. I have for a long, long time."

He wrapped his arms around me and drew me against him in an unexpected move. His arm supported my back as he squeezed me tighter and tighter. "Where's the painting?" he demanded, his lips against my neck, his mustache tickling the tender skin.

Reginald knew! He understood what was happening to me. His words galvanized the shred of will I had left. If she could share this body with me, I could also possibly share her memories. I had to try.

I pushed back my fear and sense of suffocation and went into her memories. The tiny bits left of Nora involved Francis Norquist, a handsome man. He adored her, and she was deeply in love with him. Longing, keening sadness, shame, horror—I felt it all. But I had to go deeper. Nora was window dressing. At the crux of the horror I faced was the demon.

Even though Reginald's arms held me in a terrible grip, he sounded far, far away. He was having a coughing fit. Wisteria's sweet scent gave way to a more sulphuric odor, and I knew the cloying sweet smell of what was choking him. I had to be quick. His hold on my physical body was the only anchor I had. If he let loose, I would be lost forever. I pushed deeper into the entity, down into the blackness of past events. Her craven lust, her machinations to satisfy her insatiable desires. She was a pit of dark impulses. And she hated the Norquist girls. She was inflamed by their privilege, their beauty, but most of all she hated Nora Bailey.

Images and emotions whirled around me, leaving me dizzy and weak, but I had to grasp one and hold on. It was the painting of Nora I sought, and at last I had it, hanging on the wall beside the magnificent spiral of the staircase. I was close enough to touch it, and I reached out. Nora's flesh was indeed warm. Beneath the oil, I felt her struggling for escape. She was there, trapped in the painting by some curse or trick. But where was the painting?

I nudged the memory forward, past the crying and screaming as Nora was dragged up the stairs to the second-floor balcony by men hiding behind hoods. I could smell the liquor that came off them in waves. They went right past the painting and up, up, up with Nora struggling and screaming for help. Bjorn and Marketta rushed to the foot of the staircase, and he pled with the men not to hang her. Marketta wept against his chest. The daughters had hidden in a room on the fourth floor. Francis was tied to a tree in the front yard with his two brothers. The mob ruled and it would have a hanging.

I didn't intend to leave the painting, but I found myself on the balcony with a struggling Nora. She fought to prevent the noose from being lowered over her head and tightened around her slender throat. The rope was tossed over the limb of a big tree. Before I could fully grasp the scene, Nora was picked up by the men and hurled off the balcony. Her neck snapped when the slack was gone, and she swung back and forth, her feet kicking briefly.

Francis, fighting against the ropes that held him, uttered one lone cry.

Olivia stepped out onto the front porch. "Get her lover, the other spy. Calvert Marcus! Hang him!"

"Get the doctor! Get Marcus! Get the spy!" The men tied off the rope to the banister and hurried down the stairs. Five minutes later a posse rode out. I knew what would happen. In half an hour they'd return with the doctor, his hands tied behind his back, mounted on a horse. They'd put the noose around his neck, as they did for Nora, and they'd slap the horse's rump and send it running. The doctor, the man that Olivia Norquist loved, had killed her own daughter for, would hang in her front yard. I didn't have to watch to know how this would play out.

A commotion on the lawn told me Bjorn had freed Francis. He ran to Nora's body and tried to hold her up. She was dead; there was nothing he could do to save her. But he would take her body down and hide the corpse in the back yard where a young Amos Plackett would watch from behind dense cover. This was when Nora's painting disappeared. I had to get down the stairs, to force that memory up from the darkness, to see where Olivia took the painting.

My fingers twisted in Reginald's dark hair, pulling hard, forcing his neck back. Even though I fought against the entity's strength, I couldn't stop myself. Reginald's response was to tighten his grip so that my ribs pressed hard into my lungs. Another bit of pressure and the bones would snap. He knew it, but he had no option. This was a fight for my soul, and Reginald would not abandon me to the darkness. That was my ray of light.

"Your uncle is at Waverley, looking for the painting. Isabelle too. Fight for your life, Raissa. Find the painting."

The staircase! I saw it and the painting. I saw Olivia pulling it off the wall, knowing what truth it contained and determined that no one would ever free Nora Bailey. She slipped out the backdoor and into the night. Instead of moving in the direction where Francis was hiding Nora's body, she went right, past the kitchen, past the woodshed, and deeper into the woods. She put the painting on the ground, brushed back leaves and limbs, and opened the double doors of an old root cellar. Trusting to the darkness, she dropped the painting into the cellar and then shut the doors, re-covering the area with debris.

"Raissa, find the painting," Reginald prompted.

The entity told me to sink my teeth into Reginald's throat, to bite through the jugular. I opened my mouth, his tender neck only an inch from my teeth. I didn't want to obey, but my body responded to the urging of the demon. My teeth weren't sharp enough. I would have to bite and tear, bite and tear.

"Root cellar," I managed to blurt out. "Behind wood shed."

Reginald thrust me away from him and his right fist punched me hard on the jaw. My head snapped backward and there was nothing else.

"A LITTLE MORE ETHER."

I recognized the man's voice. It was someone I should want to be with. But I was way down in a deep, dark place, and I knew he couldn't help me.

"Where is the root cellar?"

It was my uncle Brett who asked. He held a white cloth in his hand. I was tied to a tree. Not far away was Waverley, a huge white ghost in the night. Reginald stood a short distance away. I could hear Isabelle sobbing, though I couldn't see her.

"Do you have to do this?" Isabelle asked Uncle Brett.

"There's no other choice, unless you want Reginald to slug her again. She has to stay unconscious. That thing is burrowing into her. I can only hope that while she's not aware, it can't do damage."

"The painting must be found. Now." Madam Petalungro stepped into my range of vision. She was sweating in the intolerable heat. I knew instinctively that she was dangerous. My body hissed at her. She shook her head, a mist of tears gathering in her eyes.

"Make her talk quickly," Madam said. "She's strong, but no one can hold up for long to this kind of thing."

A priest stepped toward me and hurled water at me. The burning sensation weakened the demon's hold on me, and I gasped out, "Behind the wood shed. Covered in leaves."

Before I could say anything else, Uncle Brett forced the cloth to my nose and mouth. A soft, warm blackness claimed me yet again.

IT WAS TOTALLY DARK when I came back to consciousness. I recognized the back of Waverley. We weren't far from the kitchen and wood shed. Reginald and Uncle Brett had built an enormous bonfire of fallen limbs and leaves. The portrait of Nora Bailey was atop the fire. They'd found it!

"She's awake," Madam Petalungro said. "Reginald and I are ready. I know the incantation that Olivia used to call the demon to her. I can send her back to the hell she came from."

"Light it up," Uncle Brett said. Reginald stepped out from behind a tree with a wick of paper and his cigarette lighter. They'd obviously seeded the bonfire with some kind of fuel, because when he threw the lighted wick on it, the flames roared up twenty feet in the air. The painting was instantly consumed.

As the oil began to heat and bubble, I felt pressure in my head and heart. She meant to kill me rather than leave me. I looked at Reginald, and he read my distress.

"Madam! Hurry. Raissa can't last long against it."

Madame squatted down in front of me, an older woman stressing her aching joints, as she used a sharp stick to draw in the dirt as she mumbled words that seemed a mixture of Latin and the lovely Creole of New Orleans. As the flames rose higher, her voice increased in power.

The priest stood over her, reciting in Latin from a book.

His voice was strong, but his face held panic. He'd not bargained for this hellish scene, but he was either well paid or a true believer. He continued chanting, holding his rosary and making the sign of the cross. The pressure in my chest and head increased, and I felt the blood pulsing behind my eyeballs. I wanted to tell Uncle Brett how much I loved him. And Reginald that he had more talents than he ever imagined.

I wanted—

Before I could react, Madame grabbed my hand and sliced across my palm with a knife. Holding my wrist, she forced the blood to drip into the symbol she'd drawn in the sand. She stood up, over me, chanting fiercely. I was paralyzed and couldn't fight or even attempt to crawl away. I fell back, my eyes finding the bright lights of the Milky Way far above me in an inky sky. I would be there soon, away from the pain. Away from the fear. I could go, and I would not remain earthbound for any reason. At least I wouldn't be trapped like Nora had been.

"Hang on." The voice was soft and sweet, and the scent of wisteria was the sweetest thing I'd ever smelled. She came to me, hovering just above the ground. "Don't quit. She's not strong enough to take you."

It was a nice sentiment, but not one I believed. I tried to smile, but I was too tired. I wanted only to let go and ease up to the stars.

"Raissa, you must not let go. You've defeated her." I felt the brush of her hand across my face. She was warm and soft and tender. "You've defeated her and freed me. Francis is waiting. And Nan. She's just there, beyond the trees. And Alex. Your Alex."

I tried to sit up, and suddenly Reginald was beside me,

lifting me into his arms. "Raissa, come on. Come back to us. You can't leave us. We need you."

Uncle Brett chaffed my hands. "You can't leave your uncle alone," he said, rubbing warmth back into me.

"Stand back," Madam said, and she put the rim of a glass to my lips. The white heat of good whiskey exploded in my mouth and I coughed and dragged in a lungful of air.

"Here, here!" Uncle Brett said. "You know your business, Madam. Thank you. Give the girl another swig of that whiskey. It'll bring her right around. Good whiskey cures a lot and one thing about Royal Sheridan, he knows how to make good whiskey."

As Reginald helped me sit up, I realized that the pressure was gone from my body. My arms and legs had returned to my command. The entity was gone. Madam had cast it out. "Where is it?" I asked.

She knew what I meant. "Back in hell, where it can rot."

"Nora Bailey has been freed. She's gone with Nan where she belongs."

"And you are here with us, where you belong," Reginald said. He leaned close to whisper, "Don't ever try to seduce me again."

The shock of his words made me push away and sit up. "Trust me, that wasn't my idea."

"I know." He rumpled my hair. "But it's great ammunition, isn't it?"

I looked around at my friends and family gathered around a bonfire where a painting worth thousands of dollars burned to ash. It was good to be alive. Good to be with those I loved. Good that Nora had been freed and her story could be told.

"Let's go inside," Uncle Brett said. "Our work here is done."

Reginald bent to pull me to my feet, and the priest stepped in front of me just as the sound of a gun blast reverberated through the night. The priest stumbled and fell to the ground, his thigh opened to the bone by the shotgun blast.

We hit the dirt, but not before I saw the woman on the back porch of Waverley holding the shotgun.

CHAPTER 30

Reginald and Uncle Brett dragged the priest behind the bonfire and made a tourniquet to stop the flow of blood from his leg. From what I could see, the spray of shotgun pellets had torn into his thigh. Had he not stepped in front of me, I would be dead, because I had been sitting. The blast would have splattered my head.

Constance had tried to kill me.

I crawled behind the bonfire with the men, making sure Madam had taken refuge behind a tree. She was in the safest position of all if Constance tried again.

"That's Constance," Reginald said. "What the hell is wrong with her? Do you think she's possessed?"

So many different things suddenly made sense. "No. I think she killed Ashland Pratt and Fancy. And she means to kill us if she can."

"Why?" Reginald released the tourniquet for a moment and the priest cried out with pain as he retightened the ligature. "Why would she want to harm those people or us?"

"It's Waverley. She wants Waverley."

"She could have bought it." Reginald was stressed and furious.

"Once the Sheridans lose it, she can get it for a pittance. No one will want a partially renovated mansion where several murders have been committed by a bootlegger. The events here will drive the price so far down she can buy it for a song."

"She killed a young man and Fancy for a financial advantage?" Uncle Brett asked. "If that's the reasoning, she should be flogged."

"And to frame Royal Sheridan." I motioned Madam to come to me. "Can you hold the tourniquet? I need Reginald."

She looked into my eyes, the flames of the fire dancing in her own. "Be careful. She isn't possessed, but that doesn't mean she isn't evil."

"I understand." I turned to Reginald and whispered because I knew Uncle Brett would try to stop me. "Let's go." I tugged at his sleeve. He gave the tourniquet to Madam and Isabelle and when Uncle Brett was distracted, we slipped away from the fire and behind the wood shed.

"We have to stop her." My body was still weak. The entity hadn't possessed me long, but it would take time for me to probe the damage left behind. I'd been violated in a most intimate way. "Reginald." I made him look at me. "I'm so sorry."

"What are you going on about?" He smiled that rakish, dare-devil smile. "Apologize if I get shot. Otherwise, I don't want to hear any more apologies. I'm just glad Brett thought to bring Madam. She saved your life."

"She had some help." I stood on tiptoe and kissed his cheek. "Thank you."

"It was my pleasure to coldcock you." He nudged my arm. "Let's get Constance and that gun. We need to get the priest to a doctor, and she's not going to let us get into the cars if she can stop us."

"Do you have a plan?"

"As a matter of fact, I do. We have to get her out of the house and into the woods, and I think I know how."

"How?" I asked.

"I need for you to hit her. Hard. I'll get her to chase me. You whack her with something. I know you can do it."

"You're going to be bait?" I was a lot more worried about Reginald than I was my ability to sack a woman who'd tried to shoot me. I definitely could whack her good.

"I'll be fine. It's dark. She's only got two shells in the gun and I expect she's not great at re-loading. She won't fire unless she has a clear shot."

It was too much of a gamble. "If we can get in the car, just drive to town for the sheriff."

"And whoever is left here could die. No. My plan is better."

Precious time was wasting. The priest was injured, and while it wasn't a fatal wound, infection or blood loss could easily kill him. "Okay."

We searched the ground until I found a stout limb. We slipped to the front of the house and I stationed myself on the side of the main path that led to the stables. Reginald positioned himself beside me.

"C-c-c-constance!" He called to her, sounding remarkably like Newly. "Please come to me."

Movement on the second-floor balcony told me she'd heard. The curtains moved back and then the door opened and she stepped out. "Come in here, Newly."

"I l-l-love you. Please. I need help. I'm hurt."

She hesitated. "Come out onto the lawn."

"I c-c-can't. I'm bleeding."

She disappeared. I wondered if she'd ever cared for Newly and if Reginald's clever trick would work on her. She wasn't a sentimental woman.

The front door opened and she stepped onto the porch. "I know what happened between you and Elodie. I forgive you. And her. It wasn't your fault."

I frowned at Reginald. Elodie? Who was that? He shook his head.

"I'm s-s-so sorry."

"Meet me halfway."

"I'm h-h-hurt. There's blood. So much blood." He imitated Newly's slight stutter and let his voice fade.

"Newly!" She came down the steps. "Dammit. Newly!"

We hid in the brush, hardly daring to breath. Reginald moved away from me, deeper into the woods. "Help me!"

"If you're in cahoots with those private investigators, I'll kill you." She opened the shotgun, checked her shells, and snapped the breech shut. Reginald was wrong. She was proficient in the use of the weapon.

"C-c-constance. I love you." He was thirty yards into the woods and his voice sounded terribly weak.

Constance marched across the lawn, the shotgun held casually, but in an instant she could lift it and fire.

"B-b-baby. I'm not gonna make it." Reginald played it to the hilt.

She hesitated on the edge of the woods, but then stepped onto the path and walked directly toward Reginald, who had laid down in the path with his back to her, curled into a fetal position. "I see you."

The moment she passed me, I rose from the bushes and brought the limb in a wide swing that connected with her skull. There was a snap, either the limb or bone, and she went down to her knees and over. I pulled the gun from her grasp. I thought I had killed her.

Reginald was at my side, taking her pulse. "She's alive, but out cold. Good job, Raissa." He unhooked his suspenders and tied her hands behind her back and her feet together. "That will hold her."

"Is she really alive?" She looked dead.

"She is. Now let's get those cars and get to town."

"You're going to leave her here?"

"Damn straight, buckaroo. We'll send the sheriff for her. There's room in your uncle's rental car for all of us, but not for her. And to be honest, I don't really care. She tried to kill you."

Constance wasn't worth an argument. "I'll get the car started and pull around back. You help Madam and Uncle Brett load the priest. I think Isabelle is in shock."

"Go." He sent me on my way.

Once I hit the clear lawn, I sprinted. The cars had been parked haphazard in the front, and I had the key to the car Reginald and I had rented. I started the car and drove back to the bonfire. Uncle Brett's relief made me even more worried as we loaded the priest into the back seat.

"The bone is shattered," Uncle Brett whispered. "He needs a surgeon. A good one. If we were in Mobile, I'd know who to call."

"If we get him to town, we can worry about the rest from there. Constance is unconscious in the woods. I hit her with a limb."

He patted my back. "That's my girl. Isabelle, let's go."

"I never want to come back here," she said as she got in the front seat beside Uncle Brett. I assisted Madam into the back seat. "Take this car, Uncle Brett. Drive to the hospital in West

Point. Reginald and I will load up Constance in your car and pick up Newly and meet you at the hotel."

"Yes." He didn't even argue but gave me the key to his car. He hit the gas and sped around the house, the tires spewing mud after the recent rain.

I headed to the house. I'd collect Reginald and Constance, but first I'd collect our things. Like Isabelle, I'd had enough of the mansion. I would be happy never to return. I stopped in the rotunda and looked up. Moonlight filtered down from the fourth floor. It was a magnificent house. I hoped the Sheridans could find peace. Soon Royal would be freed to return to Waverley.

I went to the parlor and poured two drinks. We could sip them as we drove. I needed the strength, and some food. I couldn't remember the last time I'd eaten. As I passed the piano, I brushed the ivories with my hand. I remembered play-ing. I'd been quite accomplished—when I had Nora's ability. That was all going to take some sorting to figure out.

I felt the barrel of the gun against my spine, and I froze. There was no one else in the house. Constance and Reginald were in the woods. Uncle Brett, Isabelle, Madam, and the priest had gone to town. Newly was at Coralee's. There was no one here. Except for the person who had a gun barrel pressed into my back.

"Where's my mother?" It was a young woman who spoke.

I closed my eyes briefly. I'd missed the most important part. I'd conquered Nora and the entity and captured Constance. But I'd forgotten the girl. Elodie or Penelope or whatever her real name was. She was the one who'd made certain Ashland Pratt was on the Waverley property. The bait.

"Hello, Penelope," I said, without turning around. "We've been looking for you."

"I'll bet you have. Where's my mother?"

"Unconscious in the woods. I hit her hard with a big limb. I hope I didn't really hurt her."

The barrel punched in my back with brutal force. "If she's hurt, you're going to die."

"I guess you'll have to go look."

She brought the butt of the gun against my cheekbone with quick and efficient force. The skin split and blood flowed down my face. The pain was intense. I'd learned something about her. She wasn't rattled easily, and she would kill me. Would likely enjoy killing me.

"Why?" I asked her. "Why would you lure a young man to his death? What's in it for you?"

She leaned closer. "This is my family home, and soon, it will legally belong to us."

At first I didn't get it, but realization came swiftly. "You're an heir of the Norquist family."

"Well, aren't you the cat's meow?" she asked sarcastically. "You finally understand. You shouldn't have come here. Mama had it all worked out. The Sheridans were at their wits' ends. Royal's reputation was ruined with the sheriff. He was a hothead, a man who shot at young students. And then he killed the most influential man in town's precious son."

"You brought Ashland here so he could be killed. You murdered him, didn't you? You're the one who shot him."

"He needed to die. What a privileged daisy he was. He used girls, ruined them, then couldn't be found. You have no idea. He thought he was such a Valentino. Pitiful. His whole life, his daddy bought him out of everything. He never suspected I was setting him up. He was such an easy mark."

I wanted to turn around and look at her, because I couldn't believe the ruthlessness she espoused. I didn't turn. I was afraid she'd pull the trigger. "What are you going to do now? Royal and Anne will return to Waverley. Like it or not, Reginald and I did our jobs. The entity is gone. Nan is gone. There's nothing to interfere with their lives."

"Except me and my mother and a murder charge that carries the death penalty. That's a lot to bargain with."

"So take Waverley. I'm sure once Royal and Anne know the score, they'll walk away."

She laughed. "Right. And the sky will be green tomorrow. You don't have the gift of making applesauce taste like steak."

"What are you going to do?" I asked. "My uncle has left here. He'll bring the law back. Even if you kill me, what will you gain?"

She pressed the gun into my spine. "Satisfaction. You and your handsome fella. If you hadn't come here, this would all be over. The house would be ours."

All of these years, Constance and her daughter had wanted the place. Like trees planted in bad soil, they'd spent their lives growing into twisted, awful people, wanting something that was far out of their reach. "Who is your grandmother? Olivia, Marguerite, or Helene?"

"Olivia. My grandmother died in exile from her home, never allowed to return to the place her father had built, meaning for her to have it, to raise her children in it, to continue the Norquist line. Nora Bailey stole the man she loved. Nora seduced him, and in one act, she destroyed my grandmother's dreams and great-uncle Francis's heart."

"Nora Bailey was possessed by a demon your grandmother called forth. Your grandmother set up an innocent woman to be hanged."

"So says you." She pushed the gun harder into me. "Let's go

outside. I'm not in the mood to clean up blood. Take me to my mother."

I wondered where Reginald might be, but I didn't call out for him. She would pull the trigger. I didn't doubt it. At her prodding, still holding the two glasses of whiskey, I walked out the front door and onto the porch. The night was filled with the sound of insects and birds. It took all of my restraint not to call for Reginald. "Your mother is in the woods, tied up. And gagged." The last part was a lie, but she'd wonder why Constance didn't answer her if she called. What would she do when she realized how hard I'd struck Constance?

"Show me."

Once she had her mother, she'd kill me. I walked slowly, trying to think of an out. "You could leave. You and Constance. You could make a run for it. Take the Sheridans' car and start a new life."

"Shut up."

I had to reach her some way. "I'll take the blame for the Pratt boy. I swear it. I'll write it down in a statement that you can give to the law. You and Constance can start clean."

"Shut up." She smacked the gun butt into my skull. Not enough to stun me, but it hurt. "I mean it. Shut up." She pushed me toward the path that led to the stables. "Move or I'll drop you here."

There was no option but to walk forward. We entered the woods, surrounded by the swarm of flying insects that had come out after the storm. Yellow flies hummed around my head, diving at the tender skin of my neck and upper arms.

The sound of hoof beats came to me. I did stop and turn to Penelope. Or Elodie—now I could see the resemblance to Constance. "Who is that?"

She pushed me off the path and onto the ground. "Stay

there and shut up." She took a position in the center of the path, bringing the gun up in front of her. She meant to shoot the horse and rider.

The hoof beats grew closer, the earth trembling at the weight of the animal that pounded toward us. "Get out of the way." I rushed her, tackling her just as Moonglow rounded a curve and came straight at us. Together we rolled into the center of the path.

"I'm going to kill you," Elodie grunted.

She wouldn't have to. The horse was going to trample us to death. I threw my arm up over my face and waited for death. The hoof beats stopped and I looked up to see the horse's belly sailing four feet over my head. She landed on the other side of us and stopped. Before I could recover my wits, Newly was beside me. He had Elodie's wrists held firmly behind her back.

"Get your sash and tie her," he said. "Quickly."

"Why aren't you dead?" Elodie asked Newly. "Mother said she killed you."

"She tried." Newly took the sash from me and jerked it tight around her arms. "She tried and failed. And now the two of you are going to town to pay for all the terrible things you've done here. You're going to die in a prison."

CHAPTER 31

S till looking a bit frail but much happier, Anne Sheridan served glasses of her husband's finest whiskey over chipped ice. She went around the room until Uncle Brett, Isabelle, Madam, Reginald, Royal, Newly, and I were all served. We sat in the parlor in Waverley Mansion, enjoying the cool breeze that was pulled into the house. The room where the Norquist family had anticipated celebrating weddings and christenings—but had never had a chance—was peaceful and serene. I wondered if it was my imagination that the colors were brighter, the light a little softer, or was it merely the first hint of autumn creeping in.

Several days had passed since Constance and Elodie had been charged with the murders of Ashland Pratt and Fancy. In that time, Tennessee had voted to ratify the 19th Amendment, the last state necessary to give women the right to vote. We would cast our ballots in the election between Harding and Cox—the first time a woman in America had a say in who would lead the country. And it had passed with hardly a notice by me as I sorted through evidence and testimony to free

Royal and make sure Constance and her daughter, Elodie, paid for what they had done.

The cold-blooded calculation of their plan had left us all feeling queasy and unsettled. How strange that they'd ultimately been thwarted by the very force of evil Olivia Norquist had set in motion. Had Pluto's Snitch agency not been called to Waverley, they would likely have succeeded in setting Royal up for murder.

When we all had a glass, Royal stood and lifted the crystal. Sunlight glinted off the liquor. "To Raissa and Reginald. They ridded Waverley House of unwanted spirits, sent a young girl's ghost on to the other side, and managed to prove that I was no killer."

After the congratulations died down, I stood. "Madam, Uncle Brett, Isabelle, and Father McNeill get a lot of the credit. And Newly." I lifted my glass to him. "That was some jump he took over us. Elodie would have killed me had he not arrived."

"To Moonglow," Newly said, without a trace of his stutter. Since the incident with Constance and Elodie—which he refused to talk about—it had disappeared.

Anne timidly stood. "Thank you all. It will take us some time to adjust to all of this. I miss Fancy every day. Why did Constance have to kill her?" Her voice quavered.

"She was afraid Fancy would tell us about the spell Olivia and Fancy's grandmother, Bertha, cast to call forth the demonic entity," I said. "Constance realized that if we knew about Olivia's terrible actions, we'd dig deeper and her role would be exposed. I don't even know that Fancy knew the history. Amos didn't. Thank goodness Madam was here to cast the twisted spirit out of me or I would have been lost forever. There are many heroes here today."

"Here, here!" We sipped the fine whiskey. All charges against Royal had been dropped, but Sheriff Gaines had made it clear that Royal was walking on the wrong side of the law with his bootleg operation. Not that Gaines cared—except that other bootleggers supported his run for sheriff and Royal was mucking up his funding. Somehow, I figured Royal was clever enough to prevail.

Uncle Brett looked around the room, and I could tell he had something on his mind. When he stood, we gave him our attention. "I want to say that Raissa has brought new life into my world. She is like my own daughter, and I love her with all my heart. And it is with her blessing that I wish to invite Isabelle Brown to be my wife." He eased to one knee and reached into his vest pocket. His face clouded for a moment and he brought out an envelope and a ring box.

He put the envelope on the floor and opened the ring box as he looked up at Isabelle. "Will you be my wife?"

"I will." She bent down to kiss him and he slipped the engagement ring, a huge diamond, onto her finger. I thought my swelling heart would break my ribs.

"Congratulations! I am so happy!" I kissed them both.

"Raissa, I am remiss. This came for you in Mobile and I should have given it to you immediately, but I forgot all about it.

I took the note, which was addressed to me and mailed from Mission, Alabama, a place I'd never heard of. The handwriting was clear and elegant but the paper was cheap. I stepped back so others could congratulate Uncle Brett and Isabelle, and I opened the letter.

My dear Mrs. James,

I have heard of your remarkable talents and I am desperately in need of your help. Two years ago I began a new life in Mission, Alabama, leaving behind my past. This is a religious community of those who believe firmly in Satan and his desire to corrupt all human flesh. We have isolated ourselves from the real world for many reasons, and for two years, I've led a quiet and uneventful life. Unfortunately, I am now viewed with suspicion here.

I hope you can understand when I tell you I suffer from prophetic dreams--dreams that show me the true course of events. I did not ask for this gift, but I can no longer ignore it and what I am meant to do with it. This has put me at odds with my community. Last month I delivered a healthy baby girl. I am not married, which has caused many rumors and much animosity. My child was born with webbed hands and feet. The combination of my child and my dreams has left me in a precarious position.

But that is not why I seek your help. There is a man here, Slater McEachern, who is falsely accused of murder. You must come and help him or else he will hang for a crime he did not commit. I know the identity of the true killer, and I fear I will not live long enough to help Mr. McEachern or my own child.

I have no money to pay you or Mr. Proctor, but I can tell you of my dreams. I know a future event that will gravely impact both of you. With foreknowledge, I hope you can prevent it. If you can come, I will find accommodations for you. The community is very insular and doesn't react well to strangers, but I know your talents. You can help. You can save an innocent man. Perhaps even me and my child.

Make haste.
Elizabeth Maslow

I READ the letter twice before I realized everyone was looking at me. I passed the note to Reginald, who read it without expression.

"This woman is very educated," he said. "What is she doing living in that kind of isolation?"

"That's a good question, Reginald. We'll have to find out. It's another case," I explained to the others. "In Mission, Alabama."

"That's Sand Mountain," Uncle Brett said. "They say there are lost tribes of people there hiding out in the hills and valleys."

"Like Indians?" I asked. I knew the Cherokee had once roamed the area and the brutal Trail of Tears had gone through a portion of that area.

"No, like religious tribes. People who have cut off all contact with the rest of the world. They believe strange things. They have rituals and god knows what else."

"This is such a case," I said. "A man will be hanged for a murder he didn't commit."

"It's too dangerous," Uncle Brett said. Isabelle merely laid a hand on his arm, but said nothing. "Come back to Mobile and rest for a spell. Then, if you must go, go."

"This is a matter of urgency." Reginald sighed. "I don't want to go, but I feel we must."

The two men stared at each other for a moment, reading the situation and their emotions

"When will you leave?" Uncle Brett finally asked.

"In the morning," I said. "I need to go to West Point or Columbus to do some research into the area first. Madam, I'll need your help with prophetic dreams." The local libraries would be very helpful, but Madam would be invaluable.

"After Sand Mountain, you're returning to Mobile to celebrate my engagement. No excuses." Uncle Brett sounded stern, but he was never stern.

"I promise." I was ready for a break myself. "Hopefully we can wrap this up quickly."

"Then it's settled. Now let's have another drink," Royal said. "Amanda wants to play the piano for us."

He motioned her into the room, an average eight-year-old girl who rode horses like she was born in the saddle and played the piano like a child without a single desire to achieve any musical success. Still, it was a joy to see her struggling through the piece and rolling her eyes at her mother. Things at Waverley, at least, had been set to normal.

ABOUT THE AUTHOR

 Carolyn Haines is the *USA TODAY* bestselling author of over 70 books in a number of genres. She grew up in a rural Mississippi town with a family devoted to telling ghost stories and creating adventures. Her Scandinavian grandmother combined history and local legends for many bone-chilling evenings spent in front of a fireplace with a cup of hot choco-late. And it didn't hurt that she grew up in a haunted house where she first began to see spirits.

The Pluto's Snitch mysteries combine her love of spooky moments and puzzling mysteries. She is also the author of the popular Sarah Booth Delaney Mississippi Delta mysteries and the Trouble, black cat detective, multi-author mystery series. Haines lives on a farm where she cares for dogs, cats, and horses. She urges everyone to please neuter their companion pets to help cut down on the suffering of unwanted animals.

www.carolynhaines.com

Thank you for reading this KaliOka Press book. To receive

special offers, bonus content, and info on new releases, sign up for her newsletter.

www.carolynhaines.com/subscribe
carolyn@carolynhaines.com

facebook.com/AuthorCarolynHaines

twitter.com/DeltaGalCarolyn

instagram.com/carolynhaines

amazon.com/author/carolynhaines

bookbub.com/profile/carolyn-haines

goodreads.com/CarolynHaines

ALSO BY CAROLYN HAINES

PLUTO'S SNITCH NOVELS

The Book of Beloved

The House of Memory

SARAH BOOTH DELANEY MYSTERIES

Them Bones

Buried Bones

Splintered Bones

Crossed Bones

Hallowed Bones

Bones to Pick

Ham Bones

Wishbones

Greedy Bones

Bone Appétit

Bones of a Feather

Bonefire of the Vanities

Smarty Bones

Booty Bones

Bone to be Wild

Rock-A-Bye Bones

Sticks and Bones

Charmed Bones

A Gift of Bones

A Game of Bones

THE JEXVILLE CHRONICLES

Summer of the Redeemers

Touched

Judas Burning

NOVELS

Revenant

Fever Moon

Penumbra

Deception

FEAR FAMILIAR MYSTERIES

Fear Familiar

Too Familiar

Thrice Familiar

FAMILIAR LEGACY MYSTERIES

Familiar Trouble

Bone-a-fied Trouble

HORROR NOVELS

The Darkling

The Seeker

Made in the USA
San Bernardino, CA
18 April 2020

68385377R00214